Killer in the Sheets

ROSE CHASE

Also By

Volkov Bratva Series:
The Bratva's Bride
The Bratva's Beast

East Coast Syndicate:
Cardinal (Summer 2024)

Umbra Demon Series:
Under My Bed (Summer 2024)

Content Warning

This book is a contemporary dark romance that contains content that
some may find triggering or disturbing.
Contents include but not limited to: explicit violence, sexual violence,
abuse, alcohol and drug use, explicit sexual scenes, dub-con/CNC, BDSM
elements and tones, assault, Daddy, primal, anal.
If such content triggers you then please do not continue any further!

Dedication

To those who want to be the exception to his darkness.
P.S. I'm talking about y'all who want the psychopathic serial killer Daddy to
love them and only them.

Blurb

"IF ONLY OUR SECRETS can stay buried like dead bodies."

My stagnant life finally moves in the right direction after finding my match in Julian Smith.

I write twisted fairytales for a living, but never get the chance to live my own story until I matched with Julian through an app that paired people based on their internet history.

The flashing red signs are right in my face, but I blissfully ignores them. I can finally be weird and free without judgement, something I never could do growing up. Then when Julian feeds my passions, I can't ever leave.

Thing is, not all fairytales are perfect, something I find out when the edge to Julian's eyes become sharper than a blade and pierce me.

I know I need to run.

But can I?

More importantly: do I even want to run?

Killer in the Sheets

Serial Lovers Book 1

Rose Chase

Contents

CHAPTER 1
Avery

WHERE IS THAT- AH there it is!

Instead of a book's spine, my fingers brushed against something warm, soft yet firm, and fleshy.

When my eyes met a pair of enchanting hazel green eyes, the hairs on my neck stood and sent a chill down my spine.

Run.

My logical side screamed at me to tuck my tail between my legs and bolt away from this strange man.

Yet, the moment his fresh, earthy scent of soil and cedar invaded my system, I felt all my apprehension melt away instantly.

"S-sorry, I didn't mean to get in your way." For some reason, his eyes gained an edge when I hesitantly took a step back, as if he was angry at the fact I put some distance between us.

The hardness was gone in a blink, though, his iris dilating a little when his eyes softened with his friendly smile that felt overly warm. "No, please, it was my fault. I should have been more mindful of my surroundings. I guess I let my eagerness get the best of me." His voice was so rich and deep, which made my body tremble with pleasure as my ears ached with a yearning to hear him again.

"I'm the one with the bad eyes, I mean, I wouldn't wear glasses otherwise." I forced out an awkward chuckle while mentally beating myself up for sounding so stupid in front of this handsome man.

Well, not like I even have a chance with someone like him, so I might as well make a good fool of myself, right?

"But then your beautiful eyes wouldn't be so perfectly framed." He shot back smoothly, catching me off guard.

I couldn't control the happy little smile pulling at my lips as I shied my face away from him, letting my dark brown—nearly black—hair curtain over my face to further shield it from his vision.

"Don't get shy on me now." His melodic chuckle made another shiver of pleasure shoot down my spine.

Heat filled my cheeks when his fingertips gently brushed across my cheek to push my hair back before tucking the straight strands behind my ear.

"What book were you trying to give your attention to?" He asked with genuine curiosity as his head turned towards the bookshelf area where our hands had touched.

"Oh, uhh." I stuttered momentarily while my thoughts gathered back into my muddled mind.

Biting my bottom lip between my teeth, I directed my attention to the library's bookshelf, glancing over the titles and nervously searching for my intended book. "Oh," I said happily, pointing at a book just out of my reach. "It's that one."

"Serial Methods and Madness?" His voice was piqued with interest as he pulled the book from the shelf. "What interest do you have in this little masterpiece?" He looked at me with a bright face filled with genuine curiosity and eagerness.

"Oh, just—"

Ring. Ring. Ring.

Fucking great. Just fucking great.

Even though my phone had been on do not disturb mode, work could still get through to me along with some other whitelisted contacts.

"I'm sorry, I have to get this. It's work." I quickly apologized with a smile before picking up the work call.

Stepping away, I turned my back to the man and spoke in a hushed voice that grew softer with disappointment with each response to the other line.

With a heavy sigh and frown, I tucked my phone into my bag after hanging up the call. Then, I slowly turned back to face the man with a sad smile, "I'm sorry. Work needs me. I hope you find the book you're looking for."

I didn't give the man a chance to respond, having already turned my ass around and hightailed it out of there before I made an awkward fool out of myself.

The temptation to glance back to get one last peek at the hunk of a man tugged at my head the further I ran until I rounded the corner.

Damn it, Avery, you shouldn't have been a chicken. It's your day off. You didn't have to accept the assignment. You could have been cozying it up with the hot library dude. Ugh, this is why you're still single, god damn it. The world drops a handsome hunk in front of you, and you run.

A wave of disappointment washed over me like the cold Washington air when I opened the heavy doors of the library to exit the place.

I probably blew the one chance I would ever get at talking to a man out of my league, all because I got cold feet. Granted, work did call me in, but it wasn't as urgent as I made it sound. It might have been for the best, though, because I'd only make a complete fool out of myself the longer I engaged in a conversation with him.

Honestly, he probably only entertained me out of pity because, well, who would want to talk to me willingly?

I was a plain Jane, a run-of-the-mill Asian with straight-ass black hair, upturned brown eyes, on a roundish face. Nothing about my small 5'4 frame stood out in the crowd, or the background for that matter.

That man wouldn't have paid me any attention if I didn't get in his way just now. He looked like a model out of a magazine with his built 6'1 stature. One quick look at him and I could more than appreciate how well his seemingly bulky body filled out the black and blue plaid shirt of his. His strong arms, especially those muscular forearms, were on pristine display because of the way his sleeves were rolled and pushed up his arms. Then, those captivating pair of smoldering hazel green eyes made me want to drop to my knees.

God, those eyes were something else.

I could spend all day and night just staring at them while being wrapped up in his arms and held against his powerful chest.

Goddamn it, stop it. You just literally saw the man for less than five minutes, probably. You cannot be fantasizing about some goddamn stranger like a desperate idiot.

I scolded myself with a frown while trying to shove away my budding arousal.

I need to forget about him. I mean, I'll probably never see him again, ever.

Anxiety coursed through my body as I pulled up to the small little house sectioned off by yellow police tape and saw the lead detective pacing about. "Hey, hope I didn't take too long," I said between my soft pants after I exited my vehicle and approached him.

A string of incoherent grumbling mumbles came out under his breath before the detective looked up at me with slightly narrowed eyes. Then, in a rather snarky voice, he responded to me, "Another damn feathered murder. Fucking bastard got another one. Just go process this scene... You should have been here fifteen minutes ago, along with the rest of us."

"Excuse you, I know you're frustrated about this whole case, all of us are if you haven't noticed, but that doesn't give you the right to be snappy like this. Mind you, I came in on my day off because you scared off the last assistant." Well, not like my department had much luck to begin with. There were only two main CSU workers, myself included.

Everyone else filtered through for short periods before moving on to bigger opportunities—or they got scared off by Detective Carl Bornes over here.

Giving me a pointed look, which sent a shiver of unease down my spine, Detective Bornes somewhat snapped at me, "Shut up and do your job, don't talk back to me when it's not your ass on the line for catching this bastard. All you have to do is comb through the scene, and that's it. You don't have any other responsibilities besides that." His chest heaved with a heavy breath, and I swear I could see steam coming out of his ears. "Everything. I want everything. Just because you got called in on your day off doesn't mean I want you slacking on my scene, especially one this important. You better not fuck up my case because you're too busy ogling at the stupid feathers."

Not gonna lie, I felt a little offended at Detective Bornes undermining me like he always did. Usually, I wouldn't care; he was just a grouch and talked down to everyone under him—at least those he considered under him, which was nearly everyone. It was subtle before, and I chalked it up to bad days until it became a clear pattern. I don't know what his problem was, besides having a stick up his ass, but he's been rather hostile towards me as of recently—as in more than typical. Whenever I would arrive at the scene, he would make some kind of remark about my eagerness with almost an accusatory tone to his voice.

Yeah, I might be a little eager at these serial killer scenes than I am at others, but the scenes were usually fun to process. Most scenes I went to were almost an open and shut-case in terms of finding things around the place. Nearly everyone was sloppy to some extent that gave them away, but not this serial killer. Whoever this person was, they were basically perfect with their method. We only ever found what they wanted to be found and nothing more, nothing less. Every time I came to a scene, I always got my hopes up about possibly catching a slip-up.

These scenes were a nice challenge from the norm, and I loved that.

Maybe one of these days, I will find something to crack the case fully open, like a partial print, a single strand of hair, some magical spot of saliva—anything!

I wanted to figure the person's identity out, find them, and figure them out.

Why? What's the reason? Why do you set your scenes like this? Why these victims specifically?

Once I was home and settled in bed after my nightly routine, I pulled my phone out after I got comfortable under the covers in bed. After scrolling through my various social media apps for probably an ungodly amount of time, I moved over to my little folder of dating apps to filter through them. By filter, I meant delete.

Search for my Match

Just as I was about to hit the delete account button, something in me moved my thumb to the back button. I got nowhere with this stupid dating app, but maybe one last look at my messages wouldn't hurt. After all, it was going to be gone in a matter of minutes.

At least, that *was* my decision.

90% match with Julian.
Julian wants to swap histories.

My finger hit 'yes' before I could even think about it. Something about the high match gave me a false sense of hope in my desperation.

Not even seconds later, our internet search histories for the past year were revealed to each other. It was only then that some regret sank in because my search history was weird. Granted, he had to be strange as well if he matched with me that well.

Wow, that's a lot of murder.

CHAPTER 2
Julian

THREE DAYS LATER, AND I still had huge regrets about not chasing after the woman at the library. I don't know what came over me that day, but my feet refused to move when the small thing took off faster than a scared bunny.

Thinking back, I was surprised my instinct to chase and hunt didn't kick in like it usually did in such situations. She shouldn't have gotten away; my prey never escapes. Yet, this one did.

Why?

I remained perturbed even now when I should have been looking forward to this first meeting with my miracle match on the silly dating app my workers put me on. My annoyance with them has continued until now, even though their stunt was weeks ago. I only found out because I randomly got a notification on my phone. Further prodding revealed the app hidden within a folder.

I wasn't about to entertain this whole thing, but when I saw the premise of how matches were made, I went out on a whim. In all honesty, the fact a match was made with me surprised me a little after reading through the process of matchmaking.

The app wasn't as popular as Tinder or other top-ranking dating apps, but it still ranked well with the amount of people registered. Basically, the app takes your internet history—about a year of it, from what I could find out—and runs it against other applicants and makes matches based on the history.

Now, my history—after a quick look through—was filled with subjects related to crime, crime scenes, law, serial killers, construction, lands and lots, various materials and items, and the occasional shopping. A huge bulk of it pertained to all things crime and crime-related subject matters and serial killers.

Crime junkies and fans of serial killers existed out there. No doubt my internet history could be similar to many others, so I wasn't concerned or anything. What surprised me with my match was how much we matched up.

90%

That's how much our history matched up. I won't admit it, mainly because the feeling was foreign to me, but seeing the high percentage and seeing that it came from crime and serial killers made my heart flutter for some reason. The only time my heart ever fluttered was when I found a victim and killed. I've never had such a reaction—or any reaction—to the prospect of dating someone. Yet, seeing another like-minded individual out there in the very same city match up with me *and* agree to go on a date made my heart jump in my chest with eagerness.

The last thing on my mind currently was this stupid date because the mystery woman took precedence. All I could think about was how to find the woman and catch her to see exactly what about her captivated me so easily with just a glance and whiff of her.

I've never been one to be easily enamored by anyone, no matter how stunning they may be. A supermodel could cross my path right now, and I wouldn't bother with a glance, or if I did, that'd be it. My loins wouldn't stir like they did with the library woman.

When I caught her small stature in my peripheral, I instantly locked onto her fully before a strange warmth engulfed my body. I found my back tensing itself to appear taller even though I towered over her. Then, my chest instinctively puffed out to make myself bigger.

I fucking peacocked. Never in my life had I ever tried to do anything to appear standoffish or anything to make myself more known. If anything, I wanted to make myself unknown. Blending into the crowd and background made it much easier to get away with things.

Yet this woman, who I had no name to, only a fleeting face of innocence, had me wanting to stand out from all the other men in existence.

Ding!

At least my phone did a decent job of keeping me from going down the rabbit hole. It also served as a reminder of this damn date.

> Hey :) I am here. I got us a small booth in the very back corner by the windows. I am the only one with a pink bow in their hair. I haven't ordered, just got us some water.

The thought of ditching my date occurred to me briefly, but I was much too proud to do something so low. It was just one date; there was no harm in seeing it through. I could always send her a rejection later tonight, something along the lines of 'Hey, I had fun tonight, but I don't think this will work out, sorry,' and tack on more empty words before deleting the app from my life.

> I'm almost there, got caught up with some work.

Minutes after responding to her, I pulled my truck into a parking spot right in front of the little restaurant—a local hotspot, smart. The place was crowded enough to give her a sense of safety no doubt.

Upon entering the place, my eyes slowly scan the nearly packed place, taking note of my surroundings out of habit. I would have lingered at the back of the line more to spend more time taking in every inch of detail of the place and some of the patrons if it weren't for *her*.

Surely, my eyes played tricks on me, and I kept telling myself that repeatedly until *she* didn't disappear after a couple hard blinks.

Tucked neatly in the corner booth with a book in hand was a petite woman with a pink bow pinned against the side of her head, holding her bangs back.

The fact my date looked as she described herself didn't catch me off guard.

It was the fact fate had brought my prey directly to me.

I wanted to laugh and scream at the world as if this was some cruel joke, karma for my crimes.

But it wasn't. This was no joke. Karma definitely wasn't rearing her ugly head, either.

My date was my runaway library girl.

My prey.

CHAPTER 3
Avery

My heart seemed to beat in tandem with the ticking secondhand of my watch the longer I sat alone at the booth with my face buried in my book, hoping to avoid drawing attention to myself.

Oh God, what if he's standing me up?

No, he just said he was almost here.

This whole date started to feel stupid with each passing second as I began to doubt myself. I don't know what made me try the silly app.

When I came to my senses to delete the app, a message from one of my many matches stopped me. I've gotten a few messages before this Julian messaged me, so the fact I got a message didn't stop my intended course of action, but we had matched so well that I kept the app to set up a date with him.

Ninety percent was a huge match, according to the app. The app matched people up if they scored around forty or so percent with each other, and the average match scored around the high fifties, and the higher end of the data was around the high seventies if I recall correctly. It was incredibly rare to score anything higher than eighty, let alone ninety fucking percent.

I don't know if my desperation or loneliness won in entertaining this stupid idea, but here I was, sitting alone in hopes my date would show up.

11

Peering up from my book, I quickly glanced around the place again, hoping to spot a lost-looking guy who'd become my date. So far, no luck. Everyone had their place or quickly found it.

I should've asked him for a picture so I'd at least know *who* to look out for. The app didn't have any profile pictures, and it actually banned pictures because it wanted to match people up based on likes and personality rather than looks.

At this point, I only hoped he looked decent. I know not to judge a book by its cover, but I still had my type at the end of the day. It's not like I asked for a handsome model or some buffed-out star. At the very least, I just wanted someone easy on the eyes and average in the body department.

Of course, that was me asking for a lot already, given how I was chopped liver—trash, basically.

Sighing, I closed my book with my thumb jammed between the pages as a temporary bookmark. I just needed a second to myself before going back to my book. At least, those had been my intentions before they got derailed.

"The book not to your liking?" There was no mistaking that deep, soul-shaking voice.

Some of me thought maybe I hallucinated if it weren't for the fact that he stood right at the tableside.

Then I thought maybe I needed new glasses because there was no way the handsome man from the library stood a mere foot away from me.

"H-hey, library dude err man err I'm sorry that's rude of me, I—what are you doing here? Wait, don't answer that, that's a stupid question. You're obviously here to eat or because you want to because this is a public place, stupid question—"

My rambling cut off when the man chuckled and sat across from me.

How could I tell this man the seat was reserved and to leave me alone without sounding rude or like a total bitch?

For once in my life, something went right, shockingly.

My heart nearly stopped with the flash of his friendly grin. "It's nice to actually meet you, Avery. I am Julian."

I've never believed in God much growing up, even though my parents were religious as fuck and shoved it down my throat, but thank you, God, if you really are out there.

The pessimistic side of me wanted to laugh and tell him to cut the crap, that this joke wasn't funny. But I was too hopeful. Plus, when I really thought about it, there's no way this could be a fucked-up prank. I didn't know the man across from me, and I never met or crossed paths with him until today and the day at the library. I couldn't see a motive for him to pull some stupid prank on me by claiming to be my date. So I could shove my worries away for now.

"Wow, I don't know what to say, just, uhh hi, yeah, nice to see you...again." Fuck, could I be any more awkward? My first date in forever, and I blew it surely. "Sorry... I honestly wasn't expecting you. Not that there's anything wrong with you. I mean, you're perfectly handsome and all. I just didn't expect the hot man from the library to be my date."

Realizing what I just said, I quickly slapped my hands over my mouth, not caring that I'd just lost my spot in my book. Oh yeah, I definitely blew this date before it even started. Fuck me.

Groaning internally, I sank in my seat a little to try and hide my embarrassed self. I wanted to cry when I heard him chuckle.

God, he's probably going to leave because I'm such an embarrassment.

The fire in my cheeks flared intensely when I felt a roughness curl under my chin, bringing my face up to meet those piercing hazel-green eyes.

"There's nothing to be embarrassed about, Avery. If it helps any, I didn't expect my date to be you either." At least he didn't sound disappointed or look at me pityingly.

If anything, his soft smile eased my nerves some. Although, I couldn't find myself to fully relax under his gaze for some reason. Something about him had me on edge. Perhaps it was his intense gaze as if he was burning me into memory. He looked at me like I would be gone in the next second.

"Sorry I'm not what you expected. I'm not much of a looker, but I'm somewhat interesting." Barely.

Nothing about me was fascinating.

"Avery, anyone who likes to search for ways to kill someone from A to Z is very interesting in my books, especially if you try to find the reason behind the madness." A part of me wanted to shy away again at his chuckling words, to deny that I was such a weirdo.

That was until I remembered the whole premise for all of this. He wouldn't be here if he weren't as weird and strange as me. He knew my dirty secrets of the web, and it was why we even matched. Our tastes were the same, so I didn't need to hide any of it from him, right?

"As for being a looker, you're perfectly beautiful the way you are, and I don't see why you don't give yourself more credit. You really are stunning. I already thought so that day in the library, and you have no idea how much regret I have for not chasing you that day and letting you get away. So, to see you here tonight as my match, well, I'm more than surprised, in a good way." At least his eyes and charming smile seemed genuine, which melted away my anxiety.

Relaxing in my seat, I leaned back into the booth's corner, tucking myself into it after he let go of my chin. "So, this isn't some joke someone put you up to? You're really Julian from 'Search for My Match?'" The question felt stupid to throw out there, and he could lie to me for all I knew. I just had to know, though.

With a reassuring smile, Julian shook his head in response. "No, this isn't some cruel joke. Why would you think this was some joke?" His head tilted softly to the side while his eyes furrowed with concern.

Averting my eyes, I let out a long, sad sigh as my eyes followed the random patterns of the wooden table. "Not many people in this town want to date me, and I've just kind of been the running joke ever since I can remember. I mean, you wouldn't be the first handsome man to take me on a date to win some stupid bet."

I found my head lifting on its own accord when the sight of Julian's finger sliding under my chin came into view. My gaze locked up with his before he got another chance to fluster me with his touch. "I am so sorry that has happened to you. I can promise you that I am here of my own accord, no joke, no prank, just here because you happened to match very well with me through the app." His genuine voice and smile melted into my body once he was sure my gaze stayed on him.

A warmth spread through my body at the security his words brought me, and I couldn't help but smile shyly at the fuzzy feeling in my chest. "So, what's a man like you doing searching for burial methods? By the way, the articles you were looking at, I wouldn't take their advice much because they're amateur."

No point beating around the bush. At least, that was one good thing about this app and its matching system. I knew his interests, or at least had an excellent idea of them from his internet history. Obviously, since we connected then, he's seen a glimpse of my history.

"Oh? Amateur? How so? How would you effectively bury a body to ensure it never gets discovered?" He sounded a little too intrigued, but he probably overplayed it to try and get me to ease up fully.

"Well, personally, I'd get a little dirty and dismember the body to pieces to make detection by radar and satellite damn difficult and near impossible. As for burying, I'd dig a hole at least fifteen feet deep, though I'd go to twenty because cadaver dogs can sniff up to fifteen feet, so the deeper, the better." I paused with a sheepish grin and sipped at my water before adding on, "Of course, gotta toss on dead animal corpses with the layers, so if for some reason the dogs discover something, the numerous animal corpses will deter the search after they keep uncovering them. It's much easier to bury a piece of a body rather than a whole body. It's a little more work, but better safe than sorry."

I half expected him to look horrified after I explained myself a little too eagerly and giddily, but Julian was full of surprises. There weren't any signs of disturbance or disgust on his grinning face full of awe.

CHAPTER 4
Julian

FOR ONCE IN MY life, I was at a loss for words because I was too busy trying to figure out this mess in my head.

Hearing and seeing her joy and excitement when she answered my question stirred something within me, an excitement of sorts that made me smile unconsciously as I looked at her with wonder-filled eyes.

It felt like I was on a hunt, a chase through the woods at night, knowing my prey was close. I've never had this thrill outside of hunting and discovering a new potential victim.

Maybe that was it. Maybe sweet little Avery was to be my next victim.

No, that made no sense. I had my specific criteria for victims, and Avery did not fit any single one of them. I've never deviated before either, not ever since I figured out my niche.

Besides, I didn't feel murderous towards her, even though I had this strange itch in my fingers to lay my hands on her—not in a harmful way, no. I wanted to feel her again to see if she was actually real, to see if this feeling of intrigue would dissipate if I sated my need for contact.

The thought of touching her brought a whole new feeling of arousal to me, one that ran straight down my body to my crotch, where it pooled into a hardness. Why did I get aroused by the mere thought of touching her?

I've always been odd in the sense that I didn't get sexually aroused by typical means such as porn or such materials. The only thing to ever get my blood pumping to the right places were prospects of a kill or harm to a target. If the need for a release ever annoyed me too much, then I'd either take care of it myself; *if* I were in an odd mood for a lay, then I'd go down to the local club to snag a one-night stand, but I'd still have to think about other things to fully get myself to an orgasm.

A physical need with physical solutions, nothing to it. I could go through the motions just fine; I just never fully understood what people craved about it so much or what the rave about this 'attachment' was about.

At least, that was the case until now. I could only surmise that this is what people meant when they talked about feeling 'attracted' towards someone. Granted, I felt the same way toward her as I did any victim, almost. There was this underlying need for her, but not the need to kill. I don't know what it was or how even to start justifying it.

"Apologies, that was too much and weird of me, I don't know what came over me." She nervously apologized as I continued to look at her with the utmost intrigue.

"Avery." I don't know what came over me to reach out and grab her face and squish her round cheeks together to get her to stop her cute mouth from running. "You didn't weird me out. I'm sorry for my silence. I was just... Amazed. You talked with such passion that it took me off guard. I am not put off in the slightest, just very awe-struck."

The way her eyes sparkled with gratefulness and relief had that strange feeling in my chest stir up again. "I'm curious, why are you so into everything? Crime junky? Serial killer enthusiast?" She didn't look like a killer like me, not this tiny thing.

Then again, I should never judge a book by its cover. No one would ever suspect me, a highly successful business owner of multiple construction companies, to be one of the most notorious, uncaught criminals out in the world currently.

I was charismatic and intelligent enough to keep up a good façade. I knew how to pick and choose my victims, and I had good options of dump sites either through my home, which sat on the outskirts of town on 30 acres of land, or through my company, where we were constantly contracted to build various things.

My victim pool probably helped my evasion, too, since I only went after convicts, more so those who managed to evade the law, like assaulters who barely slip away because of their connections or because mommy and daddy afforded the better lawyer. In all honesty, I was doing the world a damn favor by ridding it of the scum that plagued it.

Not many people were keen on hunting down a killer doing justice's work.

Letting go of her face, I pulled my hand back to clasp it under my chin on my propped elbows before urging her to respond with a warm smile.

Smiling back brightly, she quickly replied, "Personal interest: I always loved all things crime-related growing up, particularly forensics and the psychology and pathology behind criminals, and I'm kind of writing a book, an aspiring author if you want a label. I'm not some strange fangirl or anything."

"But what about you? Why are you interested? I mean, judging from your history, you've been looking at a lot of the things I have." She shifted her tone to a more cautious one when she tossed her question at me. "You don't have to answer if you don't want to. I don't want to seem too prying on our first date, possibly our only date, maybe, too."

Well, that didn't sit well with me, the idea of this date being our only one. Was she not interested like I had been reading her out to be? No, the disappointment in her dulled-out eyes meant otherwise.

"Hey, I'm an open book for you, so don't worry. As for whether this date could possibly be the last, it'll only be so if you don't wish for a second one. I, for one, would love a second date, probably a third and fourth too." And forever.

I wanted to spend forever in her presence to pick at her seemingly intelligent little brain. I also had a feeling she'd be useful to me. I mean,

I knew to bury a body deep, but not *that* deep to the depths she talked about; if she hadn't provided a reasonable explanation, then I would have been inclined to argue with her a bit, but her reasonings were more than valid.

"You don't find me too weird yet? Or worried about ending up in my plastic-wrapped basement to be meticulously dismembered?" She joked with a forced chuckle to hide the awkwardness in her voice. "I'm sorry, that probably sounded so creepy. I swear I'm not a killer."

Strangely, I found her adorable too. Even though she talked too much for my usual liking, it didn't bother me one bit when the words flew out of her mouth like a train speeding down the rails. I'd barely met this woman, yet I could feel her presence digging deep into my black soul.

"Avery, I wouldn't be here if I found you weird after seeing your internet history. And if I were to wake up in your basement like so, then at least I'd die somewhat content if a pretty little thing like you were to end me." Then, I let my curiosity peek out a little, "Although, I'd be more curious as to how you'd even get me there in the first place because I'm twice your size and weigh a few hundred pounds." Another little prod to see if more magic would spew from her lovely, rosy, pink lips.

Pursing her lips slightly, she tapped her index finger on the table-top while humming softly in thought. "Well, depending on how your dead weight actually is, I could do it the old-fashioned way and drag you by your ankles. But I'd probably go with the good old tarp method, lay ya on one and roll you up to roll you around."

With a nervous chuckle, she looked at me sheepishly. "I mean, getting you down into the basement would be easy. I could either slide you down a homemade ramp or, if I was careless, then kick your body down, but if I did that, then I'd have to worry about you leaving behind traces of hair, blood, or fibers. So, the best thing would be to slide you down a homemade ramp wrapped in plastic. And if worse comes to worse, then I could start chopping you up early."

I couldn't bring myself to stop Avery from rambling on about the things she could do and why she'd go that route or not based on valid factors and reasons. Hearing her prattle on and on was... soothing, strangely.

Avery didn't make chatter annoying, somehow. I always hated hearing people talk and engage in overdrawn conversations, but Avery's voice and words didn't bring the irritated buzz to my mind. I didn't want to strangle her to make her shut up. If anything, I wanted to sit on the couch with her in my lap, wrap my arms tightly around her, and hear her drone on and on to her heart's content.

I almost frowned when Avery realized what she had done and stopped her lips from moving. Shying her face away, she forced out a nervous laugh, "Please, don't be afraid to tell me to shut up if or when I annoy you too much."

If it were anyone else, I would've told them to shut up or get up and remove myself from their presence, but not Avery.

"If I wanted to stop you, then I would have. By all means, continue, please. It's refreshing to see someone so invested and passionate." I smiled warmly as I reached out to tilt her head back up with a curled finger under her chin when she started to drop her head again.

"Stop hiding your cute face away from me, Avery. I don't want your pretty little eyes to be anywhere but on me, alright?" I couldn't help but wonder why she had that habit. Well, I guess that's another thing to add to my list of figuring out Avery.

"But to answer your question from before, I'm interested because most of the time when I am researching for my company, I tend to come across interesting facts about the land involved or the area. Unfortunately, I am the cat that would be killed by curiosity because I can't stop myself from grasping at a thread and unraveling it completely." Another well-crafted lie I had no trouble spilling; it was a good lie, though, in my opinion.

"And you're not afraid of ending up in my basement?" I shot her question back at her with an edge of playfulness.

"If I end up in such a predicament, then that's on me at that point because I should know better. It would be pretty ironic given my profession and who I work around, that and my endless research should have been enough for me to know who to avoid." Her voice started to trail into a string of incoherent mumbles as she began to get lost in her little world again.

"You work with law enforcement." I brought up the subject of her career. "CSI, if I remember correctly from your profile, right?" She hung around cops and others on the 'right' side of the law yet fell prey to me. How ironic, indeed. The irony was almost enough to make me laugh.

A lot of people like to think they'd know or spot a serial killer if they ever encountered one, and though valid to an extent, most of us go unnoticed by society. At least the smart ones—like me—do. I doubt Avery knew of my true nature and hobby just sitting across from me right now.

"Hm?" Snapping out of her little daze, she locked her big, innocent, brown eyes into mine. "Yeah, I'm an investigator in the CSU for the Laud Police Department. You're in business, correct? Construction, if I'm not mistaken."

"Yes, I own and run a bunch of construction firms all over Southern Washington and Northern Oregon," I confirmed with a soft nod before looking over at a group of waiters and waving my hand at one of them to come over.

"Wow, lots of options for body disposal there." Avery joked with a short giggle before her face turned crestfallen. "Sorry, I—bad joke."

Amused, I softly chuckled before pinching her cheek playfully to get her full attention on me before pulling my hand back. "I found it funny, so not bad to me." Funny and true because the reason I grew the company was because it gave me ample options in terms of dump sites. Also, nothing hides a body better than to build a whole building on top of it.

"Curious, you searched a lot about methods of murder, but there wasn't much to point toward the method you'd chosen for yourself." Everyone had a dark touch to them, was my belief, and though innocent looking enough, I wonder if Avery had that speck within her I could expand.

"Personally, poison. I mean, yeah, kind of typical for a woman, but I'd probably like to draw things out. So, either poison or death by some very slow and torturous means." Avery sounded comfortable as if she answered typical job interview questions. "You?"

"I prefer a game of chase. I always liked hunting growing up, and still do hunt to this day. Something about giving chase gets my adrenaline pumping just right. Then a quick stab to the heart if I was in the mood to get up close and personal. If not, then probably a bullet." I could feel the corners of my lips stretch wide in a delighted smile as I spoke.

My heart thrummed within my chest with excitement as my mouth moved happily to spill a drop of my real self to her. It was difficult to hold myself back from going into details, but I had to if I wanted to avoid suspicion.

"Well, I definitely wouldn't mind a chase from you." Avery giggled softly with a shy smile and flushed cheeks. But then, just like before, she pulled herself back before I could enjoy her boldness enough. "Sorry, that's probably a little too much for a first date."

"Avery, nothing will ever be too much coming from you, so quit holding back. I won't judge you for anything, and I'd be the very last person on this earth to do so. I want you to be open and free with me, alright?" I liked seeing her little spark come to life in her eyes; seeing her joy made my chest feel warm and fuzzy for some strange reason, but I enjoyed the peculiar feeling more strangely.

With a soft, reassuring smile, I reached out and held her dainty chin, stroking the tip of it with my rough thumb before tracing the outline of her bottom lip. The corners of my lips lifted with some satisfaction when my action got a shiver and blush out of her.

"Now, let's order some food and see where the rest of the night takes us."

One thing's for sure: it won't be with Avery's cold body in my trunk.

CHAPTER 5
Avery

"Whelp, another one bites the dust."

My coworker's remark was probably not appropriate for the situation, but no one was around besides my coworker and me.

Sighing softly, I pulled my gloves on while slowly following a trail of black feathers from the couch in the victim's living room to the kitchen, stopping once I hit scattered sheets of paper two feet away from the backdoor.

"Well, wherever he is, I hope he's suffering." My coworker commented from beside me behind a clicking camera.

I couldn't respond to my coworker because I couldn't think of a good response. I agreed with her to an extent, but it felt wrong. I shouldn't be feeling bad about the fact the missing victim was a criminal probably getting his dues, but that's what our justice system is for. Albeit a shitty justice system, but still a system to manage things like this. If everyone took matters into their own hands, the world would be in chaos.

"Crow killer has a ring to it, right?" She continued to push the subject matter about our unknown subject.

"We are not putting a label or name to him Liz, we can't. What he's doing is wrong and against the law." No matter how righteous, this uncaught serial killer broke the law with every victim, no matter how deserving they may be.

"Oh, come on, we gotta call them something. Oh, do you think they're a girl or guy?" Liz was into this mysterious killer a little too much, in my opinion, but I couldn't blame her.

In this small town of Laud, Washington, not much excitement happened. So, having a serial killer in the midst was probably as exciting as a celebrity scandal.

However, it didn't bode well for our police department because a serial killer on the loose with no signs of us coming close to apprehending them made the public frown on us greatly. It also didn't do wonders for the community because everyone was on edge and suspicious about everyone around them. The once-friendly town was definitely more hostile than ever.

"Crow Killer wouldn't work because these are raven feathers, so you don't even have the right bird." I pointed out her little hiccup after briefly picking a feather up and pointing it in her direction before slipping it into an evidence bag.

"How can you tell? Unless you're the killer and know because you put them there." Then there was the running joke that the killer could be one of us in the department, me being the prime suspect, given my extreme interest in serial killers.

Being reserved and quiet didn't help the notion of 'oh, it's always the quiet ones' being the least expected. But I didn't care much about the idle chatter behind my back and the fingers that pointed my way when I walked down the streets. I have nothing to hide. I was no serial killer, so it wasn't like they could hold any evidence against me for a charge.

It sucked to have most of the town whispering about me, but it wasn't something I wasn't familiar with. I was bullied my whole life growing up, so I was conditioned to it now at twenty-eight. It still hurt, but not too much where I was immensely irked by it. I hated how I'd become numb to nearly everything, but what's done is done. I couldn't turn back the clock and turn my younger self in a different direction.

"Raven feathers are bigger and have more of a sheen to them. Also, if I was a serial killer, then the last place I'd want to be is at a job with law enforcement." At least, personally, I wouldn't put myself in such a dangerous zone like that.

Granted, having access to the scenes could work in my favor to collect and clean up on things I might have missed during the activity. Hell, I could even go as far as altering the reports to cover my tracks or throw suspicion off of me. But that would be very high stakes for me if I were a serial killer.

"Come on, let's get everything bagged up and cataloged." I urged with a small huff as I got up from the floor from my squatting position.

"You do that while I finish taking pictures and making notes. Oh, but how did your date go last night? I've been meaning to ask you all morning, but you've been occupied at your desk." Yeah, I kept myself busy to avoid this question.

I knew Liz meant well with her curious question. She cared for me much like I imagined a good younger sibling would. Unfortunately, I wasn't used to having someone in my corner. I've never been close to anyone or had anyone who would be considered a friend until Liz came along three years ago. I tried to keep her at a distance because I wasn't used to socializing and making friends, but Liz was persistent ever since her hire to the team and stuck herself to me like glue.

It was rare, but I do let Liz know how grateful I am for her putting up with me. She made my life slightly less lonely and made work more bearable. I also have to thank her for pushing me out of my comfort zone, too, because before her, I never really ventured out anywhere between work and my little studio apartment. To be fair, I still don't do too much, but the occasional trips to the local cafes were almost becoming a regular thing for me.

Usually, I would shut myself at home or the library when I'd do research or work on my manuscript. Recently, though, nearly the past year, I've pushed myself—with Liz's help—to go out to the cafes and sit out there to do work or even the local park.

That aside, Liz wondered about last night, in which I couldn't help but smile at the memory of. "Oooooh, giiiiirl, spill!" Liz demanded with a squeal while bouncing on the ball of her feet.

"I mean, there's not much, just it went real good, and it was real nice, like really nice. Julian's just perfect." It was almost too perfect, but I played off my paranoia because I wanted to be happy for a sweet moment in my dull life. "He and I clicked a lot last night, and we're actually going to meet up again later tonight for a small dinner picnic at his place for a second date."

I was still shocked that we were going on a second date, even if it was hours away at this point. I barely comprehended him asking me last night before we parted ways after dinner and a very long chat.

"Okay, not that I'm not happy for you, but you sure that's a wise idea for a second date? I mean, dinner at a stranger's place when we've a serial killer on the loose?" Liz did pose a good issue, a *real* and valid issue.

"Liz, I'm not going to end up going out with some serial killer. I mean, come on, I can probably see a serial killer a mile away with how much research I've done on them. Julian is completely normal." Okay, I might be tooting my own horn and eating my own shoe and whatnot, but I had a good feeling about Julian—not counting the day at the library.

Waving my hand dismissively, I scoffed playfully at Liz, "Besides, I'll have my gun on me, and I know how to defend myself." I really wasn't too worried about being murdered on my date tonight—or ever.

"I want updates, hourly texts, if I don't hear from you on the hour then I'm sending the calvary your way." Liz's lighthearted voice took a serious dip when she gave me a stern look with her words.

"Fine, if it makes you feel better," I assured her with a firm smile.

Again, I had a good feeling about Julian, so I wasn't worried one bit. Okay, that was a lie because I had an icky feeling deep down in my gut, which I ignored actively.

Julian had seemed a little too perfect. Handsome as fuck, successful, had his life put together, not living with his parents—or God forbid his mom's basement—or anywhere close to them, a crime lover and junky like me, and wasn't put off by my weird little rambling habit so far. Sure, he could have been a good sport last night, but from what I felt, he seemed genuine.

There had to be something wrong with him; no one so perfect could fall into my lap so easily. I wasn't a special gal, so I don't see myself deserving someone so perfect and high standing like him.

"Just be safe out there tonight, alright? I mean, like I said, I'm happy that you've found someone who isn't a jerk to you, but just be careful. Something kind of smells fishy." Liz worried with a crooked frown, patting my shoulder before going off to finish taking pictures of the rest of the place.

Unfortunately, something was very fishy, but I'm pretending I don't smell the rotting bucket of fish in the corner.

CHAPTER 6
Julian

"I am so sorry. I swear, I wasn't trying to flake out or anything, and you really didn't have to do this. I'm sorry but thank you, but still, I'm so sorry."

Avery immediately shut her mouth when I chuckled and grabbed her face with both hands. "Avery, it's fine. Cars break down all the time, especially old ones. Besides, I had to head into town anyways to grab stuff for our dinner date, so offering you a ride works out."

Okay, that was a lie; I was cozy at home, waiting for my prey to show, with no intentions of going into town until tomorrow morning. Last thing I expected was a frantic call from her profusely apologizing for her unfortunate life events with her car. I'm not gonna lie; I was slightly peeved at the change of plans, and if it were anyone else, I would have canceled. Yet again, Avery was a strange exception; I found myself offering her a ride and to have the date at a nearby park or her place before my brain fully processed my own words.

Never, and I mean *never*, have I ever done or said anything without extensive thought.

"I'll make it up to you, I swear." Oh, that got ideas flooding into my mind, rather sinful ones in nature.

An image of hers on her knees before me saying those exact same words before taking my cock out and servicing me like a good little slut—scratch that, servicing me like *my* good little slut.

Fuck, there I went again with my uncontrolled sexual thoughts about her. I didn't have to try when it came to Avery; they just appeared in my mind randomly whenever I thought about Avery's name.

Much to my frustration—emotionally and sexually—my thoughts have been erratic. Since our first meet-up last night, getting Avery off my mind proved impossible. If I thought she occupied my mind a lot before when she was the mystery library woman—I was wrong.

Avery still snuck through even when I tried to distract myself with my latest victim. When I thought about the hunt I would have with my victim, they would slowly morph into the petite Asian next to me currently. Then, when I would finally catch her, instead of sinking my knife into her, I'd be slicing through her clothes before running the blade against her body to her precious neck. Death never followed in my fantasy; no, only a savage beast taking what was rightfully his.

Mentally slapping myself, I snapped myself out of it before I got too riled up and did something impulsive and stupid.

Tension filled my jaw as I gritted my teeth and shifted a bit in my seat to hide my painful hard-on as I continued to drive us to a nearby field of a park. I tried to talk her into letting me take her back to my place, but she denied the idea because of work the next day. However, she agreed to give me her upcoming weekend when she took notice of my displeasure with her rejection.

Two and a half days with her. I would have Avery all to myself for sixty whole hours. Just me and her, out at my house in the forest, no one but us for miles. She didn't know it yet, but she was headed right into the beast's den. Whether or not she'd make it through the weekend alive was yet to be determined.

Fortunately for her, the thought of wringing her life out brought me no joy. Actually, it brought on a new slew of emotions I didn't know was possible to feel: remorse, shame, guilt, sadness, disgust, the whole slew of it.

I finally figured out what that gnawing feeling was the night before; I felt guilt and remorse when I thought about killing Avery, something I have never, ever felt in my life before towards *anything*.

I wanted the icky feeling to go away. Initially, I thought killing Avery would be the way to go about unloading those very unnecessary emotions. However, any thought of ending her life intensified those feelings to where they'd haunt me to madness if I were to carry through with my diabolical plan. So, fortunately for her, she got to live for the sake of my sanity.

Then, I entertained the idea of forcing her to move far away or even relocate myself. It was a brilliant idea if it weren't for the fact that knowing she existed somewhere in the world but not being able to see, feel, hear, or taste her was enough to drive me up the wall that instant.

Death and distance weren't an option, so I guess I had to learn to live with Avery around me.

Maybe I should lock her away in my basement until I could figure out my madness with her. Actually, that wasn't a bad idea. With her safely tucked in my basement, I wouldn't have to worry about her safety when she wasn't with me. More importantly, I wouldn't have to worry about her talking to other men.

Once again, Avery brought out a new feeling: jealousy. I never cared enough for anyone to feel an ounce of the nasty emotion; I also never saw a need to feel jealous of anything. I was more than successful and content in my life, and I could acquire a life partner *if* I wanted to torture myself with monogamy—something I found myself inching towards with Avery.

I wanted her—no, I needed her. My desire for her burned at me like how I'd burn the bodies of my victims. Did I want to wed her? No, not exactly, but I wanted her to be mine and only mine. She could slap whatever label she wanted on us as long as she was exclusively mine.

"Hey, Julian?" Her soft voice was like a new ripple in my sea of thoughts.

"Hm?" My tense face softened instinctively when I turned to look at Avery, who sat in the passenger seat.

"Are you sure this is no bother? It's getting later into the night, and I'm sure you have much better things to do than to waste your time on me." Her eyes slowly swung away from me to her lap, where she fiddled with her fingers.

Throwing the vehicle into park, I killed the engine before reaching over to grab Avery by her hips and slide her across the seats until she was next to me. "Let's get one thing clear between us." Gently grasping her chin, I trained her curious gaze on me. "You are never a waste of time to me, ever. I'm not the type of man who wastes his time, either. If I don't want to give my attention to anything or anyone, then I don't."

Granted, she was an exception because I had no particular end goal for her just yet. Everything I put my time into has a gain for me. Time put into my company resulted in profits and growth; time towards people usually gave me information pertinent to planning out their deaths.

Avery, though, what gain did I get from this engagement? I have gained nothing good besides an endless thread of unanswered questions, emotions I never thought possible that chewed at me like rats, and a strange urge to lay my hands on her—not in a violent manner. Well, I should give this *thing* between us *some* kind of benefit because I reaped a strange warmth with her presence. Her voice and face brought some sort of delight that made my heart flutter—or maybe it was an impending heart attack.

"Julian?" My name coming from her lips made my pants tighten with need again. "Why do you look like you want to eat me?"

Fuck me.

Did she know what she was doing? How could she possibly ask a question like that without any intent behind it? I wanted to gouge her innocent eyes out—no, her eyes were too beautiful to take away like that; I wanted to make that innocence morph into lust and sin, make them roll to the back of her head with pleasure.

Cupping her face, I stroked my thumb across her bottom lip before pressing against it softly. "Because you are looking like a whole feast right now." Screw the sandwiches and pasta in the basket; I wanted to lay her out on the blanket and feast on her sweet pie—a very shocking urge and thought. Growling softly, I could feel my gaze darken, "I am not hungry for food anymore."

Her reddened cheeks couldn't be hidden from me under the bright moonlight streaming through the windows, even when she tried to turn her face away. "I-it's late in the night, a-and this is only our second time meeting each other." Her shyness did little to deter me, but the nervousness and sheer fear in her eyes pierced through me like an arrow.

Unable to help it, I leaned down and ghosted my lips over hers because I wanted to steal her breath and get a quick feel of her lips against mine. God, I wanted to grab her face and slam our lips together after the fact, but I couldn't, not yet. I had to control myself.

"I'll set up in the back of the truck then." Walking away from my prey like that felt awkward, but it also felt right, strangely enough.

Running my fingers through her messy ponytail, I softly pinched her cheek before flashing a quick smile. "I won't do something that makes you uncomfortable, Avery, so don't worry about any of it. I'm not going to force myself onto you, either. I'm not that kind of scum. I'm more than happy," *very fucking debatable*, "To take things at your pace."

The starkness in her eyes melted at my words, and I nearly went back on what I just said when I realized the awe and desire that replaced the anxiety from before.

So, she wanted me to be sweet, thoughtful, gentle yet firm, and patient. I could work with that.

Her search history was no mystery to me, thanks to the app. Besides all things crime-related, she dove a lot into the kinkier sides of things.

How to know if you got daddy issues?
What are daddy issues?
Daddy kink right or wrong?
How to find a good Dom?
Local BDSM community?
Kink club?
Do I want a Dom?
Why do I like the thought of being taken not so willingly?

Shockingly, I spent much of my time scrolling through her search history once I uncovered those questions. Now, some of the questions were debatable as to whether they were research-related or not to her book, but some seemed obviously personal.

"Bring the blankets out with you when you hop out," I told her with a quick smile before getting out of the truck after reaching into the back and grabbing the picnic basket.

It didn't take me long to open the back of my truck and set everything out. What did take long was her appearance. She didn't call for help or anything, and I didn't see her pull her phone out through the back window. All she did was sit there staring off while hugging the blankets.

"Second thoughts?" I teased when she finally rounded the truck and climbed onto the truck bed.

"N-no, just a little nervous... Never had a nighttime picnic in a field." She replied in a quiet voice as she scooted close to me.

"I haven't either, so another first for us." Her tense body calmed with a look and chuckle of disbelief when I gave her a warm smile. "What? Don't believe me?" I wouldn't believe myself either, but it was the truth.

"I really don't, but you are just full of surprises. I mean, a dashing man like you is usually taken, married with kids, or has something else going on. Hard to believe that you haven't done something silly as a nighttime picnic date." From playful to cautious, she warmed up and chilled within a minute. "Though, which begs the question as to how a man like you is still single?"

"Got too busy with life, and I was nearly forty by the time I sat back to take a breath. I fell into the statistic of a busy businessman who had no time for anything but my company. Never bothered too much with relationships because no one wants a workaholic, and I knew I couldn't give the needed attention to my partner if I were to have one. Also, I got tired of the gold diggers that came around once my bank account grew to the size of my buildings." Another crafted story with the truth weaved in.

I did get too busy with growing my own business, but my time was grossly occupied with research on my victims, stalking them, planning their deaths, and carrying out said plan. I barely had time between those two, so adding a woman into the mix was out of the question.

The part about the gold diggers was very true. I had many women from my past, exes I was stupid enough to give my glance to, people I went to high school with, workers, fans, and just too many annoying people.

I never cared much for deep relationships, so I wasn't bothered by being single; it was better that way, given my hobby. At least, that's how I felt until Avery.

Once again, always 'until Avery' with me lately.

Fucking Avery, what are you doing to me?

Taking a deep breath, I wrapped an arm around her shoulders and pulled her close before throwing the blanket over us. "I'm curious why you're still single." It was time to keep the ball rolling, a game I hated, yet I made an exception for this woman yet again.

"I'm the awkward butterfly no one wants. I mean, nothing about me is exciting. I'm nearly thirty and single, live in a tiny studio apartment, bury my face in books whenever I can, awkward, quiet, shy, not outgoing one bit, like murder and crime a little too much, and just stagnant in life. I'm just there, and not like I score good in the looks department either. Nothing about me makes someone do a double take or makes them want to go 'yeah, I'd definitely want her' after a few dates." She admitted with a frown and heavy sigh. "I'm really shocked you didn't stand me up on the date or try to dip halfway through. I mean, granted, we had a lot to talk about and a lot in common, but still, a handsome guy like you should be with someone looking like the Kardashians or some shit like that, not some wallflower like me."

"Well, maybe more of a shocker to you, but I prefer simple, which is you." The last thing I needed was a partner who was over the top and attracted more attention to myself.

"But you really have to give yourself more credit, like I said before." Though simple, she was beautiful and perfect to me—which was a lot coming from me because nothing and no one was ever perfect in my eyes. "You're more than enough in my eyes, everything about you to me is flawless."

"Okay, now you're just trying to butter me up, mister." She remarked with a giggle, softly slapping my chest with the back of her hand before picking up the little Tupperware of spaghetti to settle it in her lap.

A peaceful silence filled the air between us as we ate, with an occasional comment from her about how tasty the food was after an initial bite.

Done, the two of us sat in each other's arms, gazing at the clear night sky. "You know, you're making it hard not to sink my claws into you. Handsome, charming, independent, financially stable, don't live in your mom's basement, nor do you stink, and you can cook? I don't want any other girl out there to get a chance at you." Her tiny body shook against mine with her chuckle.

Leaning my head over, I settled my chin atop her head as I held her tightly. "You don't have to try to keep ahold of me. I'm not going anywhere. If anything, good luck getting rid of me." I remarked with a chuckle of my own.

"What kind of story are you writing anyways to be doing so much research on killers like that?" Might as well try to sate my curiosity for her.

Avery's body deflated against mine in a squirm. "You're gonna think it's stupid." She spoke into my chest as she buried her face in it.

"Avery, I'm on a date with a girl who could murder me and get away with it because we matched on a dating app based on our internet search history. I should be running for the hills and hiding as far away from you as possible." I joked with a deep chuckle while rubbing her shoulder. "I'm not going to think it's stupid unless you're gonna tell me it's about people eating dirt."

Looking up at me, Avery rolled her eyes and chuckled in response as she twisted her body to face me fully. "Okay, one, ew. Two, I don't even know how that story would even go."

Leaning in, she settled against me again with her head on my shoulder. "It's about a pair of serial killers. One of them is a judge who is tired of seeing people get off the hook, and he has this cop friend who he talks to about it all who understands where he is coming from. Now, the cop friend has a daughter who's a little obsessed with the judge, like a huge crush on him and whatnot, so she seeks out these people she always hears him complain about and kills them and gives little trophies to the judge. He doesn't know it's her at first, and he's horrified at first, too but then he takes a liking to it. Then he finds out that it's his friend's daughter, and they kind of go into business together, and their relationship takes off because of it."

And there's that passion I loved hearing from her. I could glimpse at her bright face out of the corner of my eyes, an image I wanted to capture and hang on my wall. God, that sounded gaudy, but I didn't care—shockingly.

"That's not stupid one bit. I'm not much of a romance reader, but I'd give that story a try. The basis of it sounds intriguing, really. I mean, a judge turned killer and the daughter of a cop, that's all quite a combination of things." Now, I was curious about the finished product.

"You don't have to try and stay on my good side. I already like you enough to not give you a watery grave. If you don't like it or think it's stupid, then just say so." She tried to cover up her doubt with a dry joke and chuckle.

"Oh, so no more burying me in the forest twenty feet under?" I joked back with a quirked brow, settling my hands on her waist.

"The river currents are more than enough to carry your body parts far and wide at this point in the year, so it's an idea." She threw back at me with a sheepish grin and giggled before bursting out in full-blown laughter when I sank my fingers into her sides.

"Julian! Stop it! That's not fair!" She stuttered out between her laughs while trying to pry my hands away.

"Are you going to stop doubting yourself? Because I meant it, that idea is intriguing and in no way stupid." I eased the pressure of my fingers a bit, but not enough to entirely stop tickling her.

"Y-yes, just no more tickling, please." She panted while begging me with playful eyes.

"If you keep putting yourself down or anything like that from now on, then I'm tickling you." I threatened her with a playful yet stern look as I pulled her into my lap.

"I'm only stating facts." She retorted with pursed lips.

"Then I guess I just have to tickle them out of you." Her body jumped from the slight pressure of my fingers when I twitched them mockingly.

Why am I so peeved about her having low self-esteem? Why should any of that matter to me one bit? Why am I offering to waste my time correcting her bad habit? I wasn't her parent or teacher or something.

The answer to my questions smacked my mind like a bat to the face, but I refused to acknowledge it because it wasn't rational or practical.

Avery was to be mine, so I had to build her up to my standards. She had a perfect foundation, but no one bothered to put the effort into building up from it. I was more than happy that no one took a chance with her because it meant I had a clean slate to work with.

I will fix her to my image and make her perfect for me as she is meant to be.

CHAPTER 7
Avery

Yep, I am going to be killed.

The deeper and deeper I drove down the road of endless forest of trees, the dreadful feeling in my chest grew heavier and heavier until my arms ached to move on their own accord to turn the steering wheel fully around and drive back to the safety of the city.

It's fine. It's just your anxiety and paranoia. You're just out of your comfort zone. You're going to be okay. He's not going to kill you. Help is only a phone call away. You're fine.

I don't know if my attempt at a pep talk helped because my nerves continued to stay on edge until I reached a moderately sized cabin house with a wrap-around porch. The place was huge for one person, in my opinion, but it looked nice, like some camping vacation home you'd see in the magazines.

Not knowing where to park in the open area, I settled for the area in front of the garage and hoped I wasn't blocking him in.

Julian was already outside on the porch, occupying one of the many chairs that scattered the place methodically. Upon laying his eyes on me, he offered a warm smile that I couldn't help but return with my own as I ascended the stairs to him.

"Hey there, beautiful." He greeted me with a tight hug when I was within range for him to reach out and snag me.

"Hey yourself, handsome." Oh God, did that sound too cheesy of a response?

"Relax, I'm not gonna kill ya out here." He joked with a lopsided smirk, making me giggle—a little too nervously—in response.

"Oh? I haven't thought about that one bit driving down into the middle of nowhere to meet Mister Dreamy." I joked back with a roll of my eyes.

Chuckling softly, Julian cupped my heated face in his burly hand, leaving one arm secured around my waist as if to prevent an escape. "I am so glad you didn't change your mind. I know it's kind of fast for a second err third date, but I figured you'd much enjoy something more private and intimate." His deep, velvety voice melted me as much as his wonder-filled eyes.

God, his voice sounded so clear and better without all the background noise of the public muddling it. He really could talk gibberish, and I wouldn't care as long as I could hear his soul-shaking voice. "I have to admit, I'm really nervous. I've never done anything like this before, ever." I shamefully admitted with burning cheeks.

"Well, just think of it as any other date with any other boyfriend you've had and shit. Nothing to be nervous about. Just a nice dinner between two people who obviously like each other." There was a slight edge to his voice when he mentioned my previous dates before it smoothed back out to his joyful self.

Pretty sure if someone snapped a picture of me right now, then they would mistake my face for a cherry with how red it probably is. "I uhh... I've never been asked out before, nor have I ever had a boyfriend or anyone remotely close to intimate. The only time I have ever been on anything remotely close to a date, besides last night with you, was senior prom night, but that was with a group of friends, and it was a planned thing for all of us." I wanted to run away and hide in a hole for the rest of my life because I basically admitted to being a total loser to the hottest man I had ever talked to in my life.

God, I probably just blew whatever hair of a chance I had with my stupid confession. Stupid. Why the hell had I done that!? This was only date two. Shouldn't I have waited for date five at the very least before uncapping the stupid shit in my shitty life? God, why am I such a fuck up?

The disturbance in his eyes caused mine to avert as I steeled myself for the rejection. I shouldn't be bothered by the idea, but my heart clenched at the thought of him rejecting me.

"I-I'm sorry, I'll go... You'll never—"

The sudden grab at my face promptly shut me up, a sharp gasp leaving my open mouth from Julian's grip. One look into his darkened eyes, and I could feel my knees become mush as my blood redirected itself to my core and breasts, tightening my nipples under my blouse.

My survival instincts screamed at me to flee, to hop in my car and drive as far away as possible. The way Julian looked at me right now, as if I was prey, was like a hungry wolf looking at its first real meal in forever. There was a dark, burning need in his eyes, a desire, a possessive edge.

But fuck my instincts because I wanted to let him consume me, to see the extent of his desire for me. Was it as intense as his eyes reflected? How badly did he want me? How did he want me?

Some inner part of me purred at this twisted attention, the part that wanted to roll over and expose myself to him completely.

Leaning down, he pressed his forehead against mine, hovering his lips just inches from mine. "You shouldn't say such things to a man like me, Avery. You have no idea how riveting it is to hear that. You have any idea how crazy you drive me? From the first time in the library to last night, something about you has ignited this inferno in me. Hearing you admit all you just did is going to drive me beyond the brink of insanity." His intense words hit my lips with his breath, making me tremble in his arms.

"Y-you still want me? I'm a twenty-eight-year-old virgin who never had a single boyfriend or dating experience in her life. I'm annoying, don't know when to stop rambling, look like a plain washout." I have no idea what else left my running mouth because my brain couldn't keep up with the stupid shit spewing out.

A sudden chill ran down my spine, making me shut my mouth when I noticed the heavy shift in the air. Then, focusing my attention back on Julian, I saw the intensity of his gaze as he pressed me harder against his body, letting me feel how sturdy he was, especially down south.

Letting out a shaky breath, I let Julian take my hand and place it against the bulge in his pants, moving my hand so that I palmed him through his jeans. "Avery, you feel what you do to me? That is all you, from having you in my arms to hearing that I am your first real experience." Pleasure shook at my body when he hissed out a growl. "God, you have no idea how much you've fed my ego and desire for you. I don't ever want to let you go now because the moment I saw you skitter away from me at the library, I knew I had to catch you and make you mine. Now, knowing that I am going to be your first, god, just fuck." Even through the thickness of his jeans, I could feel the subtle throbs of his hard-on with his words filled with utter lust.

Lust for me.

Taking my bottom lip between my teeth, I breathed in deeply, taking a long hit of his intoxicating scent that instantly set my aroused body ablaze. "I'm scared... But not how I should be. I'm not scared of giving myself to you, even though I should. I should be scared of getting hurt, but I'm not."

I had to pause for a moment to swallow my stupidity and ridiculousness. "For some reason, a part of me screams at me to run away from you to protect myself. Yet, I feel safe with you, within your presence, even though I've barely known you for three days. This could end badly for me, yet I don't care. I want to be hurt. I want to be hurt by you."

My body shook like a leaf in his arms, and I wasn't sure why. Excitement? Arousal? Fear? Nervousness? Immense happiness?

"I am fucking scared about how much I'm going to enjoy this. Enjoy you." I don't know what compelled me to confess it all to him; something about the safety of his warmth made me want to open up. "And how much I want and need all of this with you."

His chest rumbled with his growl as he moved his other hand up so both cradled my face as if I were a precious jewel. My tiny body stood no chance against his brooding one as he backed me up against the railing of the porch, causing the wood dig into my lower back as he trapped me.

"You shouldn't say such things to a man like me, Avery, a man on the cusp of losing all control. God, you should be fucking terrified, and I am so glad that you are." His raspy voice should send me for the hills, yet they sent shockwaves of electrifying excitement straight to my aching nipples and throbbing pussy. "You have any idea how turned on I am by your fear little one? Fuck, I want to devour you right now. Fuck dinner, I want to eat you."

"What would you do if I ran right now?" I whispered breathlessly, leaning my face in and ghosting my lips dangerously against his, earning another growl from him.

"I won't be responsible for what happens if you rip open the cage door, baby." There was an excitement to his grave warning, one I should take with earnest.

Instead, I found myself stepping into the ring of craziness.

Slowly, I felt my hands up his body, reveling at how his muscles tensed in reaction to my touch. He made me want to submit, yet he made me feel so damn powerful. No man has ever reacted this way to me before, not truly, at least. Everything from Julian was genuine; there was no hiding the want in his lust-blown pupils.

A smirk pulled at the corners of my lips a split second before I shoved at his chest with all my strength, creating the tiniest opening for me to slip from him and take off down the porch to the tree line.

The adrenaline pumping through my body made my feet run in tempo to my thumping heart as I grinned crazily.

God, what the fuck am I doing?

Looking back, I could see Julian slowly stalking me with a dangerous, feral grin.

He was game, and he gave me a head start.

"Run, little one, run. Spread your wings and fly as far and high as you can before I catch you."

43

CHAPTER 8
Julian

IT'S ONLY A MATTER of time, Avery.

My heart raced in my chest like a horse on the track as I kept my eyes locked on her fleeing body. The thudding in my chest echoed against my eardrums with each heavy step I took toward Avery as her little form grew smaller and smaller from my line of sight.

The fog of her breath filled the air around her with every heaving breath she took. Her luscious, silky ebony locks whipped around wildly with her darting head, reminding me so much of the wings of ravens spreading for flight.

Too bad I won't let this one get away, ever.

She might think this to be a game, but she's about to be proven so wrong. This little game of chase was a hunt to me. Only difference this time was my prey won't be dead by the end of it. Even though the thrill of a kill pumped at my blood and moved my feet forward, my hands didn't itch like usual. No, this excitement, the anticipation, was for something greater than to wring the life out of her once I would get my hands on her.

When I would get my hands around her neck, I'd choke her, but not for the sake of cutting her precious air from her until her eyes rolled back and her lips turned blue with her paling face. No, I wanted to hold her life in my hands and play with it; I wanted to feel her life pulse under my fingers as I held her delicate little neck. I couldn't help but wonder how she would look in that position. How much fear would fill those warm brown eyes of hers?

Fuck I need to find out.

My feet instantly kicked into a full sprint when I deemed her head start good. Even though she had put an excellent distance between us, my long strides made closing the distance easy.

"Shit." I could hear her faintly through the rushing wind and buzz in my ear.

"Got—" Just as my hands were about to clamp down on her shoulders, she made a sharp turn and ducked under my arms in the nick of time.

Her little squeal of excitement in light of her victorious escape was like gasoline to the fire within me. The need to successfully capture her and take her under me burned into every inch of my body.

The rush I felt was indescribable. No matter how many hunts I have been on, nothing has come close to comparison. The mere thought of chasing Avery had me hard already, but now that I was actually chasing, well, fuck. I was probably going to embarrass myself by prematurely ejaculating the moment I buried myself fully inside of her, but that's how wild she drove me.

"Come here, little birdie."

Come here so I can pluck your feathers out one by one, tie your wings down, or better yet, break them so you can't ever fly away from me again.

Yet again, I find myself repulsed at the thought of ending her life. I rarely killed women, very rarely because the crime often didn't justify death by my hands, but that's not to say I haven't. Avery wasn't a criminal, though; she was squeaky clean. Besides being beyond my norm, I didn't want her gone forever

For lack of better terms, she was boring, plain, average. She worked a good job as a CSI, made fair money to keep herself cushy enough, lived alone in a quaint studio apartment decorated to reflect her simple and cute lifestyle, and was a bit estranged from her family from what I gathered with the scattered and unanswered letters from home that she had tucked away in an abandoned drawer.

Yes, I broke into her place, sue me. I had to see who I intended to get involved with. She seemed too ordinary and sound on our first meet, and it could have all been an act or front for all I knew. So, I grew kind of cautious and paranoid. Thankfully, and much to my disappointment, she was as boring as she appeared. Okay, I should take that back; she wasn't dull; otherwise, she wouldn't indulge in a chase. Appearance-wise, yes, she was more on the plain side, but I had a good feeling that deep down, she was filled with surprises that never got the chance to bloom after my little break-in.

Even though I had this need towards her, a very similar need to seek, hunt, and kill, the image of her dead by my hands twisted my gut uncomfortably—yet again. The feeling still confused me and scared me because I had never been repulsed by murder ever before—even when I was a child, killing rodents and stray animals out of sheer curiosity. My first actual human kill didn't bother me either; I didn't even twitch or blink the moment I slit the man's throat so horribly with a dull, rusty knife.

Gore never bothered me or made my stomach queasy; nothing in life could make my steeled stomach churn. At least, not until I met Avery. The thought of harm coming to Avery gave my chest this sinking feeling, one that worsened if the source of the harm were to be me. No matter how much I wanted to wrap my hand around her slender, delicate little neck, the intention behind the need was something more primal and sensual.

I wanted—no need—to control her life. To have her life in my hands, at my whim, to have such control over her. Fuck. The thought of it all amplified my need and excitement for her, and it gave me the motivation I needed to push myself to pursue her harder than ever before.

Her delicate body came closer and closer with each stride, and her sweet face slowly morphed from fun and excitement to fear and arousal the more I closed in on her. Those pretty eyes of hers widened so much that I thought they'd pop out of her head, and her chest heaved more with her panicked breaths.

Avery gave out a short scream when I reached out and grabbed her, wrapping my arms protectively around her and tackling her to the ground with a grunt. I didn't want to damage her, not yet.

Slapping my hand over her mouth, I press her into the ground and pin her struggling body using my own to weigh her down. "Gotcha little bird, no escape now." Unable to help myself, I press my hips into hers, grinding into her covered core with a strained grunt.

Much to my surprise, Avery returned the action with her own moan and roll of her hips despite the fear pinpointing her pupils. With my control slipping—another shock to me—I slip my hand into her jeans after hastily undoing them. Shoving over her pubic bone, my fingers found their prize. I didn't even have to try to part her folds because they slid apart so easily from how slick she was. "Fuck." I hissed pridefully with a dark chuckle. "You're fucking soaked, you little slut."

Pulling my hand out, I grabbed her face with a firm grip, making her watch me suck each finger clean of her delicious nectar. One taste and I knew I was fucked. The moment her unique taste hit my tongue, I was hooked.

Ecstasy flooded my system like never before as I savored every bit of her taste on my fingers. This feeling of euphoria went beyond my expectations. The taste of fear paled in comparison to Avery.

Was this the start of a new addiction? The taste of a woman?

No, not just any woman: Avery. Just Avery. The thought of shoving my face between anyone else's legs repulsed me to where my arousal threatened to flee. I only wanted to taste and feast upon Avery and her forbidden fruit, and only I could do that. The thought of anyone else having such a pleasure made my rage simmer to the surface.

Focusing back on Avery, I studied her closely. Her sweet, plump lips were parted with her heavy breaths, her brown eyes were nearly black with how blown her pupils became with need, and how she looked at me with such awe and desire drove me mad.

Using my thumb and fingers, I force her jaw open and shove the fingers I had just cleaned into her mouth until she gagged and teared at the eyes. I expected her to bite my fingers and fight to get free, so I was a little bewildered when she brushed her tongue along my fingers and wrapped her lips tightly around my digits.

If this was some dream, then it better not end until I have buried myself deep in her and spilled my seed into her. Otherwise, I will hunt her down upon waking and take her wherever the hell she is like a damn savage.

Pulling my fingers from her mouth with a soft pop, I slowly trail it down her body to her breast. With no mercy, I roughly cupped her small breast into my big hand and squeezed until she squirmed and whimpered a moan out under me.

Easing my grip on her jaw, I slid my hand down to around her throat, cutting her airflow off with a firm squeeze as I leaned down and hovered my lips an inch from hers. "If this wasn't your first time, then I would tear your clothes away right now and fuck you like a beast in a rut. But the only place I want to spill your virgin blood is on my sheets, where you will be able to witness our sin the morning after." Fuck, the thought of staining my sheets with her blood nearly had me coming.

Her little shiver with the glimmer of excitement brightening her eyes didn't go unnoticed by me. "Oh, you like that, don't you? The thought of me taking you like an unhinged animal." I don't know if her little smile was purposeful or not, but seeing it with the flutter of her eyes made my cock twitch in my pants.

Gathering her wrists in one hand, I pin them above her head while shoving her legs wide open to give myself room to roll my hips into her fully.

Once again, I found myself doing something very much out of character for me. Never in my life would I ever dry hump someone like some overly hormonal, horny teenager with no control. Yet, for some asinine reason, I was more than content with grinding against her with our clothes on. Fucking insane, honestly. Her clothes should be in tatters right now, and the sounds of our bodies clashing should fill the area and echo for miles. Or, at the very least, we should be back at my place because I hauled her back over my shoulder like a prized kill.

Yet I am humping her on the forest floor because I couldn't get enough of her flushed face under the moonlight that streamed through the trees. Her lust-filled pupils were blown so wide that her eyes almost looked black from between her half-closed eyes. Her perfect little heart-shaped lips were so sweetly parted with her breathy moans that I could see because of the cold night air. What really ensnared me was the way her sweet eyes begged me for more.

I didn't want to stop to strip her and enter her, not while her face twisted so sweetly with pleasure as her orgasm approached. I wanted to push her over the edge to see the release wash over her face and paint the image in my mind forever. If I stopped now, then I'd lose what I've got, like cutting a movie off in the middle of something good.

"Julian, I—oh fuck." Her body shuddered and trembled under me as her hips bucked at me needily with her release.

Seeing the bliss soften her face was my breaking point. I came with a groan through my gritted teeth. The smooth movements of my hips became jagged and erratic as I rode out both our orgasms.

Fucking hell, what is she doing to me?

CHAPTER 9
Avery

"ARE YOU OKAY?"

Julian's concern warmed my molting heart and deepened the heat on my face.

With a happy hum, I nodded in response and smiled at him widely because I couldn't control the spread of my lips with the immense happiness I felt. "Yeah, just kind of processing all of it still, in a good way. I mean, I've never done anything like that before, nor did I think I'd like it that much. I loved it a lot, don't get me wrong, it's just a lot for little virgin me to process. I mean, I haven't had sex yet, nor have we fucked yet, and I basically let you chase me like some animal and hump me on the forest floor until I melted under you. I enjoyed it so much, and I don't know why, but I want to do it again even though I hate running, but—"

My rambling was cut short by a pair of lips sealing my own. "If it makes you feel any better, that was a first for me too." He chuckled against my lips before sitting beside me on his couch. "Not the chasing part, the humping and coming in my pants part." I was tempted to call bullshit until I saw the sincerity in his eyes.

Both of us were back in the cozy comfort of his home now. After we came down from our high, Julian hauled me over his shoulder and took us back, where he settled me on his couch with a blanket after a heavy make-out session with another orgasm by his hand. Then he made me wash up and change before tending to the little scrapes and cuts I had gotten on our little run with some healing ointment and antibacterial cream. Afterwards, h left me to my thoughts when he cleaned up and changed himself.

"You scare me," I admit with an excited tremble in my voice. "You are bringing out a side to me I never thought possible, and you make me feel things I shouldn't yet. All rationality goes out the window when it comes to you."

Who in their right mind would agree to a third date at a private residence in the middle of nowhere? This idiot, me, that's who.

Who fucking entices their date to chase them through the damn forest at night on the third date to get hunted down like some animal? This fucking idiot right here.

Sure, my life was simple, boring, average, and it could use some excitement, but still. I shouldn't be tossing everything out the window because of one man I met over a dating app and have barely known in person for a full twenty-four hours; honestly, it all sounded like a hor-ror movie in the making or a nightly news segment about a homicide.

This fire Julian had lit in me terrified me because I shouldn't be this reckless, not at this age, and definitely not if I want to keep my head on my neck. I should run, but I was a damn moth being drawn to his flame. And the scary thing was, I didn't care for when I would get burnt to ashes.

"You scare me too, Avery. You're bringing out a side to me I've always tried to keep locked away." Though he was truthful, I could see some kind of restraint in his eyes, as if he kept something from me. "On a different note, happy I didn't slit your throat in the forest and bury you beneath a tree?" He joked with a soft laugh.

Unable to help it, I rolled my eyes and laughed in response. "Yes, thank you for saving your diabolical plans for murder for another date. At least bury me in a bed of flowers if you do kill me and bury me. A tree is so mediocre unless that's how you see me?"

"Oh baby, you are anything but. I'd bury you in the stars where you belong if I were to take your pretty little head off, not that I'd ever do that. I much prefer your neck intact for me to wrap my hand around and maybe put a collar around." The little smirk on his face widened at my little gasp of excitement. "Did the thought of that excite you?"

Whimpering, I shamefully admitted to his question with a nod while averting my eyes. It shouldn't excite me, the thought of him collaring me like some pet to keep. Yet, I reveled in the idea deep down, no matter how wrong and somewhat depraved it may seem.

I have dove into the world of BDSM, and by dove, I meant researched extensively. My interest in the community grew with my research, and soon, I found myself having a personal curiosity. Unfortunately, the only experience I had was in my mind with my fantasies, thinking about how things *might* feel.

Another wave of shivers rippled throughout my body when his finger traced across my neck. "I've never done anything before." I whimpered with an aversion of my eyes. "I want to, but..."

"You're scared. Afraid that you'll love it more than you think. Afraid of making yourself vulnerable." Well, way to hit every nail on the head there buddy; or was I that easy to read?

"It's embarrassing." I couldn't believe I was having this conversation with him.

Chuckling lowly, he eased his body over mine, forcing me to lay back on the couch. "Nothing to be embarrassed about. I'm not judging you. There's nothing wrong with curiosity and wanting to explore. So, what if you end up liking things? Nearly everyone has a kink or fetish, nothing to be ashamed or shy about."

Swallowing the lump in my throat, I reached out with shaky hands and gripped the collar of his t-shirt, playing with the neckline of it. "Is it wrong that I want you to chase me again through the woods?" Even though I hated running, and exercise in general because I was a lazy ass, I wanted to feel the burn of cold air scratching at my lungs while my heart pounded with anticipation and excitement.

"Did you enjoy our little chase?" He may have held back his excitement from fully showing on his face, but his eyes lit up like a Christmas tree.

"Is it wrong to say I loved it? I never thought fear and anxiety could turn me on so much. The adrenaline pumping with each step sent my blood rushing to all the right places. And every time I searched for you, to see how close or far you were sent a rush through me, especially when I saw the excitement on your own face." Scratching the side of my face with a finger, I grinned sheepishly at him. "I really don't know how to explain it fully, but it was such a thrill unlike I've ever felt before. When you finally caught me, fuck, my heart was about to explode with an orgasm. I was ready to strip, spread my legs, and beg you to fuck me right then and there." Again, reckless but exhilarating, liberating, absolute freedom.

Julian's chest rumbled with his humming growl as he trailed kisses from my cheek to my ear. "That's the joy of it all, to be free, no constraints on your urges. Should have added primal play to your search history along with daddy issues."

"Oh God." I was pretty sure my face was beet red because of his words. "You looked at all of that?"

"I was a little curious about what else you looked at." He admitted with a chuckle. "But no judgment here from me, promise. If anything, it all just made me more drawn to you. I am only holding back because I don't want to scare you off, nor do I know how fast or slow you want to take all of this, and talking while we're in a heated moment wouldn't have been a good idea."

He wasn't wrong there. If I let my emotions talk, I'd be making regretful decisions. I was ready to give him my virginity in the forest, but now that my adrenaline had died down, oh man, I probably would've crawled into a dark corner and died of shame or something. I didn't necessarily want the full romantic dinner and rose petals with Mister Right, but I didn't want to lose it out in the open on a dirt floor.

I barely had an idea of my limits, yet I was about to throw everything out the window earlier. Julian could have done whatever the hell he wanted to me, and I would have been okay with it all because of the adrenaline clouding my mind. At least he had enough of a clear head not to take things to God knows where earlier.

"Also, there is nothing wrong with consensual non-consent. It's more common than you think." His deep voice brought me out of my head, and his finger trailed down my face. "It's just one of those things that *needs* to be discussed before hand, and boundaries and rules *need* to be set in place for such things."

"But I shouldn't want any of that, it's so wrong, and I don't know, it makes me feel so dirty and tainted. But I mean, it's not like I'm asking for it or anything. God, no, that's not it. Like I want it, but with the right person and not just some random person off the street or have it actually happen to me." It sounded more confusing said out loud, and I expected a look of confusion or judgment from Julian but got none of it.

Understanding and amusement filled his eyes, along with a flicker of lust. "It's a very touchy kink and one not to be taken lightly. Yes, assault is wrong and should never be wished upon someone, nor is it ever truly wanted by a person, but CNC is a scene where there is still an element of consent and control, so it's not truly an assault." Smiling warmly, he kisses my cheek. "Just because you fantasize about something doesn't mean you are asking for it, so get that out of your mind, and if anyone ever tells you otherwise, then you stab them in the eye for being stupid."

Cracking a smile and chuckle, I returned his eyes with my grateful ones. "So, seeing the little thing about daddy issues didn't weird you out?"

"Baby, we all got some kind of issues. So, what if you need a little more love and attention from me? I won't be complaining about that one bit any time soon." Something in his eyes unsettled me.

Even though he seemed fully accepting, an edge darkened his eyes and made him feel dangerous. He looked at me like prey before, and when he chased me, but this was the look of a predator out for blood. It made me feel like some prized game to be caught and hung on the wall or something to be chased and captured to be locked away in a dank basement.

But why? Why did I get this strange feeling again when I was more than comfortable and open with him seconds ago? Like our date last night, he felt warm and comforting one second, then cold and menacing the next. It wasn't a huge shift in his behavior either or a subtle change in his voice. It was his eyes; something about them haunted me and drew me in, yet served as a stark warning for my self-preservation to kick in and force my legs to carry me as far away from Julian as possible.

"You make it sound like you'll give me all I ever need to where I wouldn't need to ask or seek it elsewhere." The nervousness was hard to hide from my chuckle as I focused my eyes on everything else but his eyes.

My eyes snapped up to his when his finger tilted my head to meet his devouring gaze. "Because I am all you will ever need in your life, little one. I *will* give you all you need and ask for, keep you more than happy every second of the day, shower you with all the affection in the world, and show you a whole world of pleasure you've never seen or experienced before. I want to take care of you, Avery, if you'll let me."

Talk about putting me on the damn spot.

Tucking my bottom lip between my teeth with worry, I couldn't stop my nerves from flaring up. "Way to play on my daddy issues." I joked with a dry chuckle. "And what happened to pacing it? Or is asking people for something serious a third date what you do?"

"Can you blame me? I just so happen to like taking care of people, especially those I take a particular liking to." Though lighthearted, there was an edge to his words that sent a chill down my spine. "But you don't have to decide tonight. I am just putting it out there so you know. But also, I never make this kind of offer to anyone, never have. You are the first, once again. Something about you makes me want to hold you in my arms forever to shield you from the world and keep you safe."

Well, either he was a terrific liar and smooth talker, or he was truthful; I had an inclination toward the latter, given the genuine vulnerability in his eyes that tore into me like meat shredders. "Can I have some time to think about it? I want to say yes, but I want to spend some time to think about it deeply when your dominating presence is not persuading me."

"Of course. I apologize for putting so much out there on our third date, so let's just put that at the back of our minds for now and enjoy the rest of our weekend together, alright?" His melting smile made it hard not to relax and comply.

Nodding with a small hum, I gingerly traced the seam of his lips. "Just... I want you to be sure as well. I really am a lot for a simple girl. Emotionally, I'm probably gonna demand a lot, and you're probably gonna have to slow your roll with sex and kinky shit until I figure out my limits."

"Little bird, I wouldn't have said anything if I wasn't sure. It'd be pretty fucked up of me to get your hopes up like that and waste both our time if I wasn't serious." The trembles from his voice tickled the tip of my finger that continued to dance along his lower lip.

"What if I turn out to be all vanilla?" Okay, I wanted to laugh at myself for asking that question because no way was I vanilla in the slightest, not after that chase.

At least he did the laughing for us, filling the area with his deep, bell-tolling laugh. "Oh, I doubt that will ever be a problem. Don't worry. I'm not some extreme sadist or anything like that. Nothing too heavy. We can talk more about our likes and dislikes if you choose to pursue this relationship of ours. Like I said, I don't want to get too deep tonight."

Humming softly with a smile, I nodded before eying his lips with hungry eyes. "Can we still kiss? I think I'll go crazy if I don't feel your lips against mine the rest of the weekend." To tempt him, I leaned up and held my lips to his; the only thing keeping our lips from touching was my finger lingering against his lips still.

His chest rumbled with a growl as his lips tensed. Then, his pupils widened with a burning lust that made me gasp with a shudder as I sank back into the couch cushions.

Removing my hand with a firm yank, he pierced straight into my soul with the intensity of his eyes. "If you think you can stop me from claiming your sweet lips to my desire, then you've got another thing coming. Just because I agreed to give you time to think about this relationship and whether or not you're willing to risk it doesn't mean I won't take you all that I can this weekend."

Grinning darkly, he held my face tightly. "I am going to kiss your lips, face, and every inch of your body until the feeling of my lips is burnt into your body for you to feel and fantasize about when we are apart. No skin of yours will be left untouched by my hands, not until you are perfectly painted in my mind." Kissing me with a growl, he smirks against my lips. "I am going to make you addicted to me and the pleasure that my hands and tongue can b,ring you, so your decision regarding us will be a no-brainer."

"Fuck." I gasped with a whimpering moan from all the dirty images flashing through my mind like a movie reel.

The tension on his face eased into a smirk with his tilted head. "I never said I was going to play fair. I will give you time, but I am sure as hell going to do all I can to persuade your answer." He chuckled before threading his hand into the back of my hair and pulling slightly to give a soft tingle to my scalp.

With my head tilted slightly, he leaned in fully and pressed his lips against mine in a breathtaking kiss.

If his kisses could steal my soul, I would be a goner.

CHAPTER 10
Julian

Why does it feel so cramped?

And what is this warmth?

It smells like my home, but it can't be. It's too comforting.

Smokey wood, cotton, and fresh bitter tea; the scents kept my sleepy mind lulled, giving me the peace I usually felt after a successful hunt and kill.

Breathing out a growl, I tightened my arms around the body of scent to press it closer to me. Something soft touches my face, adding another layer to make everything all the more intoxicating. Instinctively, I buried my face more into whatever it was to surround myself more with the rich smoothness.

On their own accord, my hands started moving between layers of fabric along a smooth and soft surface. My fingers dipped and curved around this delicate thing as my hands wandered without any given direction, as if they just wanted to feel and touch it for the sake of it.

A body.

It was a body in my hands. A body was the source of the warmth. A very soft and delicate body that was on the top of me, trapped in my arms.

But wait, why is there a body against me?

The thought was enough to flick my eyelids open from the sudden chill that shocked my body. Instantly, relief rushed over me like a tidal wave the moment my eyes landed on the curtain of silky black hair across my chest that was connected to the lovely head of my date.

It was a strange feeling to wake up with someone next to me, let alone on me. I liked my own space, so why the hell would I let someone else invade it? Also, sharing my bed space with someone did *not* sound pleasant in the slightest to me, ever. Secondly, I never could relax enough to sleep next to someone, no matter how comfortable I was with them.

Yet, somehow, I passed out on the couch with Avery in my arms. The living room was dark, with only the flickering light of the TV lighting up the area last I remembered. Now, sunlight streamed through the windows and filled it with natural warmth from the sun's rays.

The TV screen had the movie's menu screen on repeat. If either of us had been awake by the time it ended, it surely would have been turned off.

God, I didn't even remember when I began to doze off. We were cuddling one minute, then I kissed her, touched her curves, laid my hand on her bare belly, then my face was in her smooth hair, and I remember saying something to her... But what?

Well, it didn't matter now, surely. What I needed to figure out was why the hell I slept like a damn hibernating bear around her. I wasn't tired. Okay, never mind, I was always tired to some extent because of work and my hobby, but never to the point of passing out or anything.

However, this strange exhaustion fell over me like some guillotine the moment I had Avery's body molded perfectly against mine and my arms around her. The weight of the world disappeared with her presence, and for once, I felt a constant solace drowning me in bliss.

Fucking hell, there I go again.

Groaning internally with rolling eyes, I curiously stared at the sleeping beauty.

What are you doing to me, Avery?

God, please don't let this be a cruel joke from the universe or Karma finally fucking me over. I didn't want to have to end Avery's life if her intentions with me were ill. Doubts were high about that, though; she seemed too genuine. As corny as it was to say, sunshine, rainbows, and butterflies trailed behind her. She truly was a woman who was yet to be jaded by the world.

A twisted smile danced on my face at the fact I would be the one to taint her. My bloody hands would be the ones to soak her white wings red before I'd lock her away in a gilded cage for my sick pleasure.

Granted, she was no angel, but compared to me, she was. Well, she won't be once I was through with her. Poor thing won't know who she committed herself to until it was too late, and at that point, I'd never let her escape—ever. As if I had any intentions of it in the first place.

I didn't know it then, but the moment I spotted her in the library was the day our fates were sealed together. Whatever higher being out there sent her to me, put her right in my path to take and have. That's why I've become so obsessed with her; my mind was priming me for everything. It was also why she seemed to be an exception to everything in my life. Yes, that had to be it: a gift from those above or whatever; otherwise, there was no sense as to why I would react so well to an average woman like her.

Average or not, she did have a certain charm to her, one I couldn't quite place my finger on. Maybe it was her love for crime and murder, who knows, but as long as she intrigued me, it was all I cared about.

"Julian? Shit, what time is it?" Her sleepy eyes shot open after a slow blink. "Oh my God, I'm so sorry! I fell asleep on top of you. I could have squashed you or suffocated you."

The amused laughter erupted from me before I could tame it. "Avery, you do realize you weigh less than an average human being, right? You're what? A hundred pounds soaking wet?" I teased, tightening my arms around her squirming body to keep her firmly planted against me. "You felt like a nice, weighted blanket to me. If I got bothered or didn't want you on me, I wouldn't have held you. If anything, I would have removed you."

Again, I wasn't one to put up with nuisances, minor or not.

With a soft groan, I sat up on the couch with Avery straddling my lap, which turned out to be a big mistake because she pressed right against my morning wood. "Avery." I hissed through my gritted teeth as I dug my fingers into her plush bottom to make her grind her hips against my bulge.

It'd be so easy to rip her shorts off and make her sit fully on me, and the idea was very damn tempting. Growling softly, I pressed her harder against me, bucking my hips against her to rub along her covered center. "Julian." Her sighing moan made pleasure ripple through my body as I fought for the control I always prided myself on.

My mind jarred with my body, snapping my focus back to Avery, who pushed me away with a little sheepish smile. "No funny business, don't care if you're not playing fair and all, but I still want to spend time with you that doesn't involve us doing something dirty."

Rolling my eyes with a groan, I pulled her flush against me again and quickly fisted the back of her head to tilt her head up towards me. "As much as I want to ravage you for twenty-four hours straight, there are plans I have for us today that don't involve my hands pleasuring you. Of course, those plans only take a few hours, which leaves us plenty of free ones to work with." I spoke against her lips before running my tongue along her bottom lip, eliciting a shaky gasp from her.

"You do this with all your dates?" Her voice tensed the air with apprehension, dimming the mood some.

"No, you are the first and the last." Because like hell would I do anything like this ever again with anyone. For one, I didn't want to. Two, it wouldn't be Avery the second time around. And I wanted no one else but Avery.

"You seem really sure of me even though you barely know me." She giggled, sticking her tongue out and flicking the edge of my lip with the tip of her tongue. "Again, I could be a serial killer for all you know, and you're my next victim."

Oh, the fucking irony in that.

I wanted to laugh my head off, but I only let a small one slip. "Again, if I fall victim to you, then I wouldn't complain one bit." I lied about the reason behind the little laughter.

If I had no moral compass and killed at my whim, then maybe she'd be a victim in the end, but fortunately for her, I was a good killer. Unless she was some serial abuser or assailant, which I very highly doubt because she looked like she lacked quite a bit to pack any kind of damage.

"Stop me any time you want, but you are a reserved person, shy with a wild side just waiting for the right moment and people to unleash it around, smart, ambitious, a little jaded from the sad and dull look in your eyes at the time, curious with a sense of adventure, careful, organized, a crime junkie to the soul, crafty. That's just the gist I've got of you so far in the past few days we've been texting and from the two dates we've had. I still sense there is a lot to you that you keep buried, and I intend on slowly uncovering it all to know every inch of you inside and out." Grinning playfully, I chuckled and press a kiss to her neck. "Yes, it's a little crazy for me to be going in this hard and fast with someone I just met, but I'm the type of guy who knows what he wants and is always sure about it. I will wait forever for you if I have to because you'll be more than worth it." Some sweet truth sprinkled with sugary lies to melt her enough into my hands.

"Now you make it sound like I'm easy." She remarked with a playful scoff and roll of her eyes.

"I only make it sound easy because I'm very observant. Also, you're only more open around me because you already knew my interests from my search history through the app, so you already had a gist of me. If we were to meet through any other dating app where all you knew was my basic info and simple hobbies that'd make me sound like every other man on earth, then would you have said anything about your passion for crime on our first date? Let alone be so eager for future dates?" The point of the app using an applicant's search history as a method to make matches was that a person was much less censored with their internet privileges.

We, as humans, were creatures of habit, falling back into comfort in the safety of privacy. Yes, there were the oddball searches, but for the most part, we tended to look up things of the same nature to read, watch, or research to sate our curiosities. Hell, I thought I was good at covering my tracks by searching for random subjects or things in construction and business to throw off my digital trail of serial killers and things of that nature. Still, I guess not if the app managed to pull that much information out to make a good match.

Pouting with defeat, Avery relaxed into me and shook her head. "No, if I didn't know all I did beforehand, then I wouldn't have been so free and open. So, you're right about that. Hell, I don't know if we'd go past a first date." She admitted with a sheepish chuckle.

Smiling softly, I press our lips together for a brief kiss before patting her ass to get up. "Fine, no funny business this morning, but only because you made me feel soft and mushy." I still desired her greatly, but it simmered down enough to where I could ignore it well enough.

Once she was up on her feet, I quickly joined her. "I'll make us some breakfast. Anything in particular you want? If not, then I'll make us some omelets." I asked while stretching my arms above my head, smirking when I noticed her eying me.

"Omelets are good." She answered with a dazed smile.

"My eyes are down here, sweetie." I teased with a hearty chuckle when she blushed a nice red.

"God, I hope you know I don't exercise, so don't expect a gym buddy out of me." She forced a chuckle out to hide her cute awkwardness.

"Then I'll consider that my me time away from you to keep my sanity intact, just like how your office time for your author activities is your me time away from me." That and my time at night when she'd be asleep.

Damn, maybe I should think about this more carefully, as she suggested. Being single with all the time in the world made picking, tracking, and killing my victims easy because I didn't have to worry about entertaining another body, coming home to someone, or worrying about someone questioning me. Right now, I didn't have to hide anything from anyone because I kept everyone at arm's length. If I let Avery in, then I would have to figure out a whole new routine.

I really shouldn't be sure about this, a relationship, but damn myself if I wasn't because the thought of life without her seemed dead. Not even the prospect of victims to come made the clouds go away. After so many years of perfecting one, I didn't want to create a new routine. I fucking hated change, especially big ones.

Yet here I went, making an exception for Avery.

Always the fucking exception.

I wanted to run a hand down my face and groan at the world.

Did I want to do all of that? Make a whole new routine and list of lies to feed Avery for when the questions will come? No, not particularly, no.

The logical thing would be to cut this off, but I might as well take a knife and plunge it into my chest. If only logic worked when it came to Avery. I had already committed myself to shifting my life around for her when she hadn't even given me an answer yet.

I've never done drugs in my life, nor did I have the inclination to explore that cursed avenue, but I'm pretty sure Avery would be considered my addiction with how I couldn't bear the thought of living life without her in it next to me. Every inch of her felt like a hit to me.

If my hands weren't itching to take the life from someone, then they wanted to be on Avery's body. Even my mind couldn't escape her because she'd become a permanent placement in the cycle of work and murder, from things to do to woo her and make her smile to all the depraved things I wanted to do to her, like play an actual game of hunter and prey and claim her like a trophy when I would catch her in the forest.

I could imagine it now, the sound of her clothes giving away from the pressure of my hands, the struggle she'd put up; oh, she better fucking struggle; otherwise, half the fun would be gone. I wanted to make her submit to me, wanted her to fight to take that all away and tear away at her until she gave in.

Thwump.

A winded grunt cut out of me at the feeling of the throw pillow hitting me square in the chest. Zoning back in, I playfully narrowed my eyes at the giggling woman before me. "Go take a cold shower first before you pounce me. You're starting to get that intense look in your eyes again."

Smirking, I opened my mouth to suggest that maybe she should join me, but she got the jump this time. "No, I am not going to join you for a shower because you and I both know where that would go. If you want to see me naked, then you gotta try harder than that." She teased with a grin and giggle before sticking her tongue out at me.

My hands shot out as my eyes rolled, grabbing Avery by her hips and pulling her into a quick kiss before lightly smacking her ass and leaving before I wasted any more time this morning chasing a flying bird with no means to shoot it down.

I made the shower quick, not wanting to leave Avery alone for long. The temptation to stroke one out in the shower crossed my mind before I dismissed it because I had Avery to get back to. I didn't want to spend any time away from her this weekend unless I absolutely had to.

Avery quickly hopped into the bathroom to freshen up when I finished, and I busied myself meanwhile in the kitchen to whip both of us a hearty breakfast to fuel us for the little hike on my property. We'd be back at the house for lunch, but it was still a bit of an adventure, and I didn't want her dropping out on me halfway through.

She entered the kitchen area with a hum of delight and a playful giggle. "Just so you know, I might start whining halfway through and demand a piggyback ride the rest of the way." It took me a second to fully figure out that she was joking to respond with my own chuckle.

"If you're gonna make me carry you, then I'm going to chase you until your legs give out." I joked back with a hint of seriousness.

"Okay, I might hate exercising and just doing anything more than I have to, but I'd gladly run for you any day, any time." She admitted with a shy smile and pink cheeks.

"That's because it's not work. It's fun with a reward out of it all." I remarked with a deep chuckle as I approached her and pulled her over to the kitchen island.

Hoisting her up onto the surface, I leaned in and kissed her softly. "It's just a small hike, probably about an hour or hour and a half tops." The river embankment wasn't too far, to me at least.

"Where we going?" She questioned with a tilt of her head and furrowed brows.

"A river on the property. I was actually thinking about having a picnic lunch there. Though I also planned on having us back here for lunch if you get too exhausted from a little walking." I bit out the last part with a teasing grin and chuckle, earning a roll of eyes and a light smack to the chest from Avery.

Humming softly in thought, she pursed her lips slightly for a moment before responding. "I wouldn't mind that. I mean, we're already going out there, so we might as well sit and enjoy the scenery with some food to make the trip worth it." At least she seemed easy to adapt, which was good.

Smiling, she leaned in and settled her forehead against mine. "Let's eat our breakfast, which smells amazing, by the way, and then I'll help you throw some lunch together, and we can go. Yeah?" She suggested while her finger traced along my jawline.

"Sounds perfect to me." Surprisingly, it wasn't a lie.

The quick flash of us being domestic in the kitchen made my heart flip—if that was even possible—and flutter. Honestly, I still think my body attempted to warn me about an impending heart attack with these strange feelings.

Cliché sayings like 'my heart melted' or 'butterflies in my stomach' were only in fiction to play on a reader's emotions. In no way, shape, or form were they real...

Right?

CHAPTER II
Avery

"Oooh! That's a sharp knife. It'd cut a finger off like butter."

My intrusive thoughts slipped from my mouth before I realized I wasn't home alone.

Hanging my head from the embarrassment, I glanced over at Julian out of the corner of my eyes, catching his amused smirk and adoring eyes. At least, they looked adoring with how they lit up and sparkled almost.

Gasping, I quickly slapped a hand over my mouth and blushed. "God, I'm so sorry, that was weird of me to say, it just slipped out. I don't plan on cutting your fingers off or anything like that, not that I want to. Otherwise, you can't use them to like touch and stuff, and I kinda need you to have your fingers still to touch me because I like it when you touch me." I quickly shut my mouth when I noticed his smirk widening into a smile before his chest shook, and chuckles started to come out of him.

"Oh sweetie, to anyone else, yes, a little weird, but not to me. I found it amusing and adorable. Honestly, you could have said something about how easily it would glide across the neck enough to sever the head cleanly, and I wouldn't find it off-putting. Actually, I take it as a compliment because that means my knives are nice and well-kept, which is my intention." I don't know if he entertained me with his response; a part of it sounded like he played along, but he also sounded somewhat serious about keeping his knives sharp.

Well, I wasn't weirded out one bit because sharp knives were an excellent thing to have if he cooked a lot; cutting with a dull knife is a pain in the ass. If I took care of myself more and actually put more effort into cooking meals at home, then I'd probably give some attention to my neglected knives.

"Just so you know, I'm probably gonna say a lot of weird and random things. So, you gotta be fine with that if I'm to stick around." Better for him to know now than to get annoyed later when he finds out about my awkward habit.

Socially, I've always been awkward my whole life. Growing up in school, I barely had any friends because I was never good at talking and connecting with people; when I did, I'd get too eager and scare them off. I didn't know how to properly interact with people for the longest time because my parents fucked me over by keeping me sheltered until they couldn't. Then my gross interest in crime and murder at a young age and all things related, and a liking for anime and all things of that nature before it became popular, put me towards the edge of the ring when it came to social circles in school.

Actually, I was part of the outcasts in school growing up, the running joke with them—the little boyish freak. Even now, I still get called that by those I went to school with—coworkers included—if they ran into me and recognized me. Even though I looked nothing like how I did back then, I couldn't escape it.

I learned to live with the bullying after so long, and for the most part, it all bounced off the shell I had put up. Still, just because I became mostly numb to it didn't mean I wasn't affected to an extent sometimes. My self-esteem never recovered after two decades of being smacked around by my peers and family.

"Hey." The rough pad of Julian's finger brushing along my jaw before my chin got gripped made my attention go to his mossy eyes. "If I wanted normal, then I wouldn't have gone on that app or agreed to a date with you after seeing all the things you searched up. I don't know what others have said about you, but I quite like your little quirkiness and weirdness so far. It adds a nice spark to you and makes you uniquely you."

Well, ain't that just sweet.

Even though I pressed my lips together to suppress my smile, it powered its way through in the end until I smiled like a goof. "Keep being sweet like this, and I might have to agree to stick around and see where we would go in a relationship." I teased with a nervous chuckle.

"Well then, guess I just have to sugarcoat everything from here on out." He joked with a chuckle before giving me a ghost of a kiss. "And it would be a shame if you cut my fingers off. You'd be denying yourself a whole world of pleasure if you did."

His deep words against my lips made my knees weak with a shudder. "Well, that's what your mouth and tongue are for, right?" I don't know where the boldness came from suddenly, but no complaints here, especially after seeing how his pupils melted his darkened eyes from my words.

"Cheeky little one, aren't you?" He chuckled out a growl before fully grabbing my face and crushing my lips against his in a heated kiss.

My bottom lip tingled from him tugging at it—hard—with his teeth when he pulled away. "Did you sneak some fruit?" He mused with a chuckle and quirked his eyebrow.

"Uhh... No...?" I lied badly with a smile that I tried to hide, poorly.

"Lying to me already, little bird?" His voice rasped and dipped low in a playful manner as his hands shot out and grabbed at my sides to tickle me. "I can taste it on your lips." Then, his lips curled in a playful smirk. "Or were you hoping to get in some trouble?"

"Maybe just a little to test your hand." I shouldn't be playing with fire, but screw it; I needed to live a little.

"If that's all you wanted, then all you had to do was bend over and ask me to spank you like a good girl." The hunger in his eyes made my aching pussy clench as heat pooled between my legs.

Fuck me. No, seriously, fuck me, please!

Lordy, since when did I become such a depraved, horny teenager? I wanted to slide off the counter, bend over it, and beg him to spank me like never before in my life. Have I ever been spanked before? Yes, and no. Yes, by means of my parents punishing me as a child for fucking up. But no, in a sexual sense. I probably shouldn't be wanting a man to lay his hands on me physically, and in a way, this wasn't like that; at least the meaning behind it wasn't the same. I couldn't explain it, but the thought of him turning my cheeks burning red made me soak my panties.

"But I have a feeling you don't want to be spanked like a good girl. Otherwise, you wouldn't have lied to me just now." Slowly, his hand brushed down my hair and wrapped around my neck. "You want me to grab you by the neck or your hair and force you over my knee, hold you down with one hand, and spank you with the other until you're crying or truly sorry for sharpening your tongue at me, don't you?"

Holy shit, could he get any hotter?

I probably shouldn't tempt fate, but God was it hard not to when he said all the right things to get my body to heat up perfectly in all the right places. I shouldn't be leaning my body into him or wrapping my legs around him, let alone lean my neck into his hand more to make him grip it.

"God, I hope you make your decision soon so I can do all the sinful things to your beautiful body to make it all mine." His hand tightened around my throat for a brief second before he slid his hand up to grab my face—squishing my cheeks together—and kiss me with a deep groan.

Fuck me.

Moaning softly, I wrapped my arms around his neck and frantically grabbed at the back of his head to deepen the kiss as I slid my tongue out and ran it along his bottom lip.

Julian quickly opened his mouth with a chuckle, but I didn't get a chance to slip my tongue into his mouth because he shoved his way into mine. My whimpers became muffled by him as he dominated every inch of my mouth with his tongue while his free arm snaked around my lower back to keep my body pinned against his. I tried to fight back, but the futile attempt only amused him and spurred him on more until I tapped against his shoulder repeatedly.

Instantly, he broke the kiss and rested his head against mine as he breathed heavily. The moment he removed himself, I took in a sharp breath of much-needed air, making my head dizzy from the sudden rush of oxygen.

"Finish with the fruit, Avery, and no more spoiling your little appetite." He chuckled breathlessly before leaning in for another kiss and stepping away from me completely to return to his side of the kitchen counter to finish the sandwiches.

Shockingly, we didn't make out again and cut the hike from the day's itinerary. As tempting as it was to try and get him out of it, I was kind of curious to go out on a stroll with him and see what he had in his backyard—literally.

"Just curious, and you don't have to answer if you don't want to, obviously, but why so much land if it's just you? I mean, even if you don't like neighbors, this is a bit excessive; I mean, what was it again? Like twenty-something acres?" I couldn't remember exactly how much he'd told me the night before when I asked how big his place was, but it was quite a bit for a single guy living on his own in a two-thousand-square-foot cabin house.

Was it a little creepy? Eh, maybe a little, but who was I to judge when I lived in an apartment the size of his closet? So, what if he just liked his space? Granted, it still gave off creepy vibes, ones that I should heed, but oh well, for now.

"A little over thirty acres. Besides wanting to be far from other people, the space is nice and gives me a lot of my own land to do what I want without many constraints. I can camp out in my own backyard without worrying about other campers around or hikers coming across me randomly. I could hunt from my own window practically if I really wanted, and I just get to have all this nature and peace to myself and hopefully you." A quick flash of his charming smile was all my stomach needed for the butterflies to storm around.

With some quickened steps, I caught up to his side and took one of his big hands into mine, letting him lead us to our destination. "You really have it set on me, huh? Not that I'm complaining. It just feels kind of weird and strange to have a man like you hung over me and actually pining for me."

"Come on, you're really telling me that *no one* had a crush on you growing up or in school or anything? I know you said you never had a boyfriend before, but come on, a small crush from a schoolboy or something?" Julian prodded at me with a glance of his curious eyes.

Heaving out a sigh, I looked down at our intertwined fingers as I fidgeted with them out of habit. "I didn't always look like this growing up. I was skinny as a stick with little to no figure, weird ass shit Asian bowl haircut, and clothes that didn't fit me right. Pair my awkward looks with an awkward personality and hobbies, and I basically became a natural repellent to everyone, even my own friends, or at least those I considered friends back then."

I only had a 'glo-up' after I finally cut my parents off for good when I turned twenty and got a shit ton of therapy. Once I was finally on my own, I put on a healthy amount of weight to be average for my height and age. Then, I learned to properly dress myself and figured out my own style, which did wonders and showed off my body, which I didn't know I had. The real cherry on top of it all was my hair; I finally got to grow my hair out.

Unconsciously, I reached up with my free hand and stroked it down the length of my long hair, from the top of my head down to my lower back. Since growing it out, I've never gotten it cut shorter than my mid-back.

As stupid as it sounded, I was a little obsessed with my hair because it gave me my femininity, the one my parents had denied me all my life growing up.

"Your hair is so lovely. Has anyone ever told you that?" The dreamy far, far-out look in his eyes and a matching smile meant he was truly enamored. "It's so dark like the night sky, with just a hint of a blue sheen when the sunlight hits it just right. It's so soft and silky, too, like feathers. Then the way it flares and sways in the air when you run reminds me so much of the wings of ravens spreading and taking flight."

Then, his soft eyes darkened with an edge that sent a wary shiver down my spine. There it was again, the little flip in him, which I couldn't place my finger on. It's as if he held something back within him whenever he got that glint in his eyes.

Though I feared the dark look in his eyes, there was something about it that soothed me, oddly enough. I don't know why because I shouldn't find such a possessive look so lovely. I knew I was deprived of everything, but something about seeing a man like him look at me with such want and promise made me want to purr with delight.

Fucking hell, am I really this fucked up?

I didn't care for the fact that my first potential and only boyfriend in my life might be a crazy lunatic. Hell, I found the thought of it endearing, for fuck's sake. Like, what the hell was wrong with me?

Swallowing hard, I quickly shove my thoughts away to try and reel the conversation back in. "N-no one's ever really said anything nice or good about me to me, especially anything physical about me."

His eyes softened again, settling my edged nerves. "Well, start getting used to hearing and accepting them because I am going to shower you with them until I lose my ability to talk and think straight." His chuckle echoed through my body like it did the air around us.

Holding my hand tightly, he continued to lead the way until we reached a river with a slight embankment perfect for a picnic setup. "Can't believe this is basically your backyard." I could definitely see the appeal in wanting land to have all this to himself.

"Also, a nice place for me to dispose of a body. Not saying I'd toss yours in the river, but just saying." He joked—I think—with a chuckle. Okay, he did joke with me, but there was an edge of truth almost to it, but I wasn't sure which part.

"The river wouldn't be ideal for disposal at this time of the year anyway. The current is almost stagnant. Your body would just float there asking to be found, and the levels are low, too." Forcing out a dry chuckle, I smiled at him nervously. "Honestly, it's a bad disposal method at this time. I'd be kinda disappointed if you did throw me in right now after killing me." I half-joked with him, tossing in facts with my response.

Chuckling, he shook his head before reaching out and grabbing me to pull into his lap as he sat down on the picnic blanket after laying it out. "Smart little bird, I'm going to get one over you one day." He said, resting his chin on my shoulder as he had my back to him with his arms around my waist.

"The cold and chilly weather, along with the water, might throw off the time of death, though, and the water would wash away evidence or make it very damn hard or near impossible to get anything viable. Granted, you'd have to be very meticulous with the actual killing part, though, to make sure you minimize any traces to you." I added with a soft giggle when his stubble tickled my neck from him rubbing his chin into me.

"Smart and beautiful, you really are so perfect." Sweet words with the eyes of darkness.

I might be smiling at his little compliment, but I felt so unsettled underneath it all because of the hungry, possessive pull of his gaze. I don't know how it was possible, but he looked at me with the greediest green eyes I've ever seen, as if I was the most precious thing in the world.

But... Why did the idea appease me? It's a damn red, blaring alarm for me to run, and a part of me wanted to hop in a plane and fly across the world from him. Yet, the insane part of me that was so touched by his attention wanted to stay. Deep down, I loved and craved for someone to look at me with such passion, adoration, and desire. I was too starved for attention, and I wanted all of Julian's attention, which he seemed more than willing to give me.

I wanted to be his possession; it sounded kind of crude, but I liked the thought of it. To be desired and kept, prized and treasured. Unless he just wanted to lock me away to keep me like a forgotten pet, which could be the other case I didn't see because of my own depravities.

"What's got you quiet, little one?" He sounded too curious like a cat toying with a mouse before it would kill it.

"J-just sorting out my thoughts... Just... This all feels so nice, and I'm just not used to it. I'm not ungrateful for it or anything. It just feels so comfortable and so soon, like is it weird for me to feel as if we've been doing this forever and not the first time?" Was I just so desperate for someone that I instantly latched onto the first person to show me kindness and regard?

One reason why I didn't give Julian an answer quite yet was because I needed space from him to think about my decision thoroughly. His presence influenced me way too much. I was too heavily infatuated with this fine man. I needed to decide while of sound mind without my hormones and emotions pulling my strings.

I shouldn't be this comfortable around a man I haven't known until the past few days and with whom I've only spent a little over twenty-four hours with physically and personally. Yet, being around him felt so fitting, as if we'd been friends since childhood or something like that. I mean, I had no idea about how all of that felt since I never had a childhood friend to grow up with; I only assumed this is what it would have felt like.

Chuckling softly, he held me lovingly in his arms, drawing circles on my hips with his thumbs. "Some people are just meant to be. You know the cliché saying, your other half is out there somewhere in the world, and you'll just know when you find them." His low, gentle voice rumbled against the shell of my ear.

Cute, but something about this also didn't feel right. Well, it felt right, but *too* right. It was just *too* perfect. Yes, we were technically in a honeymoon period where most things wrong would be covered up, but surely, I should have picked something up. The only thing off about him so far were those moments where his eyes would look funny, almost malicious. He also seemed too well put together, almost like it was all an act, a front. What if he had some kind of explosive temper that wouldn't show until a few months into the relationship? Or what if he was some kind of serial abuser?

I mean, the fact that a seemingly amazing guy like Julian remained single was strange to me, and even though we clicked, there was still some kind of disconnect between us. Granted, I probably wouldn't figure out any of his bad habits, nor would he reveal them to me until we were past this honeymoon period, which could be next month or next year.

A gasping shudder pricked at my tense body when Julian slipped his hand under the waistband of my pants and cupped my hot sex over my panties. "Let me have a taste of you." He growled against my neck before running his tongue up the length of it.

Holy shit what happened? What the?!

My squirming body remained trapped in his arms, making my escape attempt futile. "Juli—ahn!" His palm rubbing against my throbbing clit made my body jerk with a squeal.

What happened to just having a pleasant conversation? Where the fuck did this side of him come from?!

"B-but lunch—fuck!" His thick fingers stretched me with a sudden intrusion, causing my aching walls to feel a slight burn from the sudden thrust of his digits.

"You'll always be a meal for me, baby. Breakfast, lunch, dinner, dessert, everything." His raspy voice hit my ear hotly, making me tremble and whimper as he continued to thrust his fingers in and out of me. "That's it, don't hold it back. I can feel you throbbing around me. Just let it go, ride it out on my fingers. You can do it."

I don't think I could hold it back even if I wanted to, not with how deep his fingers were going and how he hit the right spots enough to tighten the knot in my stomach painfully. "Fuck, Julian, you're going to make me soak myself, it'll be so embarrassing."

I might be a virgin in the sense that I've never had a cock inside of me, but I was no stranger to masturbation and some toys. I knew when an orgasm was coming and just what kind of orgasm I'd have depending on the stimulation and feeling in my tummy.

"It'll just be a small damp spot unless I really get you to cum all over." His twisted chuckle sent a shiver of pleasure down my spine right into my aching clit that his palm rubbed against with the movement of his fingers.

"No, fuck, you're gonna make me squirt...!" I squealed as I grabbed onto his arm and dug my nails into him.

I've never held back an orgasm before, but the thought of walking around with a huge wet spot in my pants, looking like I peed myself, had me tightening my muscles in an attempt to keep my orgasm at bay.

Unfortunately, I think that was the wrong thing to say because he let out an animalistic growl that had the knot in my stomach tightening further. "I'm definitely not stopping after hearing you say that." His fingers slowed to drag me along the edge as his other hand worked my leggings down to my knees.

Removing me from his lap, he laid me down on my back on the blanket and shoved my legs up so my knees were pressed against my chest. "Wait, Julian, I didn't—" A silent moan arched at my body at the feeling of his tongue licking the entire length of my pussy from bottom to top, where he wrapped his lips around my clit and sucked.

"Shut up and feed me your sweet juices, baby." His growl sent vibrations against my throbbing love button, making me gasp and squirm from the sensation.

Julian wasted no time placing his mouth entirely over my pussy, his tongue lashing against my clit to work me up before dipping into me to press against my throbbing walls. He ate me out like a starved beast as his arms remained wrapped around my thighs to keep me trapped against him.

No matter how much I squirmed and jerked my hips away from him, I couldn't budge from his death grip. I even got a threat from him when I reached down to push at his head. "Keep shoving my head away, and I'll tie you up to eat you in peace until I have my fill."

I thought threats were supposed to be, well, threatening, not fun and enticing. Being tied up in the middle of the forest with a sexy man between my legs sounded like the perfect dream.

"Naughty girl, what did you just think about?" He chuckled against me before giving my engorged clit long licks of his tongue.

"I didn't—ah!" A sudden wave of pain shocked my body. "Did you just bite me?" I asked in disbelief, lifting my head to peer down at his grinning face.

"Don't lie to me, and I won't have to punish you. You clenched around me just earlier after my little threat, so what were you thinking about, hm?" Reaching a hand between my legs, he pinched my pulsating clit between his fingers and rolled it.

Throwing my head back, I let out a deep moan as I bucked my hips at him. "About your threat, about you tying me up out here and having your ways with me while I'm helpless to stop you." Maybe I could entice him into another chase.

Oh God, to have him chase me, catch me, then wrestle me into some rope or cuffs before taking me until I relented fully to him. Of fuck that was hot.

"Say yes, and it'll be your dream come true and whatever else your little heart and mind desires." Releasing an arm from me, he stretched his other one across to properly anchor my hips before shoving his fingers back into me, making me arch my back with a moan.

"Time, Julian, time." I reminded him with a weak chuckle before giving out a slight yelp when he pulled his fingers back and slammed them back into me, getting my sweet spot deep in there. "But fuck, please make me come, please."

Twice, he's denied me an orgasm, so I was needy and overly desperate for one. "Please, show me why I should say yes." I purred wantonly with a roll of my hips. "Have to taste a sample before buying the whole cake." I giggled playfully before squealing into a moan when he pounded his fingers into me with—what felt like—no mercy.

A subtle jerk started to hit my body from the force of Julian's finger fucking. Fully taking in the overwhelming pleasure, I moved my hands to my breasts and started to fondle them over my shirt and bra; they might not be much, but they gave somewhat a small handful. "Fuck, fuck, fuck,

Julian, I'm gonna come." I whimpered with a tense face as I felt myself hanging over the edge of pleasure.

Growling, Julian picked up the movement of his tongue against my clit and pushed his fingers faster. "Then fucking come, I want to taste and swallow every single drop of you, so give it to me, give me your orgasm like my good girl."

Well, that definitely did it. I couldn't hold back another second after hearing those words from him. My head threw back with my arched body, my loud moan filling the forested area as I let myself freefall into the endless pit of pleasure.

Julian's groan became faint as the haze of pleasure clouded my senses. Every aftershock of my orgasm pushed me further and further away from reality as my juices gushed and squirted out of me. My legs ached with a painful pleasure from being tensed up from the drawn-out orgasm that Julian forced upon me. Every time my juices stopped spraying out of me, he'd plunge his fingers back into me and slam against my G-spot before withdrawing and causing another stream of juices to squirt out of me.

Fuck he would drive me insane if he kept it up. I've never came like this before, ever! My body always stopped me whenever I got too far into the pleasure at home, but I had no control this time. No, it was all in Julian's hands—literally.

I could feel myself becoming delirious from the onslaught of rapture and bliss. "Julian, please, Julian, Julian, please, please, please." I sputtered helplessly, unsure of even what I begged for at this point.

Did I want him to stop? Or continue until I became insane with lust?

CHAPTER 12
Julian

Fuck, if I had a choice, then I would never stop, but I couldn't do that to Avery, not yet. She wouldn't be able to handle it. No, she needed more practice and training before fully taking all I had in store for her without losing her mind forever.

But fuck me, seeing her body spasm uncontrollably from the aftershocks of her orgasm while her face twisted with pure bliss and pleasure was a divine sight. I only wished I pulled my phone out to record her to keep the footage for myself in my late nights or whenever I felt a need for Avery. And the fact I caused all this made my pride swell in my chest.

I was the one breaking her apart, driving her mad with pleasure to where she couldn't control herself. She was at the mercy of *my* hand and whims. Fuck I didn't want to stop, not when I saw those sweet tears spilling out the corners of her eyes, probably from me overstimulating her so much.

Reluctantly, I slowed to a stop and withdrew my hand and mouth from her cunt completely.

Sitting back on my knees, I looked down at her with darkened, hungry eyes as I wiped my mouth with the back of my hand. Carefully, I watched her slowly come back to reality as I sucked and licked my fingers clean of her, groaning to myself as I savored her taste bathing my tongue.

Just as she started to come to, I could see the crash happening, probably before she even knew it herself.

Shoving my lust down, I reached down and grabbed her to bring her up into my arms and lap, cradling her as I sat down fully. "Shh, come back to me, listen to my voice, focus on me, breathe in through your nose, out through your mouth." I soothed and instructed her as she shook and cried in my arms.

I continued to soothe her and mutter sweet nothings as I rubbed her back. I waited until she came down enough before grabbing the water bottle, holding it up to her lips, and feeding her slowly until she turned her head away in refusal.

Putting the bottle down, I grabbed the sandwiches and fruits I packed into my backpack. "Sandwich or fruit?" She probably needed actual food in her, but something sweet right now might settle her some more.

"Sandwich." She mumbled in a slight daze, her hands gripping my shirt's front tightly in her fists.

Unwrapping the item, I tore off small pieces and fed her until the whole thing was gone. "Good job, baby." I'd only expected her to finish half before turning her head away, but more was better for her sake right now.

Surprisingly, I wasn't bothered by her clinginess, not that I minded before—oddly enough. She got even more attached to me after her drop, and I thought I'd grow tired or annoyed sooner rather than later, but later never came.

Instead, I enjoyed her tiny body in my arms, and I didn't want to let her go. I discovered a fondness for this side of her, for this intimacy between us. I didn't think I'd enjoy bringing someone to an orgasm like that, ever. I mean, what purpose did it serve me that they got their pleasure and release if I'd gotten my fill? Yet, I wanted to keep pushing her until she'd break. I found a twisted joy in it all.

God, then eating her out and drinking every last drop of her addictive nectar like a depraved man with no control. Fuck, I would have laughed at myself or cringed in disgust before Avery if someone had ever described how fun and good eating out a woman was. Now, I fell into the same circle as those fools.

Me, a fool, never. I was above all those idiots. I'd never stoop so low. Yet, for Avery, I'd revert to being a neanderthal if it meant getting a chance to taste her pussy again.

Fucking hell, what is she doing to me?

Slowly, I pulled her pants back up, making sure everything was in place for her comfort before kissing her forehead. "How are you feeling now?"

The intention was to fake some concern to make it believable, but somehow, it turned real. The genuine concern slammed into me like a tsunami the moment I carefully looked over the delicate woman in my arms. I worried about her. Why? Like truly worried, something I've never felt or done for anyone before. Yet, I wanted to ensure her safety and comfort after everything.

A bright smile graced her lips after she tilted her head back and looked up at me. "Good, really good." She giggled, breaking out in a grin. "That was, just, wow, so intense, I've never came so much like that and so many times in a row, just, wow."

I couldn't help but let these strange emotions control my expressions in response to her. The strain in my facial muscles from smiling registered in my mind, but whether I smiled like a cute goof or a deranged man was unbeknownst to me.

Leaning down, I brush my lips across hers before taking her bottom lip between my teeth and tugging at it. "And that's just a taste of life with me. Imagine that every single day, every morning, every night, and just whenever I want." I whisper against her lips with a smirk.

"Whenever you want? You make it sound like you're gonna be in control." Oh, the little minx knew exactly what came out of her mouth with her little giggle. The little teasing, playful sparkle in her eyes was a challenge.

Soft trembles moved at my shoulders with my chortle. Seeing the little uppity smile was cute because it was as if she thought she won, but the smile fell with a surprised shock when I shot my hand up and wrapped it around her succulent neck. The inevitable smirk spread madly on my face as I felt the thrumming of her pulse under my fingers along with the nervous swallowing bob of her throat. "Oh, you'll be singing a different song sooner than later with me if you agree. I don't mind a little brat to break." The excitement crept out of my darkened face as I leaned down and hovered my lips over her quivering ones. "I love it when they fight."

A fully submissive victim who never gave a chase wasn't fun. I always preferred a struggle, no matter how small or big, as long as they fought back as if they could escape from me.

Wonder how Avery's eyes will change when she realizes what monster she crawled into bed with. How sweet will her fear smell and taste? Will her eyes widen to where they'd pop out of her head? Will she fawn? Fight? Freeze? Take flight like a good little bird?

No.

I shoved the thoughts of chasing her away or her running away from me in true terror out of my mind the moment they tried to settle. Nasty claws fought their way under my chest—like spiders trying to explode out of me—when the images of her terror and escape fully flashed in my mind.

Once again, I felt a repulsion at the thought of doing anything to elicit an ill reaction from her. I didn't want to terrify her or see her flee from me with pleas for her life falling from her lips and tears coming from her eyes.

I wanted to chase her, yes, but not to hunt her down like an animal like all the others. No, I wanted to hunt to capture and keep Avery, for now and ever, until we both take our last breaths. Then, I'd chase her through the fields of hell because I've bled too many lives—no matter how deserving—to have a place in any holy land. I'd sure as hell drag Avery with me; fuck happiness in the skies, she belonged next to me and only me no matter where I ended up.

I might have given her the choice of making a relationship between us happen or not, but I already had my mind made up about us. At this point, it'd either occur naturally and easily, or it'd be a hell of a fight. Her decision will decide which route we go.

No one would hear her in the basement, and there'd be no escape for her if I were to shut her down there. She would be mine one way or another.

The growl of my words scratched at my throat as they left me. "You really make it hard to hold back when you look at me with those eyes." Not an ounce of fear, or a mere hint of it, presented in her sparkling eyes, which looked at me in wonder and want.

"Like what?" Her voice was so soft and innocent, but whether it was an act or not eluded my lust-filled mind.

"With those fuck me eyes. Eyes that are begging me to fuck you within an inch of your life." Needing something, *anything*, I snag her bottom lip between my teeth again and bit—hard—making her whimper with pain with fluttering eyes. It wasn't enough to make her bleed, but it would definitely swell.

"Would you do that? Screw me so good that I forget my name and very existence?" She needed to cut this shit out before I started toeing the line of control.

"Until the end of our lives." They weren't empty words; no, it was a filled vow to her.

Keeping her neck hostage, I use it to bring her into another kiss, letting my tongue spear itself into her mouth again as my other arm tightened around her as if she'd slip away if I didn't.

Her tiny hand assaulted my chest with feeble hits when she tried to pull away but couldn't. I forced myself to remove myself from her with a chuckle when they became too annoying to ignore.

"Suffocate me with kisses, why don't you? Guess that wouldn't be too bad of a death, but still." She joked with a giggle through her soft pants as she looked up at me with a big smile filled with adoration.

It was tempting, but I'd much rather have the chance to steal her breath away every single day—which wouldn't seem like a hard task, considering one deep kiss was all it took to get her eyes to daze out with unadulterated bliss. I would give anything to cause and see that wonderful look on her face every day, and I couldn't do that if I killed her.

So, once again, death for Avery was off the table. Well, actually, I could kill her to preserve her beauty forever, but the thought of her lifeless corpse bored me. I wanted to see her lips curl at the sight of me, the natural reactions from her; I could pose her dead body however I wanted, but it wouldn't be genuine. Her cute and soft face wouldn't blush up with life at my touch, and it wouldn't be warm or responsive.

No, Avery couldn't die, not unless I wanted to destroy what little soul I did have in my fucked-up shell of a body.

"You're doing it again." Avery's soft voice brought me out of my thoughts, making my eyes zone back into her curious and wary scrunched face.

"Hm?" I questioned her further with a short hum while I continued to stroke her face slowly and carefully with my index finger.

"Staring at me, as if I mean the whole world to you, but also as if I were a piece of meat after you've starved for eons." From appreciation to apprehension, the emotions rose and fell from her eyes in a blink.

"Because you are the forbidden fruit I've been trying to find my whole life. Now that I have, I'm sprinting to you to grab you and never let you go." And I sure as hell won't share.

There was only one Avery in the world, and she *will* be mine, all mine. It wasn't even a matter of if, it's when. I'll indulge her, let her come easy of her own will, but if she resisted or turned for the hills, I'd have to force my hand.

"You know, you're bat shit crazy and insane out of your mind for being so infatuated and sure with me after a short time. Not complaining. It feels so good to be wanted and desired, almost like I actually feel alive now." Avery seemed to have an answer to our relationship already, but I could see the hesitation and hurt pinching at her eyes.

Smiling softly, I leaned down and kissed her lips tenderly before patting her leg to get up. I won't push the subject matter any further; she needed to hang onto things without pressure from me. So, time to change the subject, "What do you want to do when we get back?" I asked as I began to pack things up.

"Hmm, can we watch the new Serial Minds episode? It just came out last night, but I totally forgot about it because my mind was too caught up in you." She asked while rocking back and forth on the balls of her feet with a sheepish smile.

"Are you still having some trouble fully flushing out the character in your book?" Avery was demure about her story, but I coaxed some of it out of her when we got a little more comfortable texting each other throughout the week.

"Y-yeah, like I want to make her not just some weird psycho, and the new episode is about Dennis Rader, who I haven't really dug into much yet, so I wanna see what they have to say about his psyche." Even though she claimed the interest and research were all for her book, she truly enjoyed peeking into the minds of oddities like me.

She *loved* serial killers, though she didn't admit it, and chunked it into her crime interest. A bulk of her crime interest consisted of serial killers, particularly their psychology.

Likewise, people like me sometimes wondered about the minds of neurotypical people like her. "I'm curious, why don't you just make her a killer with a hero complex or something simpler?"

A slender finger tapped her bottom lip as she hummed in thought before giving me a pensive answer. "Well, a murderer without purpose is just a nonsensical person, a fluke, a lapse in control. A serial killer has a reason behind his madness, a compulsion that can only be sated with certain things. I want to give my character that extreme depth to her, explain her reason beyond being some vigilante who was wronged by the laws of society. It's hard to explain, and sorry if it sounds muddy, but I really like to have a reason to things and not just because something is right or wrong. We as humans are all driven by something, but sometimes those things aren't typical, and I just like knowing and trying to figure out the why to that or seeing the why from others who have gone through it."

No arguing with her there. I didn't kill for the thrill of it—okay, that's a lie, I did it for the thrill. But! I did it to help cleanse this forsaken world of scum that the system failed to prosecute. When the judge and jury fail, the executioner must step up—and that is me.

Killing for me was like a good meal to 'normal' people. We all have cravings, and though we may try to ignore them because of other factors in our lives, we eventually face them and indulge in them to satisfy the urge and itch. It's like having the goal of eating a meal at a five-star Michelin restaurant; not everyone can afford it, so those who can't have to save money and carve out time in their lives. Then, when the time comes to finally sit and enjoy that meal, the immense pleasure of gratification of all the dopamine in the brain tears at the body.

Now, obviously, I wasn't saving up to go out and eat. No, but my process was similar. I set a goal, in this case, to find a victim, then I dug into every little inch of their lives, and stalking them was the equivalent of me saving money and making plans. Sitting down at the table and looking at the menu was me waiting in my victim's homes and giving them false hopes of an escape before knocking them out and taking them back to my place. The full course meal was the chase and actual killing, where my flood of dopamine gave me a high like never before.

I was fucked up, no denial there. I already knew something was wrong with me in my childhood years when I couldn't comprehend or understand my peers and their reactions and stupid emotions. Given my murderous tendencies, I should probably be locked up in a mental facility somewhere to be kept under watch 24/7. It almost did happen after my parents made me see a damn shrink, but I was too clever. I played them all with a stupid little act.

Society only wanted 'normal' people, so as long as I could act 'normal' or neurotypical, as many would label it, then I could remain. Tasteless beyond comprehension to me, but I sucked it up for my own sake because life in a mental ward wasn't what I wanted. After all, then I'd be surrounded by crazy people who would drive me truly insane.

So, I faked it for the past thirty years until I made it. There was a point in time when I'd been hopeful enough to think my urges would fade with time or into the background if I kept this normal act up enough.

Unfortunately, it rebounded like a taut rubber band right into my face with a steel ball.

Hunting and animals did it for me for the longest while until that one fateful night when I spilled human blood for the first time. There was no going back after that night.

Slaughter and carnage gave me the sweet release my mind and body craved and needed.

Until a little raven flew into my path.

Oh, Avery, you flew right into your own cage and locked it.

CHAPTER 13
Avery

FIVE DAYS LATER, AND I still haven't given Julian a definite answer.

Five days since I had the best time of my life because Julian gave me the most mind-blowing orgasms I have ever had in my life.

Granted, he was the only one who ever gave me any orgasms because he was the only one I have let go so far with my body.

My thoughts were snatched away along with my phone from my hands. "Girl, if you don't tell him, then I will." Liz snapped with a groaning sigh. "Honestly, it's just a yes we'll be exclusive, not yes we'll get married and shit. Even then, you could still divorce his ass if worse comes to worse. Seriously, you act as if this answer will merge your souls or something."

Needless to say, she'd grown tired of my constant bitching about the whole situation. I thought being away from Julian would clear my head enough to come to a sound decision, but the mere thought of him made the inferno of lust consume me.

Every single time. The answer was always the same: yes.

I was so sure of it down to my very bones—no, down to the last fiber of my soul.

Yet, I couldn't bring myself to tell Julian because of this anxiety that held me back. My sense of self-preservation prevented me from telling Julian to meet up to give him my answer.

Only question: why?

Why was that sense of flight still so prominent in my system whenever I thought about Julian?

"Done." Liz beamed with a cheeky grin, shoving my phone back to me.

Done? Done what? Oh my—

"Liz!"

Sure, we can meet up at the library after you're done, then head to my place. Do you want me to pick you up or meet you at the library?

I had to quickly scroll up to see what the hell Liz had sent while impersonating me.

We need to meet. I have my answer. Library then home?

Puffing my cheeks out in anger, I let out a seething breath while glaring spitefully at Liz, who still had a shit-eating grin plastered on her face. "What? You'll thank me later. If he were to wait for you, then it'd be a damn eternity."

Arguing with her would be useless because she was right. I've been chickening out nearly the whole week; every time I typed up the message to send him or hovered my finger over the call button, I'd pull away at the last second or erase the whole message.

"Come on, we have a date to dress you for." Liz eagerly pulled at my arm towards the door. "We're basically done for the day, and you got about two more hours before you have to meet with Julian, so hurry up and answer him as to where you want to meet and let's hit the mall real quick."

"What? What for? I don't—" I didn't get a chance to protest because she practically dragged me out.

"Your sexy wear is lacking last I checked, as in you have none, nil. Seriously, not even a thong." Liz chided me, rolling her eyes and giggling at the glare I threw her. "See what his favorite color is when you respond to him."

"Ugh." Never in my life did I think I'd listen to Liz.

> Can you pick me up from my place at 5? Also, what's your favorite color? I know, silly question, and you don't have to answer if you don't want to.

The three dreaded dots bumped along the screen on his side of the messaging app for a moment before his response popped up.

> I will see you at five at your place then. And I've never really had any favorite colors, but if I had to say, then black and green. Why?

> Just for future reference. I'll see you later :)

Sighing out of relief, I tucked my phone into my back pocket before letting Liz drag me to her car to take us to the nearby mall.

"Liz, really, why does it matter if I have something sexy on underneath it all? It's all going to come off and end up on the floor at the end of it all." I complained as I let her drag me into Victoria's Secret, straight to the sexy outfit section.

"Because it'll help you feel confident and sexy for le deed. Also, everyone loves lingerie on a sexy woman. Also, imagine how turned on he's gonna get seeing your gorgeous body clad in skintight lace or sheer." Liz continued to drone on and on as she ran through the racks of outfits with speedy hands.

"Liz, I have the body of a teenage boy, or did you forget the flat chest and bleh ness?" I sighed heavily with a drag of my hand down my face.

"Girl, a 32C is not flat. Is it big? No, but it's not flat. You have subtle curves on that pear-shaped body of yours with a bubbly ass that's all nice and tight, perfect for a spanking." Liz snickered deviously at me when I snapped her name with a red face filled with embarrassment. "What? It's true, and those big hands of Julian's would be perfect at turning your bottom red like an apple."

"Oh my god," I exclaimed into my hands, wanting to duck into a dark corner and hide for the rest of my life.

I didn't even bother trying to fight Liz as she tossed—what felt and seemed like—endless garments into my arms. I was about to argue and put nearly all of it back, ready to pull out the 'this is all too expensive' card, but Liz beat me to it by grabbing everything and paying for all of it herself. I also tried to argue that, but she quickly shot it down, saying it was her money, so she could do whatever the hell she wanted with it.

Liz shut me down one last time with a determined look, making me shut my open mouth before a word got out. "Avery, you never get anything nice for yourself or let anyone spoil you, so just let me do it this once because I want this thing with Julian to work out for you. I mean, is it kind of fast? Yes, but I can see how your eyes light up like the stars on a clear night whenever you look at your phone or talk about him to me." Smiling warmly at me, she gave me a quick hug. "You're head over heels for this man, and he's already tripped to your feet."

Sighing in defeat, I accepted my fate, letting Liz drag me back to my little studio apartment, where she proceeded to quickly wash one of the lingerie sets and toss it into the dryer while I showered and put on some light makeup. And by light makeup, I meant lining my eyes with black liner to give my sharp eyes a cattier look and smearing some ruby red lipstick onto my lips.

Standing before the floor-length mirror, I smoothed out my light gray, knee-length skirt to make sure it wasn't snagged somewhere in my panties or something.

Hesitantly, I peeked out from my hooded eyes to take in my entire appearance. My long, black hair was thrown into a side braid going down my right side, with my bangs loose to frame my delicate face.

I might not have the bombass hourglass body of a model, but I had enough curves with my pear-shaped body that Liz claimed was oh-so-cute and hot if I dressed more to show it off. The fitted long-sleeved shirt was ribbed and soft pink and tucked into my skirt. Now, it wasn't the outfit I fretted about. It was the fact my nipples could be clearly seen through the shirt because the lingerie outfit I had underneath had no bra cups, or a crotch for that matter. At least I had the luxury of being able to pull a pair of forest green panties over the whole bodysuit with garters attached to it.

Appearing behind me like some phantom, Liz slapped her hands down on my shoulders and rubbed at them. "Breathe, you got this. And hey, if for some reason he's a flop in bed, then all you have to do is lay there with your legs spread and toss some fake moans here and there and pretend to have an orgasm to stroke whatever little ego he has." Liz encouraged me with a happy, cheeky grin filled with more confidence than what I felt currently.

A playful laugh of disbelief crossed out of me at her words. "Liz, I very much doubt, like very highly doubt, that Julian is a flop in bed." Not with the weapon he packed in his pants. Also, I didn't get that feeling from him.

"Don't count your ducks before you have them, or whatever that saying is. I mean, he could just talk a good game but is a one-pump chump or something or is just a bad fuck 'cause all he can do is move his dick in and out without thought." Liz gave an uncaring shrug of her shoulders before helping me clip the lacy top of my black sheer stockings to the garters of the outfit.

The soft ding of my phone distracted me from picking at my outfit.

> Do you want me to come up?

> No, that's okay :) I just need to throw my coat on real quick and I'll be down.

"No." I deadpanned with slitted eyes when I spun around and saw Liz with a suggestive grin while holding up a pair of black heels.

"Oh, come on, it'll give the right amount of sexy to your cute!" She protested with a pout while dangling the pair of heels inches from my face.

"No." I remained firm in my decision, crossing my arms as I looked at her sternly.

Maybe if this were some sweet date where he'd whisk me away to bed at the end of it all, then I'd suck it up and pull the four-inch heels on and work them like I had a clue about my actions. But not tonight, not with what I had planned.

Bypassing her, I pulled on my black combat boots to give my cute look a bit more of an edge to the softness. My sneakers were a good second option, and they would have seen some action tonight if they were more comfortable to run in. Well, that and I didn't want to spend forever scrubbing them clean.

"I'll tell you about it later," I replied, giving Liz a quick hug to thank her before flashing her a smile and grabbing my backpack.

"Sorry, Liz was trying to convince me to—are you okay?" I was concerned when I saw his slightly unhinged jaw and stunned expression.

His jaw slowly closed as he smiled appreciatively at me, the corners of his lips curving increasingly with each step I took toward him until I was right before him. "Yeah, just, you always take my breath away. You always look good with whatever you wear, but this is a different edge to you, and I really like it. Cute but with an edge of adventure and sexy."

Strong hands envelop my waist, pulling me into a kiss with the handsome hunk before me—hopefully *my* handsome hunk by the night's end.

"So, what are you plotting in that beautiful brain of yours, my little bird?" Julian chuckled, softly tapping my temple with his finger before running it down the side of my face and along my jawline.

"If I should kill you before or after you give me the best night of my life, or maybe during it." I joked with a roll of my eyes.

"Oh? A little praying mantis now, are we?" He played along with an amused smirk. "At least let me have my fill of you before you do end me. Can you at least grant me that one last wish?"

Giggling a laugh, I leaned up and quickly kissed him with a nervous smile. "I was thinking we could go to the library for a bit so I can check out some books, then dinner at Girlie's Grill before heading back to your place for the weekend and for a little dessert tonight, too." God, that sounded weird and awkward. Did I even say it right?

If I didn't, he showed no motion of correcting me as all he did was chuckle and nod before urging me into his truck after a kiss. I also took that as he was fine with my plan because our first stop was the library.

The intention was a quick in and out because I knew which books I needed and wanted, but I found myself pressed against the bookshelf with Julian's mouth on mine the moment we got lost in the far shelves.

"Julian," I gasped between our kisses. "Fuck me." I groaned softly so as not to let anyone hear.

"Later." He mused with a chuckle before he went back to devouring my lips. "I just couldn't help it, reminds me of the very first time I saw you and felt that instant spark the moment our hands touched. I definitely have to fuck you against these shelves one day."

"But someone could walk in on us, and we'd be banned and charged with indecent exposure and shit." As hot as it was, we'd get in way too much trouble, and the risk was way too much.

"Then I guess you better keep quiet while I make it quick for both of us." The mischievous gleam in his eyes told me enough.

Fucking me in the library wasn't an issue of *if* but a matter of *when*.

"You got all you need and wanted?" He asked against my lips before occupying them again, making my reply come out muffled. "Then let's get some food in you for fuel. Can't have you passing out on me mid-orgasm."

Gasping playfully, I smacked his shoulder. "Julian, someone can hear us."

"So? Let them know who's the lucky bastard who gets to have you all to himself tonight and forever. Let them hear what they can't possibly ever have." Julian chuckled deeply before stepping away to let me breathe comfortably.

Thankfully, the rest of our library trip went smoothly, as in no more surprise make-out sessions against the shelves or wondering hands on my body from behind when I'd be reaching for something on the shelf.

Dinner went by in a blur, mainly because both of us were eager to finish to get to the main course of the night: dessert at Julian's place. I kept my meal on the lighter end, too, not wanting to stuff myself and end up in a food coma or throw up from all the activity.

"So, I'm assuming your answer is yes to a relationship?" After eating my face off and getting handfuls of my body, now he finally asks? This man.

Rolling my eyes, I reached over and lightly smacked his arm. "Would I be letting you take me out and back to your place for a weekend getaway if the answer was 'Sorry bud, I'm not interested,' Julian?"

Keeping his eyes trained on the forested road, he rolled it before reaching over and sneaking his hand under my skirt to rest it on my nearly bare thigh. "Oh?" There was a faint curve to his lips as he splayed his fingers out to explore my leg, tracing the edge of the lace of my stocking and following the strap of the garter. "Planning far ahead for something?" He asked with a teasing glance at me.

"If I was bold enough, then I would have gone pantiless." I threw out at him with a giggle and playful smirk of my own, making him groan and dig his fingers into my plush flesh in return.

"Avery, I'm only a man at the end of the day, and I am trying to take it at a decent pace for you. But by God, if you keep pulling shit like this or go without panties under your clothes and I find out, mhmm fuck, I don't know how much I can control myself around you." A veiled warning to me to knock this shit off unless I wanted to set him off.

Too bad that's what I intended to do.

Slowly, I bit my bottom lip and reached over to run my hand across his thigh to his tented pants. "Would it be crazy of me to say that's what I want? Even with my first official time, every time I think about you taking me, it's never nice and slow. I tried to think of you 'making love' to me and all, but it never got me off as hard as thinking about you tying my wrists up or holding me down and taking me like an actual man with needs to fulfill."

The bulge in his pants pulsed under my palm as the tent grew more prominent and harder with my words. "I want you to take me, like really take me. Break my body to you, make it submit to you along with my mind.

I don't want the slow, sensual kissing and touching before the slow thrust when you'd inch yourself in." Dangerous words to a dangerous man, like pouring gasoline into an already out-of-control fire.

Racing in my chest, my heart pounded against my ribcage like some prisoner hammering away at the bars in an escape attempt. To say I was nervous as hell would've been an understatement. I shouldn't be trying to draw the beast out, not for the first time like this, but I wanted him to ravage me, no matter how much it would hurt at first. I was sick in the mind, but I didn't care.

"I don't want to hurt you, Avery, not yet, not until I know your limits and boundaries, which is going to take a little while to work out, considering how you've never really explored or have much experience." Of course, he had to be a decent and perfect man—not fair!

Groaning, I threw my head back before letting it slump against the window. "Isn't that what safe-words are for as well? And it's not like I'm asking you to go completely unhinged on me, at least for tonight." Now, that would indeed be a bad idea, considering how I didn't know all he was capable of.

"If we're going to do this and make it work, this relationship and everything involved in it, then we need to be open and clear with each other." He stated firmly with a quick flick of his finger between him and me. "So, before we do anything tonight and dive deep into this new relationship of ours, think of a safe-word to use from here on out, and tell me any limits or boundaries you can think of at this moment."

The drive to his place would be another thirty minutes or so, so I had the time to go through my mental kink bank quickly. I haven't tried a lot, but I've definitely researched a lot for both personal and non-personal reasons.

A calm but somewhat tense silence filled the air as I pondered, quickly fabricating the list. "Well, obviously I'm fine with you chasing me through the forest and just chasing me. It's fun and really gets my blood pumping and whatnot. Roughness, hair pulling, teeth in the right places, being held down, cuffs and ropes, and being restrained, a little iffy about spanking mainly because I don't know how hard you hit, so maybe if you do, then take it a little easy on me tonight."

A quick pause to rack my brain one last time before wrapping up. "Other than that, definite hard no's would be fire, mutilation, feet play, and just anything with the feet and toes, so don't go getting any ideas about stepping on my face anytime soon or ever. Piss and shit is a very hard no, no drugs either."

Nervously, I glanced at him out of the corner of my eye to catch his reactions as I listed things off. Julian's face remained indifferent, or at least he didn't show any signs of judgment as he hummed and nodded along with me to show that he paid attention to my words. "That's all for now, but I'll probably come up with a full list later of yes, no, and maybe for you, but those are the definite ones that I know for sure."

Julian ran a hand across his jaw and rubbed his stubble for a moment before giving a firm nod of his head. "I can work with all of that tonight." He agreed, reaching over and grabbing my face to force my attention on him as he glanced at me from the corner of his eyes. "At any point, I don't care if I'm a thread of a second away from coming or you're close. If you ever feel an ounce of discomfort or pain or anything beyond what you can possibly handle, you use the safe word. I don't care if you agreed to it beforehand and we get into it, and you change your mind, you scream it as if your life depends on it, understood?" His straight and serious face locked with my nervous one fully for seconds when he'd tear his attention away from the road entirely.

"Promise you won't get mad or upset if I do?" I worried with a shaky voice.

His head instantly snapped to me, letting me see his tense eyes. "No. Never. And if anyone ever pulls any kind of shit on you for using your safe-word because you feel unsure and unsafe, then you throat punch them and run. No one and I mean no one, should ever shame you or give you any kind of backlash for using your safe-word, *ever*. Consent can easily be taken as it is given. Don't you ever forget that."

"Am I clear and understood? Yes or no, little bird?" He reiterated his question with a firm squeeze of my cheeks.

"Yes, sir, loud and clear." I shuddered my reply, chewing at my bottom lip to hold back a little groan.

"Good girl." The low growl in his voice made me clench my thighs together at the growing ache between my legs. "Now, what exactly did you want to happen when we return to my place?"

Sucking in a sharp breath, I removed his hand from my face and placed it in my lap to play with his fingers while I recollected my thoughts fully. "Well..." I started with a devious little smirk. "I was hoping you'd chase me through the forest, and if you catch me, then you'd tie me up, throw me over your shoulder, and drag me to bed where you claim your prize."

It sounded silly now I said it out loud, but the scene in my head was very vivid and lovely. I might or might not have gotten myself off a few times late at night thinking about the same scenario.

Chuckling, Julian moved his hand back under my skirt, where he stroked the inside of my thighs with his fingers. "For your first time? You want to lose your virginity like that?" Again, not judgmental, just very interested and amused in my choice.

"Yes, but only because it's with you. I trust you enough to not abuse me. And, I don't know, just the thought of vanilla sex in bed is boring and doesn't quite get me aroused and ready to be taken." I admitted sheepishly with a nervous chuckle. "I much rather get a little crazy and make my first time as memorable as possible."

Julian let out a deep groan as he gripped the steering wheel until his knuckles went white. "Fuck baby, you have no idea how hard it makes me to hear all of that. I swear, I will do right by you always." His voice was laced with sincerity as he gripped my soft thigh. "You are so fucking perfect. I'll show you how grateful I am tonight and every night after."

With one more firm squeeze, he retreated his hand fully in order to navigate the hidden road to his place. Once we were in front of his home, he threw the car in park and killed the engine. Then, he sat there in silence with his paced breathing, just looking off into the distance. "Last chance, are you sure? Because the moment I start the clock, there is no going back. Unless I hear your safe word, I'm not stopping."

Julian slowly turned his head over to me as his tongue swept his lower lip before disappearing behind his hand when he ran it across his jaw. There was a darkness to his eyes veiled behind a look of restraint. It was the look of a predator, a beast ready to spring from its open cage.

A ball of hesitation and reservation clogged my throat until I forced myself to swallow it. "I understand." I nodded in earnest with a confident and sure smile.

"Ten minutes, that's how much you'll have before I go after you. Keep your phone on you just in case you change your mind and need to call me." He laid things out for me and waited for my response—to which I agreed—before continuing. "What's your safe-word?"

Taking in a trembling breath, I licked my lips and swallowed a gulp again. "Guilty."

Julian snorted out a chuckle before pulling up a timer on his phone and setting it for ten minutes. Hovering his finger over the start button, he looked at me with an unhinged smile and crazed eyes that sent shivers down my body with my initial adrenaline spike.

A faint click echoed throughout the car when Julian unlocked the doors.

"Run."

CHAPTER 14
Julian

A FERAL GROWL RUMBLED out of me as I watched Avery's body disappear into the forest.

Ten minutes. Ten torturous minutes. Fuck.

Taking a deep breath, I held it briefly until I felt dizzy before letting it go. I needed to keep it all under control if I wanted to work her into my life to where she couldn't escape.

I hadn't expected the car ride to go how it did. Her telling me how she wanted me to take her, despite it being her first time, nearly had me pulling over to grab her and force her onto my throbbing cock. Vanilla, that's what I expected, completely vanilla sex. So, it was a huge shock to hear what she put forth.

My eyes drifted over to my phone in my lap, and a deep groan followed shortly.

Fucking hell, it's barely been a minute.

Clicking my tongue against my teeth out of annoyance, I forced myself out of the car to get what I needed. I could use the rope in my trunk, but that was meant for my victims, which Avery was not. Also, I didn't want to chaff up her porcelain skin and risk damaging it with the rough rope. Not like I tied my victims up with soft rope meant for bondage.

Forcing myself to take my sweet time to burn time, I slowly went into my house and up to my room, where I kept the special rope. The tightly braided length had me shivering at the thought of winding that around Avery shortly. Her lightly fair skin will make the black rope look so sexy.

"Fuck." I growled to myself as I could feel my rampant lust for the woman storming up again.

Pulling my phone out, I let out a frustrated growl when I saw only a little over half the time had passed. I began to wonder if I added time by accident at this point because it felt so much longer than ten damn minutes.

Making my way outside, I stood at the front door with the rope in hand while I waited for the rest of the time to pass.

The cold night air stung my lungs with each inhale, but that only further fueled the adrenaline buzzing through my body as my heart rammed against my ribcage like a bull. It damn well nearly exploded when the timer went off.

Like before, my feet took off toward the forest before I could even think about it. I went off pure instinct like some deranged animal with a single goal in mind: hunt and claim Avery.

Following her trail was easy until she grew intelligent and tried to throw me off with the randomly disturbed ground and broken branches. Too bad I was no amateur.

"Cute trick, little bird, but don't think it'll be enough to escape me!" I shouted into the night as I closed in on her.

Out of the corner of my eyes, I could see the soft gray of her jacket sticking out from behind a tree.

Note to self: Teach Avery how to hide effectively in the forest.

Stalking up to the tree, I let my grin widen madly before swinging wide around the tree trunk. "Boo!" My excitement dropped with confusion briefly before being replaced with amusement and pride.

"Smart trick, little bird!" I shouted as I picked up the jacket she'd discarded.

Then, I could hear some rustling and shuffling a little distance away. Don't know if she was just sloppy or being so on purpose because this wasn't an actual chase for a kill. Either way, at least she was taking it somewhat seriously.

Turning in the direction of the sound, I didn't hesitate to take off in that direction. It could have been an animal for all I knew, but the idea was tossed when I saw my cute prey skittering away.

Her braided hair whipped around violently with her head, and the look of shock widened on her pale face when she spotted me. Avery looked forward again and ran with—what I suspected—all her might.

She could run all she wanted, but she couldn't escape me unless she could run at the speed of light or had the superpower to turn invisible.

With the rope tucked safely in my pocket, I took after her at full speed, gaining on her with a few long strides. "Shit." I faintly heard her cuss when she whipped her head around and saw how much distance I'd closed between us.

Shooting my hand out, I grasped the sleeve of her shirt, causing her to yelp and scream out a laugh as she jerked out of my hold and ducked off to the side.

"Oh no, don't fucking think so," I growled under my breath, quickly turning my feet to adjust myself to her direction.

Tiny and fast, I'd give her that, but I've been at this game far longer than she had.

This time, I closed the space between us completely before throwing my arms around her midsection and picking her squealing and kicking body into the air. "Let me go!" Her feisty body thrashed against me.

I had to tighten my hold so much to keep her petite body from slipping out from under me with how she kept twisting her body and kicking at my legs.

I should have known better than to underestimate her, though. My ass ended up on the ground with a winded grunt when she managed to throw a foot behind me and kick the back of my knee. The impact caused my arms to loosen enough for her to slip away.

As she tried to scramble away on all fours, I quickly lunged at her and grabbed her by the ankle, earning a squeal from her when I pulled her towards me. Her legs kicked out at me, but I learned my lesson the first time.

Climbing on top of her, I kept her front side pressed to the ground with one hand while my knees pinned the back of her thighs. "Quit struggling and make it easy." Or don't, please don't.

Looking back, she bared her teeth at me in a snarl as she threw an arm around to try and snag me. It was adorable, her attempt, I mean. Although, she did come close because I didn't expect her to be so flexible. No matter; she wouldn't get another chance because my free hand caught her wrist and pinned it to her back before I wrestled the other one behind her and held both wrists in one hand.

Seething with a throaty growl, she tried—and failed—to buck me off of her. "Get off me you big oaf!" Very adorable considering how I had her completely pinned and helpless.

A dramatic sigh escaped my lips as I allowed a mischievous smirk to spread across my face. "Looks like we were doing it the hard way," I said in a playful tone, pretending to be annoyed.

Carefully, I pulled out the rope from my pocket with my free hand and shifted my position to tie her wrists better together. However, I underestimated her finesse. She used the small distance I had created between us in a split second to twist out of my grasp and shift onto her back.

If my reflexes weren't faster than a cat's, then I would have gotten a slap to the face from the feisty woman. My body leaned back an inch, barely avoiding the tips of her fingers that brushed past me with a slight whoosh. Before she could fully retreat it, I trapped it in my hand and pinned it above her head with a smug smirk.

Gritting her teeth into a scowl, she lashed her other hand out at me with a snarling grunt. Too bad I saw that coming a mile away. Her hand was captured before it came close to my face. Even though I had the rope in my hand, it was easy to use half my fingers to grab her small wrist and pin it above her head.

Her face twisted with fury, and her lips pulled back in a snarl as she glared at me in mock anger. "Fuck you." She spat through her clenched teeth.

A mischievous glint shone in my eye, and a sly grin spread across my face. "If you behave like a good girl, then maybe I'll let you." I taunted playfully, letting out a light chuckle.

Keeping my weight fully on her hips to keep her fully pinned. I firmly grasped her wrists and laced the rope around them, leaving enough room for circulation. Then, I tested the knots for sturdiness and noted where the safety release was located, just in case.

Hauling her up to her feet after I got up on my own, I wound the unused length of rope in my hand to draw her up close to me. With her face inches from mine, I leaned down closer until I hovered a mere inch above her after I wrapped my free hand around her neck to assert some control over her—to show her who was in charge.

The tip of my tongue lightly brushed her lip when I licked my smirking lips. "Now, we can do this the hard way or the easy way. You either walk like a good little girl on this makeshift leash, or I throw you over my shoulder." I didn't mind either, they'd both appease me greatly in the end.

Avery's mouth remained in a tight line with her playfully harsh glare. I opened my mouth to repeat her options but was cut short by the sound of shuffling. The hand around her neck quickly dropped to catch her leg before it could connect with me.

Tutting with a soft shake of my head, I let out a small sigh of disappointment before giving a small grunt of effort when I picked her up and threw her over my shoulder.

Her struggling resumed the moment her face hit my back, and I started to make my way back to the house. The small whacks and kicks from her felt like annoying little flicks to my sturdy body and only served to rile my amusement.

Once we made it back to the house and to my room, I unceremoniously threw her down onto the bed, causing her to grunt upon landing.

Quickly, I pulled out my pocket knife and grabbed at the front of her top. "Julian, I swear to God, if you—"

A shocked gasp filled the room, along with the sound of fabric tearing as I split her top right down the middle. "Julian!" A look of disbelief hung on her face as her eyes swirled with arousal.

"Oh, don't worry, I'll buy you a thousand more to cut off your body all the same." Something about unconventionally removing clothes gave my body little ticks of excitement.

Grabbing at the edges, I tore the rest of it off her entirely before yanking her skirt off and tossing it onto the floor.

Fuck me.

Now, it was my turn to be stunned. Her delicate body was clad in a forest green bodysuit, the thick lace strings wrapped down her body in such a way to extenuate her subtle curves just perfectly, and the way they framed her small breasts in a cupless manner made them pop. Then, the thick lace band of the sewn-in garter ran down to her matching panties and black stockings.

I could have spent forever taking in every inch of her body if it weren't for the painful ache between my legs reminding me of my task at hand. "I don't know if I want to keep you in this or rip it off of you so that you'd be bare." My deep voice rasped as I ran a hungry hand down her arching body.

I didn't think someone could look so divine in lingerie. Usually, I hated barrier and layers between me and my partner for the night, but something about taking Avery dressed like this—looking like some perfect little sex goddess—got me more aroused than ever.

Actually, a better idea came to me after admiring her for a while.

Gripping the sides of her panties, I gave her a devious smirk, which caused her to glare at me in protest. "Julian, I swear you---"

Rip!

"Julian!"

"You're not getting this outfit back, baby." I grinned at her wolfishly before looping the end of the rope around the metal bars of my headboard to secure her arms above her head.

Whining and whimpering, she pouted at me while stomping her feet. "You're still fully clothed, and it's not fair." I could argue that she was dressed still with the tantalizing lingerie on her body, but I figured I should give her something to look at.

So, with a chuckle and a soft roll of my eyes, I took my shirt off in one swift motion and discarded it onto the ground with her clothes after setting the torn panties onto my nightstand. The rest can come off later after I take her fully. I wanted a trophy of tonight, and nothing would be better than her sexy little outfit after I make her bleed and fill her with my cum.

Softly, I slapped her inner thigh and gripped at it. "Spread your legs, baby, show me what's going to belong to me." Oh, every inch of her would be claimed tonight by my touch until I seared my very essence into her.

"What belongs to you? Last I checked, it was my pussy." She remarked defiantly, sticking her tongue out at me and going as far as closing her legs and clamping my hand between her plushness.

My body shook with a dark chuckle as I slipped my other hand between her legs, pushed them open, and pinned them to the bed. Slowly, I leaned down to brush my lips against the shell of her ear while using my hips to pin her open. "The moment I caught you, you became mine, all mine. Every inch of your body, from head to toe, to your heart, and your very soul, all belong to me now. Especially after I break your innocence with my cock and make you bleed and come all over my cock."

Our groans simultaneously filled the air when I rolled my hips into her hot sex, getting some of her arousal onto the tent in my pants.

The only thing keeping this moment from being extremely picture-perfect in my eyes was the lack of a collar and leash around her succulent neck. Perhaps at a later time if that's her thing—God, I hoped to whoever was up there that it was her thing.

For now, a hand collar would do just fine.

A riled growl ached at my throat as my hand squeezed her neck softly to where I could feel the hard thumps of her pulse. With her firmly pinned, I ground my hips into her, causing her breathing to hitch with her soft moans as she bucked her hips back at me.

Gritting out a low groan, I released her neck to fist her hair and tilt her head down. "Look at how wet you are, baby. See how much you've soaked me? Did you really get that turned on with the chase and me tying you up? Are you so desperate to be my little slut that you're wet enough for me to shove my cock into you without any foreplay?" I could feel her juices soaking through to my boxers underneath the more I bucked my hips into her.

Her body shuddered under me with a strangled moan as her hips jerked erratically. "Fucking hell, are you gonna come already, baby? Just from some filthy words thrown at you? You needy little vixen." Moving my other hand across her hip, I pressed down on her pelvis to keep her firmly pinned to the bed so she couldn't move. "Not yet though, not until I've got my cock fully stuffed in your sweet cunt, only then can you come like a good little slut for me."

Definitely adding dirty talking to the list of kinks for her, given how sweetly she reacted to my filthy words.

"Please, take me, please. I need you in me so badly." I wanted to tease her some more, maybe finger her a little to get her nice and ready, but my control became nonexistent at her sweet plea.

Moving my hand off her hips, I undid my pants in a flurry and kicked them off before settling the length of my shaft against her wet slit and slickening myself up using her own arousal. Then, I reached up and untied her from the bed but didn't remove the rope completely from her wrists, so she was still bound. "Put your arms around me. I want to feel your nails on my back when I take you." A little pain for the pleasure always did wonders for me.

Avery smiled up at me with her bottom lip tucked between her teeth, and she looped her bound hands over my head and around my neck, splaying her fingers across my upper back and shoulders. Then, her eyes widened slightly when she spotted the monstrosity between her legs. "You're going to hurt me so good with that big thing." I could see the wariness and fear in her eyes, probably from her wondering if it would fit if I had to guess the reason behind her expression.

For a split second, I hesitated after I pressed my bulbous head at her opening, giving her one last look. Nervously, her tongue flicked out before her shaky breath released with a determined nod after she locked her gaze with mine.

Her nails instantly dug into me like talons the moment I breached her, especially when I broke past her maiden barrier. "Fuck!" I hissed under my breath when I felt her tight walls resist me with every inch I tried to work in.

"Oh God." Her feet kicked under me as she let out a choppy moan with ragged breaths. "Julian, fuck."

Exhaling deeply through my nose, I gave out a low, groaning snarl the moment I felt my hips press against her. "That's right, little bird, I am your fucking God." She definitely made me feel like one with how wonderful her soft walls gripped at my girthy member.

It was a high I had never experienced before. I didn't think it was possible to feel such blissful lust without dying.

I couldn't help but feel a little prideful seeing all nine inches of myself fully seated in her. She must be in so much pain from being forced to take all of me like that, but from the way her face twisted with agonizing pleasure, I doubt she minded.

Giving her little time to adjust fully, I pulled back until her tight entrance gripped around my tip before slamming back into her and making her scream out a moan. Then, the feeling of something dripping down my back was felt before a faint pit of a patter registered. Glancing over, I couldn't help but smirk when I noticed the red stain on my white sheets.

The stinging pleasure of pain from her nails raking at my back pushed me to slam into her again after pulling out nearly all the way.

Releasing her hair, I dug both my hands into the back of her thighs and pinned them to the sides of her hips before leaning down and taking her mouth in a passionate kiss filled with hunger. I didn't wait around for her to let me in this time, just shoving my tongue fully into her screaming mouth and swallowing her sounds of pleasure as I took her with hard and rough thrusts.

"Come all you want baby, as long as it's all over my cock." I wanted to drive her delirious with bliss and lust, something feasibly easy considering the way her body trembled with her rolling eyes as I split her in half with my dick.

"Julian!" She gasped sharply and cut her breath short with a deep moan as her body pressed into me fully with her tightening walls.

Fuck. If she kept this up, I would blow my load a lot sooner than later. I hadn't expected her orgasm to feel so riveting to me until her pussy squeezed me in a vice grip.

My hips continued to drill into her mercilessly as I released one of her thighs to wrap my hand around her neck, choking her softly until she was gasping with a fucked-out smile on her face. Once I was sure she wouldn't move her legs, I used my other hand to grab the length of rope still loosely wrapped around the metal bar and pulled at it until her arms were fully above her head again before tying it to the head of the bed.

Settling a hand back on the back of her thigh, I press into her more and pound her into the bed with each thrust. My other hand grabbed at her breast, palming it roughly in my calloused hand while I pinched and pulled her hard nipple between my fingers.

"What's got your tongue, little bird?" Her mouth kept gasping open but always shut before the word could slip by.

"I can't, it's embarrassing." She whimpered with a squeal when I angled my hips slightly to get a different spot in her.

"Baby girl, I just hunted you down like an animal and threw you onto my bed to take you like a savage. Nothing's gonna stop this moment." Unless she wanted me to stop and put a clown suit on or something along those lines.

"Or is this about your little daddy issues?" I don't know why that came to mind, but it was out there now. The way her face flushed as her eyes looked away in slight shame confirmed things.

Releasing her breast, I snaked my hand up her chest to around her neck and grabbed her jaw to force her attention back to me. "Call me Daddy, and you won't get any sleep tonight or walk at all tomorrow."

The devious gleam in her eyes challenged me with the wide spread of her bratty grin. "Is that a promise? Or are you just talking shit? Hm, Daddy?"

Little brat.

Choking her firmly, I slam my hips into her harder than before at a punishing pace, making the bed jolt with each movement while her screams and moans fill the air. "Guess we'll see after tonight, won't we, baby? That is, if you can even think straight after I'm done with you."

A look of regret and horror crossed her face when she caught sight of my wicked grin before I doubled down on her. Well, she had no one to blame but herself for this.

"Daddy! Too much! Coming!" She sobbed through her release as her poor body writhed under me.

"That's it, ride it out so I can get another one going. Come on, you can do it. Give me one more to squeeze every last drop of cum out of me when I come with you this time." I couldn't hold out much longer with how frequent her orgasms kept hitting her and squeezing at me.

God, I hoped she was on birth control or had a Plan B stashed away in her bag because I didn't slip a condom on, not that I wanted to. I wanted to take her bare to feel every little inch of her and make this moment more intimate. Also, I wanted her blood and our mixed juices to stain my length by the time I was done with her.

A short roar cut out of me as my hips faltered in their pace with my release. Keeping myself fully buried in her moaning body, I let my seed flood her with every throb and squeeze from her.

Pulling out with a groan, I sat back on my knees to look at the mess of our mixed cum seeping out of her used and bleeding pussy. Biting my bottom lip, I suppressed a groan when a flood of our cum came out of her twitching pussy when her body jerked and clenched from the aftershock of her orgasm.

"Daddy," she gasped with a cry when I swiped up some of the cum and shoved it back into her needy sex with two fingers. "I'm sore." She whimpered while bucking her hips away, only to be held down by my hand.

Grinning darkly, I curled my fingers against her g-spot while rubbing at her swollen clit with my thumb, making her arch or moan deeply.

"And we are far from done, so you better brace yourself, baby."

No warning, I thrust myself back into her fully.

CHAPTER 15
Avery

OH GOD, WHY DID I have to open my mouth?

I didn't think he was serious about screwing me utterly stupid for hours on end. Somewhere in between my orgasms and mindless blabbering, he stripped me completely naked; I think it was after he painted my body with his cum, but I wasn't entirely sure because everything was a pleasureful blur of orgasmic madness.

My poor body felt broken after the third round, but he still took me like his little fuck doll until he was satisfied. The constant ache of my body, especially between my legs, meant last night wasn't some hot dream. No matter how much it hurt—but it hurt so good—I didn't stop him. I never felt the urge or inkling to use my safe-word. Julian might have pushed to my limits and maybe a bit beyond, but I still felt safe with him because he never gave me more than what I could handle, somehow.

Julian seemed to know when to lighten up when I seemed to be along the edge of what I could take, and he always struck before I came down too much. From whore to princess in seconds, soft strokes and kisses to his hand striking down on my body while his lips gave me bruising kisses before his teeth would mar my body with love bites.

Wincing, I hissed and groaned in pain as I tried to untangle myself from Julian's heavy, muscular arms. Of course, the only thing my struggle did was wake him, which made my escape attempt futile because he pulled me back tightly into his arms. "Where do you think you're flying off to, little raven?"

"I have to tinkle, but I can't move, and everything hurts. God, I'm so sore." I whined with a pouting squirm, wincing as a result of it.

A pained yelp squeaked out of me from the sudden intrusion of Julian's fingers inside my very sore and aching pussy. "Ow, Julian, I can't. Oh fuck, Daddy!" Apparently, I could, no matter how much my spent body protested. The painful ache of pleasure clawed at my sleepy body as Julian pulled an orgasm out of me.

"Don't forget who you belong to now, Avery. I can and will do what I want whenever I want. If I want you to come, you come, no matter how tired you are." His deep voice rumbled at my ear, making me shiver and moan back a response in my little orgasmic haze.

I didn't bother to—more like I couldn't—fight Julian when he climbed out of bed and picked me up to carry me to the bathroom. "Don't let me go." My arms locked tightly around his neck and shoulders, afraid that if he set me down, then my legs would fully give out from under me.

"Never." He chuckled against my forehead before kissing it.

Thankfully, Julian didn't try to pull anything funny the rest of the morning as he helped me shower and go through my morning routine before depositing me onto the couch with a blanket bundled around me and my laptop next to me.

While Julian made breakfast, I busied myself with some lazy typing as my fingers still felt heavy from my exhaustion. Letter by letter, the words to my story slowly appeared on the screen as I struggled to string out my thoughts coherently.

A deep chuckle pulled my focus away from my laptop screen to face an amused and proud Julian standing before me with two plates of food. "Guess I didn't do a good enough job if you can still use your fingers and brain." He joked with a laugh, making me scowl and pout playfully as I lashed my hand out at him weakly.

"You didn't have to screw me that hard. It was only my first time." I remarked with a roll of my eyes before taking a plate from him with a small thanks and snuggling up to him after he sat beside me.

His lips curved into a sly smirk as he leaned in close, locking his gaze with mine while his hand grasped my chin and his thumb brushed my bottom lip. "I warned you what would happen, yet you still challenged me," he said, his voice low and confident, sending a shiver of unease and excitement down my spine as memories of last night flooded in like a broken dam.

Couldn't argue there because I did push him, mainly because I didn't think he was serious, but also because I was a brat and wanted to push his buttons and challenge his words. To be honest, I never expected him to go so far. Not that I was complaining about last night; in fact, I enjoyed it immensely. But after the high of everything had died down, I do have quite a few complaints.

Wrenching my face away from his hand, I side-eyed him. "You say that as if you expect me to learn a lesson from it," I grumbled with a pout before digging into the berries and stack of pancakes on my plate.

Julian's dark chuckle sent a wave of nerves that pricked at the hairs of my neck. "Are you saying last night wasn't enough to make it clear to you?" The way his voice settled eerily made me regret my words instantly.

Nervously, I inched away from him with a sheepish giggle and smile. Abruptly, he snatched my plate of food from me, set it on the coffee table with his own, and grabbed my ankles to drag me towards him. Throwing my legs around his waist, he cages me between his arms and looks down at me menacingly. "The lesson was as clear as day, darling: be a good girl and obey me, and don't challenge me," he said while trailing a finger down the side of my face and along my jaw until his hand secured itself around my neck, choking me lightly, "Guess you're a stubborn girl who needs a *very* firm hand."

Coughing out a gasp, I loosely grab at his wrist to keep myself anchored and give myself an illusion of control. "B-but I'm still sore from last night, you wouldn't give me a lesson right now, right? That wouldn't be fair." I rebutted weakly with a skittish chuckle.

With a sneer, he pulled me forcefully and crushed his lips against mine with a hot, bruising pressure. His tongue invaded my mouth, probing and dominating to show me who was in charge between us. "What gave you the idea that I played fair?" His voice rasped, giving my body a nervous shiver. "Now, we can do this the easy way or the hard way. The easy way is you get over my knee willingly, and the hard way is I grab you by your hair and force you over. Then after your spanking, you go on your knees and choke on my cock."

Fuck, just exactly what did I agree to?

Chewing my bottom lip deeply in thought, I weighed the options he gave me before deciding not to go with either. Keeping my playfulness hidden with a pensive expression, I slowly shifted from his hold, waiting until he sat back with his lap open and ready for me to crawl into before sitting up fully. Mustering up as much adrenaline as possible because I sure as hell needed it to push through the discomfort of my protestant body, I grabbed a throw pillow and threw it—hard—at Julian and bolted off the couch towards the hallway.

Unfortunately, I didn't make it far before I was yanked backward by my hair and landed on my ass. His deep voice rumbled with a primal hunger as he locked his intense gaze on me. "Fine, the *very* hard way it is then," he purred, a seductive spark in his eyes daring me to resist.

This time, I did heed the warning storming behind his challenging eyes. Resigning myself to my fate, I let him drag me back to the couch by my hair, stumbling on my aching feet and knees behind him until he sat back into an armchair and pulled me over his knee. "You're lucky I am too impatient right now to grab my belt or a flogger to bite your sweet bottom with." He chuckled lowly as he threw a leg over the back of my knees to keep me locked down completely.

My heart pounded heavily in my chest in tandem with the ticking of the clock as he pushed the bottom of my—his shirt that I wore—shirt up and pooled it around my waist. That's all I had been wearing after the shower, along with a black thong. "I... Wait, I'm sorry, I changed my mind. I'll be good. I'm sorry for throwing that pillow at you. I won't do it again. Please take it easy on me, I'm sorry." I profusely apologized in hopes of a lighter sentence from his hand.

"If you were actually sorry, then I might take it into consideration, but you're just apologizing because you want to try and save your ass. Granted, you will learn your lesson after I am done with you." His rough hand palmed and rubbed at my round ass, building up the anticipation in my tense body. "If you take the first few spanks well, then I might take it a little easy on you, just maybe."

"Count." After one firm grip, I felt the air hit me from how fast he pulled his hand away before bringing it back down on me—hard.

The pain stunned me so much that I couldn't even let out a proper scream as it got caught in my throat. My body jerked in a stupor at the second hit, and it wasn't until the fifth hit that I managed to get ahold of myself and start counting each slap.

"Ow, seventeen. Daddy, ple—ah! Eighteen! Please, no more, Daddy, it hurts. I learned my lesson, no more. I won't disobey you, I won't challenge you, I'll be a good girl." I cried through my tears of pleasureful agony as I clung onto his legs for some kind of reprieve.

My ass was on fire! It hurt so much; every snap of his hand made the burning ache worse and worse. The worst part was that it hurt if he spanked me in quick succession, but it also hurt like hell if he waited to let some of the pain spread and linger; there was no win in the situation for me.

"And just exactly how are you going to show that you have learned your lesson?" He questioned with an interest in his dominating voice.

The weight of my vulnerability carried through my pathetic little whimper when he grabbed a fistful of my hair and pulled my head up to meet his fierce gaze. "On my knees like a good little slut, sir." I wondered for a second if he heard my tremble of a whisper, but his release on my body answered the silent question.

Sliding out of his lap, I got on my knees between his legs and looked up at him with eagerness. Wasting no time, I reached up and pulled the waistband of his sweatpants down to free his thick member. His thick mushroom tip glistened with his arousal as his length pulsed and twitched in my hand while I stroked it slowly.

It was one thing to see this monster plunging in and out of me last night, but now that I had him in my hand and right in front of my face, I couldn't help but pale at the sight of it and clench my thighs together. I could barely wrap my hand around him fully. Granted, I did have somewhat small hands, but my slender fingers made up for the small size.

God, it was unbelievable to think I survived my first time with such a thing. Although, I couldn't help but feel some pride warm my body at the fact of it.

Leaning in, I pressed my tongue against the underside of his cock and dragged it up from base to tip. My tongue flicked across his slit, picking up his precum and swallowing his addictive seed with eagerness before taking his bulbous tip into my mouth with a groan.

Julian hissed under his breath as he placed his hand on the back of my head, gently fisting the back of it. "Think you can take me all the way in, baby?" He chuckled after tossing the challenge for me out there.

The thought of it unnerved me, but people in porn do it all the time. So, it was possible. Therefore, I could do it... I hope.

With a shaky inhale through my nose, I slid more of him into my mouth until I felt myself gag from him hitting the back of my throat. Instinctively, my head reeled back or tried to. The jerk was cut short by pressure from Julian's hand which forced my head down onto his cock entirely.

Panic gripped my body like cold, bony hands as I gagged and choked on him. Tears blurred my vision before hot streaks trailed down my face again as I looked up at Julian helplessly.

Groaning, he held my head firmly in place with my lips right up against his pubis. "Relax, breathe through your nose, but you have to relax first." Yeah, easier said than done. He wasn't the one with a massive dick down his throat!

My fingers dug into his thighs, holding back my struggle to tap at his leg so he'd let me up. I could do it; I could take his prick deep and make him proud to call me his woman. Well, I could do it after I breathe and stop choking on it. Fuck I really needed to breathe. Maybe I should tap out this once for my sake.

As if he sensed my internal turmoil, he pulled my head off in one swift motion. My lungs burned from the sudden intake of air as I reinflated my lungs faster than I ever had before, making myself a little dizzy in the process. "Guilty yet?" His eyes softened with concern as he let my hair go and cupped my face sweetly.

Assuring him with a confident smile, I shook my head and leaned into his touch. "No, Daddy. I'll tap your thigh if I need a break." I needed his forceful hand in this matter; otherwise, it'd take me a hot minute to take him back down my throat.

My lips wrapped back around his cock after I stroked it a few times, and I took him to the back of my throat before I felt my panic rise again. "Baby, relax, it's not going to kill you." He soothed, chuckling at the end as he tenderly stroked the back of my head.

"Relax your throat fully and breathe evenly through your nose, then slowly take me in." He urged with a soft shove, so his tip breached my throat.

Squinting my eyes shut, I paced my breathing to keep myself from hyperventilating before sucking it up and taking more of him in with his help. Though, no matter how hard I tried, I couldn't not gag and choke on him. However, it didn't look like he minded one bit, with a maliciously satisfied grin on his face as he continued to fuck my mouth.

Disappointment weighed my eyelids down as my eyes dropped down to his abs, tracing each muscle's subtle lines and curves to distract myself from my ill feelings. "Baby," he spoke up after forcing all of himself into me and tilting my head up a little to snap my eyes back to him, "You are doing so well. Keep those pretty eyes on me while you keep choking on me." His soft encouragement and proudness faded over to full-blown devious lust right before he resumed fucking my face.

"Your mouth feels so good, best ever. Fucking love hearing you gag on me. Turns me on so much with how filthy you sound trying to be my good little slut." He growled through gritted teeth as he picked up the pace.

Whatever reservations I had disappeared in the blink of an eye as I melted at his words and tender touch. One hand gripped the back of my head while the other cradled my face preciously with a thumb stroking my cheek. "I'm gonna come in your mouth, and you're going to swallow all of it, understood?" His pupils were fully blown, making his green eyes darken in color as he glanced down at me.

Eagerness filled my chest, pushing me to take over the motions more on my own and eagerly suck at him. "Oh fuck, that's it, baby." He chuckled breathlessly with a groan, tightening his hold on my head as his hip movements became more jerky.

"Shit." He groaned deeply with his release, pulling my head back until only his throbbing tip remained in my mouth to spill his seed into me.

I sucked and licked his spurting cock to get out every last drop as my hand stroked at his shaft, forcing the remains to push to the top. "Greedy little one, aren't you?" He chuckled between his pants as he looked down at me almost lovingly in an appreciative way.

Pulling me off completely, he grasped my chin and pressed on it softly with his thumb. "Swallow and open, I wanna see that all of it is gone." His finger swept across my trembling lip as encouragement as my throat bobbed with each earnest swallow.

With a happy and proud smile, I opened my mouth, stuck my tongue out for him to see, and giggled softly at the look of approval from him.

Grabbing my arms, he pulled me up into his lap and kissed me feverishly. "Finish your breakfast, then I'll eat you out while you work on your book." He whispered with a smirk against my lips.

"Gentle?" The thought of him eating at me like a starved man made a zap of pain ache my beat-up pussy.

"Yes, I'll be gentle." He assured me with a smile and kiss before moving us over to the couch and giving me my plate of food again.

Now, at the time, it sounded divine, but once I saw how hard it was to concentrate with his tongue exploring every inch of me, I made him stop after some soft orgasms. It didn't help that my body was hypersensitive from last night's activities. So, we ended up cuddling on the couch with him watching a show as I laid in his arms with my laptop set up awkwardly to accommodate my position.

"You know, as fun as that scene sounds, it's not too feasible since the person would bleed out way before the fun could start." It took me a second to figure out what he talked about because it came out of nowhere.

"What you mean?" Not that I was butthurt about him criticizing my work; I was genuinely curious because I wanted to fix the mistake and learn something.

"A person wouldn't survive long enough to be buried alive if they have that much of their legs mutilated. They'd bleed out before their head was completely covered, which takes away the point of a live burial." He wasn't harsh with his words, more intrigued and amused. "I would either have less damage to the legs to keep most of the blood vessels intact or change the motive of wanting to bury them alive to suffocate with dirt." He suggested after a moment in thought.

Pondering his words, I reread what I wrote and really thought about everything. "You know, you're right."

With that in mind, I turned my head to face him completely.

"Can you double-check this other scene for me then?"

CHAPTER 16
Julian

LIFE IS GOOD.

Never thought I'd say or think that ever in my mundane and psychotic life.

I'm a whole new man.

Okay, maybe not that far because I was still the same murderous bastard from before I met and got Avery in my life. Still haven't changed there, nor will I ever because killing people is like air to me; I can't live without it.

This nagged the question at the back of my mind: how the hell would this relationship work?

Obviously, I couldn't hide this forever from Avery. Actually, well, I probably could, but it wouldn't be ideal if I wanted a healthy relationship with her. Also, how long until she started questioning me about my late nights or the questionable state I would inevitably come home in? I could only lie to her for so long before she'd poke holes into my answers and pry at me until the horrible truth came out.

Avery wasn't stupid, a little oblivious, but not stupid by any means. I needed to figure out how to deal with the fallout before she shook the blindfold off. The threads for her to grasp were there, and it wouldn't be long until she unearthed an end and followed it to the source.

Speaking of Avery...

"Hey, little raven, everything okay?" I didn't hesitate to accept the call when I saw Avery's name flash on my phone's screen.

However, my attention never left my victim fully as I kept my stark orbs trained on his pathetic body as he crawled very slowly on his forearms towards the backdoor of his house.

My ear trained to her sweet voice as I stalked up to the victim, who started to nod off from the drugs I spiked his drink with. "Yeah, sorry I'm gonna be a little late to your place. I got held up at work a little bit, the processing took a little longer because someone thought they lost something, and it was a whole manhunt for it because it was something like suuuuuper important. I'm gonna swing by the bakery, though, on the way to your place. Do you want anything?"

"He—mhmpfh!" A foot into the mouth was always an effective way to shut someone up.

"Oh, shit, did I interrupt you? I'm so sorry, you're probably so busy, and I just called you to bug you about something stupid." Avery's apology flew out of her mouth a mile a minute.

"It's alright, don't worry about it, you're not interrupting me. Funny enough, I actually got caught up in the office as well, so don't worry about being late. As for the bakery, get me something light and fruity. You drive safe now, alright? The roads are still kinda slippery and messy from the heavy rainfall yesterday." Worrying about her well-being was second nature to me after a whole month of being together.

It always slipped out even when I tried not to think about her much. Have you eaten yet? Have you drunk your water? Snack? Drive careful. Don't forget to sleep at a good time. Don't stay up too late.

I excused it as me digging for reasons to turn her bottom red or for her to get on her knees and choke on me, but somehow, it turned into actual worry and care for her. Not going to lie, it felt weird to honestly care for someone other than myself. Even when it came to myself, I only really ever cared about sating my need for bloodshed and justice that the system failed to deliver.

The law and system in place never did its job correctly. Otherwise, scum like this pathetic man would be behind bars and scampering away from me like an injured dog after I removed my boot from his face.

"I'll see you later at the house, little raven, be safe." I quickly hung up the phone after Avery said her little goodbye to give my full attention back to my victim.

The man whimpered weakly at me, feigning innocence. "Why are you doing this? What did I ever do to you?" Why is it always the same questions from these guys?

Who are you? Why are you doing this? What did I do to deserve this? Can't you spare me? I was let off, so I'm good.

It bored and irked me to no extent.

With an empty sigh, I squatted down to him. "Liza Kil, Heather Gath, Gerry Lon, and Jillin James, just to name a few. Do they ring a bell?" His list went much further, but those were his most recent 'conquests' as he liked to refer to them.

The way his face went whiter than a ghost meant he knew why I was present. "Y-you're... I... No!" The budding panic was too short-lived with how fast he passed out. Maybe I should have waited until he freaked out before drugging him. Oh well, I could incite the horror later before his execution.

"Pathetic." I thought aloud with a disappointed sigh and shake of my head.

At least he made it to the area rug I had set out, so rolling him up in it was easy after a bit of positioning. It was also a good thing he was on the smaller end of the average; it made hauling his dead weight with the rug a whole lot easier.

Once I had him loaded and secured into the back of my truck, I booked it home in hopes of beating Avery. I still needed to transport the guy into the basement holding area, which would have been tricky if she had been present.

Thankfully, I beat Avery home. Come to think of it, and maybe I should have given her a bit of a list when she asked me what I wanted to bide for more time. Too late now, but not like it mattered since—shit!

The hairs on my neck stood with a chill down my spine at the sound of dirt and gravel groaning under heavy weight.

From fake to genuine, the shift was uncontrollable when my eyes landed on my woman as she exited her car. "Hey bub, got done faster than I thought." Avery greeted me with an innocently bright grin filled with blissful wonder.

I couldn't be upset after seeing her face, as if I could even get upset with her in general. Her bright and cheery face always helped lighten my mood, which was another strange thing I found happening with Avery's presence in my life. A ray of sunshine to my darkness, as many would say in books. A bit preposterous, in my opinion, because no one could be as harsh or bright as a ray of sunshine or as blinding. At least, that was my opinion until Avery; now I understood the stupid words I once mocked.

"More time for me to steal from you." I charmed through my teeth as my grip on the rolled-up rug tightened unconsciously.

Good thing the area rug was bigger than the man it consumed, so Avery wouldn't be able to see the man unless she looked directly into the center hole. But fuck did the thing get a hundred pounds heavier? With each peppy step Avery took towards me, I felt a drag to my shoulder until she stood before me.

"I think I spoil you too much with my time." She teased back with a giggle before leaning up and kissing my cheek.

Then, the dread rolled over me like a heavy fog when her eyes drifted to the rug. Instinctively, the file cabinet of lies within my brain flung open, and my mind was hit with a flurry of words to string along.

A cute little tilt of her head did nothing to ease my nerves as she studied me with a tapping finger against her lips. "Oh, is that the new rug you were talking about for your little man cave or whatever in the basement? I thought you weren't going to pick that up until this weekend?"

The drawers in my brain slammed shut with my small exhale of relief. "It came early to the office, so I figured that I might as well lug it home." It wasn't a total lie; the context was *way* off, but she didn't need to know that.

Honestly, I didn't plan on striking today, but the man was smart and took my warning seriously. He made plans to flee, and I couldn't risk my target getting away. The slight shift in the timetable peeved me a little, but nothing I couldn't handle. I had done it before: move up a hunt because of the target.

Of course, I could do so freely before because I only had myself and my own time to worry about. Somehow, I underestimated my relationship with Avery, a nearly fatal flaw on my end. I needed to be more cautious unless I wanted to end up on death row.

"Why don't you go put the food away while I toss this down there? Then we can settle on the couch and watch the new documentary episode, yeah?" That should give me more than enough time to secure the victim in the holding room until I could deal with him later.

"Mhmmkay." A quick flash of a smile, and her body bounced right past me with her luscious hair flying behind her like a dark veil.

Fuck that was too close.

My chest ached from the breath I kept holding back from fully releasing because of my anxiety about her being mere inches from me with an unconscious body over my shoulder. I remained glued to the porch momentarily, unable to work my legs to move to my basement. All I could do was stand there and watch Avery from the open front door.

It was strange how fitting she looked in my home, as if she was meant to be there. My home was where she belonged, the missing touch to make home, well, *home*.

"Sweetie, I know you tell me you don't get cold, and I'm sure your burly ass body has enough insulation to keep you from freezing out there, but you need to come inside before you become a frozen statue. Also, it's cold, so come in and shut the door." Avery shouted from the kitchen with a playful smile and chuckle.

Her words snapped me out of whatever stupor came over me, and I found my legs moving on their own accord across the house's threshold. "I'll make us some crab soup while you busy yourself in your little man cave. Honestly, don't know what's so interesting down there to keep you away from me so long, but as long as it keeps you happy." The faint wisps of disappointment sliced cleanly through the air right into me.

Avery didn't like me keeping my 'man cave' a secret from her, but she understood my need for alone time and space away from everything. So, she didn't ever push much, but her discontent was clear as day whenever she touched the subject of my little getaway room. She kept up a fake smile for me, which I was grateful for, but not at the same time.

I made her sad, but I couldn't do anything about it. Showing her my basement, aka my prison/holding area, was definitely out of the question. I might be new to long-term relationships, but I was pretty sure showing your girlfriend your torture and sometimes kill chamber was a huge no-no, unless I wanted a prison sentence or planned to kill her, neither of which I had an inclination to.

"I won't be long, promise. I really just need to set up this rug, and I'll be back up. Don't worry, no man cave disappearances while you're here this weekend." Fucking hell, why did I say that with no guarantee? I couldn't leave the guy in my basement for three days straight.

Okay, never mind, I *could* leave him for three days without too much worry and hunt him after Avery left. Not ideal, but if it kept my girl happy, then I would make it work. If anything, sneaking out of bed in the middle of the night to ensure my prisoner was fine would have to do.

Pepping up, Avery bounced a bit in her spot. "Promise?" Internally, I groaned at her overly hopeful eyes that shined like the stars with her bright smile.

"Of course, I wouldn't say so otherwise." I might as well cut my heartstrings while I was at this.

Fucking hell, why am I punishing myself like this? Just, what the fuck am I even thinking about with this relationship? It shouldn't even be happening in the first place!

The mental beating I gave to myself drew out more and more as I crept further and further into my basement. My mental anguish came to a halt with the frigid air of the prison room biting my face like fangs when I opened the secured door, which remained hidden behind a false wall in my basement.

Yes, my basement was an *actual* basement that I had converted into another living area. I wasn't stupid to have my prisoners directly under the floorboards of my house; I would be asking to be caught with that idiotic of a move.

The fully furnished basement was a front to throw people off. Behind a false wall, which I secured heavily with safe measures like a hidden finger-print lock, was a dark, concrete hallway leading to another basement-like area with a trapdoor outside into my backyard. The concrete room housed a prison cage along with a chair with straps and a wall completed with a table filled with various instruments to inflict inhumane things.

Usually, I would wait until my victims woke up to have a little fun with them, but not today. Not when I had Avery upstairs waiting for me. I threw the rug with the man rolled up inside into the cage without a single care and locked it before rushing back upstairs to get my little bundle of happiness in my arms.

Bundle of happiness. Fuck, something really is wrong with me if that's what I referred to Avery as. It wasn't wrong, but by God, I have never been so cliché and cheesy in my life. Honestly, I probably needed to be lobotomized to stop the dopamine from eating away at my brain.

"Is the rug what you hoped for?" I wanted to mock her obliviousness and innocence, but that'd be too cruel.

Still, our situation was very ironic. She was a CSI processing crime scenes of my crimes while dating me and being under the same roof as me. Hearing myself say it in my mind cracked me up because it was one of those things that seemingly only happened in movies or fiction. Yet, here we were, a serial killer and a CSI, blissful together like two doves in love.

Also, I think it was funny because her job literally required her to be highly observant and have an eye for detail, yet she couldn't pick up shit about my deadly hobby. Granted, I was extremely careful around her, but never once had she questioned me deeply enough.

At least, not yet.

Which brought up the issue of this strange relationship of ours. Logically, I shouldn't entertain it any further. I got my fill of her physically, which was all I needed from her because I sure as hell didn't need affection or emotions from her. Well, maybe that was a lie to myself because deep down, the thought of her not giving me any attention, happy smiles, or adoring eyes cut at me.

But people like me didn't need those useless things, emotions, I mean. Emotions did nothing but hinder and hurt, so why bother?

Plush clouds pressed against my lips, stealing my breath and filling my chest with happiness.

There. That. That's why I should bother.

Avery.

"Can we cuddle on the couch with our soup now? I want you to hold me." If only she knew; she wouldn't be asking for my embrace if she knew how bloodied and dangerous my hands were.

"Of course, let me wash up and change real quick. I'm all sweaty and dirty from work." Again, it was not fully a lie; stalking and kidnapping people was work. It might not be legal work or my official job in the books, but I considered it a job I thoroughly enjoyed.

"Hmm, can I shower with you?" I'd be a stupid man to turn that down.

Unfortunately, I would have to be a stupid man today. "Maybe next time, sweetie, I've got some chemicals to scrub off of myself that I don't want getting onto you." Okay, I needed to be less stupid with my excuse.

"Why the hell have you been busying yourself in your little man cave then if you had chemicals like that sitting on your body and clothes?" The fact that she didn't grow suspicious of me made me question her intelligence a tad bit. She wasn't utterly mindless by any means; just the things that flew over her head sometimes had me wondering.

"Slipped my mind in my excitement." I shrugged it off coolly before dragging her over to the couch and forcing her to settle. "I won't be too long, promise."

The man didn't bleed too much on me earlier when we got into a minor tiff when he walked through his front door and lunged at me. He came home much earlier than I'd expected and planned for, so things got dicey for a moment before I managed to knock him out to continue setting things up. Then he woke the second time with my phone call with Avery, and that's when the realization hit him of who I was, the reason for my visit, and the rest was history.

I wonder if Avery would eventually become history to me.

Okay, maybe I shouldn't wonder about that because I didn't like the heavy feeling it brought to my body.

Actually, any thought of Avery not being a part of my life as a partner or anything less than a partner made me frown.

I hated the idea of Avery not being mine.

Was it annoying to work out a new stalking and killing schedule with this new relationship of ours? Yes, very much so, yes, but I wasn't bothered by the fact of it one bit as I should or usually would be. Why should I change my life to make someone happy and make some stupid romantic relationship work out? I shouldn't, that's what; at least, that was my answer before I came across the little raven bundled up on my couch.

Of course, any plans or schedules I made now would have to change later when—not if—Avery moves in. I haven't brought the subject to her yet since I didn't want to scare her off with the sore subject. Honestly, I don't get why couples made such a big deal about moving in with each other.

Avery lived in a shitty little apartment in a somewhat sketchy—in my opinion—part of town, and I had a nice, cozy, safe house big enough for the both of us. From what I observed, she already spent two or three days out of the week here, and she was comfortable around here. So, it shouldn't freak her out *that* much if I asked her to move in with me sooner than later, right?

Obviously, we have feelings for each other, and I doubt that would change to nothing with time. She didn't have any unsavory habits from her time spent here, and from what I had seen through her window and the video feed I got from the camera I snuck into her apartment.

Avery kept her living area neat and organized, mostly. She had her stacks and piles of books and papers here and there in an organized chaos, but they stayed in their corner and never cluttered the place. Well, she occasionally left her cups and mugs around and forgot about them until the cleaning day of the week—even then, she forgot sometimes.

For an intelligent woman, she was a scatterbrain more often than not. A little annoying, but cute. But only because it was Avery. I found it very unbearable in everyone else.

Shit, what was I—oh, right, Avery moving in.

I needed to pop the damn question to work out a new stability in my life. Otherwise, I'd end up caught.

CHAPTER 17
Avery

SOMETHING ISN'T RIGHT.

"Avery!" The starkness of Liz's voice snapped me back to reality.

Slowly, my head turned towards her as I twirled the black feather between my gloved fingers.

"Did Julian screw out whatever little brain cells you had over the weekend?" She teased with a snicker while holding an evidence bag out for me.

Pretty sure my brain still ran in the forest, but she didn't need to know the details of our crazy sexcapades. "Har har, missy, just thinking about this scene, that's all."

"What about it? It's the same as always with the score on the floor with how far the victim got along with the pile and trails of feathers." Liz pointed out the obvious with a shrug of her shoulder before grabbing the feather from me and putting it into the bag. "Besides, it's not our job to figure all that shit out, that's for the detectives and big shots. Don't forget, we're just the clean-up crew basically, gather what's needed and leave."

Valid point. Working out the crime and the scene wasn't in my job description. I only had to collect and catalog everything for the 'brains' of the department to figure out. Which I thought was kind of stupid because they weren't here shifting through everything with a fine-tooth comb. Liz and I had good ideas that didn't get heard, or at least we were refused to be heard.

"It's small, but the red string, they've never done that before, and the feathers, they aren't the same either. Also, the scores on the ground, I don't think they're intentional. They're too random and erratic, almost like scratches from wear and tear." Scrunching my face up, I huffed out a sigh. "I don't know, I just don't think this is the same perp as before." It wasn't the same killer.

The one that's eluded us so far has been meticulous to a fault. There was no way he would change his M.O. up so suddenly like this. Also, the scene was too disturbed, as if there was an intense struggle, which I hadn't ever seen before with the killer.

"Honestly, you're probably just thinking into it too much, and it's not odd for killers to switch things up a bit to throw police off their trail." Liz dismissed me with a wave of her hand before she went back to snapping photos of everything.

There was no point in arguing with her, not when she wasn't as invested as me.

"Hey, Avery, wasn't this the guy who raped that poor college girl who's the police chief's daughter?" Liz inquired with a nod towards a knocked-over picture frame on the floor.

"The one who's rich Mommy and Daddy got him off the hook?" I deadpanned with a scowl as I carefully picked up the shattered frame.

"Yeah, that one," Liz replied while studying the photo of a young blonde man in a graduation gown with his parents on either side of him. "Yeah, pretty sure that's the guy. I mean, he looks a little skinnier in the picture, but this picture is like four years old."

The target would fit the usual M.O. of The Omen—the nickname the media has dubbed our elusive serial killer—but everything else didn't. It could be some copycat, which would be a disaster because we haven't even found the original. So, to chase after a second killer psycho in the midst of this one would be a headache and a half.

"I'm not one to root for the bad guy, but good riddance." Liz huffed with a scoff before returning to the task at hand.

I had nothing to say back to her because I—begrudgingly—agreed with her. Whatever this guy had coming to him, he deserved it. He shouldn't be free to live after drugging and raping all those young girls. The only reason why he got off with a shit ton of probation and community service was because of the money his mommy and daddy had. Poor victims got torn into ruthlessly on the stand, and the damn bastard gets away scot-free, basically.

I shouldn't be condoning this behavior of the killer, but it wasn't as if they went after innocent people. Granted, they shouldn't be killing anyone, period, but better those deserving than those not.

God, what's wrong with me?

Looking past a murder and agreeing to it. A killer was a killer in the end. Why should it matter who they went after? Murder was murder.

With a heavy sigh, I forced my brain to shut down to process the rest of the scene in peace. I'd never get done if I kept wandering into the gray zone of morality.

"How are you and Julian doing, though? You don't seem too peppy like all the other times you've spent the weekend with him." Liz noted, worried with a soft frown and furrowed eyebrows.

Forcing a smile, I waved her off with a floppy hand. "We're good." It sounded more like I was trying to convince myself at this point.

Leave it to her to know when to press. "But?" Although I was an easy person to read.

"It's good. I mean, a month or so now? Right? And I still feel like I'm living on cloud nine whenever I'm with him, and our conversations over text aren't dull or forced, even if they are curt and simple most of the time. He's so sweet and caring, always with the good mornings and good nights, checking in on me throughout the day and making sure I'm taking care of myself and eating properly." Brightening up with a smile, I jumped a bit in my spot. "Oh! And the little surprises at work were so freaking nice, I love it!"

Realizing that I was rambling, I quickly reeled myself in. "But sorry, not the point. The 'but' to it all is the whole relationship. Like it's lovely, and I just don't want the honeymoon period to end. And I'm afraid of it ending and blowing up in my face if I agree to move in with him." And therein lies the problem to it all.

"Whoa, whoa, whoa, whoa, whoa! Whoa! Back the fuck up! Move in? Hold up, what? Okay, start from the beginning, girl." Liz gave me a bewildered look as she hooked her hands on her hips.

"It's what has been eating at me the past few days ever since I came back from his place." I admitted with a heavy sigh. "Before I left Sunday night, he asked me if I wanted to move it. He knows it's kind of fast, and it's like super fucking fast because I mean, come on, we've only been at this for a month, and he's already asked me to move in. Granted, I kinda live with him half of the week when I go over to his place over the weekend. But still..."

Looking down at my feet, I shuffled them uncomfortably. "The thought of going back to him every night, like I love the thought of it, don't get me wrong, but it's just... I don't know... Like what if for some reason we can't stand each other after we move in and start living together? I just... Oh my god, I'm gonna have to eventually fart in front of him and take a shit, oh my god!"

A slap to the face promptly stopped my rambling. Okay, let me clarify: a slap to the face from a rubber glove, not an actual slap to the face with a hand.

Straightening her face at me like a parent getting serious with their child, she let it loose. "Girl, he's serious then if he wants you to move in! And who cares about flatulence and toilet use, everyone does it. If he makes fun of you for doing normal human shit, then shove his head in the toilet and give him a swirly before leaving him."

Reassuring me with a smile, she lightly bumps my shoulder with a giggle. "Now, I can't speak about your stupid honeymoon period and whatnot, but I say you take the chance because I mean, when are you going to find such a perfect man like Julian? You two have gone strong and good so far, so I have no doubts about you two lasting after adjusting to each other fully. Besides, beats going home to your little closet of an apartment every night."

I couldn't help but catch her infectious smile. "Shouldn't you be talking me out of this? Like 'hey uhh this is kinda fast are you sure' or some reasonable shit like that?" When I needed her to be my voice of reason, as she always is, she shoots me in the knee.

Her cheeky little face turned towards me as she gave out a teasing giggle. "Well, I mean, if you weren't so in love—"

The brakes were slammed full force on that. "Whoa! Hold the fuck up. No."

Did I like Julian? Yes, a lot. But love? This soon? I mean, sure, I was severely infatuated and enamored with him, and there wasn't anything to him to *not* love... But to say that I loved him right now was way too soon.

"Girl, if I could take a pic of you whenever you talk about him or see him, you would definitely see that you are in looooove. Like your eyes really do light up, and your face just does this thing that screams you're in love, just, you have to see it to know what I'm talking about." Liz gushed and squealed, her feet dancing in her spot with her bouncing body.

"It's because we're still in the honeymoon period, where you are *supposed* to be in love." Probably didn't help that Julian has been the only man to give me this kind of attention and affection.

My sudden attraction to Julian could've stemmed from him being the first person ever to show me any interest and kindness. Perhaps I've been so starved and desperate for it all that I clung to the first person to give me all I ever wanted and needed. Maybe I put my time and energy into Julian because he was the only one, and it'll all fade out with time.

Granted, I would be a complete idiot to leave someone as great as Julian because he really had nothing bad to pick at so far. He was a grown-ass man with his life together, which couldn't be said about *a lot* of men these days. Honestly, I was probably being stupid and afraid of commitment because everything was so new to me.

"Has he been pushy with it? You moving in and all, or how has he been since he's asked you?" Liz prodded with a curious tilt of her head.

I had to think about it for a moment before answering her, "Quiet, actually, which is kind of weird? He's not bringing it up, pressuring me, bugging me, hinting at it, nothing, nada. Is that normal?" Was anything normal when it came to Julian?

Looking up with a finger tapping at her chin, Liz hummed softly in thought for a minute before replying to me. "I mean, it depends on how you want to take it. I mean, kinda weird? Maybe, but it could also be him respecting your answer and space, which is a huge plus in his book because most men are idiots who won't give us girls that." With a small hum and shrug of her shoulders, she continued, "Either that, or he really didn't care either way and was just really casual about it, which I doubt because he doesn't seem like the guy to invite short-term partners to move in with him. At least, that's what I would assume, given what you've told me about him. Julian seems like the guy to act after careful thought, so I doubt he took to offering you a key lightly."

Of course, she'd make valid points. Damn her for being wise and insightful and shit. None of it helped me, though, because it still pointed me back to the crossroads of my conundrum.

Dragging out a groan, I threw my hands up in defeat and let them fall back to my side as I turned on my heel to go back to bagging evidence. No point in dwelling on this topic any further because I would get nowhere. Besides, not like I had to give him an answer right away. Which was a bad thing because that meant I would drag my feet and avoid it until he forced my hand.

"Okay, what's your reason for not wanting to move in with him?" Her voice softened with curiosity, along with her quizzical face.

And honestly? Good fucking question because like hell did I know. I didn't have any valid reasons. Julian didn't have some horrible habit that would make living with him impossible. My reasons were definitely more selfish in nature, from wanting my own space to pure self-preservation because this first real relationship was too perfect to shatter.

For once in my life, something went right, and I was utterly terrified of royally fucking it up. What if Julian's attraction to me died down after I moved in because he'd see me so often? What if he grew complacent with me because the chase was finally over? I didn't want to risk anything when it came to Julian and our relationship. On the other hand, if I didn't move the relationship forward, he could get bored and leave me.

A long sigh deflated from Liz as she hooked her hands on her hips and stared at me pointedly. "Avery, I love you and want the best for you. So, I mean this in the most loving way ever, but get your head out of your ass and treat the awesome man like he deserves because he's giving things a hundred percent from the sounds of it while you're giving like seventy-five at most." Softening her voice, she offered me a lopsided smile. "I'm not saying you don't deserve a good man in your life because you do, but you are taking him for granted, and if this is how you're going to be, then I'm sorry, but he deserves better."

Once again, I couldn't argue with her because she was correct. Julian didn't deserve this weird half-assed limbo shit from me, not when he's been perfect to me. It hadn't really occurred to me before, but couldn't I just talk to him about this? We're both grown and mature adults who could converse with one another.

Why am I even stressing over this stupid matter? If he got upset about my answer, then he obviously wasn't *the one*. If he was a man, then he'd take this conversation well.

"Finally, I was starting to think the next blood splatter would be coming from you if it didn't click." Liz joked with a chuckle.

CHAPTER 18
Julian

WHAT'S GOT HER SO stressed?

I hated how her face scrunched and twisted while she paced back and forth in her tiny little apartment—or a closet, in my opinion. I wasn't even in the same area as her, yet I could feel her stress drag me down from watching her through the camera that I snuck into her place the second time she invited me over.

Speaking of sneaking things, I still needed to get a tracker on her somehow. It'd be easy to knock her out with some drugs and give her a quick shot in her perky ass, but that was too barbaric the more I thought about it and tried to plan it. I didn't want to harm Avery or break her trust in me by drugging her and violating her body like that. I might be a monster, but I would never harm or wrong my precious little raven.

Picking up my phone, I shot her a quick text before gluing my eyes back to the screen to watch her pick up her phone and respond to me.

Hey, yeah, lunch sounds lovely tomorrow :)

Any requests?

Hmm I was thinking we could go to Lil' Louie?

Whatever your little stomach desires little raven. What time do you want me to pick you up from the station?

Oh! That's okay! I can meet you there! It's not a far walk from the station and I know you have that big project you're still working on, so I don't want you taking time out for me like that!

Sweetie, you're never a bother or waste of time. Now, what time?

Babe, you have a multimillion dollar project going on that needs all your attention and time, I'm def second to all that.

Am I going to have to teach you a lesson already?

1245.

You didn't answer the question dear.

I did. 1245 is when you should pick me up :)

Cheeky little girl, if she thought she'd get away with this, then she had another thing coming for her in the future.

Did you eat dinner yet?

I haven't noticed a delivery man or any kind of takeout on her kitchen island, nor did I see any attempts at preparations to make a meal. Judging by the lopsided expression through the camera, I was willing to bet she hadn't.

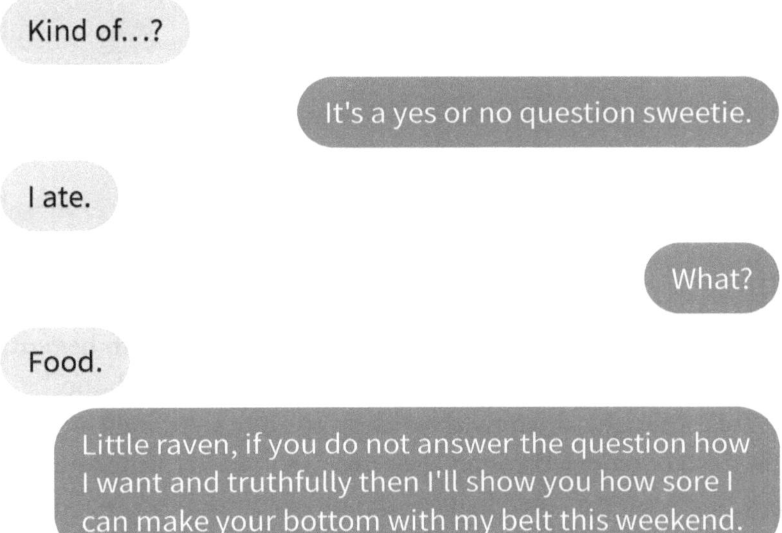

The three little dots appeared and disappeared a few times over a span of seconds as she gnawed at her bottom lip excessively. I don't know why, but seeing her take so long to answer a simple question peeved me a little. There shouldn't be much thought put into the answer, nor should she be stressing over it as much as she was.

My fingers flew across my phone screen in a fury as my breathing hiked.

An amused chuckle shook at my shoulders when I saw Avery's face drop and fluster from my message.

> Well if those are my options…

> Keep in mind sweetie, punishment not funishment.

> Fine. I'll eat some ramen with veggies and an egg. Happy?

> Pics or it didn't happen.

Even though I would see whether she obeyed or not, I wanted to see her follow through. Also, I hoped she'd send a picture with her cute face so I could add it to my never-ending album of her on my phone.

While I fought an amused smirk from fully stretching at my lips, I watched Avery trudge through the screen around her little kitchen area. Clearly, she wasn't amused by how she mocked me as she made her little packet of ramen over the stove. I couldn't even be mad at her because she looked so damn stinking cute with her face all playfully scrunched. Well, it wasn't like I could even punish her for it because then I'd be giving myself away. If she had been here in my kitchen, this scenario would have gone a lot differently.

Ten minutes later, Avery's picture came through of her sitting behind her bowl of ramen with a plate of vegetables next to it and her cheeky little face with her tongue sticking out between her curved lips.

> There, happy Daddy? :p

> Yes, very, now eat then get ready for bed, it's getting late and you still have work tomorrow.

> After I finish one more chapter of my story, I'm on a kick right now and don't want it to run away because I slept.

> Fine, one chapter only, and no energy drinks or coffee though.

> THAT WAS ONE TIME!

> Sweetie, I have a whole garbage bag full of your cans of energy drink from your late-night writings. You do know that you're only supposed to have two a day MAX right?

Cute little thing decided to antagonize me more by sending me a picture of her holding up an energy drink next to her devious little face.

> Whatcha gonna do hm? You're not here to stop me >:)

> You crack that open and take a sip then and see what happens tomorrow.

I wasn't being a hardass on her; she just had a bad habit of caring for herself poorly. This was a huge reason why I wanted her to move in. I'd have the peace of mind knowing she was well-fed and safe and sound at the end of the day. Feed her in the morning, take her to work, bring her lunch or take her out for lunch, pick her up and take her home after work, feed her dinner, fuck her senseless to tire her out, then leave her to slumber in peace so I'd have all the time to do what I needed with my hobby. I wanted to get her on that schedule for both of our benefits.

The only problem with shaving out more of my time was that it meant less time for my victims. Now, like a pan to my face, I wasn't bothered by the fact one bit when I should be bat-shit crazy about the notion. Never have I ever been remotely fine with cutting into my research and killing time, ever.

Then came along a little raven who threw my world into the sun. With each passing day, I found my priorities and obsession shifting from my forbidden hobby to my lovely Avery who somehow wormed her way into my life. Time and time again, I found myself wondering about her throughout the day, and the feeling of unease never rested until I knew she was well-fed and rested.

A soft ping from my phone took my attention away from my thoughts to read Avery's quick message about putting the drink back, which I confirmed through the camera. Unable to give her more time tonight, I sent her a quick good night text and some sweet nothings before silencing my phone. I couldn't afford any chances of a distraction tonight, lest I wanted to risk slipping.

A few days later, and still no definite answer from Avery on the subject of moving in with me. I started to wonder if it had been a little too soon to pop such a serious question. I sometimes forget how precious neurotypical people are sometimes. However, I suppose I should get used to *trying* to think about the other person since my girlfriend was indeed very neurotypical.

Even if things between us felt normal and were normal by all means, I could see some kind of discomfort, a tension of sorts tightening her eyes whenever we were together. A part of me wondered if I should tell her to forget I asked because she only got this way after I popped the question. I needed her to be comfortable around me to pull the wool over her eyes easier and keep her safe.

"So, you really are serious about Avery. What's the catch?" The police officer's question caught me off guard.

Glancing up from my seat near the front desk, I quickly scanned the officer clad in dress pants and a white button-up as he leaned against the desk across from me with his arms crossed. Nothing about him stood out, though, besides maybe his position based on his choice of clothing; he wasn't a street cop, either someone who worked behind the scenes—which I doubt—or an investigator of sorts. My thoughts were confirmed by the receptionist—a charming older lady—who smacked the officer with a stack of papers. "Detective Bornes, leave the handsome man alone. You should be happy for our little Avery, and lord knows she deserves someone good in her life."

Then, the woman turned her smiling eyes to me. "Sorry about him. He likes to play guard dog to everyone around here. Some kind of stupid macho-man bullshit. Either way, Avery is just finishing up. It won't be long, maybe about five or so minutes. Would you like something to drink while you wait?"

"That's okay, thank you for the offer." I politely rejected her offer with a small smile before turning my attention to the officer, who scoffed and rolled his eyes.

"Oh please, she's cute, I'll give her that, but she's a load of crazy. Honestly, no one right in their mind would be so obsessed with crime like her, especially her little serial killers and liking to pick apart a mind. I'm surprised she's not locked up in the mental ward or something." Detective Bornes began to trail off in a mutter; at least, it sounded like mutters to my rising anger, which caused my ears to buzz out. "Seriously, it might do us all some good to put her away before she snaps or something."

I was taken aback by how my senses dulled from my rising rage. The last time I ever felt intense anger akin to this was back in my teenage years when nothing made sense to my adolescent mind and body, but even then, my rage was bursts of explosive violence and/or destruction. Now, the current rage I felt was different because it was gradual, and it lingered; more importantly, I felt anger on behalf of Avery. Every distasteful word against Avery fed the growing fire within me.

Avery didn't deserve to be bad-mouthed. More importantly, no one should ever talk ill about my woman, ever. My little raven was a precious and perfect little thing who deserved nothing but the best and beyond. So what if her interests, likes and dislikes, and hobbies weren't like the majority of the population? She was more normal than me at the end of the day and had the personality of a little angel.

Quiet, reserved, introverted, nothing about those parts of her personality made her weird, in my opinion. Granted, I loved and appreciated those qualities about her, and it was what I liked in most people. Avery still had her little spark to her, though, particularly with Liz, who was the only person closest to a friend Avery had; the two could get into a crazy mood if Avery had enough drinks or hung around Liz long enough for the younger woman to weasel her way past Avery's walls.

Sure, Avery could be a little awkward at first, only because she got so flustered upon initial contact. Afterward, she was a ball of sunshine, as weird and cliché as that sounded. Always having a smile on her face, she was never anything less than friendly and warm to all those around her. If I knew any better, then I would let her go because she was too innocent for me; too bad I was a selfish bastard.

Sucking in a sharp breath, I gnashed my teeth together again to hold my anger at bay as the detective's words started filtering back into my ears. "There's nothing wrong with Avery. She is perfect the way she is. I suggest you stop talking bad about my girlfriend before something bad happens." If it were up to me, then threats and dead birds would be on his doorstep already, and his car would magically stop working tonight.

Of course, he didn't know when to quit. "Fine, I'll leave you two weirdos alone. You gotta be as fucking looney as her to date her, let alone have any kind of feelings towards her. Unless there's some strange catch." Looking at me with a mocking look of disgust, he scoffed at me. "Seriously, you her sugar daddy or something? A successful and well-renowned man like you should be doing better than a little weirdo crime junkie who works in a police department basement."

Clicking my tongue against my teeth, I let out a long breath as I stood up fully and puffed my chest out for some extra effect in towering over the detective, who stood a few inches shorter than me. "Last warning, pal, back off my woman. Unless you have solid evidence for your idiotic claims and words, I don't want to hear any more of it." Taking a deep breath, I calmed myself further. "Our relationship is also none of your damn business, but no, I'm not her sugar daddy. She and I are together because we are interested and attracted to each other and because we click well together. Now, back off." Or else.

I couldn't say the last part out loud, not in a full police station while all eyes were on me. I had an image to upkeep, and making a veiled threat against an officer was a surefire way to end up on a shit list, one I needed to stay off and far away from.

"Psh, hope her pussy is worth it, you pathetic—"

"Detective Bornes, that is enough and highly inappropriate in the workplace. It's also ill-mannered of you to speak to a civilian like that while on the clock. I suggest you return to your desk and leave my boyfriend and the business of our relationship alone before I report you to HR." Avery's voice snapped at the detective, who shrunk back with a glare and retreated with his tail between his legs.

Judging from the hostile gleam in his eyes, this wouldn't be the end of it.

CHAPTER 19
Avery

"Ju—"

My words were eaten up by his lips and mouth as Julian continued to kiss me ferociously.

Julian jumped me the moment he got me inside his truck. His hands grabbed at my waist and ran up and down the sides of my body while his lips ravaged mine like a starved beast. "You know how much I love it when you get a little feisty? Turns me on so much." He growled against my lips between his soft pants before consuming my breath again.

Breaking away from him, I let my forehead rest against him while I recollected myself. "H-he crossed a line, as much of an asshole as he is, that's too much and highly inappropriate. He doesn't like me much, but to hear him say that stuff to you is just... I don't know, and it rubbed me the wrong way. I know you aren't shallow and won't think much about his words because they are untrue, and you can clearly see that they are. But still... I'm sorry for his behavior."

"No, don't apologize for him, don't you ever apologize for anyone else or on their behalf. If they want to apologize for themselves or if they actually feel sorry then they'll apologize themselves." He corrected me in a soft voice before capturing my lips again in a heated kiss.

Giggling, I shoved at his hard chest, earning a chuckle from him in response. "Julian, I don't have that long of a lunch, and as much as I want to get dicked down by you right now, we're parked in front of the police station."

"The windows are tinted enough." Julian grinned playfully with a snicker before laughing softly when I smacked his chest with a scoffing chuckle. "Don't worry, I'm not that crazy to do a quickie in front of a police station in my truck and risk someone getting a peek at my girl."

Reaching over, he grabbed the seatbelt and buckled me in before turning his truck on and taking off to the little eatery around the block corner. Lunch was quick, mainly because of my schedule and time constraints, so we kept our conversation short and sweet while we ate.

"Hey babe, about me moving in..." Or maybe now wasn't a good time. I thought maybe I could just get it done and over with, and the time constraint would force my hand to be quick. I guess not, though, if I found myself wanting to sink back into the mud and drown.

Flashing me with a reassuring and comforting smile, he reached out and pinched my cheek. "You don't have to give me an answer until you are ready, and I don't want to pressure you or anything, so please, take all the time you need, darling." This man was too sweet and good for me, I swear.

A sharp breath stung gripped my throat as I steeled myself. "That's the thing, I've thought about it, and I will move in with you, but with some conditions." I waited for Julian to nod his head for me to continue. "I want to keep my place, just for an escape if I need space from you or if I have to stay late in the city because of work and such. It's more convenient than driving like thirty to forty minutes each and every time from your place in the woods to the city. If you're fine with all of that, then I'll move in with you."

Even if my little studio apartment wasn't much, it was still *my* place, and I didn't want to give that up quite yet. Besides personal reasons, I had a valid point regarding my work and the hours. I would rather be close and in the city if work were to call rather than out in the middle of nowhere and spend nearly an hour to get to a scene. It wouldn't be too often, though, but I wanted the option of my place just in case.

Cracking a smile and chuckle, he nodded his head in agreement. "And here I thought you were going to ask for a whole floor of my house to yourself or something." He joked, making me roll my eyes in response. "That all sounds reasonable, so I see no reason in not agreeing to your terms."

Glad to see he didn't blow up or become upset over it—not that I expected him to. "I'll move most of my stuff into your place, but I'll probably just keep my kitchenware and some outfits at my place, just in case."

"Or you can just get yourself a whole new wardrobe, not saying you have ratty clothes or anything, but when was the last time you got yourself something nice and new?" Couldn't argue with his little quizzical gaze because recalling the last time I went on an actual shopping trip was an impossible task for me right now—not counting lingerie shopping with Liz.

"I mean, my clothes work, and it's not like I *need* new clothes or anything. That and I just like saving money." I saw no point in spending money when, technically, I didn't have to.

Julian shifted in his seat momentarily before fishing out his wallet and a black card from it, holding it out to me with a warm smile. "Get whatever you want and like."

Back and forth, my head shook furiously as I shoved his hand back towards him. "I can't just spend your money like that. It's not right, and it's your money, not mine."

"Little raven, I wouldn't tell you if I didn't want you spending it. Besides, it's my money, so I'll use it how I want. So, I want to spend it on you. Either I go shopping with you, or you take the card and spend it yourself. And let me tell you, if I have to take you and go with you, I'll probably make you spend more than you plan because I want to spoil you." Expertly, he flipped the card into my open hand that was still pressed against his and curled my fingers around the thin piece of plastic. "Besides,

I'm sure as hell not spending it, so it's just sitting there. Oh, and none of that I'll pay you back crap either, you're my girl, so this is just me taking care of you and making sure you're happy as can be."

Damn him for having an irrefutable answer to everything.

Note to self: do not get into arguments with Julian because I will lose.

So, with a defeated sigh, I reluctantly tuck the card away into my little purse before pouting at Julian's grinning face. "What's my limit?" Not that I had any intentions of spending too much, maybe around a few hundred at most, but I wanted to know my line in the sand.

"Honestly, none. You could go buy three new cars for all I care with it." My laughter in response quickly died down when his face remained serious. "I know you won't abuse my bank account, but you really can spend however much you want."

God damn! How loaded was this man?!

I knew he was wealthy and successful from a quick Google search, but not like I dug too deeply into him and his financials because that was a big headache to think about. Of course, now I regretted the decision because the thought of being with someone of his caliber felt daunting. After all, I was a measly little CSI while he was out here being a millionaire—probably billionaire—multi-business owner.

What if I wasn't good enough for him?

What did he even see in me?

I was a little small fry while he was a shark; a bunny and a wolf.

"Hey, what's wrong?" His voice dipped low with concern as he tilted my head with a curled finger under my chin.

"I just... I'm not good enough for you." I confessed with a frown.

"Hey." Tucking my bangs behind my ear, he cupped my face and stroked my cheek with the rough pad of his thumb. "Don't you ever think or say that ever again. You are more than enough for me. You are too good for me if anything. You are a ray of sunshine while I am a lonely little forest troll in the shadows." Giving me an appreciative and reassuring smile, he continued. "Don't let our standings in society make you think otherwise because I don't care or give a shit about any of that. Hell, you could be a fast-food worker and I'd still fall head over heels for you like I have."

Leaning in, he kissed my forehead with a happy hum. "If I cared about any of that surface stuff, then I would have hitched myself off to some Beverly Hills Barbie a long time ago to keep an image, but I don't. What I want is a good person at heart, one who I click with on a deep and spiritual level almost, someone I can be free around, and that is you, Avery. There is no one else in the world I would want to call mine but you. You are mine, Avery." The way his voice dipped with his darkened eyes at the end had me shivering and melting in his hands.

Never in my life had someone looked at me so intensely with such raw passion and desire. Also, not that I liked to be treated like some possession, but it was hot when Julian claimed me as his. I was his. Julian's girl. I never wanted to belong to anyone so badly until him. He could grab me in the most obscene way, say whatever he wanted, and I'd gladly let him do it all and love every bit of it.

"Yours? You mean it? Yours for how long?" Insecurities faltered my belief that this could be something long-term.

"Forever, and you should know by now that I am not a man to say meager things, especially when it comes to you. There is no one else I want in this world but you, so I intend on keeping you forever as long as you will have me." Perhaps my ears acted up because his last few words sounded strained, but I let it go because he probably had some difficulty getting his feelings out like the typical man.

"I'd be a complete idiot to let an amazing man like you go." So far, he hadn't shown any signs of flipping some kind of switch. He hadn't abused or manipulated me any, so that was a huge plus in my books. He also had his whole life together and had the emotional intelligence of a grown-ass adult. He was truly a proper man through and through. "Besides, this is probably a once-in-a-lifetime opportunity for me. If you left me, I doubt I'd ever find someone else in my life, let alone someone as perfect as you."

Because let's be honest, I'd only attract the wrong type of men with how I carried myself or the weirdos based on my likes and hobbies. It was hard to find a decent man these days, let alone a good man. So, like hell would I let Julian go. No, my claws would remain sunk into him deeply.

"Well, I'm going to spend every second of every day for the rest of our lives to show you how much you mean to me and how much I appreciate and adore you. I am blessed to have a woman like you as mine, humble, cute, adorable, reasonable, just perfect." Julian's lips pressed against my forehead in a quick kiss after quickly wrapping his hand around my neck to pull me in.

"Now, finish up so I can taste more of you in the truck before you have to go back to work. Also, did you want to start moving in tonight or this weekend?" The fact he hadn't barged into my place and thrown things into suitcases amused me a little bit with how eager and happy he reacted when I gave him my answer.

After a moment, I responded to him while still tapping my chin. "Let's save it for the weekend. It's only a day more after today. I'll probably go shopping with Liz tomorrow after work, get some clothes for your place, then head back home and pack up things like my notebooks, laptop and whatnot, and some of my clothes and sentimental things. Then I'll head to your place probably a little later into the evening, so don't wait up for me with dinner like usual."

His face graced itself with a soft smile as he reached over and took my hand to bring it to his lips for a kiss. "I've gotten used to eating with you on the weekends, so I'll wait. It'll be fine. It just means I have more time to cook something good. Any requests on what you want? Or do you want it to be a surprise like always?"

"Surprise me, but I'll make us some food the next day. I've been craving a good bowl of Bún bò Huế for a while now. Hope you don't mind your house smelling like a shit ton of spices and lemongrass." I did know how to cook, but I was just too lazy to do it half the time. When I did cook, though, on the rare occasions I got the spur to, I made good shit.

"That's the spicy beef noodle soup we ate the other week, right?" Julian's head tilted a little with his quirked brow.

Confirming his question with a nod, I gave a small giggle. "Yeah, the one little hole-in-the-wall place. I like making a big ol' pot of broth and freezing them to pull out over time. Oh, hope you won't mind me using a bit of your freezer space for a lot of my broths."

"It's gonna be yours too now, so you don't have to ask me for anything, just go for it. My house is yours, but the only thing—"

He didn't even have to finish before I finished it for him. "Yeah, I know. Don't touch the basement. That's your space, your mancave. Don't worry. I respect you more than enough to know my boundaries." Was it kind of strange? Him and his basement and whatnot? Yes, a little, but it was his house to start with. That was his safe space, his personal area, so I figured he'd share it with me when he was ready.

"Thank you. I promise, when I am ready, I'll share the space with you." For the first time in our relationship, I doubted his words because of how empty he sounded and how voided his eyes became with his fake smile to placate me.

Never before had I questioned him until now, and it'd been a while, but I felt chills in his presence again. The little part of me that told me to scram.

What are you hiding Julian?

CHAPTER 20
Julian

Hisssssss!

Unlike the tire, my body was filled with satisfaction and content.

I thought I'd be okay with Avery coming and going as she pleased after she moved in, mainly because she only ever traveled between home and work. Unfortunately, I miscalculated because that was too much freedom for her. She came too close to discovering me too many times over the past few weeks when it came to my activities regarding my hobby. I needed to control her whereabouts more like I initially planned.

So, I returned to the initial plan I concocted when I thought about ways to force her hand to move in with me. She couldn't really go many places without her car in working order, so she would have to rely on me as a means of transport. She could travel for work via company vehicle, but that would only be during work hours and for work-related things. So, I wouldn't have to worry about her heading into the city at night or outside my predicted schedule.

Avery won't be thrilled to find her tires slashed and engine busted, but I did what I needed to ensure my life wasn't thrown off the rails because of her unplanned trips.

As I expected, around the time she got off work, my phone went off with texts from her freaking out about finding her car in an unusable state.

Now, being the good boyfriend I was, I gave her the concern she wanted to hear and gave her the solution of me being her ride. She rejected at first, not wanting to trouble me, but after some convincing, she relented.

After I got off work, not too long after she clocked out, I went to pick her up after calling a tow for her car.

"Sweetie, I'm so sorry to hear about your car. I can't believe something like that happened." I feigned a frown as I hugged her tightly once she climbed into my truck.

"I'm sorry for being a bother to you." She spoke against my chest after burying her sad face into it.

"Little raven, you are never a bother to me, ever. Besides, I was the one who brought up the idea and pushed for it." I assured her with a smile after pulling back to look down at her. "If you get called in, then you can just take one of my vehicles."

At least if she took one of mine, I could track her because they had GPS trackers that alerted me whenever they left my property. Actually, "You can have one of mine if you want. I mainly use my truck anyway, so my two others are kind of sitting there collecting dust, which isn't too good for them. It'd save you some money in getting a new car. That way you can put it more towards your book." As if I'd let her use her own money to buy another car. If anything, I'd pay for it; it'd be the least I could do after sabotaging her current one.

"I can't just take and use your car like that. They're yours. I'll just look into another car. Besides, I've been wanting to upgrade for a while, guess this was just a sign from the universe to do so." She deflated in her seat with a sigh while leaning against the window.

"Baby, I really don't mind, like I said, I mainly use my truck anyways, so please, take my car. But if it really bothers you that much, then we'll go car shopping tomorrow, alright?" Yeah, that would be a fight for tomorrow if she agreed because, like hell, I would let her pay.

"Babe, I can't let you buy a whole brand-new ass car for me, that's too much." She whined with a pout, making me chuckle when I caught a glimpse of it in the corner of my eye. "It doesn't feel right for you to spend that much money on me."

"Little raven, I really don't give a damn. As I said before, all that money is just sitting there doing nothing but weighing my bank down. Someone needs to spend it, and it ain't gonna be me. I already made my donations for the year, so you really have free reign over billions." My eyes kept flickering over to study her reaction to my wealth.

I never told her how loaded I was, but we worked on the assumption that I was filthy rich. Guess she underestimated my net worth by how her eyes bugged out of her head before she whipped her shocked expression at me. "I'm sorry, what? Billions? You can't just drop that bomb on me like that Julian. I thought you were just a millionaire. Not like any of it matters to me 'cause I'm no gold digger, but still, that's kinda important to know." Letting out a sigh of disbelief, she shook her head softly. "Lordy, just what the hell are you doing with a broke-ass little CSI like me then?"

Chuckling, I reached over and rubbed the top of her head while keeping my eyes trained on the road. "Because it never really occurred to me, nor does it matter to me how much I make. I live comfortably enough and have more than enough stashed away to last me a lifetime or so if things were to go belly-side up. Trust me, I want you to spend my money, and nothing would make me happier than seeing and making you happy." Strangely and shockingly, I found truth in my words.

I never cared for anyone's happiness, not even my own; I only sought to sate my dark desires, not make myself content and happy. Yet, with Avery, I wanted to make her smile, make her face light up with pure bliss and joy, which is why I cooked for us because I found a strange satisfaction in catching her subtle little smile and grateful eyes whenever she looked at the meal.

Avery made me happy, strangely enough, and I wanted more of that—happiness through Avery.

It was good to see Avery cave when I backed her into a corner. "You're not gonna let me off the hook unless I agree to take your car or let you buy me a new one, are ya?" She deadpanned with a defeated sigh.

"Smart girl, you might avoid punishments if you keep that up." I joked with a small laugh. "But yes, those are your two choices, well, three if you count me driving you everywhere."

"I'll take your car. At least that'll save some of your money." She grumbled, crossing her arms and sinking into her seat.

"Good girl." My hand fished blindly for her cheek to pinch before searching for her hand to hold.

"I still can't believe someone did that to my car. I mean, what the fuck, and that close to a police station too." She fumed silently in her spot as her fingers mindlessly played with mine.

"Well, nothing can be done now. What's done is done." I spoke against the back of her hand after bringing it up to my lips to place a kiss on it. "Now, when we get home, go take a nice bath or shower to relax, and we'll eat some dinner on the couch with a movie. Sound good?"

"Yes, Daddy." She squeaked softly before tucking her lip between her teeth with a smile.

I would throw together a quick meal and use the rest of the time to ensure the equipment in my car was all in working order. My supposedly daily vehicle got forgotten in the garage between my truck and my motorcycle. Working in construction, my truck made more sense for hauling things around, and my motorcycle only saw use when I needed to stalk my victims around.

"Hey, Daddy?" Avery peeped up just as we pulled into my driveway.

"Yes, little raven?" My head was quick to turn to her after turning my truck off.

"Can you fuck me later?" Her little bouts of boldness were adorable as well, mainly because she tried so hard to keep everything neatly tucked under her good-girl image.

"I was planning to either way, but now that you ask, what makes you think you deserve to be fucked tonight?" Now I was being a little asshole, but she brought it up.

"I've been good all week, though." She defended herself with a soft pout, leaning into me and hugging my arm. "And I wasn't too much of a brat all week."

"But the fact that you were even a brat at all deserves some punishment, does it not?" A smirk warmed its way onto my face as I studied Avery's deepening, pouting frown as she struggled to reply.

There was no winning for her with the question. If she agreed, then there was an admission of being a brat. On the other hand, if she denied it, then she'd dig the hole deeper for herself by lying to me. Avery knew the corner I had put her in with how she chewed at her bottom lip and darted her eyes around for an escape.

"Well, little raven? I expect an answer." I toyed with her, smirking while twirling a lock of her silky hair with my finger.

"Yes, sir, it does." She relented after a small moment of pouting to herself. "How many this time?"

"Surprisingly, only fifteen." Shame, I wished she had misbehaved more. I quite enjoyed spanking her bubbly little butt. Although, at the end of the day, I didn't *need* a reason to spank other than because I wanted to. Thinking about tying her to the bed and bringing my belt down to welt her supple ass had my cock straining for freedom from my pants.

Avery continued to chew at her bottom lip while peering up at me through her lashes. It was hard to tell because tonight wasn't particularly nicely lit due to the moon being hidden behind the clouds, but I think her cheeks blushed up. Either way, something went on in her mind for her to be so silent. Usually, she was more than eager to snark back and rack herself up a good handful of spankings before her actual punishment got dealt out.

So, her brooding silence was off-putting.

In a flash, her lips struck mine in a hard-pressed kiss, which stunned me momentarily. When I came to in the blink of an eye, Avery's little figure had already bounced towards the front door with *my* keys in hand.

When did she even take that?

Scrambling out of my truck, I took off after her, getting a door slam to the face along with an earful of her mischievous giggling laughter. By the time I threw the door open, the sound of her retreating footsteps down the hallway rang through the house. Moving on their own accord, my feet took after her like a predator chasing prey on instinct.

Unfortunately, my prey slipped with another slam of a door to my face, along with the soft click of the lock, before my fist pounded against the room door. "Big mistake, little raven, open up," I demanded as I jiggled the doorknob for effect.

"No! You're going to spank me!" Her muffled shout rang out.

"You have no one but yourself to blame. You decided to be a brat and flip me off before drinking that energy drink the other day. You know the rules baby, and I warned you before you even cracked open the can. Then need I remind you about the other night when you decided to take your own pleasure into your own hands when you know fully well who your pleasure and orgasms belong to." Honestly, her little masturbation stint was what earned her a bulk of the spankings tonight because how dare she deny me the pleasure of an orgasm by my hands.

"Hmp!" Then, the sound of something thumping hit my ear. "But you enjoyed it, so you can't punish me for it. You came too." She retorted, probably pouting and stomping her feet on the other side if I had to take a guess.

"Doesn't mean you get off the hook. Rules are rules, and you broke them. Now, open the door and get on the bed, or else." Once again, she had no one else but herself to blame.

"No!" Followed by what sounded like another stomp.

Unable to help myself, I let out an amused chuckle as I reached above the doorframe for the key. "You have until the count of three, and if I don't hear the lock clicking by the time I get to three, then I'm tripling your punishment tonight, and it'll be the bench and flogger. So, either you be a good girl and unlock the door and take thirty with my belt, or be a little brat and get forty-five with the flogger. So, what will it be."

"What? What happened to fifteen?!" She whined, this time definitely stomping her feet.

"Fifteen turned to thirty when you refused to listen to me the first time when I told you to unlock the door. Now, it's either thirty or forty-five, your choice." Either way, I get to inflict pain on her, so I'd be satisfied either way.

It shouldn't be a surprise, but I was a sadist at heart. What did come as a surprise was Avery's masochism. My innocent little raven craved pain, even if she liked to deny it more often than not.

Her sweet lips may spew the lies her tongue weaves, but the look of pure bliss and lust in her eyes couldn't be denied. That's why I loved grabbing fistfuls of her hair to force her around and to get that happy shift in her eyes when she submitted. Even when she would be a brat, it was because she enjoyed putting herself in tough situations for the consequences.

"One."

Insert the key.

"Two."

Jiggle the key.

"Thr—"

Immediately before I finished, the lock turned, and the door opened just a peep before the sounds of scuffling feet drummed the air, along with the faint *thump* of something hitting the mattress.

I hadn't entered the room fully before she started to sputter her half-assed apology. "Please, please, please, I'm sorry—"

A few long strides and I closed in on her enough to pounce on her, pinning her unexpectant body down onto the bed by her neck. "Save it for after your lashes when you actually mean it through your tears," I growled into her ear after fisting her hair and wrenching her head back. "Now, I am going to let you up, and you are going to strip and get on the bench."

Her body shivered briefly before tensing under me just as her wary eyes locked onto me. "Wait, the bench? You said to get on the bed." The flailing and whacking of her legs and arms ensued and was expected.

Being restricted on the spanking bench meant no escape, no wiggle room—literally. When it wasn't used for a punishment spanking, then Avery was more than happy to comply and settle her pretty little ass on it for me to play with her body. Needless to say, the same couldn't be said if she knew the reason for the bench use was for a punishment.

The soft *click* of my knife flipping open stilled the room before frigid air filled it as I ran the flat side of it up Avery's delicate curves to her twisting face. "That was to see if you'd obey or not. Besides, I only told you that you'd get lashings, not where. Just because I told you to be on the bed doesn't mean it'll be where I will make your bottom cherry red." Her body shook along with my shoulders when I let out a deep, dark chuckle before I sliced through her top—right down the center—with my pocketknife.

A brief flash of defiance and fight flashed in her eyes before muting back to an excited wariness when she flickered her gaze back to the blade in my hand. The quick tensing of her jaw had me smirking and mentally praising her because I knew she had just held her tongue—literally. It was a shame—kind of—that she didn't give me more reasons to add to her count tonight. On the other hand, she was learning at the very least, so I had to give her some credit there.

With her split shirt open and pooled to the sides, her supple skin was a blank canvas for me to run the flat of my knife against, painting her body with goosebumps and filling the room with her shudders. Pressing the blade carefully against her, I leaned down and took her lips with a deep groan before slowly moving the knife off to the side of the bed and setting it down. "Now, are you going to be a good girl?" My words fell against her lips after breaking the kiss.

"Yes, sir." Her breathy response fanned my satisfied face right before she slipped from under me, scrambling off the foot of the bed to shed her split shirt and jeans.

"Wait." It was as if I had hit the pause button on her with how instantaneously she froze in her half-bent position after taking her pants off. "Leave your bra and panties on."

Avery's eyes darted back at me questionably as she slowly straightened out and dragged her feet over to the padded bench that had become a new addition to our playroom. Well, the room was a guest bedroom, but I have somewhat converted it into a playroom for us after a few nights together and a drunken suggestion from my little pet.

Funny enough, I started to wonder if she ran into the playroom on purpose or if she took a wrong turn in her flurry to escape me—our bedroom was literally across the hall. Oh well, I could ask her later if I really wanted to know.

As she got herself situated on her forearms and knees on the bench, I got off the bed and grabbed the knife before going over to her. Standing before her, I took a minute to take in the precious sight of her bent-over body before me, her head perfectly leveled at my hips with how I positioned the bench. Brushing the tips of my fingers over her cheek, I held her face tenderly as I smiled down at her. "I will never grow tired of this lovely sight." Something about her being in a—physically—lower position than me made me feel powerful and appreciative of her.

She may have gotten into this position because of the threat of more punishment, but she still actively made the choice, nonetheless. Even without the shadow of discipline hanging over her head, she still willingly submitted herself to me. Something about *that* aspect of it all appealed to me greatly, and I couldn't help but feel grateful and appreciative towards her for making herself vulnerable like that to me.

Sure, it would've been easy for me to force her submission, but the thought of it didn't appeal to me, nor did it give me the same feeling of satisfaction. This notion didn't apply to only Avery, though; forcing people to do things got things done, yes, but it wasn't fun. Now, manipulating people into doing what I wanted was a whole different ball game, one I thoroughly enjoyed playing. It satisfied me greatly when people relented to me and acted of their own accord; it meant I was just that charming of a bastard.

Of course, I didn't manipulate Avery, no. But the fact I didn't have to, yet she submitted herself to me and practically begged me for it satisfied me more than enough. It was also an aspect of our relationship and dynamic that made me fall for her and cherish her greatly.

A soft, loving, and grateful smile graced my face as I leaned down and kissed her tenderly with a drawn-out groan. My fingers tangled themselves into her hair, messing it up with how much I grabbed and pulled at the strands to move her head with mine in our heated kiss.

Reluctantly, I broke away with deep breaths. I could kiss her forever, and I would later. For now, I had other matters to attend to.

Leaning over her, I began to work the straps onto her body. "Good?" Even though I tested the restraints, I wasn't the one being strapped down.

Pursing her lips, Avery wiggled on the bench and tugged at the straps. "A little tight on the right thigh, maybe go down a notch." The fact I'd be whipping her ass and inflicting a boatload of pain and discomfort on her in a minute didn't take precedence over her safety and comfort.

Listening to her, I quickly adjusted the strap she pointed out before telling her to test it again. After I got a verbal 'go ahead' from her, I promptly stripped myself bare and positioned myself right in front of her head with my legs firmly pressed against her hands until she rested them fully against the front of my thighs.

"What's the safe-word?" We had a routine anytime we'd enter any kind of scene: test out the tools and equipment to ensure knowledge and safety, a reminder of the safe-word and gestures, and one last check before things went into full swing.

"Guilty." And she knew there'd be no starting the scene unless she reiterated the safe-word. "And if I can't use my mouth, then tap your thigh three times."

Nodding and humming in approval, I leaned down and kissed her forehead one last time as a loving gesture before pressing her face into my hardened cock that stood straight against my abdomen. "Better start worshiping my cock like my good little slut." My hips rolled at her, grinding her face in a form of encouragement before picking up the knife I'd placed on a nearby table and flicking it open.

A sick and twisted grin pulled at the corners of my lips, and I ghosted the cold metal of the blade down her curved back and over the round of her bubbly cheeks, making her body erupt in goosebumps. It'd be so easy to end her right now; the blade would sink into the area between her ribs like a knife through butter with how sharp I kept my tools. Usually, the prospect of ending someone's life got my cock twitching, but not when it came to Avery.

No matter how many times I entertained the idea, begrudgingly as an experiment, the end result was always the same: pure, utter disgust. The brief thought of doing something remotely ill to Avery just now nearly pulled all the blood from my throbbing member. If it weren't for her soft tongue working the length of it as if it were the most delicious lollipop she ever had in her life, then I'd be flaccid and embarrassed.

Avery wasn't another victim, not because she didn't remotely fit my criteria. No, it was because my obsession with her went down an avenue I never thought possible.

But now wasn't the time for such thoughts.

Shoving everything aside, I bunch the back of her lacy panties in my free hand, slipped the sharp blade right under the material, and sliced it away from her body with a few quick flicks of my wrist. The scrap of fabric was soon discarded on the floor, being joined by her matching bra not long after it hit the ground.

Catching my bottom lip between my teeth, I sucked in a deep breath through my crazed face as I ran my thumb along the length of the small hairline cut I'd placed along the side of her breast when I took care of her pesky bra.

It was hard to tell in the dimly lit room, but her once porcelain perfect skin was marred with faint scratches of my knives from our other session. I was more than careful with knife play and Avery, only ever leaving cuts no deeper than a bad papercut on her delicate skin. Inflicting the marks on her tore me sometimes, though. A part of me wanted to keep her pristine and perfect, while my true self wanted to mark her up to make her imperfect like me. Also, something about her allowing me to dance my blade around her body and mark it up how I pleased, make *my* mark on her, tugged at my primal heartstrings.

After running the blade down the side of her body and outer thigh, I left some more scattered cuts to trace along with my tongue before closing the knife and setting it safely aside. "Open your mouth," I growled against her body, shooting a hand out and grabbing the back of her head to yank it back.

A hoarse, gasping moan vibrated against her throat from the action, and the sounds of her moans could be felt along the length of my shaft the moment I shoved myself all the way into her eager mouth in one big thrust. Leaning up with a groan of my own, I held the back of her head with one hand while my other grabbed my belt from the table.

Glancing down, I couldn't help but feel a zap of pleasure strike my body head to toe when I met her tearful eyes. "Fuck you look so beautiful stuffed full of my cock all the way down your throat like this." The jerking of her gags as she choked on my thick cock only spurred me on.

"If you let me fuck your mouth good while I spank you, then I might take it a little easier on you." Honestly, I probably wasn't, but it was good encouragement to get her more than eager to let me face fuck her while I lashed her bottom cheeks.

Keeping a hand buried in her hair, I held her head firm as I thrust in and out of her mouth with long strokes at a steady pace—for now. I would go harder at her once I got a rhythm going with her spanking. For now, making her swallow my cock fully with each thrust until her lips pressed firmly against my pelvis would be enough.

With the first lash, her mouth and throat instantly clenched around me in a muffled yelp as her body jerked against the restraints. The sight of her paled flesh pinkening back up stirred me forward. Bite after bite, my belt left reddening streaks and welts with each and every lash that sounded like music to my ears, along with her muffled cries as she continued to let me use her mouth like a fuck hole.

Nearly done with her punishment, I abandoned the belt to clatter on the ground and opted for my hands to finish the last ten, wanting to feel the sting of my hand against her burning bottom. "Such a good girl, taking my cock like the good little slut you always are for me while taking your spankings. So good." The way her body shuddered into me as I kneaded her warm cheeks in my large hands before dipping the tips of my fingers between her legs to brush along the length of her wet cunt.

"Fuck, so wet, all from a belt and a cock in your mouth, such a whore." Sucking in a breath through my teeth, I abruptly step back, removing myself from her fully to bend down to her level. "But that's okay," I said in a soft voice, running my hand from her hair to her tear-stricken face, "Because you're my whore. My good little cock hungry whore, hm? Always hungry for me and only me, isn't that right, baby?"

Small whimpers left her nodding head as she leaned into my touch. Her glassy eyes, full of adoration, bore into mine with a smile as she graciously took my thumb into her mouth to suck and lick at it after I swiped it across her swollen lips and pressed. "Yes, Daddy. I am all yours and only yours. I belong to you and only you. I am your little raven, your good little slut, your girl, and your cock hungry whore." She sounded so drunk on her bliss, and I couldn't be any happier.

Holding her face, I plant a deep kiss against her quivering lips before standing back up and seating myself fully into her again. "Almost done, little raven, just ten more." Then, it'd be a different kind of torture afterward, but she'd enjoy it all the same.

"Shit, that's it, baby, swallow my cock like that." I groaned at the feeling of her throat constricting around me as I slowly dealt out her last ten spankings.

Avery quickly adjusted accordingly, judging by the rhythmic squeezing around my pulsating length. With my hands firmly gripping her throbbing ass, I rutted myself into her mouth with a few hard and rough thrusts before I groaned out my release down her throat as I pressed her head right into my hips to bury myself as deeply as possible.

"Fuuuuuck." Another resounding *smack* rang through the air with her squeal and my soft laughter. "Sorry, couldn't help it, your ass was right there begging for it."

Pulling my still-hard cock free from her mouth, I stepped back and wrenched her head back to get a good look at her messy, fucked out face. "Show me." I didn't have to say more for her to obediently open her mouth and stick her tongue out to show that she swallowed every last bit of my cum. "Good girl."

Taking a moment away from my little bound beauty, I purposedly took my time searching the drawers for the magic wand vibrator. I knew where I stored it, but building the anticipation and seeing Avery squirm out of the corners of my eyes was too much fun. Once I deemed her little wait long enough, I quickly fetched the intended item and returned to the bench to strap it against her drenched pussy lips after parting them.

Petting her hair, I let her relax into my touch before running a finger down her spine to get a small mewl out of her and turning it into a sharp, gasping moan with a sudden thrust into her unexpected sex. With two fingers seated in her tight walls, I carefully curled them to stimulate her sensitive walls and tease her momentarily before abruptly pulling out to turn the vibrator onto a medium setting. "Be sure to let your pleasure known. I'm going to prepare dinner, then come back for my dessert."

"Wait! Are you seriously going to leave me like this? Wait, can I come? Please tell me I can come, please, Daddy." The fearful apprehension in her eyes was almost palpable and sweetened my almost nonexistent soul.

Chuckling deeply, I plant a quick smack on her burning ass before turning to leave. "I already gave you your punishment, so this is your small reward for taking it well. You can come all you want, as long as you don't hold back your moans. If I don't hear you from the kitchen, then I'll assume you aren't grateful for this, or it isn't enough stimulation for you and come up to either take the vibrator away or turn it up until you are screaming."

Visibly, her body relaxed upon hearing she could orgasm.

"Thank you, Daddy."

CHAPTER 21
Avery

FUCK YOU, DADDY.

The fuck is he doing down there!?

Another loud moan ripped itself from my trembling body as another wave of rapture violated my body from my orgasm. I don't know how many I had in the past forty-five minutes; I lost count after seven because my brain started to fritz out from the immense pleasure clouding it.

Yeah, this little fun idea quickly turned south after I had my short fill. Don't get me wrong, having multiple orgasms in a night was fantastic, amazing really, but to have no reprieve between each and every single one of them became torturous faster than not. Then, the feeling of being torn between wanting more and not drove me insane. During the peak of pleasure, I wanted more until my mind went blank with numbing bliss, but during the crash, I wanted nothing more than a slight breather as my body ached from the aftershocks.

"Oh God!" Also, I couldn't control them at this point; my orgasms came and went as they pleased from being overstimulated.

"God's not the one making you come! Try that again, baby!" Julian's faint, cocky laugh barely made it into the room through the open door.

"Julian, please! I—ah!" Another stream of fluids rushed down my inner thighs with every pulse of my tight walls before hitting the ground with a soft pitter-patter.

"Oh fuckfuckfuck." The rattle of the restraints jingled in the air as my body violently shook from the earth-shattering orgasms. Heavenly bliss and burning hell all simultaneously—that's what this next wave will feel like.

Uncontrollably, my hips bucked back and forth to try and get away from the vibrator as my poor body became ravaged by wave after wave of orgasms until my mind became blank.

Nothing registered to me; everything sounded so distant as I fell into a never-ending cloud of bliss. I think the incoherent sounds came from me, but I wasn't entirely sure. Nor was I sure about the sensations I felt. I faintly remembered some discomfort and pain from the aches and cramps in my stomach before everything snapped, and I felt nothing but pleasure.

Then, it felt like my body was moved after some pressure had let up around my limbs. Soft plush soon followed along with something hard and strong. Whatever took hold of me made me feel safe, so I leaned into it. It didn't take long for my moment on cloud nine to drop, like sinking down into the cold ocean with an anchor wrapped around my ankles. Only then did I realize a voice speaking to me.

"Shh, come back to me, little raven. I got you. Come back to me."

Little raven? That sounds familiar... Wait, that's me.

The voice had to be Julian's; he was the only person to call me that. "Breathe, you are okay, you are safe, I got you." Something fluttered against my face, neck, and shoulder.

Whimpering, I turned and twisted my aching and tired body to snuggle into the warmth that embraced me. Exhaustion and vulnerability swallowed me like a cold tidal wave, and Julian's presence and arms were the only things keeping me anchored to land and safety. "Don't go." I muttered into his chest before squishing my face into the semihard surface and inhaling his soothing scent to appease my rising anxiety.

"Never. I swear, I am never going anywhere. I am never letting you go, ever. I meant what I said. You are mine, for now and ever." He replied with his lips against my forehead while his hand rubbed the length of my back soothingly. "It's okay, ride it out, let it out, do what you need."

"I don't like this." No matter how hard I tried, I couldn't get my voice past a soft squeak because of the exhaustion drowning me.

"The drops are never fun, but don't worry, I am here for you. I won't let you go through them alone, ever." He assured me with some more kisses to the top of my head.

"How'd you know?" He was in the kitchen last I remembered.

"Sweetie, I always have my eyes on you. Besides, you really think I'd be that reckless to leave you completely alone fully restrained and overstimulated? If I had control over the device or you had a way to escape, then I would, but that wasn't the case this time. I turned on the camera before I left and have been watching you this whole time while I was busy in the kitchen. When I saw your posture change after your eyes glazed over and rolled to the back of your head while your face completely twisted into an uncontrolled smile, I rushed in here." Sometimes, it unnerved me how observant Julian was.

Was it weird that he had a camera in the place I didn't know about? Kinda, but it was his home at the end of the day. Granted, I would have appreciated a heads-up. Well, no matter, it was for my safety, so I couldn't complain. And as strange as it was, I found it endearing that he looked out for me like that and knew the signs of me entering subspace, even if it hadn't happened much; the fact he knew the tells meant he paid a lot of attention to me.

In a comforting silence, the two of us remained on his bed—well, I guess it was our bed now since this was my home, too. Words eluded me, which I didn't mind one bit because the only thing I ever wanted after a drop was to be held and loved in silence.

Without a single word exchanged between us, Julian got off the bed and carried me to the bathroom, where he ran me a nice bath and bathed me with utmost care before dressing me in one of his shirts and pair of panties after taking me out of the tub and drying me off. Then, he carried me downstairs and settled me on the couch, bundling me in a plush blanket with a kiss on my forehead before he disappeared out of sight into the kitchen to fetch us our dinners and a drink.

I couldn't help the pouting frown from appearing on my face at the sight of the glass of water. Unfortunately, like always, Julian didn't have any of it because he picked up the glass of water and held it to my lips. "Hydrate first, then if you want, after you've had dinner, I'll make you a little cocktail. You know the rules, baby, don't make me punish you again tonight."

Yeah, the sound of another punishment tonight had me cringing before I eagerly drank the glass of water with Julian's help. "Can you feed me?" I was being a big baby, but I didn't care. Besides, my arms felt so heavy from the fatigue.

"Did your orgasms wear you out too much, little raven?" He teased with a chuckle before holding a forkful of mac 'n cheese to my lips.

Pouting my lips out, I stuck the tip of my tongue at him for half a second before taking a bite of food. "You did this to me," I remarked with a roll of my eyes after I swallowed the food.

His body softly shook as the air filled with his warm chuckle, and the soft clatter of the bowl broke into the warmth when he set it down to grab my face. "And you could have stopped it any time with the safe-word." His lips hung dangerously close to mine, just a deep breath, and our lips would meet in an electrifying kiss. "Just admit it, you couldn't help yourself. You just wanted more and more after each and every one, chasing after the high of the first until your body and mind can't take it no more."

"Oh, shut up and feed me, you jerk." I bit back with a soft stutter while tearing my head away from him to hide my blush.

Another hard grip, and I faced his arrogant face again. "Is that how you ask me?"

Letting out a huff, I averted my eyes from him, "No, I'm sorry. Can you please feed me?" I asked in a slurry, wondering if any of it sounded coherent.

Julian leaned back with a chuckle after kissing my forehead to pick up the food bowl again and feed me while I snuggled into him. "Think you'd be up for another round later?" He tested the waters with a teasing tone and shy smirk.

Scoffing in response, I rolled my eyes at him and lightly hit his chest. "You stick your dick in me, and I'll bite."

"A little pain never stopped me before." He joked with a playful growl, burying his face into my neck and nipping playfully at me.

"I might need a nap, but that nap could also turn into a full night's sleep." Basically, no more sex for tonight. Well, maybe because sometimes my body did surprise me with rebounds.

"Don't worry about it, I'm just teasing." He assured me with a soft chuckle and kiss before returning to feeding and doting on me.

Once we were done, Julian put the dishes away before returning to me and putting on Forensic Files as he got comfortable on the couch with me. Even though it was one of our favorite shows, my attention wasn't on it, something Julian sensed after a while because of my subpar responses to him. Usually, we'd be knee-deep in nitpicking at everything wrong that the perp did on the cases in the show and have a grand time discussing how we'd do things differently. Forget fancy dinner dates—pajamas on the couch with heartwarming food, and crime shows were our thing at this point.

"Little raven, what's wrong?" He inquired with a soft frown and scrunched face. "You're not upset about earlier, are you?"

I shook my head in response to his second question with a reassuring smile. "No, nothing about earlier. Was it a lot? Yes, but I didn't stop it when I had full control, so don't worry about it. I'm just a little nervous about living with you still. Like, don't get me wrong. I'm not having regrets or anything. I'm just worried about you finding my habits too much over time after putting up with them nearly every day."

How long until my habits of leaving half-filled cups and bottles around annoy him? Or my hair shedding around everywhere? What about my snoring, which he was adamant about? He might find it cute now until he has to put up with it every single night for days on end. Oh! What about my bad habit of being lazy with chores? Oh god, the laundry! I sucked at folding my clothes and putting them away in a timely manner.

Worried thoughts came to a screeching halt at the sudden jerk of my head from Julian, who'd grasped my chin and forced my face up to him. "Sweetie, I wouldn't have asked you if I knew I couldn't and wouldn't be able to put up with you and your habits. At the end of the day, we're only humans with our own little quirks. Unless you have a habit of throwing raging parties every day or like to live in a pigsty, we'll be more than fine. Besides, you make it sound like you won't get annoyed with my habits."

Okay, he had a good point there, but still.

Huffing and pouting, I leaned into his hand until he cradled my jaw in his large hand. "I'm sorry, it's just this is so new to me, I don't want to fuck it up. You're just so great and amazing, just everything I could ever ask for and want in a man. You're more than a dream come true. I thought I'd just eventually settle into some mundane relationship and just live in a weird limbo state or stay single forever and be ridiculed by my parents and everyone else."

At twenty-eight years old, I gave up hope in finding a good man to settle with, and I knew better than to engage in a relationship for the sake of it. So, I resigned myself to the fact that I'd likely be single forever. After all, the notion was already ingrained in me. I mean, who would want to be with the quiet weirdo who wrote dark romance stories about serial killers and prisoners? Not like I did much to help myself either with being so introverted and reserved.

"You don't need a man or a partner to define yourself. It's the twenty-first century, and being a single, independent woman is more than acceptable and enough. Who cares what others think. You are your own person, Avery, so don't mind the background chatter. Your parents shouldn't have been on your ass, either. You are a successful adult who is independent and self-sufficient." Always knowing the right things to say this man of mine.

My man. I liked the sound of that a lot.

My parents weren't the nicest people to me, even if they created me and brought me into this world. "It's still a pain in the ass when my parents got on me every single time they saw me though." They weren't too present in my life after I went—very—low contact with them.

"Why? I understand that not all parents are great or good, and actually, you never really talk about your family much. Why's that?" Julian prodded with a curious voice as he turned his full attention onto me.

Sighing heavily, I snaked a hand under his shirt to mindlessly doodle on his chest to keep me distracted. "There's not really much to talk about. They weren't the worst parents, but they weren't too good either. I'm not really close to my cousins either or anything, not that anyone wants to get along with me because I'm still the weird one out of the lot of us." Scrunching my face up because of the discomfort, I shoved the icky feeling aside. "Just... My family and family life has been subpar and meh." I couldn't complain, though, not as if they physically abused me or anything.

"I always want to know more about you, Avery. I want to know everything there is to you, even if it's the past. So, please, tell me more?" How could I resist his curious eyes and eager smile?

"Well, I'm an only child, as I told you already. My parents immigrated here with the rest of the family. Everyone else lives around the Vancouver or Portland area. My parents were typical Asian parents who wanted me to become a doctor or a lawyer. Obviously, that didn't happen because I'm where I am now, not that I've any complaints about it or anything. I love my job and choice of profession and would never change it for the world." A long sigh slipped past my frown. "Unfortunately, not the same can be said about my parents' notion towards it because they still don't see it as successful or anything. They berated me whenever they could because I was 'a big disappointment and shame' to them and the family. Physically, they provided for me growing up, but emotionally and mentally, not even a good lick of it."

I had to pause for a moment to recollect myself and wonder about my life until now. Nothing was wrong with my life, especially now, so I shouldn't complain. Although, I still yearned for the love of my parents, something I knew I'd never get. "They were typical Asians in the sense that they wanted a boy as well, so I already disappointed them from the moment I popped out with the wrong parts. They couldn't have any more children after me because of health issues, so they were kind of resentful towards me in a way.

Oh no, it was that time again.

"No, please, I don't like it. Please, I want it long like the other girls. I don't want to be made fun of for looking like a boy again, please." I knew my desperate pleas and tears would do nothing to sway my parents from their set course of action, but maybe, just maybe, I would get through to them this time.

With an angry scowl, my father lurched at me and snagged my arm. "You are not one of those stupid girls, nor will I let my son be one of those who are delusional idiots who want to be something they clearly are not." His seething words burned my delicate face with his hot breath.

Even though it was useless, I flailed and struggled behind him as he dragged me to the garage where my mother waited with clippers. "We talked about this Avery. Boys don't have long hair." My mother chided in a tired voice, not bothered one bit by her own child's suffering.

"But I'm not a boy!" That snappy remark quickly earned a slap across the face and a harsh glare from my father. "I don't have a—" I didn't get a chance to finish the sentence regarding my genitals as another slap came down upon me.

My father bit out through gritted teeth, "Do not insult us by remind-ing us of your failure."

Then, just like always, my mother went at my head, buzzing my hair short until it was less than an inch while my father held my struggling body. "I don't know why you make this so hard. It's just a routine haircut. You should be used to it by now." My mother chided with her own growing scowl as she tried to tighten up the choppy areas of my head.

"I don't like it. I just want to be like every other girl."

As the flashback faded, I sighed heavily and snuggled into him more for some comfort. "Growing up, they were deluded enough to try and treat me like a boy, forced me to wear boy clothes, made me do boy activities and whatnot, and even went as far as forcing me to keep my hair short by forcing haircuts onto me. They did all they could for the longest time, until I was in my late teens, to pretend I was a boy and treat me like a boy."

Were they the absolute worst parents a person could have? No, because at the very least, they gave me proper shelter and fed me for the most part—they starved me in my teen years to keep my body from developing too much into a female's body. Emotionally, they never provided for me; I honestly had no clue or a lick of an idea as to how good it felt to have affection from your parents—I could only ever imagine.

Yeah, I probably had both mommy and daddy issues because of my upbringing and lack of support from my parents. Hence why I had social awkwardness and issues with forming relationships. Thank the heavens for Julian because he was a godsend for me, a reward for all the suffering in my life.

A frown slowly etched itself onto my face as I spoke again, and the memories came trickling in. "I was always bullied so much throughout school because I looked weird and different. My name, being how it is, didn't help either. My parents purposely named me Avery because it was a boy's name to them, their way of trying to convince and delude themselves further. The kids at school would always use that against me, too. I hated my name for the longest time and still kinda do because it's so plain, and nothing about it is special." For the most part, I was indifferent about my name because I learned to live with it.

"Is that why you like it when I call you pet names or little raven? Because to you, they are special?" It sounded more like he wondered out loud than straight-up asked me.

Humming and nodding my head, I snuggle my head into his chest. "And because to you, they mean something. You call me those things because I mean something to you, because I'm special to you. As somewhat strange and a mouthful little raven is, I like it because you thought of it when thinking about me and my features." Unsure if I made any sense, I decided to zip my lips for now before sounding like a confused mess.

Julian said nothing in response and just hummed and kissed the top of my head. "Well, forget about everyone else because all that matters now is that you are living a good life, your best life, as you like to say. You are happy with your career, you are chasing after your dream of being an author with your debut novel wrapping up soon, you are more than financially stable, and you are a darling of a woman."

"I know, but I guess I just need to be reminded of my worth some-times, something that doesn't happen often or much. So, thank you." The grateful smile spread wide before I could hold it back.

Julian's lips pressed against mine in a passionate kiss that caused my heart to flip in my chest. "I will spend every day reminding you and shower you with as much affection as possible, I swear."

CHAPTER 22
Julian

It was hard to hide the amusement in my voice as I peered over the laptop screen to look at Avery, who sat on the loveseat across from the armchair I occupied.

"It stuck with me, alright? Just one of those mysterious things from work that I have to get out somehow. So, might as well make it a calling card of sorts in my story." Avery replied with a shy shrug before sinking into the cushions more with her blanket.

"You guys still haven't found much with the feathers at the scenes?" As if I made it easy to discern the reason behind the ominous item.

"No, just that they are always present, and for the most part, they show a trail of the victim's movement. I mean, the raven feathers could mean so many things, given the history and symbolism behind them, so it's hard to pinpoint the exact point. Point blank, it means death, dead, done, end of life, but the killer is too meticulous and crafty for it to be so simple like that, in my opinion." Pausing for a second, her face scrunched softly in thought. "Then again, no one likes to hear what I say about it because I'm just the little background worker, and not like that helps them any besides giving them a headache and reminder that they still have a serial killer loose," Avery replied with a heavy sigh at the end.

"You would be on the right track, though, and it might even help if you got behind the mind of the killer to help pick them out of the crowd. You're not going to find someone that crafty and careful hanging out in the shady end-of-town gang banging all day with no education past middle school." I couldn't help myself from commenting while my eyes continued reading through Avery's story. "Should probably go into some more detail with it in your story, give more of a reason as to why the killer leaves feathers around. Maybe you could make a play on how it's an omen and the trails are a symbol of his last steps in this life, his path to death."

Avery blinked her eyes at me a few times while tapping her finger against her lips in thought. "Not a bad idea, I might just use it along with your suggestion of the dumpsites. I mean, who would ever think to look under a building."

Exactly why they made the perfect dumpsites.

No one, no one ever would, which made it a perfect disposal and burial method. I didn't go into construction and made my own companies for no reason; it was all for my own gain. No one would ever question a construction worker digging with an excavator at a site, nor would they question things being patched up unless someone knew exactly and precisely where and what to look for. The chances of my victim's bodies being discovered were practically zero. I never have to worry about them surfacing back up because of the seasons or someone stumbling upon a corpse out of the blue. Unless a massive earthquake upended the building and its foundation, none of them would ever be found unless I willed it.

Another long while passed, and Avery was immersed in her TV show while I busied myself with her book. "You're gonna have to change up this scene a bit. If the killer stabs the victim there, then there's a high chance things will get messy, and death will be quick. The victim wouldn't survive for a live burial as you write ahead." I noted out loud to her after reading through the scene of an attack.

For an untrained person and typical reader, it probably wouldn't matter, but if they were to pay attention enough and do some quick Google searches, then they could find the discrepancies of a knife into the abdominal cavity. I only knew because of experience from hunting—both animals and humans. A knife to the gut was touchy and too risky for what she was trying to achieve in the scene.

Avery's face pouted with a defeated sigh. "So where do you suggest the killer stabs them then? When you're in a struggle, the stomach is the easiest place to hit. Although, you are right about it being too messy and death being fast if the knife was that big and they were swinging the way they are. I couldn't think of anything else for the life of me, and it's not like I have a body to go stab and experiment on."

Well, it's a good thing she didn't have to get her hands dirty because mine were filthy for her in that regard. Even before I moved to human beings, I experimented the hell out of animals to make sure I had my technique down before escalating. The last thing I needed was to fuck up because I didn't have my own method down and became sloppy through exploration.

It was torturous to hold my urges at bay until I had everything set in stone. If I'd acted to scratch my itch back then, then I would probably be on death row right now. There was a list of things I *needed* in place to be successful: a kill zone, kill method, and disposal method. The zone I ended up creating my own in the safety of my own backyard when I bought the thirty-acre property on which my house sat; the area was densely forested, away from the city more than enough that a person would have to spend a day or so wandering to have a chance to make it to civilization again possibly—that is, if they even went in the right direction.

Killing animals proved tedious after a while, but I got a good feel for sinking my knife into flesh to learn fine control of my blade. The opportunity also gave me the chance to hone my skills and figure out my method of murder. Strangulation took too long and was tiring, a gun was a little too quick for my liking, and good ol' fists and feet were exhausting and time-consuming—not to mention it wasn't a guaranteed death—for me to deal with. I wanted to inflict pain and suffering on my victims and give them a fraction of what their victims felt before a crime was committed on them.

There is nothing better than turning the predator into prey. Humans thought so highly of themselves, but tear that pride away, and only fear was left in its place. We don't like having the roles flip on us from the top of the food chain to the bottom. To be turned into a helpless idiot after being a powerful person.

Oh, I loved watching my victim's body and eyes shatter and fill with fear and desperation when they'd realize what I would do to them, what their fate was. What was more fun was the false hope I'd give them by allowing them to run for me to hunt them down. Little did they know, there was no escaping me. I never took any chances when it came to my targets. I was fine letting them flee to chase down myself because I'd tag them with a tiny microchip when they'd be out cold. I never needed to use the tracking app to find them because my tracking skills were more than enough for their amateur skills and antics.

Avery's soft voice rang in the distance, pulling me out of my head. "Julian?"

"Hm? Sorry, was racking my brain," I lied smoothly with a smile, "You can adjust the position off to the side or go for the legs. I would recommend you switch it to the chest area, but given the scene, it wouldn't work either, so you would have to go off to the side or for the legs, your choice." She didn't have to be perfect; it was just a story at the end of the day, not real life.

It's ironic how fiction became her reality, and she didn't even know it. At the same time, fiction was the reason why I didn't want to pull her into the shadows with me. Yes, Avery knew that killers existed in the world, but to her, they were horrid people. I didn't want her to see me that way, ever. I didn't want to see the light in her eyes leave the moment she knew of my bloodied hands, the very hands that touch her so intimately and tenderly. How disgusted would she be knowing the filthy hands that had tainted her pristine body?

More importantly, I didn't want to lose her. She'd become so much more than an obsession to me now. She wasn't a mere want, nor did I simply lust after her with my hormones at my reigns. No, she was so much more than that. Avery had become my sun and moon, day and night, my every breath, the air I need to survive, the sweet nectar to my incurable thirst.

Avery was a need.

I *need* Avery in my life to survive, to be remotely sane.

If she ever dared threaten to leave me, then, well, I guess that's one way for her to find out about the basement after I lock her away down there. I meant what I told her before and what I tell her so many times nearly every day: she was mine, all mine, for now and ever. Not even Death could tear us apart. I'd clamor my way out of the depths of Hell to breach Heaven and steal her away back down to the fiery pits below, damn her with me for all of eternity.

Unable to refocus on the story, I shut the laptop and advanced on Avery with a playful growl, making her squeal and giggle when I scooped her up in my arms. "What are you doing? We still have to prepare dinner."

"Dinner can wait," I grunted when I tossed her onto the bed, "You can't."

No matter how many times I tasted and took her, I could never get enough. I really could spend the rest of my days in bed with her in my arms. I never wanted to stop spoiling her, showing her how much pleasure I could bring her over and over even after I've driven her to the brink of madness and delirium from the passion and pleasure.

Not wasting another second, I flicked open my pocketknife and sliced her clothes off her body in one fluid movement. Her protestant words were ignored by my own chuckle as I stripped myself of my shirt.

"You can't keep destroying my clothes like that." She whined with a pout, her hand lightly smacking my chest.

With a twisted smirk, I slid the flat edge of the blade up her stomach, between the valley of her breasts and up to the pulsating artery thrumming under the skin of her neck. "Little raven, thought I made it pretty damn clear that I can do whatever the fuck I want when it comes to you." Not like I didn't buy her a shit ton more to replace what I ruined.

Adding the slightest of pressure, I carefully pressed the cold steel into her, not enough to break her skin, though. "Now, be a good girl and spread your legs for me." To give a little encouragement, I snaked my free hand up her leg and gripped at her inner thighs, getting a soft gasp from her when I kneaded the sensitive flesh under my calloused hand.

Eyeing the knife with wide and excited eyes, she carefully spread her legs wide open for me, being mindful not to move the bed or her body much to avoid a cut on her delicate neck. I wouldn't have let it happen, of course. Her body may be littered with faint cuts, but they were in areas easily hidden with clothes. The last thing we needed in this relationship was nosy people thinking I abused Avery if they saw marks on her face and neck.

Involuntary twitches followed the blade of the knife as I trailed it down her body to her wet core, where I pressed the blunt head of the handle against her swollen clit, making her whimper and fist the sheets softly. "You're fucking soaked already, baby, and I haven't even touched you or done anything yet."

"I can't help it. You just have that effect on me." Airy words slipped out between her lips as she looked down at me with lustful eyes. "Please, touch me, please."

Sometimes, I wondered if she knew how to wrap me around her finger. Avery always sounded so sweet whenever she begged, and any resistance built up in my body melted away whenever she uttered such words in that soft 'fuck me' voice of hers.

"Please be gentle with me, Daddy. I'm still so sore from this morning." She shuddered with a blush.

Chuckling softly, I leaned down and placed an open mouth kiss against her slickened sex with a groan. "If you aren't sore after I fuck you, then I'm not doing a good job, so that's a good thing."

Peeling the knife away, I closed it up and discarded it randomly in the room before wrapping my arms around her legs to anchor her against my mouth to prevent her from escaping me as I ate her out like a starved beast. "Play with your tits, baby, play with them while I make you cum all over my tongue and face," I commanded with hardened eyes before licking down the length of her pussy and pressing my tongue into her tight walls.

"Slower, please, too sensitive still." She whimpered with a pout as her hands cupped her breasts and massaged them.

Deciding to take some mercy on her, I listened and eased the pressure of my tongue until I felt her tense body relax and buck at me. Slipping my tongue out, I pressed my whole tongue against her parted folds and gave her long licks along the length of it, careful to run it across her sensitive clit to provide her with a jolt of pleasure. Groaning, I lapped at her with my tongue gently, careful not to slip too far past her entrance.

"Oh God, I don't think I can take you again, Daddy, too sore." I could see her eyes glassing over with tears as she reached down and grabbed the top of my head to push me away from between her legs.

Relenting, I pulled away for a second before a devious little idea crossed my mind. Knocking her hand away, I leaned back in and licked all the way down past her entrance to her puckered little asshole that twitched under my tongue.

"Julian! You're too big. You're gonna split me in half if you fuck me there." Despite the fear in her eyes, her hips urged me on with how they pressed more into me as I continued to give her forbidden hole lazy licks. "I'm not ready."

"You will be once I'm done." I chuckled against her before pulling away completely to dig through the nightstand for the bottle of lube and a small pouch. "Relax, I wouldn't take you without stretching you first." I told her with a dark grin as I dumped out the contents of the pouch, a variety of silicone butt plugs varying in sizes.

"On your hands and knees at the end of the bed facing the mirror, I want you to see the pleasure break your face the moment I make your ass take the plug." I wanted her to see the wonderful sight I always saw in her each and every time I inflicted any kind of pleasure on her.

Rustles of the sheets prickled at the tense air from the movement of Avery's body. "Y-you're gonna use the smallest one, right?" Her lips trembled with her words, and her big round eyes remained locked with my reflection as I knelt behind her.

"Little raven, as much as I like to hurt you, there are limits to my sadism with you." I wasn't *that* much of a cruel prick.

Avery might be fine with pain, but they were from things she knew. Before we got deep into our scenes—or even started them—we tested her limits and experimented with all she was comfortable with. I only stocked our playroom with equipment she okayed after testing out, so anything in there was fair game to her. Her limits were clear to me after our little week of experimenting, so I knew how hard or soft I could go at her before I came close to touching the line in the sand. I knew her limits, and I knew my limits with her.

Placing a firm hand against her upper back, I pressed softly, "Face down, ass up, and spread your cheeks for me." A little humiliation never hurt, especially since I knew she'd get a kick out of this position, too.

"Yes, sir." She obeyed with a mumble, gracing me with the wonderous sight of her vulnerable asshole as her fingers dug into her plush cheeks.

It was probably easier said than done, but it needed to be said, "Relax." She nearly jumped out of her own skin the moment the lube landed on her closed hole.

Using a single finger, I slowly spread the lube around to get her used to the sensation of being touched in the area. "Breathe, I'm going to take it slow, don't worry. I'm going to push my finger in first, give you a first feel, and finger you a bit to stretch you before I put the plug in." I laid out all that would happen in the next span of time to help ease her mind.

When I got no denial or excuses from her, I proceeded to push my finger to the first knuckle into her with a deep inhale to hold back my excitement from bursting out and scaring her. "Doing okay?" My firm eyes studied her reflection closely the whole time, revealing the way her face softened and twisted with a pained pleasure as I violated her sacred hole for the first time.

Her hips wiggled in a jerking motion when I started to make small thrusts with my finger and moved it around to press against her hot walls.

"Yes, Daddy... It feels weird, but I'm okay." Her clenched jaw slowly un-hinged with each passing second until her sweet, airy moans heated the room up the more I worked her asshole open with my digit.

Soon, my whole finger was swallowed by her ass. "That's it, baby, don't fight it, just relax and take it like a good girl." A glutaral groan croaked at my throat when the image of my cock being balls deep in her asshole flashed through my mind.

Once I take her forbidden hole with my dick, then that would be it. Everything Avery had will belong to me. I would finally be her first everything: oral, vaginal, anal, all her first taken by me. The fact I'd be the only man to claim every inch of her body like that set a prideful fire ablaze within me, forcing my mouth to grin arrogantly.

"Can't fucking wait to fill your ass up with my cum later tonight and mark it as mine too." At least this was another hole I wouldn't have to worry about getting her pregnant in. Granted, I didn't have to worry much in general, even if we didn't use condoms because she had an IUD in her. I knew the chances weren't completely zero, but they were pretty damn close for me not to be paranoid.

Keeping my finger fully in her, I reached back with my other hand and picked up the smallest plug and used the lube smeared around her rim to slicken it up. "Ready?" My eyes searched her reflection for an answer as I teased the top of her opening with the tip of it.

Her head nodded with her shaky exhale. "Yes." However, she still seemed very nervous with how her eyes kept darting up and down with her labored breaths.

Leaning down, I kissed the top of her head as I removed my finger fully and pressed the tip of the toy against her opening. "Breathe, you're going to be fine, only difference from this and my finger is the big bump at the end before it gets smaller. But you can take it, I know you can." Not much she'd be able to do either if I decided to shove it all into her the rest of the way—not that I would ever abuse her trust like that.

Patiently, I waited until I saw her body physically relax with her even breaths before advancing the anal plug in, being mindful of being slow.

"That's it, just breathe, you're doing great, just keep on breathing, the hard part is about to come but then it'll be easy after that." Don't know if my words were for her or me at this point because I wanted to ram the thing into her and fuck her ass with it until her eyes would gloss over with bliss.

As I expected, I was met with resistance at the biggest part of the toy. Applying a bit of pressure, I somewhat forced it into her bit by bit while my eyes studied the way her mouth hung open with a soft moan. "Are you coming?" I couldn't help but ask when I noticed the slight curve to her lips as her body shuddered.

"Fuck, just when I didn't think you could get any hotter, you blow my mind." I mused with a soft chuckle, reluctantly tearing my eyes away from the lovely sight of her reflection to watch the rest of the toy get swallowed up by her ass until only the flared base remained outside. "Fuck, that's so hot baby. You did so good." Being a cheeky asshole, I pressed my thumb against the base to give the toy a soft jerk to mess with her.

Grabbing her hips, I turned her around and caged her in with my arms. Then I lowered my head down and captured her lips in a hungry kiss, taking her bottom lip between my teeth and pulling on it until it swelled. "That stays in for the next hour, then we'll switch it out for the next size up. We'll repeat that until bedtime when I'll replace it with my cock, understand?" I asked after I grabbed her face and smiled down at her.

"Yes, Daddy." Fear flashed and fleeted her brown orbs before pleasure dilated her pupils.

"No panties, just my shirt. Go get comfortable on the couch while I make dinner." My hand swatted at her ass to urge her off the bed before I got up myself to fetch a shirt for her to wear from the dresser.

Her sweet giggle chimed the room along with the soft pitter patter of her feet as she bound up to me. "Okay, babe."

Maybe I should warn her... Nah, I wanted to see the surprise and genuine reaction from her later.

CHAPTER 23
Avery

"You better fucking run, little raven."

Shit. I fucked up, and I was all here for it.

I might as well have cracked the belt on my own ass the moment I cracked open the can of energy drink.

In my defense, his eyes challenged me and egged me on. *'Don't you dare open that.'* Like, what did he expect was gonna happen after he uttered those words? For me to actually listen and put the energy drink away?

"Ten. Nine. Eight."

Shit! He's counting!

I'd never slipped on my shoes faster than now; I didn't even realize I did so until I felt some padding between my feet and the forest floor as I tore through the foliage. Oh God, why didn't I listen? Okay, stupid question because the answer was obvious: it wasn't fun. Yes, I knew of the consequences, kind of. I'd been prepared to accept however many lashes he'd deal out later or when he'd force me to my knees to choke on his thick dick—I was *not* prepared for a chase. But hey, nothing wrong with spicing things up.

Thump! Thump! Thump!

My thoughts raced erratically as my feet continued to carry me somewhat mindlessly through the forest. Where did the noise come from? Him

189

or me? Was it my heart or his feet bounding after me? Discerning between the two proved to be impossible in my adrenaline-hazed mind.

I shrieked instinctively when Julian appeared out of nowhere before me. "Ah!" Instantly, I dug my feet into the ground in an attempt to stop myself and shift directions as he reached out grab me. Only I wasn't as graceful as intended because I landed flat on my ass with a grunt, giving Julian the perfect opportunity to pounce on me.

Julian's body tilted off to the side with a swift kick to the top of his knee, giving me barely enough space to scramble out from under him. Unfortunately, I didn't make it far. It only took a mere second for Julian to recover and lunge at me, pinning my struggling body front side down.

"Hope you're prepared to reap the consequences of your actions, little one." His deep voice growled above me as he kept his limbs on mine to prevent another escape from me.

"Oh, bite me!" I snapped, throwing my head back and glaring playfully at him.

Shifting my wrists into one hand, he used his newly free one to fist the back of my hair and crane my neck to an uncomfortable angle. "Oh, don't worry, I plan to." His voice rasped against my ear with malice before he shoved my face into the ground.

The pressure against my head eased, and the sound of clothes rustling along with his belt being undone cut through my lustful buzz. My body bucked in an attempt to throw him off as a second wind filled my body with another adrenaline rush. The attempt didn't get me anywhere because Julian outweighed me by a few tons.

Without a falter to his movements, he quickly bound my wrists together using his belt before using both his hands to strip—cut—his shirt from my body and pin the knife through the belt and pinning it along with my wrists to the ground. I continued to struggle against him as he pushed my legs apart and forced my ass up into the air, making me shiver at the cold air hitting my exposed parts.

It was only then that I remembered the toy in my ass when I involuntarily clenched around it. Honestly, it was easy to forget my second hole being stuffed by a plug after a small while for my body to adjust to it fully. Sure, it sucked this recent time when he eased the bigger plug into me after dinner, but I quickly zoned it out after finding a good distraction in working on my story.

Now, though, all I could think about was the toy, along with what would come next. Julian would make my ass his before I'd be dragged back to the house, where he might or might not go another round at me. Losing my anal virginity in the middle of the forest at night after being chased down by my boyfriend should scare the hell out of me, but I was too fucked up to fear any of it.

Instead, I found myself being aroused like never before. "You're dripping wet baby, you want me to take your ass right here and now, don't you?" Julian questioned, thrusting two fingers deep into my twitching pussy and making me moan. "You better come good on my cock and coat it good because your cum is the only lube you're gonna get."

No warning came before he rammed himself fully into me, catching my scream in my throat as my body tensed from the sudden intrusion. "Julian!" I gasped a sob out, grabbing handfuls of the soil beneath my hands in a feeble attempt to brace myself.

Pressure from his forearm fell down onto my back to hold my body down in place just as his hips began to wildly buck at me, slamming hard into my pinned body with each and every thrust until the area around us filled with the sounds of our bodies clashing. "Julian!" I nearly screamed his name in pleasure as the sharp sting of an orgasm bit my body.

The way he had my body bent felt so uncomfortable, but it allowed him to bury himself so deep into me and get such sweet spots that made my eyes roll to the back of my head with each brush from his tip. It didn't take much for him to make a mess of me; I could feel my juices escaping my spasming walls and smearing my thighs as he speared in and out of me with no mercy.

His thickness filled me so good, and the plug in my ass only made him feel so much bigger. The added stimulus from having his length rub against the barrier between the toy and his member had my legs quivering with delight.

Unable to help it, I wondered how good it would feel to have both holes stuffed full briefly before tucking the idea away for later. I mean, it wouldn't be that hard to shove a toy in either hole while Julian took the other. I wonder if it would feel good for him to have me tighter because of the new occupation.

As the idea of being double penetrated eased my lips into a devious smile, I was ripped away from my fantasy because of the sudden empty feeling from Julian pulling the toy out. Turning my head back, I opened my mouth to protest and beg for him to put it back in, but nothing came out because my own words choked me from the burn of his cock breaching my tight ring of muscles after he withdrew from my cunt.

"Fuuuuck, so hot and tight, fuck." He hissed through gritted teeth as his hands squeezed at my chubby ass until the skin underneath paled. "Oh fuck, your slutty little ass is swallowing my cock up so well."

Silent sobs racked my body as I struggled to adjust. My body screamed at me to flee, but I was trapped. All I could do was take it, unless I wanted to end it with our safe-word, but I didn't. As much as it hurt, there was an underlying pleasure that gave my insides happy flutters. I loved the pain he brought upon my body, always, and this was no different.

A shudder trickled down my body when his hot breath hit my ear. "Let's see if you can squirt while getting your ass fucked." His dark, chuckling words snapped me to reality.

Once again, before I could try to protest, he moved, turning my words into mushy moans. I knew I could take him, but it felt like he would split me in half with each thrust. Then, when his hand snaked around my waist to my aching clit, I knew I was done for.

His fingers dipped between my cunt to gather some of my juices to make his fingers glide across my swollen clit easier and enhance the waves of pleasure. "Feels so weird, so much, but fuck so good." Sweet rapture assaulted my body from head to toe, and I couldn't get enough of it. The insanity of lust and passion would consume me sooner than later if he kept this up.

I couldn't control any of my bodily reactions to his ministrations. It was as if my body had a mind of its own with how my asshole kept squeezing Julian back in every time he pulled back. My poor, empty pussy clenched around nothing as my juices squirted and gushed out of me and onto the dirt ground below, and my juices made the sensation of his body slapping mine intensify when it dripped down my thighs.

"Shit, I'm gonna fill this needy little asshole of yours up good." He laughed boisterously before his hands came down on my bruised ass with some playful spanks. "Fuck! Take it!" He growled loudly with one final thrust before burying himself balls deep into me and emptying his load into my forbidden hole.

"Nghn, fuck, thank you so much, sir." Thanking him for filling me had become second nature, a habit I formed after our first few times together because I really was eternally grateful to him for giving me such pleasure and freedom by filling me with his essence.

Heavy pants heaved his body as he quickly freed me and picked me up in his arms. Smiling, he leaned down and kissed me deeply and passionately, "No, thank you, Avery, for giving yourself to me like this and for trusting me." Such a genuine smile melted my heart, as those were somewhat rare for him.

Julian smiled a lot, and most of the time, it was charming and lovely, but rarely were his smiles ever entirely genuine. Which, thinking about it now, was kind of odd. Actually, it freaked me out a little with how easily he could plaster an empty smile on his face to everyone, even me, sometimes.

Chalking my anxiety and paranoia up as a result of my drop, I decided to trash the thoughts for now as I leaned into Julian and relaxed with some deep breathing. "Cuddles?" I looked up at him with pleading eyes and drew small lines on his chest.

Warmly, he smiled and chuckled at me before kissing my forehead. "Of course, always." Another thing I appreciated about Julian was that he never, ever left me alone after sex. Even if I knocked out, I'd wake in his arms or with him right next to me, at the very least. Unless I slept all the way until noon, which has happened a few times in the past few months since I moved in, he usually left a small note on the nightstand and a breakfast plate in the kitchen.

He's honestly the sweetest and most perfect man ever, in my opinion. It was pessimistic of me, but sometimes I waited for the bomb to go off. Surely there's something deeper going on, or an impending breakup. No guy like Julian would settle with a plain woman like me. No matter how much he assured and reassured me with his words and actions, there was still that little thread of doubt because something in my gut didn't settle when it came to Julian.

"What? Something wrong with that one? Did you forget to wipe it clean of your prints or something?" And here I thought I'd escaped Detective Bornes's accusations today.

I don't know what his problem was, but he's had it out for me ever since he got tossed this serial killer case. Actually, it didn't really start much until he found out about my extreme liking for criminals, especially serial killers. My fascination with the case itself probably didn't help my case with the detective. It didn't bother me much initially because I thought it was joking. I mean, honestly, me, a serial killer? I might make stupid decisions in my life, but come on, I wasn't trying to be a real-life Dexter because that was beyond risky.

Besides, killing people was wrong. After all, that's what the justice system was for. At least, that was the lie I kept telling myself. It became harder and harder to deny with each passing case, though; seeing criminals get away scot-free or let off with light sentences not befitting of the crime chipped away at my belief of the justice system is fair and just. I wanted to believe the system to be flawless as it was made out to be, but seeing perps go free more often than not shook that foundation.

Clicking my tongue out of annoyance, I threw the evidence bag back into the box before whipping around to glare at Detective Bornes with a flat expression. "What is your problem with me, Carl? What have I done besides showing gross interest in cases that would indicate my hand in all of it?" I've done nothing incriminatory, nor have I displayed any suspicious or strange behavior regarding all of this.

"You spend way too much time with the evidence." Or maybe he was desperate for a suspect or dumber than a dumbbell.

Muscles in my eyes pulled them up and around. "You do realize what my job entails, right?" Usually, I wasn't so rude to people, but today, I was fed up with Carl. "It's literally in my job description to process the evidence, which, newsflash, is what I'm currently doing. So, unless you have a pertinent question then please, I have a lot to do and would greatly appreciate you leaving me to do my job in peace."

Maybe I ought to smack him upside the head with a bat to reset his brain or wake his brain up so it could actually work for once. Seriously, out of all the people on this goddamn earth, he went around accusing *me* of all people of being a *serial killer*. I don't know whether to feel offended or not at the fact he suspected me because, yay, he thought I was capable enough of pulling off such a successful series of homicides. But what the fuck for even *thinking* it was me because I am how I am.

"You can easily clean up after yourself after the fact while going through the crime scene to process things and afterward. You can easily hide things at the scene or dispose of things afterward before they are even cataloged." He stated as if he had cracked the code to it all.

Another ridiculous scoff chuckled at my body as I looked at him questionably. "Are you serious? Do you even hear yourself? You do know there are other people who are at the scene with me, and things are cataloged there before being double and triple-checked here at the processing area in the precinct. Seriously, go get a donut and a cup of coffee to wake up your dead brain and go pick on someone plausible." I was a hair away from kicking him out of the area and shutting the door in his face.

Frustrated, I grumbled to myself under my breath about the whole thing as I turned my attention back to the stack of bagged-up evidence I had to shift through. Sure, he had some good points; my profession could very well aid me in my crimes if I were to commit any. I also had valid counterpoints because it wasn't as if I was alone at these scenes, and everyone—me included—was very meticulous to a fault.

Now, shame on me for thinking Detective Bornes was finished with me. A vice grip cinched my wrist and twisted my body around where a set of sharp, glaring eyes shot fear into me. "You may have everyone else fooled, but I'm not as naïve or ignorant as them. You're gonna slip, and I'll be there to catch it. One way or another, I'm gonna get you for all this."

Wincing, I struggled to pry and pull my wrist from his death grip, which made my hand go numb and become discolored. "You're hurting me. Let me go," I said in a threatening tone, softly kicking at his shin as a warning.

Huffing out a sharp growl, he threw my hand back at me, and I instantly cradled the throbbing limb to my chest while glaring at Carl's retreating form. "Asshole." I cursed under my breath with a string of unsavory things as I slowly refocused on my task.

The audacity of that baffling man.

CHAPTER 24
Julian

"Who did this to you?"

A shiver fluttered at Avery's body as she quickly pulled her wrist back and attempted to hide the very visible handprint around her wrist.

Suppressing my anger with a deep inhale, I slowly reached back out and took her wrist in my hand again to not scare her like earlier when I suddenly grabbed the discolored limb. "Little raven, tell me who I have to put twenty feet underground. Who hurt you like this?"

Avery's eyes looked up at me through her lashes as her head had hung a little in shame almost. Her mouth opened to speak, but I cut her off, "Don't you dare brush this off either or tell me 'it's fine' or 'it's nothing' because it's not. No one, not even me, should injure your body or leave marks like this. So, either you tell me who the bastard is, or I'll go around knocking on every single door in this damn city until someone admits to this atrocity."

Welting and bruising her body up during a scene was different than outside of one, but even then, the marks made sense. Never would I ever harm her like this though, especially to this extent. I've reddened her wrists a few times from holding her down, but never have they bruised like this. So, whoever did this to her exerted a lot of unnecessary strength towards my innocent little raven.

Knowing Avery, she probably didn't give them hell either. She could hold her own battles but never snapped back until pushed to the edge and possibly over. I'd like to imagine her giving the person a good swing to the face or kick to the crotch, but in reality, I knew that would never be the scenario unless it were out of self-defense. The only time I've seen her get physically violent with someone was at a bar we went to for a work party of mine when someone didn't get the hint and kept pressing with their hands.

Although, my girl had spunk in other ways, and I don't mean in bed. Avery was a very, very, very petty woman. She might not lash out at someone violently or physically, but by God, she'd make a person wish she had by her actions and words. She liked to deny this, stating it was an unsavory thing to have, but denial was more than a river in Egypt.

Just like how I could deny my feelings for Avery all I wanted, it didn't mean they weren't there.

Yes, me, having feelings for someone nonetheless. The notion itself was insane, but it was the truth. I couldn't deny the intense fire of bliss that blossomed in my chest whenever Avery was in my sight. Even when she wasn't around me, I still felt a fierce flame of desire and adoration for her, especially when I'd unconsciously think about her. My feelings became harder and harder to deny over the past three, nearly four, months since she moved in.

I thought having her around would eventually get dull and annoying, but there was a peace to it all. There was a certain order to my place regarding my routine and physical things like decorations and the furniture, things I'd somewhat lose my shit over if someone were to tinker with them. Yet, Avery flew in and made herself at home, made *my* home *our* home. Her touch to the place didn't bother me one bit, shockingly. I thought surely my anger would blow when I saw her shifting some of the furniture around to clear some space and give the room a better flow, but I found myself smiling and offering my full help. I was still more than happy with the end result. Even now, whenever I came home and saw the pictures she'd hung around the place and the little stationary decorations she'd slowly swap around, it brought a smile and warmth to my body.

This damn woman of mine turned me into a sap, me, a cold-hearted killer. Killing had become a bit of a challenge with the huge change in my life, though. In a way, yes, it was a little simpler in the sense that I could control Avery's whereabouts or at least be more aware of them, but the questions about my late nights or long hours were slowly taking a toll on our relationship.

"There's nothing to do about it, so just leave it. I'll have dinner ready soon. Good thing I took my time with cooking. Otherwise, it would have been cold by now." And there was the subtle jab.

Sighing heavily, I pressed her wrist to my chest and hugged her tightly. "I told you a client ran over, I'm sorry." I lied smoothly with a frown to mask the strange nagging feeling in my chest.

Another strange recent development was this stupid feeling in my chest every time I lied to Avery, something I never felt or struggled with until now. Every time I spewed untrue words to her, there'd be this grip around my chest, as if someone squeezed at my heart with each and every word until it almost felt suffocating.

Why? Why am I feeling this way?

I shouldn't be feeling bad—if that's what this feeling even was—about lying to Avery. I'd done it so many times before without a hitch, kind of. I guess the feeling had always been there, but it was easier to ignore back then. Now, though, it became present at the mere thought of lying to Avery; I didn't have to perform the act for this nasty feeling to take hold of me.

Deflating her body with a long sigh, she stuffed her face into me and mumbled an apology, "I know, but it still makes me a little upset sometimes when it eats into our time with each other. I just miss you so much, and I want to see you as soon as possible after I get home and spend time with you."

"I know, darling, I want all that as well, but both you and I know how it is. I mean, the same could be said for your job, too, with you getting called out to a scene randomly sometimes and when you're on call. But that's okay, I understand. Well, I'm home now, so let me go wash up, and we can eat dinner and then cuddle on the couch while you go over your final draft one more time before uploading tomorrow, alright?" There was no holding back the proud smile from pulling at my lips at the mention of her final draft.

After twelve long months—and lots of tears—her career as a published author practically knocked at the door. I barely believed her when she told me it took her a whole year—give or take some time—to get to this point after giving up a few times throughout the past few years. Even if it hasn't officially been released yet, I still feel incredibly proud of her for getting to this point and taking the next step in achieving her dream of being an author.

"Mhmm." Her head nodded against my body before leaning on her tippy toes to give me a chaste kiss with a giggling smile. "You do need a shower, you smell like cement and iron, and you're covered in paint." She said with a roll of her eyes before slipping away from me.

Oh, if only she knew the source of it all. Unfortunately, my latest victim didn't go down without a fight. Damn idiot tried to fight death right before I threw him into his grave and bled all over me. Avery didn't need to know all of that, obviously. Getting dirty while working out on the field was all she needed to know.

"Oh," I said, stopping at the hallway entry and looking back at her, "Don't think we're done with the conversation from before. We're not sleeping tonight until I get a name from you."

No one hurts my girl and gets away alive.

The moment they laid their hand on her—no, the moment they even thought about coming into contact with her, they signed their death warrant. Intentional or not, they hurt her, so they needed to face the consequences of their actions. No matter what transpired, they shouldn't have harmed an innocent woman. I don't care if Avery had been the one to initiate it all, though very highly unlikely given her kindhearted nature and personality. The opposing party shouldn't have retaliated; they should have let it go and walked off.

My rules for target selection were specific and set in stone, but sometimes exceptions had to be made. Before, I had to look out for myself only and worry about my needs and desires, but now I had someone important to care for and worry about. Being involved with Avery meant she was now an extension of me. Any wrong to her was a blow to me as well. She might not hurt a fly, but I damn well will for her.

So, the person who bruised Avery better start counting their last seconds on this earth.

It didn't take long for me to rinse my crime off in the shower quickly. If only it were that easy to wash my sins away thoroughly, make the world forget what I'd done. No matter, it's been done, there is nothing to be done about it now besides honing my craft more to become more perfect.

Avery.

Fuck, what am I gonna do with her?

In an ideal world, I'd keep killing behind her back with no problems. She'd remain forever blissfully ignorant to it all, and we live happily ever after.

Too bad the world was full of shit.

As much as I wanted to keep the blindfold on her, it was only a matter of time before she got impatient and peaked or took it off fully. The ugly truth was that I couldn't hide this from her forever. No matter how much I tried and how perfect I became, she was bound to find out. Unless I cut her out of my life, which I never want to do or ever intend to do, I needed to figure out a plan for when the inevitable *will* happen. It wasn't a matter of if at this point, no, it was when.

"That smells good honey, what'd you make?" I attempted to clear my mind with a mundane question as I came up behind her and wrapped my arms around her waist while she plated the stir-fried noodles onto some plates.

Giggling, she turned her head back and kissed my cheek. "Figured I'd use up some of the venison to make some room in the freezer for your next one. Just some teriyaki venison and stir-fried noodles, nothing too fancy, but a nice homey meal."

"You're going to suffocate my muscles with fluff if you keep spoiling me like this." I joked with a chuckle before attacking her neck with kisses and bites, making her squeal and giggle.

It was just a joke. I wasn't worried one bit about my physique. I was average and fit enough, and my daily workouts would perfectly maintain what I had. Besides, the thought of gaining a little didn't bother me one bit, mainly because Avery seemed to love the little softness of it all. As long as I was fit enough to work, then I was more than fine and happy. I didn't need to have and keep a shredded body; it was not like I was some bodybuilder or model. I was fine being average with subtleness.

"That's the point, if I feed you enough then maybe you'll get a nice little dad bod going for me to cuddle like a huge teddy bear." Avery snickered, pinching at my sides softly.

My little raven has also made it clear that she preferred a little more chub to me to give me more of a teddy bear look and that she preferred more average, bulky-ish, gruff-ish kind of men anyway.

Personally, I kept myself fit because of my deadly hobby, but I wasn't to the point of shredded or being completely ripped. I was fit enough. My muscles were somewhat defined to the point where faint outlines of them could be seen, but again, nowhere close to a bodybuilder. No matter, I was more than content with myself. My body had enough on it to keep me perfectly warm in the cold weather of Washington, and I packed more than enough muscles and stamina underneath it all to go after and keep up with my prey.

Pressing my lips to her forehead, I chuckled against her before patting her ass to go towards the dining room table. "Something on your mind? Besides your upcoming book release, that is." I knew she'd been beyond anxious as the days crept closer, and now it was a mere matter of hours and minutes before she'd have to upload her final draft and let fate take it wherever. But how her shoulders sunk with the subtle hang of her head meant something else going on in her mind, especially with how distracted her eyes were.

Avery sucked in a breath and held it for a concerning amount of time before letting it out with a forlorn expression. Those pretty lips of hers parted for a hair of a second before clamping shut with her shaking head. "It's stupid, I don't want to—"

Stopping her with a warning growl, I narrowed my eyes softly in a playful yet steady manner. "Little raven, do you need another lesson about communication again already? How many times do I have to tell you and drill it into you? Nothing is ever a bother, especially when it comes to you. I don't care if it's something silly like you telling me how nice the damn grass looks today, if it's coming from you then I want it." Granted, I knew she wouldn't say such idiotic things, but my words were true; I would still want to hear it regardless.

"No, Daddy." She squeaked out a reply before shoving a forkful of her food into her mouth as a good excuse not to continue her thought from before. "It's just... I got an email a few days ago, and I honestly forgot about it until a reminder came through today."

"What about?" I pressed when she started to trail out and averted her eyes from me.

With a heavy sigh, she leaned onto the table and propped her face up with a hand as she picked at her plate of food with her utensil. "High school reunion. I didn't pay any attention to the first email because I completely disregarded it with the full intention to not go... But everyone around town and those in the precinct who went to school with me have been pestering me about the ten-year event in two weeks. It got more and more annoying, and I don't know why, but I stupidly agreed earlier today when a few of them ganged up on me. It feels like a copout to change my mind and not go after word spread like wildfire that I agreed." Her words flew out in a flurry of a mouthful, and I almost missed them.

"Well, from what I see, you have a few options. One is to bite the bullet and not go, make up some lie like you're sick or something. The second option would be to go, and maybe just stay for a little while, then dip. Third is to go and stay the whole thing and be a mindless drone amongst the bees for a few hours." I suggested with a single shrug of a shoulder, not really seeing too many options for this pickle of hers.

Sighing softly, she looked at me with wide, pleading eyes. "I was gonna ask if you could go with me... I don't exactly have any friends to go with, and I rather not be alone for the time I have to suffer there, even if it's just a few minutes before I try to dip. You don't have to, but I wanted to ask." She almost sounded like she wanted to say 'forget it' at the end when she turned her eyes away from me almost shamefully.

"Hey," I said in a softened voice, reaching over and grasping her chin to look at me, "Of course I'll go with you. Just tell me the date and time."

"Y-you don't have to." She argued cutely, her eyes refusing to meet mine.

"I know, but I want to. I gotta keep my girl safe in my arms out there. Besides, maybe with me around, it'd be easier to come up with some excuse to give them the slip." The thought of her classmates, particularly the boys, looking at her got my blood boiling along with the thought of her being in a sea of wolves out there, all vulnerable and ready to be torn into.

Avery's opened up quite a bit about her past to me in the past few months. The more comfortable she got with me and this relationship of ours. Her school life was just as shitty as her home life. Constantly bullied during school hours by her peers for looking and being different, then criticized and picked at by her parents at home. No wonder the damn woman had issues upon issues and kept to herself.

No matter, I had every intention of fixing those issues of hers by showing Avery her worth and by showering her with as much affection as my psychopathic self could dish out.

She will be loved and cherished by me.

And only me.

CHAPTER 25
Avery

"Oh my god, I can't believe I did it."

Was it hammers in my chest or my heart? I couldn't tell.

"I'm so proud of you." Julian's smile and kiss on my cheek almost felt as surreal as the fact of me finally being a published author.

I don't know why, but it didn't hit me as hard—or any—last night when I uploaded my final draft to the publishing site. Sure, there was a sense of relief and release, but nothing over the top as I expected. Of course, maybe it was my anxiety holding things at bay, and perhaps it didn't all hit me until now. No, that couldn't be it because I felt nothing for most of the day. Granted, I hadn't looked at my reports page until Liz called me and unloaded her excitement on me about knowing a famous author and whatnot.

It was only after the call that I pulled up the website for the first time since last night to check the status of my book sales, which blew me miles away into a different country. "Is this real? Pinch me, please, or toss me into the ocean right now. I just... These numbers can't be real, right? These reviews must be for the wrong book, and it can't be for mine, right?" Or maybe I lost my ability to read and read the numbers wrong.

Julian's amused chuckle shook me as the air while his arms kept me rooted to reality. "You're so adorable little raven. That's all for you, all you.

Those sales? Your book. Those reviews? Yours. Those blogs and posts? All about your book with your cover on it."

I knew I had quite a handful of ARC readers, which I came into contact with, and I think marketing went fine since Liz kept assuring me so—I let her be the marketing manager and do all the social media stuff for me because I was clueless. However, Liz did say she had an excellent Street Team going for me and my book.

I expected my orders to be in the double digits, maybe the low hundreds—like very low hundreds—in terms of estimated royalties. NOT IN THE THOUSANDS!!! I nearly dropped my phone when I saw the numbers and how badly I shook.

Then, the reviews were insane. It was clear whatever Liz did worked like some damn miracle because a lot of the reviews and blogs mentioned how they saw reviews from my ARC readers and reels and TikToks and some other social media stuff that really snagged their attention. Many of them devoured the book upon release, were more than eager to drop their thoughts about it on the website, and posted their own personal reviews on their social media platforms.

Pure disbelief paled my excited face as I scrolled through everything, afraid that if I looked away, then it'd all disappear because it was some dream and not reality. "Sweetie? Do you need to sit down?" His hands on my shoulders melted the frigid anxiety, making me lean into his touch more to let him lead me from the kitchen to the couch. "You're so amazing, so proud of you."

"Thank you. Thank you for putting up with my weirdness and for reading my story and helping me with it, I couldn't have done it without you and Liz and all my readers, but you and Liz put up with the most shit from me. So, thank you." I'm pretty sure my constant bugging of questions at the most random times annoyed him to an extent, even if he insisted otherwise.

Taking my phone from me, he set it down on the coffee table before taking my face in his hands. "And I'll gladly do it all over again as long as it gets you to this state of excitement. You have no idea how happy it makes me to see you this elated and thank you so much for sharing this important moment of your life with me." He leaned into a deep kiss, causing my heart to flutter and explode in my chest as I eagerly returned it.

Spurred by the sudden passion, I shove Julian down flat on his back and straddle him. "Fill me up? Please? I want to be stuffed full of you when we're out." Damn, my hormones are making me needy.

"How can I ever deny my darling when she asks so nicely like that." He chuckled against my lips, running his hands down my body to work my pants off before opening his to fish his hardened member out. "Ride me, take your pleasure, baby, use me to get off, squeeze that tight pussy around me."

His hand snuck under my shirt and peeled my panties off to the side so I could easily impale myself on him with a deep moan. "I'll never get enough of you." Shivers of delight tingled my body as I remained seated on him, not wanting to move quite yet as I adjusted to him.

"Good, means you'll never try to search elsewhere for some fun and pleasure." He chuckled as his hands snuck under my top to grope my breasts. "Fucking love your tits, baby."

Heat crept to my face at his words as I bounced eagerly on his cock. "There's not much to love about them, they're small." I remarked with an aversion of my eyes.

A sharp sting clamped down on my hard nipples through my bra, making me yelp and snap my eyes back at him. "Quit that. Have I ever complained or said anything bad about them? No, I haven't, and I never will because I love them just the way they are because they are yours. Now," he paused for a moment to swat my backside with a cheeky grin, "Shut up and ride me."

Needless to say, it wasn't a quick ride. He absolutely stuffed me before throwing me in the truck for another round before taking us into the city so I could shop around the mall for some things.

"Are you sure you're still up for shopping?" Julian teased with a smirk, seemingly a little too proud at the fact he fucked me until I could barely walk.

Rolling my eyes, I gave out a sigh and reached over to flick him on his forehead. "If I don't do it now, then I'll never get it done until probably an hour before the reunion. Besides, what better way to celebrate my book release than a nice little date out? I thought we could go to the bookstore after dress shopping, then a nice little café or bakery to grab something to-go and go to the park or something for a little impromptu picnic. Or there's also an outdoor theater showing Wonder Woman that I wouldn't mind going to watch." Probably should have planned it all out better before we left the house, but not my fault my brain was in the clouds.

"Got anything in mind?" Julian asked as we entered the mall hand in hand.

"Well, they said in the email that the theme was cosmic, so maybe just something dark with some glitter or shine? I know it sounds tacky and plain and shit, but it'll work. Besides, it's not like I'm ever gonna be wearing this dress again." Nor did I intend on staying for long. A quick appearance, smile for a bit, greet some people, then slip away with Julian.

Store after store after store—okay, it was only two, but it felt like ten to my inexperienced self—we struck out until I finally settled on a floor-length gown with a sheer illusion halter that faded into a sweetheart neckline. The gown's color had an ombre effect that made black go to blue and purple from top to bottom, and all the colors were rich and deep, which fit the cosmic theme perfectly with the sheer overlay of scattered sparkles that gave an illusion of stars; a galaxy personified, that was the easiest way to describe the dress.

Unfortunately, I didn't leave the store with one bag in hand. "Did you really have to get one in every color?" I whined with a pout as Julian piled the bags into the trunk of the car.

"Oh, come on, you're exaggerating a bit, sweetie." He chuckled with a soft roll of his eyes before steering me into the passenger seat. "I only went with the typical colors in a few shades. Besides, you really think I'd disgrace your beautiful body with a puke green dress?"

Conveniently, Julian had forgotten about his upcoming business party until I called him out on shopping through dresses. So, after I was done picking out my reunion dress, he grabbed some dresses from the rack and bought them for me. Well, at least he picked out nice ones. I had to give him *some* credit even when he was being a smug asshole about it all.

Our next impromptu stop was the bookstore, which wasn't some huge place like Barnes & Noble, but it was pretty close in terms of size and popularity for being a family-owned business. Upon entering the shop, I was surprised to see Liz chatting away at the front checkout desk.

Unfortunately, my hopes of avoiding her after a quick wave disappeared when she eagerly waved me over with a grin. "Speak of the devil, and they will appear," Liz said with a widening grin as she threw her arm around my shoulder, "Avery, meet Lacey, she helps run the family business bookstore. Lacey, meet Avery, aka Lila Moon."

I have no clue about what's going on, but I think I have no choice but to go with it. "Hi there, nice to meet you." I wanted to slap myself for sounding a little strained and awkward.

"This is perfect! Hi, sorry, Lacey, my parents own the whole store and business, but I do basically everything as well. Your friend Liz here was just talking to me about setting up an author meet and book signing for you just now before you walked in. First off, major congrats on your first book release and the raging success. Like wow, it really just blew up big time. Two, amazing book, freaking love it to bits, everything is so detailed and real and the male lead, just," Lacey paused for a second to give a chef's kiss, "I want that man so bad. But either way, sorry, I was working out the details with Liz before you walked in, which is kind of perfect because you're the author, so I might as well see your direct input."

Holy shit. A book signing?! I know Liz went ham with marketing and doing what she could do to help me with my author career, but damn. Besides Julian, she's the best person to ever happen in my life; well, she's the only other person to happen in my life who stuck around and truly got along with me.

A long chit-chat later, and we got an event set up for a meet 'n greet and signing in two weeks. It seemed so surreal for an event like that to happen so fast with the release of my book. I was beyond stoked and scared shitless at the thought of having to talk to people about my book because I had no idea what to even talk about it. Even with Liz's assurance of having my back along with Julian, I was still terrified because it would be me front and center at the table on the day of the event. *I* would be the one talking. *I* would be the one people trained their beady little eyes on.

"Honey, you have to breathe before you pass out from lack of oxygen. You're going to be fine." Julian's deep voice soothed my turbulent waves of anxiety as his hand on my lower back provided an anchor for me to keep ahold of.

Unfortunately, my anxiety won this round. "What if I say something stupid? What do I even talk about with my book? There's too many scenes to possibly talk about, but also a lot of those scenes aren't exactly rated PG. There's nothing about my book that makes it stand out. Oh God, what if people don't show up?"

My rambling was cut short by Julian's lips shutting me up after pushing me against a bookshelf. "Stop. People out there love your book. Someone, at least one person besides Liz and I, will be at that event. You have to believe in yourself more, baby. Honestly, if those rave reviews aren't enough of a flash in the face for you about your book doing well, then I don't know what it is. Stop doubting yourself, darling."

I had to admit he was right; I was freaking out too much for no good reason. Whether people show up or not was out of my control. It was clear my book did great upon release and will probably continue to do great with time. "Thank you." Leaning up, I ghosted his lips with a kiss before smiling at him gratefully.

THUD!

It was impossible not to jump out of my pants at the sudden slamming of the table in front of me.

Hand over heart, I glared at Detective Bornes through my heavy breaths. "What the fuck Carl, you could have given me a heart attack. What gives?" As if I wanted to help this fucker now after he did that.

"Explain this." His hands picked something up and slammed it back down on the table before jabbing a finger at it.

Now, it was my turn to be utterly confused. "That's a book, Carl, something you open and read its contents either for entertainment or knowledge. What about it?"

With an exasperated groaning sigh, he picked the book up and shoved it in my face, quite literally. "Not just any book. *Your* book. *Your* book about a serial killer who has a keen liking for black feathers who also goes uncaught." Okay, now I see where he was going.

Rolling my eyes, I gently shoved his hand out of my face. "It's a book, Carl, a work of fiction. What I write or what I get inspired from is none of your business. Just because it happens to line up with some things of this stupid case doesn't mean I'm the killer in real life. Honestly, Carl, use your damn brain for once and make some sense. Where'd you even get that anyway? Didn't take you for the type to read spicy books." Or read books in general, but I needed to hold my tongue around him before I dug my stupid grave deeper.

"That's none of your business." He retorted with a sneer.

"Go do something useful, like your job, and leave me alone. Go interview actual suspects who could be the killer." He could waste all the time he wanted on me, but I sure as hell didn't want to waste any of my precious time on him.

A sudden grip around my upper arm caused me to flinch and lash my hand out, slapping Detective Bornes across the face and catching the attention of everyone else around us. "Let me go. Now." I seethed through gritted teeth as I attempted to tug my arm out of his bruising hold.

Instead of releasing me, he tightened his grip and pulled me right up to his reddening face. "Or what? You'll send your ape of a boyfriend after me again?" He spat with a scowl.

"I didn't send Julian after you. Besides, it's neither of our faults you can't hold your liquor." I snapped back with a bite to my words.

Julian wasn't happy when he finally pried the name of the person who hurt me from my lips. I actually tried to stop Julian from doing anything stupid, and he assured me he wouldn't. Whatever he did, nothing Detective Bornes threw at him stuck, so Julian wasn't charged with anything because nothing could be proven.

When I pressed for details, all Julian told me was Detective Bornes had a bad drink that made him sick. Detective Bornes was found passed out in an alleyway the night after Julian ran into him at some bar; the arrogant detective was stripped nearly bare and had his things stolen. Julian swore he didn't poison Detective Bornes's drink, and CCTV proved him to be innocent and true to his words. No foul play was found, so no one was charged with anything.

Unfortunately, that didn't get Detective Bornes off my ass. If anything, he'd been after me more ever since his run-in with Julian at the bar.

"Detective Bornes! My office! Now!" The boom of our chief's voice set everyone back into motion to avoid his wrath.

CHAPTER 26
Julian

WHY?

I wanted to ask her so badly, but I held my tongue because my sensible side told me it'd be a bad idea.

Faking a convincing smile, I leaned in and kissed Avery's forehead. "Thanks, darling, but isn't it supposed to be me spoiling you with gifts?"

If it wasn't clear, I wasn't a gift person. This didn't mean I didn't give gifts at all, because I had to do it to keep up appearances and make people happy and whatnot. But personally, I never could grasp the excitement about the act. I understand neurotypical people enjoyed the simple act because it brought them joy and shit, but obviously not the case for me because I don't do emotions.

I never enjoyed people gifting or giving me anything in general either because it usually meant I owed them, and I hate being in debt.

Of course, none of that applied to Avery, fully at least. I didn't get an overabundance of joy from receiving the little black box from her, nor did I jump for joy when I saw the jewelry within. It might not have been a lightning bolt to my body, but I felt a spark of some sort along with my confusion and lack of enthusiasm. There was an appreciation and warmth felt in my heart.

"Doesn't mean I can't spoil you every now and then. I know you don't like to wear accessories much, but I couldn't help it when I passed by it. It just kind of reminded me of us since you call me your little raven and all, and we both have a strange liking for the blackbird. Also, I just thought it'd be a nice thing for you to have on your body that reminds you of me when we're not home." Her rambling trailed on, but I sensed something amiss with how tense she was as she fiddled with her fingers.

Smiling, I took the raven pendant out of the box, letting it dangle in the air by the long chain. It was a simple raven with its wings stretched behind in flight. Avery had the same pendant hanging around a choker on her neck, but hers was flipped. The raven's claws and beaks hooked together the two pendants to form a heart of sorts, and on the back had our initials engraved into it along with the date we met.

Honestly, the more I admired the thing, the more appealing it became. Was this to be something sentimental to me? Gods, that was a strange thought to have. Although, it wouldn't be any different than a trophy. For fuck's sake, I kept the bedsheet and lingerie outfit Avery wore the night she gave herself to me, and I made her innocence bleed in an airtight safe in my basement. So, I shouldn't be weirded out over this little necklace.

"There's something else on your tongue, darling." I shifted my thoughts and attention back to her to avoid the confusion swirling in my own fucked up mind.

Pursing her lips, Avery mumbled something under her breath before I pressed her again to say it louder. With a struggle and flushed face, she practically blurted her words out, "I wanted to mark you. I thought it'd be a good way for others to see you're taken with the pendant hanging around your neck."

I felt terrible for the little laugh I let out because I found it all too adorable, not because I mocked her. "Baby, no, don't get sad. I'm not laughing at you." Damn these stupid feelings. Seeing her eyes tear up from my laughter sliced my heart like a knife.

Throwing my arms around her, I held her tightly as I rocked us gently. "You're just too adorable and cute when you get possessive and a little jealous. I couldn't help it. I wasn't laughing at you, I promise." I assured her with kisses against her neck.

Taking her hands in mine, I place the pendant into her palm. "Put it on me. Mark me as yours."

Speaking of marking property, putting a band around her finger crossed my mind once more as she slipped the chain around my neck. Marriage was never really part of the plans for my life. Then again, neither was Avery. My urge to make things even more official with us deepened significantly after Avery agreed to let me collar her around the house. Seeing a physical sign of my ownership on her body like that spurred some kind of primal urge to lay more of a physical claim to her beyond screwing her senseless.

The urge was easy to ignore until recently when a worker of mine rattled on about his plans to propose to his girl. Somehow, his words made the image of Avery's hand in mine at the stupid alter with a ring around her finger paint and etched itself into my mind. Avery never wore her collar outside the house, maybe only a discreet little choker at most, but usually, she wouldn't wear anything out that would make it clear to other men that she was taken. So, what better way to completely own her than to put my ring around her finger and have her last name be mine?

I don't know if marriage was in the cards for Avery, though. We also never really talked about our relationship going beyond what it currently is. Both of us were more than happy with what we had going on, and I sure as hell had no plans on living the rest of my life without Avery in it. Hopefully, she had the same notion. But it felt a little too soon to bring up such a serious subject when we weren't fully a year into our relationship.

Breaking my train of thought, I occupied myself with devouring Avery's lips until both of us ended up on the couch with our clothes off. "I love how you're always so wet and ready for me." I groaned against her inner thigh as I trailed kisses up to her wet pussy.

"I can't help it. I always want to be ready for your cock to break me." She gasped out a sharp moan when I dipped my tongue into her wet cavern for a better taste. "Break me, Daddy, please."

Growling lowly, I sat up on my knees, pressed her legs wide open, and slammed myself into her with a hard thrust. Pressing a hand against the back of her thigh, I pressed her leg flat into the couch cushion while my other hand wrapped around her neck to choke her until she smiled deliriously at me with her moans as I slammed in and out of her with no mercy. She knew better by now than to say things like that if she wasn't prepared to take the consequences of her words.

After a few hard thrusts, I pulled out completely and brought a hand down on her pussy, spanking her hard to where she squealed and jerked under me while gripping the wrist of my hand around her neck tightly. "Fucking slut, coming from getting your pussy spanked," I growled with a dark grin as I watched her jerking body gush her juices out with the impact on her throbbing cunt.

Then, without warning, I entered her again and rutted into her again like an insane beast. "That's right, come around my cock like a good little slut. This is the only cock you can ever get pleasure from, the only one allowed to be inside your pussy, you got that?" I growled against her lips before kissing her hungrily with a deep groan as I slowed my hips down to give her long and slow strokes while pressing down on her stomach with the hand not around her neck still, making her feel every little inch of my length. "Feel that baby? Every little inch of this cock, of my cock, belongs to you. This is your cock as well, little raven, your cock to suck and fuck whenever you want and please. All you have to do is ask or beg for it."

Her dilated eyes looked at me with such happiness at my words, as if I'd dosed her with dopamine and gave her the best high of her life. Her mouth hung open in pleasure, and they twitched slightly as if she wanted to say something, but no words ever came out. All she did was reach out, take my face into her tender hands, and stroke my cheek while her bright eyes bore deep into my soul, touching it and mingling with it directly.

My discomfort didn't let the situation last, though. One hard snap of my hips and our deep moment was shattered to bits. Whatever I felt just now freaked me out, scared me even. I needed to distract myself before I unraveled before her because of her damn eyes. What did she do? There's no way a look could touch my insides like that.

"Julian, coming." Avery whimpered under me just as I felt her walls clamp around me. "Please, can I come, please." Now, these desperate eyes of hers I didn't mind staring upon all day.

"Not yet baby, just a little more, I'm close." I whispered against her lips before taking them and shoving my tongue into her mouth to claim it.

Even though my release had been close, I paced myself to hold back to drag out her torment a little for my twisted pleasure. It didn't take long for her sweet pleas to flow from her mouth, a sweet song from my little raven just for me. "Daddy, please, it hurts, please let me come, please." The sight of her tears was the cherry on top that broke me.

Pressing my body into her more, I pin her body down into the couch as I picked up the force of my thrusts until my release crashed into me. "Fuck, now baby, milk all the cum out of me." I strained out a groan as my hips erratically came to a stop, flushed against Avery's trembling body.

"Julian." The way my name fell so softly from her sounded like a choir of angels to my ears. "Thank you, thank you so much." It was a strange habit of hers, well strange at first when I questioned her about it, but I've come to appreciate and love it because why shouldn't she thank me for bringing her such rapture? She probably didn't help with my ego, but I didn't fucking care.

Shifting around on the couch, I lay with her atop me, my arms wrapped securely around her. "Thank you for the gift, I will cherish it forever." I whispered against her forehead before kissing it. "Rest, nap a little before the event tonight. I'll wake you up in a few hours." I lulled her reluctant body to slumber, stroking her arms and rubbing her back.

Once she was out, I carefully slipped away from her to prep my truck for my victim tonight. Was it risky to kidnap someone tonight while out with Avery? Very much, but he was ready to flee. I couldn't have that. It was either tonight or never since I'd conveniently be in the city.

So, while Avery slept soundly, I gathered everything, tossed it into my truck's covered trunk, and locked it up before going to my basement to prep the area. Unfortunately, a recent storm decommissioned my extended area until I drained the rainwater and fixed it back up. I wasn't comfortable with the fact I had to use the actual basement, but it was my holding and kill chamber before I made the extended one. So, it was well equipped, just unused for a while for its initial intended purposes.

With everything set, I washed up and got myself ready before waking Avery and waiting for her to wash up and get ready herself. At least Avery wasn't the kind of person who took forever to get ready for a night out or anything of that nature. So, it wasn't long until she came out of the closet with her dress loosely around her body. "Zip me up, please?" Her voice was small as she showed her back to me, holding the front of her dress with one hand while the other bunched her hair up messily.

"You should do your hair up like that, a messy bun, I mean." Probably should have told her before she put her hair in loose curls. "Or a half-up kind of do. I think it would pull everything together nicely and give you a good frame." I added as I pulled the zipper up and placed a kiss on her shoulder.

"Hm, I was thinking half up and pinning it with that hair clip you gave me a little while back," Avery said with a hum before kissing my cheek and stepping away to go to our dresser and finish doing her hair and finishing touches on her makeup.

Soon, we were on the road. "So, an hour? Then the typical excuse of work tomorrow and whatnot?" I wanted to confirm our plan of escape before going into the fray.

"Yep, an hour should be more than plenty. Honestly, I was thinking of dipping after thirty minutes, but I guess an hour would work just fine." Avery sighed softly, slumping in her seat and poking at the window with a finger. "Thank you for agreeing to come with me tonight. I know you probably had better things to do, like stuff for your business."

True, I did have much better things to do, but for some odd reason, the thought of being there as support for Avery appealed to me more. Well, that and this being a way to let others know she was taken and by whom. Yes, I was using this opportunity to peacock and scare others off from Avery. "It's fine, and you don't have to thank me for doing something I'm supposed to do as a good boyfriend. Besides, it works out fine as long as you're still fine with me running an errand before we go back home." I assured her with a smile, reaching over and pinching her cheek softly.

Unfortunately, the more we drove, the more tense Avery grew until it suffocated the air and made me feel uncomfortable. "Little raven, breathe, it's going to be fine," I said in a soft voice while placing my hand on her thigh. "Or do you need some help relaxing?" My fingers slowly dug into her plush thigh, pulling a long, sighing moan from her.

Avery chewed her bottom lip momentarily before shaking her head and taking my hand in hers to play with my fingers. "No, I'm a little too sore from earlier, maybe later." She gave me an apologetic smile before kissing the back of my hand.

Frowning softly, I weaved my fingers with hers and held her hand tightly. "Honey, don't ever be sorry for rejecting my advances. I love sex with you and all things around it, but only if you want it in return. I'm not with you for the sex. I am with you because I like you for you. Even if it wasn't me, you never apologize or even look apologetic for rejecting someone because you're not in the mood or comfortable." Never have I ever, and would I ever, force her into any situation that'd bring her any kind of discomfort.

"Thank you for being a great man and for being mine." Avery's lips fell upon my cheek after the sound of shuffling filled the car cabin.

CHAPTER 27
Avery

MY LIPS REMAINED PINNED in a painfully fake smile as I forced the laughs through my façade.

The plan had been to stay for an hour, tops, yet three hours later, I was still at this stupid reunion in the stuffy gym of the high school I attended. Julian and I had made our way to leave after the hour was up, but we were promptly stopped by the event coordinators, who prevented our early departure. Apparently, there would be awards and silly things like that at the end, and I was down for one of them. So, I couldn't leave.

Hopefully, this torture session would end soon because my nonexistent social battery was empty; I ran on fumes at this point. To make things worse, I ran on fumes without backup.

Stupid vultures knew when to swoop in for their damn meal. "So, umm I guess congrats on your latest venture. Best-selling author, who would have thought. I mean, you were always a bookworm in school, but who knew it didn't all stay in your head. What even gave you the idea to write a story, let alone such a... interesting one?" I barely recognized the girl who spoke through the plastic surgery she put her body and face through. Reading her name tag rang the bell a little bit only because I recalled her to be one of the bitches who picked on me more than the others.

Well, I can't exactly go kill someone now can I?

Yeah, not the most appropriate thing to say, so I kept my lips shut for the sake of keeping some kind of peace between us all—for now. "Just something I thought up over the years of working. A work of fiction, that's all." I replied with a flat smile.

At least I have a functioning brain to imagine with, unlike you.

"So, Julian Smith, is he... Straight? Or? 'Cause aren't you gay?" Some other woman prodded at me with an awkward tone to her voice.

Rude, but I didn't flat-out call her out on it. "I don't know what gave you that impression of me, but it's not nice to just assume those things about people. There's nothing wrong with swinging the other way either, so I would watch your tone. Julian and I are happy with how we are with our relationship, and that's all you need to know." I should really look for a way to bail out this stupid group before I snap at them.

My eyes whipped over to another woman as she spoke up over the deafening music. "Okay, but like, how did you even get a man like him? No offense, but someone like you ending up with a man who's been on Forbes and their list of successful businessmen? There has to be something going on there."

"Hey, where is your little fake date? Had enough of you already?" Another asked before I could answer the one before her, turning the attention of everyone around the small area to me.

Unfortunately, being on fumes meant my patience for people was nearly nonexistent. "At least Julian's more real than your poor boob job Laylie." I snarked with a smirk before sipping on my water. "Julian had a quick errand to run, he'll be back in a bit." His plan was time restricted, so us being kept here would have screwed it up. Julian promised it wouldn't take long when I told him to go do what he needed to do. According to his ETA text he just shot me, he should be here soon.

"Okay, but come on, there has to be something going on between you two, like some kind of arrangement. No way some hotshot guy like that is with a girl like you, or does he not know how weird you are yet?" Another woman piped up after laughing along with the others at my comment about the other's plastic surgery job.

Dragging out a sigh, I simmered my anger before it could boil over. "You know, I thought after all this time you would all have grown up, but seems like I had too high of expectations. Honestly, I don't even want to imagine how you treat your own children if this is how horrible you treat me after all these years." I couldn't help it, but I was fed up with their stupid mean girl shit.

"Excuse you, we are wonderful mothers with *normal* children." One of them scoffed with a look of disbelief.

"Oh? You mean your group of children who are all friends who hang around the manga section at the library? Last I recalled, you guys called me a dweeb and tossed rumors around that I got off on hentai at night because I can't afford to watch real people do it or get some on my own." I snapped back with a tightened chest. I don't know where this confidence came from, but I'll fucking take it all.

"Oh please, that shit is weird back then and now, but they read the normal comics, so it's whatever." All the stupid harpies looked and sounded the same to me with their shrill voices. "Besides, you're the weirdo who looked like a confused trans with how you dressed and had your hair. You were a freak at school. You look decent now, but you're still weird with your likes. Honestly, what kind of girl likes all the nerdy shit like that? And then the serial killers and all the crime junky stuff? Come on you stupid detective wannabe. Seriously, you're still as much of a loser now as you were back then. Well, guess we can add extremely pathetic to that list to. I mean, faking your boyfriend to be Julian Smith? Be real."

Not wanting to further engage them, I turned around to walk off, but a set of arms around my waist and a solid wall of muscle prevented me from doing so. "Sorry about that, but it was an important client whose schedule was tricky to work with." Julian's voice rang out from behind me before a kiss came down on my cheek.

Looking up, my smile relaxed to a genuine one as I basked in the comfort Julian's presence brought me. "That's not a nice thing to insinuate about our relationship earlier, nor was it mature of you to spat at my woman like that," Julian paused for a second to squint his eyes at the dimly lit name tag on the woman's dress, "Milly. There's no such thing with Avery and I. I am with her because she is a wonderful woman who has a fun and quirky personality that I quite love. I know about her hobbies and all that. It's actually how we met and clicked. I know about her author career, too, and how it's taken off, so I know about all she writes as well."

Looking down at my lovingly, he tightened his hold around me and kissed my temple. "Avery's not with me because of my money or anything, nor is that even close to the nature of our relationship with each other. We truly care for each other and get along very well, unlike you and your estranged husband, who is busy snogging with some other woman in the bathroom hallway."

Milly gasped and stomped her foot before marching off with a puffed-out face. Then, Julian looked at everyone else with a saccharine smile. "Anyone else want to question our relationship? Not that it's any of your business in the first place, but what Avery and I have is very real. There's no sugar daddy arrangement going on or any such exchanges, and you best nip such rumors going around before I do. I don't know why you're all so sour towards Avery, who's nothing shy of an angel, but you best change your tone with her with me around, or things will happen that are rather unsavory. Now, unless you have something nice and real to say, go back to your half-filled marriages that are on the cusp of divorce."

Wow. Julian was always so cordial; honestly, I didn't think he had that kind of snap. Sure, he was a businessman and all, so he probably could hold his own more than enough and has some sass packed away for good times. But he's never shown such an extent of it to me.

I giggled with a grateful smile. "My man." Reaching an arm up, I wrapped it around his neck and brought his head down to a deep kiss to shove it in the others' faces.

Smirking, Julian glanced over at the stunned crowd arrogantly. "Real enough for you ladies? Or do you want to turn into voyeurs to see how a real man pleasures a woman, maybe you might even want to drag your pathetic excuses of a partner so they can learn a thing or two. I mean, maybe if your men actually pleased you properly, then you wouldn't have your panties in a bunch and take your jealousy out on poor women like Avery, who has a man who can actually find the clitoris and know how to properly use his dick to get his woman the big O." Okay, this little spicy side of Julian was hot.

I mean, men in fiction getting all snappy and protective of their woman was always hot, but seeing and experiencing it in real life was a whole different thing altogether. Then, the fact it was *my* man getting all sassy with my high school bullies and rendering them speechless made me soak my panties right then and there.

Before everyone could scamper away with their tails tucked between their legs, microphone feedback sent the whole place into silence as we all looked towards the stage. "Hey, everyone! Hope you have all had some time to brag about the new rocks on your fingers or the new Benjamins you're all now making! It's time for the award ceremony! So if everyone can take a seat, we'll get started!"

Stones weighed my gut down to where I wanted to throw up. Something about all of this gave me a bad feeling, as bad as I felt about Julian initially. Honestly, the strange feeling about Julian never fully disappeared, but I actively ignored it at this point because nothing was wrong with Julian.

Although, even after ten months together, I'd occasionally get a bad feeling about Julian randomly. There's nothing wrong with him, though. He was perfect... Maybe a little too much, but why should that matter? He kept and made me happy, put me first, and cared for me greatly, and obviously, the sex with him was beyond perfect and mind-blowing. Our relationship was perfect after the honeymoon period. So, why should it matter if he had late nights at work or disappeared sometimes in the middle of the night because of work? He was a busy man, and he had to work hard to keep his business running smoothly and well. Nothing wrong with being diligent.

"And now, for the big moment of tonight, we're going to have our prom king and queen come up for old time's sake, then we'll have our reunion king and queen join them! So, Harry and Gia, come on to the stage and do us the honors of announcing the reunion king and queen nominated by none other than our lovely class of 2013 tonight!" The emcee's words almost made my stomach drop into some random pit of despair, and I was about to get up to run to the bathroom to hurl when my name was called.

"Avery Le! I see you over there, girl! Get yo pretty lil ass up here!" Oh God, maybe I should just run—shit! Blinded, I covered my eyes briefly until I adjusted to having the spotlight on me, literally.

With no escape, I made my way to the stage, which felt like the gallows right with each echoing step I took toward the raised platform. "The reunion queen, as chosen by the people, Avery Le!" Claps and cheers filled the gymnasium, but the beady little eyes I caught sight of didn't reflect their enthusiasm.

"Now, before we announce the reunion king, Harry here has something he'd like to say to you, Avery." The emcee stepped back, and Harry stepped up to me with a microphone in hand.

Wariness drowned my body in cold nervousness as I held my feet in place to prevent myself from stepping back from the sight of Harry's malicious smile. "Avery, congrats on your newest ventures as a published author first off. Who knew our shy little bookworm would become so famous overnight like that." I caught Julian's tensing jaw out of the corner of my eyes when Harry threw his arms around my shoulders as if we were old buddies. "After ten years, people change. Many of us grew up with adulthood, and many of us moved up in life to grasp at our dreams. Avery here, she hasn't changed much, which is a breath of fresh air because she somehow achieved so much while still staying weird. I mean, who would have thought our little boy here would be dating *the* Julian Smith instead of Jeffrey Dahlmer. Gotta say, it definitely makes this a little awkward since we found your perfect match for tonight with tonight's reunion king."

Before any words came out of my open mouth, I was shoved backward into a pair of arms. Ridiculing laughter filled the gym after I screamed in horror in reaction to a masked face shoving itself at me while I remained trapped in the arms. "Ted Bundy here's gonna be so sad you're taken, he was looking forward to meeting his new bride. Oh well, guess you'll just have to end up like the others who broke his heart."

A pained yelp sobbed from me when my ankle buckled under my body from having it shoved in another direction. A big clash and clatter ramped up the laughter when my body landed into a pile of bones set up in a clear kiddie pool with water and feathers. The black feathers clung onto my soaked body as I quickly removed myself from the pool in a panic, screaming again when the guy in the Ted Bundy mask made another grab at me and pulled me up to his face.

"Well, at least now maybe The Omen will come for you now that you're all covered in his favorite things!" Harry's cackling echoed inside my head as I struggled against the man who held me.

Going off my adrenaline, I shot my hand out and punched the person across the face as he made kissing noises and motions at me, knocking the mask clean off his face. Then, my knee met whatever poor excuse he had between his legs, which forced him to release me completely. Not wasting another embarrassing moment, I scrambled off the stage and ran straight for Julian, who made it onto the stage all red in the face with a murderous rage boiling in his usually charming eyes.

Julian's arms instantly wrapped around me protectively as he glared at Harry, who was busy laughing his ass off. "Hey, I'm just trynna help ya man, you've no idea what a weirdo she is. I'm saving you a lifetime of disappointment." Harry said through his fit of laughter.

"Julian, no." I firmly pressed my hands against his chest when he made a move towards Harry. "He's not worth it, just leave it... I just want to go home... Please." I should have listened to my gut and left the reunion despite the pressure to stay.

Still as a statue, Julian remained rooted in his spot while his chest heaved with heavy breaths. "Julian, please," I begged through my burning tears, gripping the lapels of his jacket tightly.

He didn't seem happy about it, but he relented. Knocking my hands away, he shrugged his jacket off and draped it over me before escorting me to his truck. In the safety of his vehicle, I broke down completely in body-shaking sobs as the event replayed itself in my mind like a damn movie on repeat. "Why? What did I ever do to them? Why am I so fucking stupid and naïve to think nothing bad would happen?" What sick joy did they get from picking on me? I honestly didn't understand their aim at me throughout the years, and I thought maybe things would've changed since we were all grown up now.

Julian's embrace was like a warm blanket, enveloping me in a sense of safety and comfort. His strong arms held me tightly, and his hand gently rubbed circles on my back. The steady rhythm of his touch slowly broke my horrendous sobbing into soft hiccups, and the gentle strokes of his hand in my undone hair brushed the shame and anxiety away with each movement. In that moment, I felt truly and utterly physically and emotionally embraced by the man I've grown to adore greatly. No words were needed; his silent comfort was more than enough to provide for me.

Pulling away, he took my face into his hands and wiped my tears away with his thumbs while his concerned but hopeful eyes mingled into mine. "They're the losers and idiots who can't get past high school. They haven't gotten far in life and are jealous of you and where you are, so they had to knock you down to make themselves feel better."

Tightly, he hugged me and peppered my face with soothing kisses. "They can embarrass you all they want, but that doesn't change the fact that you are a successful and independent woman who has their life together, living their dream and best life. What happened tonight will slowly fade, but their sad lives won't. They have to live with their choices for the rest of their lives while you get to enjoy yours. I know it's hard to look forward right now in this moment, but you'll get through it. We'll get through it. I won't let you go through it alone. I will be with you every step of the way." His deep voice wasn't enough this time to keep everything at bay.

Through the cracks of my weakness, the demons of my insecurity broke through to the surface. "I don't get it. Why are you with me? I'm socially awkward and would rather talk to the imaginary characters in my mind or shove my nose into a book than talk to actual people. I look like a teenage boy with how flat my boobs are, and I have an ass that's too big along with my fat thighs. I look like a turnip, probably."

Frustrated gasps and breaths heaved from my body for a second before I recollected myself to continue. "You're such an amazing person who's so confident and charming, and everyone's fawning at your feet when you flash a smile, and women throw themselves at you. You're hot and handsome as fuck you literally belong in some movie like 365 Days. I'm just a plain old girl who deserves to be passed by—"

Julian's lips crashed against mine with a fierce intensity, and my body froze in response to the unexpected kiss. Chills pricked down the length of my spine at the jolt that his lips sent through me. All thoughts and words disappeared as he continued to press his lips against mine, silencing me completely. More and more, his lips pressed into me, the more he stole every outgoing breath from me until I laid flat on the seats with his body nearly crushing mine. "You better be prepared for a lesson when you get home because I thought I made it damn clear to you that I do not give a single shit or flying fuck about any of that. I will fall for whoever I want and whoever my heart pines after, whether that be the next Hollywood actress or the simple small-town girl who slaves away in a café to make ends meet."

Resting his forehead against mine, he continued to burn me with his genuine, loving eyes. "I chose you because you are uniquely you. I do not care about your looks, and I actually find them fitting and cute and more than perfect for me. I love your plush thighs and plump ass, they make the perfect pillow at the end of stressful workdays, and your ass is more than the perfect target for my hands. There is nothing about you that I would ever change, from your looks down to your personality. I admire that you don't crave attention from others or seek to go out every night. I love how cute you are curled up on the couch or at your desk with your books and laptop. Quit worrying about all that stuff because I really don't give a damn about any of it." He assured me with the most joyful smile ever.

He gave me no chance to respond as he descended his lips upon mine again in a heated and dominating way, leaving me breathless as I struggled to swallow the immense passion pouring out of him into me. "You are not the same person you were back then, and that's the person they are stuck on. They may have reigned the hallways and the years then, but they are nothing but the peasants now while you are the reigning queen. You have so much potential buried under years of neglect and hurt. It's time to bring it all out and show them all how much better you've become than all of them."

His eyes soften with awe as his thump strokes my cheek. "Also, at the end of the day, you have something many of them lack and want: true happiness. You're in a relationship with a man you have no regrets about, you're fine with your career as a CSI, and now you've achieved your dream of becoming a published author that will only grow from here on out. You come home with me every day with a bright smile on your face, and you don't complain about stressful things like our relationship falling apart, losing a spark, or stupid finances. You want for nothing because you have it all."

Damn him for being right and giving me no room to argue. How in the world did I become blessed with such a perfect man who has a rebuttal for every little insecurity I have? It's unfair how safe and sound he makes me feel because then I never want to leave. Fuck, now my tears of shame and sadness turned into sappy tears of joy as I threw my arms around Julian and held him tightly while I buried my messy face into his chest, getting his chest all dirty and wet with residue water, washed off makeup, tears, and snot.

I love him.

I love Julian, and I was terrified of it.

CHAPTER 28
Julian

"Again? Babe, this is the fifth time this month you've dinged your truck."

Avery's groan dragged out with her hands going down her face as she stared at my truck's dirty and slightly dented grill.

"It's deer season, and we live in the middle of prime deer land. I mean, you know how it is around these parts of the woods. Deer everywhere. I mean, you get them destroying your garden while I encounter them on the road. Seriously, the Buck came out of nowhere." It's a shame I have to clean the evidence off my truck sooner than later. Oh well, I can fuck the buzz out of me using Avery later.

Funny enough, his name was Buck, or at least he liked to go by that name. Poor Buck stood no chance against a three-ton truck going seventy miles an hour. The cleanup at the scene was a little messy, but nothing some dirt and cement couldn't cover up.

"I have never hit a deer in my ten years of driving or hit anything. Seriously, and you call me the bad driver." Avery sneered with a joking snicker and roll of her eyes before disappearing back into the house to leave me to clean my truck in peace.

At least that's another name off my never-ending list. It won't be long now until another body drops because of me. I can worry about that later. I have blood and guts to wash off of my vehicle and a lovely girlfriend waiting to spread her eager little legs for me to dive between.

As fun as it was to kill people, the aftermath of it wasn't too bad. Sure, clean-up was never fun, but watching my crime be covered or washed away was kind of soothing, like how the blood from my truck's grill faded away to nothing with the water crashing against it. Off the truck and into the earth, back to the earth, where it would sink back to where we were made, according to the bible and whatnot.

Evidence of my crime gone before anyone could even get an inkling of a clue or idea, I went back inside the house with a content smile on my face, one which grew at the sight of Avery chewing on a piece of licorice while her face twisted with cute confusion as she had her eyes narrowed at her laptop. "Darling, I don't think you can scare your story into writing itself." I teased with a chuckle as I came up around behind the couch and hugged my arms loosely around her neck and shoulders.

"Well, maybe if I stare at it hard enough then the words will just start appearing on the screen as they should be." Avery pouted as she wrapped her hands around my forearms and leaned her chin on them. "Hate writer's block." She whined with a string of inaudible mumbles before opening her mouth and chomping down on my forearm playfully to vent out some of her frustration.

"Well, why don't we take a nice, long bath together to unwind and relax before I make dinner while you relax on the couch in a post-orgasmic bliss." I suggested with a low growl into her ear, followed by a not so gentle nip to it, making her shudder and shrink a bit under me.

"You are insatiable, I swear." She chuckled, tilting her head back to smack a kiss against my lips with a smile.

"Can you blame me when I've the perfect, sexy little girlfriend like you around me?" I threw back with my own chuckle before plucking her off the couch with a soft laugh at her squealing.

No, we did not screw in the tub, not our thing, because Avery hated how the water got into her and dried her out. I didn't mind; shower sex and bath sex weren't my favorite anyway. However, she wasn't safe before and after the bath. Something I thought she would have learned by now with our routine.

"Daddy! No more, please." She begged me through her tears as she clung onto the edge of the counter to keep her body from hitting it too hard from the force of my thrusts.

"One more baby, you can give me one more, I know you can." Pretty sure her body would give me one whether she wanted to or not with how she started to twitch and pulse around me. "That's it baby, one more."

Reaching over, I grabbed both her wrists and pinned them behind her back in one hand before slipping my hand around her hips between her legs to search for her little hidden pearl. "Sir, please, gonna—fuck!" Her body suddenly jerked violently in my grasp when my fingers pressed firmly against her engorged clit and rubbed firm circles on it.

THUD! THUMP! THUMP!

"What was—" Avery was still in a daze as she lifted her head and looked around, all confused at the sudden noise.

It most definitely wasn't an animal, but she really did *not* need to know anything about it. "Probably just an animal, don't worry about it." I lied, increasing the force of my thrusts.

Words disappeared from her blabbering mouth as her orgasm took over and sent her into a high, evident by how her eyes glazed over before rolling as her mouth hung open in sweet bliss. Her erratic hips tried to jerk away from me, but there was no escape. A forward buck of her hips would make her meet my hand while bucking backward or any other way would force her to grind on my throbbing cock, which remained buried deep within her suffocating walls as I released my cum into her.

Stilling my hips, I remained in her and released her wrists to fully wrap my around her to pull her up against me. "Shh, come back to me, baby, come back to me." I soothed her while petting her head.

Avery wasn't fully gone into her subspace, but there'd still be a drop. "Daddy, I'm so sore and full of you." She whimpered through her small little hiccups as she leaned into me. "I wanna nap."

Cradling her face, I peppered her face and neck with kisses as I slowly pulled out of her with a soft groan and picked her up into my arms to carry her out to the bedroom to dress her in a pair of panties and my shirt, then to the couch where I bundled her up in her blanket. With her in my lap, I held her tightly as I fed her some juice and chocolate.

After pampering her on the couch for a while, I settled her down with her favorite TV show to disappear into the kitchen to prep and make dinner for us. I looked over to check up on her, and my shoulders shook with my amused chuckle when I saw her passed out.

Such a cute and innocent little thing. How unfortunate she fell into my hands. Honestly, if I were a decent person, I would let her go. Too bad I'm a greedy ass demon who's selfish as fuck. I cared too much for my own needs and survival, and unfortunately for Avery, she has become a need for me to survive. Imagining a day when I didn't wake up to her or have her to come home to gave me physical pain in my chest, as if someone busted my chest cavity open and reached in, grabbed my heart, and literally squeezed at it. I literally cannot imagine life without her.

Yet, at the same time, I couldn't imagine myself holding her against me if she did not wish so. I wanted to keep her—no, I *needed* to keep her. Yet, the thought of her not wanting or reciprocating any of it ached my heart as much as the thought of not having her.

I never cared for the other person, yet Avery broke the damn rule like she did all the other rules in my life. For once in my life, I actually thought about the other person or found myself wanting to think about Avery and her feelings. She's turned me into a sap, for her only, of course. I couldn't think objectively and selfishly when it came to Avery; it wasn't hard the first few weeks we were together, but the more intimate we became, and the longer our relationship dragged, I found the task of not caring or worrying about her and her opinions to be impossible.

The shift perplexed me greatly because no one, and I mean *no one*, could ever get me to behave differently, not even my own parents or my therapist, when I saw one. Yet, here came along Avery, the little ball of sunshine of all things right; it infuriated me how she had such an effect on me without actively trying. All she had to do was exist.

Discerning why she was different from literally everyone else was a headache and a half for me. Don't even get me started on learning to deal with the new onset of emotions she threw into my life, emotions I never thought possible for someone like me to feel. Granted, I still don't feel or have these emotions with anyone else, not as if Avery made me a changed person. No, I only felt these stupid neurotypical emotions with her and no one else—and yes, I have tried very begrudgingly so to test out my stupid theory.

No matter how many avenues I ventured, they all led back to the same answer.

God, dare I say it: I'm in love with Avery.

I avoided the conclusion as long as possible, dancing around every stupid little theory and grasping at any and everything to avoid reaching and accepting that answer. I practically laughed at myself when the realization dawned on me. Me, in love!? Un-fucking-believable. Yet, the more I stewed on it, the more sense the answer made.

Avery had become the exception to everything in my life thus far, so it made total biological sense for me to feel such an immense attraction and devotion to my perfect match in life.

But by God, love!?

I'm fucking losing it, but I didn't care or mind it one bit because, once again, it was Avery.

Fuck me.

"Going somewhere, Harry?"

The man nearly pissed himself with how terrified he looked when he whipped his body around from the front door to face me, who leaned against the railing of his stairway a few feet away from him with half my body obscured in the shadows. My new target dug through his little bowl of keys at the table next to the door in a frenzy before I interrupted him.

"Y-you! G-get out of h-here! I'll call the cops! Charge you for breaking and entering!" His trembling body backed into the door as he backed away from my daunting advance towards him. "I mean it! Stay back!"

"Now, now, that's not nice to be so hostile towards me after you invited me into your house. Or did you forget about the fun we had just now after a few drinks when you invited me back to your place after running into me? I mean, I know I'm not neurotypical, but I was sure we were having a good time with how you were laughing so carefree as you egged on my girl and spilled to me all the nasty little things you did to her in high school." I was like the sea right now, calm on the surface but turbulent underneath.

Initially, he became my next target because of what he pulled at the high school reunion. I thought about adding more names to my list, but after digging around, I found Harry here to be the grand mastermind and puppeteer. Everyone else got a scare of their lives with a little present from The Omen, the dubbed name the media had given my serial killing ego. Ted Bundy wannabe got a good beating though because he dared lay his hands on Avery and scare her further with his little tactics that night. Needless to say, he won't be grabbing anything for a while until his broken hands heal. He'll forever remember to keep his ugly mug hidden, lest he want to face ridicule by showing the lovely, jagged scar I gave him that ran across his face.

Devolving would have been so easy during the moment, and I could see how others like me in history fell prey so easily. The urge to become violent for the sake of it never burned the tip of my fingers so badly until I avenged Avery. Unlike the others who've been caught, my control kept me sane. Actually, Avery kept me sane. The thought of losing her, because I ended up in prison, was more than enough to reel myself back in and keep from going berserk.

With everyone else scared shitless, Harry was all who was left for me to torment—and kill. Yeah, he wasn't a criminal by the law, but he was in my books for embarrassing and bullying Avery at the event. My conviction grew beyond solid after I got chummy with him tonight, and he spewed all the horrible things he used to do to Avery, along with what he had planned to do to her on their prom night. He definitely had to die after hearing all of that. Fuck it, who gave a damn if he fell outside of my typical range of victims, an oddball kill won't hurt me, not with how careful I'd be like always.

"W-wha... Fuck... What'd you?" And that would be the sedative kicking in with his increased fumbling and stumbling and slurring of his words as he tried to scramble—and fail miserably—away from me.

"People always think they'd be able to easily tell if their drink has been spiked or not or that they'd see it coming a mile away. The truth is, you don't tell until it's too late, not until you feel its effects. Then the other thing is, you shouldn't drink something you have no idea about, which was your grave mistake when you woke up and took a giant swig of that glass of water that was conveniently in front of you." Of course, like all my other victims, he was stupid, irrational, and too easy.

My carefully curated and perfected method never went astray or wrong. Most of the time, I'd charm my way up to the victim to where they'd invite me into the house—saves me the trouble of breaking and entering—where I'd proceed to dose their food and/or drink with some Rohypnol.

Once they were out, then I'd situate myself and them in the center of their home, usually their living rooms, and wait for them to wake up, where I then give them my little spiel of why I did this, why them specifically—usually this entails outlining the bulk of their crimes—before giving them some false hopes by telling them to make a run for it. They never successfully escaped; I just wanted to see and taste some of the fear of their pathetic attempts before I stopped them a little ways from the door.

A trail of raven feathers to mark their final steps and journey in this life, a score to the ground with my knife to mark the exact spot their lives ended in this world because once I tied them up and hauled them into my truck, then that was it for them. Then, I'd leave a file of their crimes for the law enforcement to find when they'd inevitably come across the scene of the abduction.

Like I stated before, I had my clean-cut list of criteria for my victims: criminals the system let slip. Harry didn't fall into any of it, but he committed a more heinous crime in my books by wronging Avery.

An exception for my little raven.

"Did she tell you to do this? Is she making you do this? Listen, man, if she's making you do this, then just let me know, and we can go to the cops together and get her incarcerated for good before she creates more trouble. Listen, I told you about how weird she was in high school, and I know how much of a tease and bitch she can be. So, I can understand if she manipulated you." Harry blabbered on and on as I hauled him to his feet and dragged him to the back of my truck.

With a grunt of effort, I threw him onto the truck bed and climbed up into the space. Menacingly, I stood over his quivering body with my eyes narrowed in a harsh glare. "If you bothered to get to know her, then you'd know she's none of all of that. I'm doing this of my own volition because Avery's too nice to do anything. This is for my peace of mind, knowing a piece of her trauma will be dealt with. I was mainly doing this because of what happened at the reunion, but after you ran your mouth about what you did, what you planned to do. Well, you definitely dug your grave tonight."

The anger still simmered beneath my calm. "You're going to regret everything before I'm done with you. You're lucky I'm above having people rape you. Otherwise, I'd make it happen for you even thinking about defiling Avery." I wasn't *that* much of a monster.

Bending down, I grabbed his face and held up my knife to his pressed-out lips. "These are going to be the first to go along with your tongue for kissing and tasting her when she didn't want it." Then, I hovered the knife over his hand, "Then these go next for touching her." Then, the most precious place for any man, though I doubt he had anything usable between his legs. "Your pathetic boyhood will join you next in the grave.

I'll be sure you use the dullest knife I have to saw it off before shoving it into your bleeding mouth to let you suffocate while I bury you alive."

If it weren't so messy to hack a body up into multiple pieces, then I might indulge myself with Harry, but mutilation to that degree wasn't my forte. I only wanted to go after what mattered. Harry forced himself onto Avery on their prom night after stringing her along and tricking her. Things didn't go the way Harry planned, though, because Avery refused to drink anything alcoholic; he never went beyond shoving his tongue into her mouth and cupping a few feels.

He'd planned on drugging her and taking her that night, get some pictures and videos to spread around, smear Avery's name further than it already was, along with some other outcasts. Unfortunately for him, Avery stood her ground and fought back, so he never got to carry out his whole plan.

No punishment came for him back then, so he was long overdue for justice.

Standing back up, I delivered a swift kick to his face to stun him before stomping on his hand and crunching it under my foot until I felt his bones shift and give under my weight. With one hand broken, I quickly moved to the other hand. "Quit your screaming, no one's gonna help you. You're making my ears hurt." I noted out loud, with boredom lacing my voice as I stared down at his struggling body.

He lived on some property, and his closest neighbors were gone for the next few days. Literally, unless someone decided to jog by, no one would hear him. Just because no one could hear his cries didn't mean I wanted my eardrums rupturing. And, of course, he doesn't listen because they never do, which earned him another kick to the face.

Luckily for him, I wasn't one to make a mess of my truck; otherwise, I'd slice him up and gut him right here and now for disposal. Usually, I was more patient with my victims, but Harry pissed me off too much. Avery deserved justice now, not later.

Too bad killing him here and now would be overly sloppy of me.

So, after a brief struggle with Harry to bind him up more, I began to go about my typical routine of setting up the final scene before starting my final walk-through to ensure I picked up after myself and left nothing damning behind.

Harry wouldn't be the only exception and deviation from my norm tonight, either.

I never had my phone on during my little moments to fully submerge and enjoy myself, but Avery's call came through because I'd set her to bypass my 'Do Not Disturb' function because, well, she was my woman.

"Hey, I'll be ho—"

"JULIAN HELP! HE'S GONNA KILL ME!"

CHAPTER 29
Avery

"You should just let me at 'em still. I can't believe they did that to you, you're such an angel."

Liz huffed and puffed to herself as the two of us prepped the van to head out to a scene.

It'd been a few weeks since the high school reunion and my whole ordeal with everyone. Yes, it still stung to think about, but nothing could be done after the fact. So, I've learned to just put it behind me and move on. Obviously, Liz wasn't too happy about it because she wanted to go egg some houses, bash a few windshields in, maybe slash a few tires, and terrify the living shit out of those involved on my behalf. Well, I'm pretty sure she's put a few laxatives in some of our coworker's drinks the past few weeks as revenge because I did work with some of those I went to high school with.

"It's okay, I'm used to their antics..." It was the sad truth. Even if it had been a decade since I'd last had any pranks pulled on me, I'd been desensitized to it all by now.

Pulling a smile on my face, I threw my arms around Liz for a quick hug. "I saw Loreiz taking multiple bathroom trips earlier after his coffee." I snickered, giving Liz a knowing look, which she returned with a cheeky grin.

"Hm? Bad coffee? Told you the department needs a new coffee machine." She feigned innocence with a bit of snicker of her own before the two of us piled into the van to head off to our latest scene, some burglary and homicide in a rather decrepit place that looked like some drug den.

"Damn, what a sad life to live in a place like this." Liz sighed with a heavy heart as we entered the place with our equipment cases in hand.

"Not much of a life to live, I'd assume, once you hit this low. I mean, on the bright side, at least the holes in the place provided a nice ventilation. No dead body smell trapped in a rotting place." The smell never bothered me much to the point where I've had to puke, but it was still a horrendous smell I'd rather avoid getting hit in the face with full force.

It took us a while, but we managed to comb through every inch of the place from the bottom up to the second floor. We took longer than we'd like and longer than usual, but it was hard to shift through the place and discern what was actual evidence and what was residue or crap from patron activity. I can't exactly bag the whole house and every speck of dust it produced.

We were exhausted after hours of work and from working through our lunch hour. Unfortunately, the world wasn't kind to us today because we realized a grave mistake by the time we got back and unloaded the van.

"Fuck. We're so going to get our asses handed to us for this." Liz worried with a frown while pulling at her bleached blonde hair.

Removing her hands, I patted them down to her side before snagging the keys to the van from her. "It's fine, I'll just run back to the scene real quick and grab the case. God, I hope no idiot came across it and decides to jack it." A whole suitcase filled with evidence. We'd forgotten it in our tired haste to get back to the station to get some food in us. "Just grab something to eat real quick and start processing what we do have. I'll be back before you know it."

Please, please still be there.

I prayed to all that was holy and unholy out there in the world that the case would be sitting there fully intact when I got back to the scene. The place was still taped off to prevent people from wandering in, but it was in a shady part of town where people wouldn't give a shit about any of that. Worst case scenario: the case would be gone, and we'd be punished. We'd probably get suspended at most because this was our first offense, and we were the only two CSIs in the department; we were overworked by the hour, so we ran on fumes most of the time at scenes. As sad as it was to admit, we were bound to fuck up eventually—I just hope this wasn't it.

Frantically, I tore through the crime scene in search of the stupid case with bated breath. "Where is it, where is it, where is it?" I muttered to myself as I went through my third run of the place, refusing to accept that the case was gone.

"Looking for this?"

"Holy fucking shit!" Placing a hand over my exploding heart, I spun around with my exhale to face Detective Bornes. "Jesus fucking Christ, Carl, don't fucking scare me like that! What are you even doing here? You were on desk duty the last I remembered."

Yeah, the department chief wasn't too happy to witness Detective Bornes grabbing me as he did and throwing such accusations at me, so he was suspended from fieldwork for a month as a penalty. He wasn't one bit happy about it, and he made his detest very known every day from when he clocked on to when he walked off the premises. The brunt of it went towards me because, well, obviously, I was the reason for his suspension, which was stupid. After all, it was all his damn fault for being an asshole and grabbing me in the first place. He had no one but himself to blame for the consequences of *his own* actions.

"Yeah, how very convenient for you huh? What were you gonna do with this? Dig through it and scrap anything incriminating?" He accused me with narrowed eyes as he trudged up to me with the evidence case clutched tightly in his hand.

"Are you serious right now, Carl? I'm not the damn serial killer! How many times do I have to tell you that for it to sink into your dense ass brain? Also, nothing about this crime is related to the serial killer, it was burglary homicide." Pausing for a breath, I let out an annoyed huff before continuing. "For Pete's sake, we have the perpetrator in custody with a written and signed confession. It's an open-and-shut case. So, give me the damn case of evidence back, and I won't tell the chief you defied orders and came out here." I fibbed a little to threaten him into complying, but he didn't need to know that.

My outstretched hand for the case retreated at the sight of his gun being pulled out and pointed at me. "Carl," I said tersely with my hands in the air, "Put that away." This wasn't good. Having a gun pointed at you was never a good thing, ever.

With a shaky breath, I held my hands out towards him in a calming motion. "Carl, put the gun away, let's be reasonable and talk. I get it, you're pissed about the suspension, but there's no need to point that gun at me. All I want is the evidence case to take back to the station to process. So, please, put the gun away, I'm begging you." I pleaded with scared eyes while I struggled to keep my breathing paced.

Unfortunately, the soft *click* of his gun's safety being clicked off meant my words flew over his head. "Carl, please." My voice shook and cracked as my heart raced into my throat.

"Not so fun being on the other end, is it? Tell me, how much did your victims beg and plead for their lives before you ended them? Were they as pathetic as you right now?" The edge of his voice and eyes unsettled me greatly, causing my adrenaline to surge through my body.

Just in time to spur my body into action as he pulled the trigger. The deafening gunshot rang in my ears as I made it for the broken stairs, frantically scrambling up the uneven and broken steps with my sobs choking out of me with my mindless pleas for him to stop as he continued to shoot bullet after bullet at me.

Rounding the hallway's corner, I ducked into an open closet and nearly slammed the door off its hinges. Safe in the closet, the instinct to go for my own gun kicked in. Frantically, my hands patted my body down, my face growing heavy with a frown when I realized that I had left my gun in the car. Panic set in again, and my tingling hands crept around my body to pull my phone out of my pocket where my fumbling fingers struggled to dial the first person to come to my mind.

Julian.

911 would have been the better and more reasonable choice, but my one-track mind zoned into Julian. My fingers tapped away at the screen on autopilot before I even realized it, and by the time I did, the line was already ringing.

Well, at least if death were to happen, then I'd have my final moments with Julian.

THUD! THUD!

The door moving against my back, along with the pounding, had me screaming in terror and straightening my legs more against the wall opposite of me to keep my body pressed more against the door. My stiff body made the perfect doorstop with how my legs propped against the wall and kept my body pinned. "Open up you little bitch! Help won't come before I get to you! You can make this easy on yourself and agree to confess and I'll let you live!"

"You're insane!" I shouted back with a sob. "Please! Carl! You've got this all wrong! Please st—"

THUD!

"Ah!" Shaking, I clutched my phone tightly in my trembling hands as I sobbed helplessly.

Reprieve breathed fresh air into me for a split second before the horror of the situation slammed into me again when the line picked up. "Hey, I'll be ho—"

"JULIAN! HELP! HE'S GONNA KILL ME!" I blurted before letting out another terrified scream when the sound of gunshots rang out, and the door vibrated under me.

A violent shaking of the door causes my phone to slip out of my grip from my body, abruptly jerking in response to the force exerted by the door. Instinctively, I reached for my phone, only to discard the idea when I felt the door give from the little space I made from leaning forward. Locking my legs straight again, I pinned myself flat against the door again. "Julian! I—"

"I'm on my way! Stall him!" I faintly heard his voice through the phone's speaker, which was muffled a little by a pile of discarded clothing.

"No! Julian! I l—"

"Hang in there little raven, I'll be there before you know it!"

Beep beep beep!

My last shred of hope burned up as my walls came crashing down. "No, Daddy!"

That was it. I had my chance, and I completely blew it.

I'm gonna die here, and Julian will never know. I'm gonna die with such a huge regret.

Hopelessness settled deep into my bones as I felt them tire and ache from keeping myself propped against the door like a stopper to prevent Detective Bornes from busting the door down.

No! Nononono!

Snapping to my senses, I literally slapped myself with a hiss of pain from the sting.

No! I am not going down like this! Not by this pathetic cop who can't get a grip with reality! No! I refuse to go down like this!

Deep breaths puffed at my chest almost painfully as I forced myself to inhale more than usual to get oxygen rushing into my body and brain.

Think Avery, think, you have a brain, use it.

I told myself as I shuffled through my options mentally.

Wrestling my way out of this is definitely on the 'I think the fuck not bitch' list because, well, I might as well be running into a brick wall if I tried to take Detective Bornes on in a game of strength. No weapons on my body either, so I was already at a disadvantage to him having a fucking loaded gun.

Fuck me.

Dragging out a groaning sigh, I cleared the fog in my mind further until it was nearly empty because all the ideas were thrown out the moment they filtered in.

"Carl, you want a confession?!" Stall, I had to stall. Reasoning with him would be walking on eggshells, and with how strung out I was, I'd crack them. So, I had to appeal to him, feed into him, just long enough for Julian to get here.

"Finally realized you've got no way out huh!?" Damn maniac laughed on the other side of the door. "Come out here and we'll chat then with the whole thing recorded."

Yeah right, you damn psycho.

Crossing my arms, I let out a huff. "No. We're having this conversation right here, right now, through the damn door. I don't trust you as much as you don't trust me. I'm not going anywhere because I'm trapped in a fucking closet, so don't worry about me booking it. You, on the other hand, have a loaded gun that works, and you've shown many times that you're not afraid to lay your hands on me. So, I'm staying in here where it's safe." I argued with the refusal to budge.

A scoff could be heard before the door shook again softly after a hard *thud* hit the door. "Fine, but you're gonna have to come out of there eventually so I can take you down to the station. But fine, stay in a dingy druggie closet for your confession." The barrier of the holey door provided me with a false sense of security and safety from Detective Bornes.

"What do you want to know?"

Okay, you can do this, you see it all the time in Criminal Minds. Just talk to him, appeal to him, you can do this, just stall, that's all you have to do.

Yeah, way easier said than done.

Time dragged as my words flowed out of me almost robotically as I crafted some stupid but believable confession to him using known knowledge from the case and evidence I'd processed. I was a damn author who pantsed my story, so I can definitely weave a stupid confession on the spot like this with prior knowledge. Just another story; that's what I kept telling myself.

On the other hand, this conversation gave me a good story idea for a third book.

Suddenly, while I was in the middle of some stupid garble, Detective Bornes shouted at someone to stay back before the sound of gunshots filled the air, then what sounded like bodies hitting the ground. Abandoning the safety of the closet, I scrambled to my feet and threw the door open, afraid that what I heard was Julian's body dropping because who else would be here? Well, maybe some unlucky idiot could stumble upon us, but they wouldn't have warranted gunshots or the amount of shouting I heard.

The sudden pressure around my body caused me to startle with a bone chilling scream as fear gripped at my body. I thought the sudden force slamming into me was Detective Bornes until the familiar scent of soil, wood, and spice calmed my nerves like a warm wave of smooth water. Immediately, my arms threw themselves around my lover, and my body buried itself into him.

The calm washed away faster than I wanted, and tears burned their way down my cheeks as I broke down in sobs from my adrenaline crash. "Don't let me go, don't let me go, please tell me this is real," I begged while fisting his clothes.

Movement descended on my head, and a hand petted my hair while an arm remained anchored around my lower back. "Shh, shh, shh, I am here, it's me, I am real, you are safe, it's okay, you are safe. I got you, Avery, I got you. You are safe, my little raven, safe in my arms." Hearing his rich, deep voice filter into my ears sent a shiver down my spine as I melted into his embrace.

Before I could fully relax, my body was filled with fear again. Sucking a sharp breath, I shoved myself away from Julian to dart my head around for any sight or sign of Detective Bornes. "Hey, it's okay, he can't and won't hurt you anymore." Julian grabbed my shoulders and forced my wide eyes back to him.

Peering behind him, I could see the body of a familiar man. "Oh my God, did you—"

"No." Julian tersely cut me off. "I didn't kill him, just knocked him out."

I shouldn't be relieved at the fact, but I couldn't help the way the weight rolled off my shoulders, knowing Detective Bornes wasn't dead. With him out of the way, though, I shifted my attention entirely onto Julian, running my careful eyes down his body from head to toe multiple times. The only reason why I stopped was because Julian grabbed my face to keep my head still.

"I'm fine, he was a lousy shot." Julian let out a dry chuckle before pulling me into a tight hug. "Come on, let's get you outside, the others will be here soon to take care of everything."

"Hm? What do you mean?" I asked with a tilt of my head as Julian led me out to the front lawn by my hand.

"I called the cops the moment I hung up and sped over here." As he finished speaking, an unmarked car pulled up to the curb.

CHAPTER 30
Julian

"Where's your necklace bub? You haven't been wearing it lately."

Fuck, fuck, fuck, fuck, fuck.

Nothing else ran through my head but my own panic as I frantically searched for a valid excuse that didn't tear at my heart. I hated this stupid consciousness I've developed with Avery, because it hurt my heart to do this.

For once, lying to someone with a straight face seemed nearly impossible because it felt so suffocating. "It's at my desk at work. I've been helping my men out a bit lately and it kept getting caught and snagging, so I had to tuck it away somewhere safe." I gritted my lie through my teeth, forcing my tongue to weave the untrue words against my heart's protests.

"Oh... Okay." Fuck, the way she hung her head and frowned further gutted me.

Don't make it worse, don't—

"Come here." I continued to scream at myself mentally as I pulled Avery into my arms in an attempt to comfort her from my own lie. "I'm sorry. I will be more mindful of putting it back on after work."

If I can find the damn thing!

I have searched everywhere for the damn thing and had no luck. I spent a whole day while Avery was at work, tearing apart every inch of the house and nothing. Nothing at the office either. I could not, for the life of me, find the little trinket that I've actually come to treasure greatly. It hurt me to lose the pendant when I realized the lack of restriction around my neck.

Kissing her forehead, I patted her bottom playfully before taking a step back. "Take the car to work today. I'm gonna work from home today to get more business done. If I show up to the office, then the others will drag me out into the field, and I can't resist an opportunity to get my hands dirty." Another damn lie; I needed the time to myself to sort out this whole mess.

Avery's sad little pout made her look like a kicked puppy, and I couldn't help but reach out and wrap my arms around her waist. "You holding up okay darling?" Swaying her a little, I kissed her forehead. "They're not giving you too hard of a time at work, are they? Any word on what's going to happen to Detective Bornes yet?"

What happened at the crime scene caused quite a stir at the station and city because the detective had been a prominent figure around the place. Him losing his shit like that with Avery caused a lot of concern about the city's police department and what they could possibly be covering up if such an event like this occurred. At least the chief was adamant about taking Avery's side and tossing Carl Bornes to the wolves, which was an easy feat considering how he was in the wrong for his accusations against Avery and going about things the way he did.

Unfortunately, things haven't been easy for my poor Avery ever since the incident. Some people blamed her for everything; others took her side about how Carl was indeed a Grade-A douchebag. Of course, besides all of that, she started having nightmares that left her screaming every night until she woke up drenched in sweat and pale as a ghost or until I shook her awake and dealt with the minor panic attack that would ensue.

Sighing heavily, Avery wrapped her arms around my waist tightly and buried her face into my chest before letting out another loaded sigh. "I'll be okay... I just never thought he'd go so far as to corner and attack me like that. I mean, if he could do it, then the next cop could damn well do it too."

Taking a moment to breathe, she chewed at her bottom softly. "It's just a scary thought not to trust the people I work with, trust the good guys and all. Work's just been really tense for everyone since the whole thing. I'm also pretty tired of all the pity and sympathy from everyone. But, I'll be fine." Though present, her words sounded so distant with how cold and almost monotone and rehearsed they came out.

Something wasn't right. The whole air in the room shifted uncomfortably with each passing second as if this whole thing between us right now felt forced and out of place. "Is there something else on your mind, love?" Something festered under the surface, and I had to uncover it for the sake of my sanity.

"No." A lie.

Avery didn't elaborate or say anything else as she pushed away from me to grab her bag and head for the front door. "I'll be home for dinner." She hesitated for a moment before opening the door and leaving, shutting me inside the house with the suffocating silence.

Why would she lie to me? Why did she lie to me? Avery's never lied to me before, so why? Why the cold shoulder? Have I done something? No... I couldn't have... What the fuck was going on?

One train wreck after another, my erratic thoughts raced around my head and further fueled my rising frustration until I burst out in an angry scream that echoed throughout the house.

Taking in deep and controlled breaths, I gripped the back of my hair until I felt the sting of pain. I needed the stimuli to keep me rooted in reality right now. Otherwise, I would fly into a frenzy because of this damn confusion overfilling me.

What did I do? I have been nothing shy of being the perfect supportive boyfriend to her this whole time. Literally, there had been no deviation from our typical routine besides her nightmares, and maybe some extra time for herself, but other than that, nothing has changed. So, why? Why did she refuse to meet my eyes just earlier? Why did she lie about something not being wrong?

"Graaaaah! I don't get it!" I shouted at whatever phantom or ghost hung around my house.

I needed to distract myself. Work. Yeah, work.

Provided no such distraction.

The hours flew by at a numbing pace with my irritation. My mind paid no attention to the papers I pushed through over the hours or any of the appointments I made. I couldn't focus, no matter how hard I tried. The only thing—well, the only person—on my mind the whole time was Avery. I fretted over her nonstop behind my desk with my head in my hands.

Tension in my body strung tighter with Avery's arrival home that evening because she continued to give me the cold shoulder. I wanted to push the issue but didn't know how without sending us into a full-blown argument. Yes, arguments were a normal relationship thing, I know, but it didn't mean I wanted to have one. Though, it seemed to be an impending storm after a very tense and silent dinner.

I needed to get out of here and get some fresh air and space, and maybe my mind would clear after a bit of it. "I'm gonna head into town for some last-minute supplies and to grab some paperwork from the office... Uhh do you need anything?" My words dragged awkwardly as I lingered by the front door with my keys in hand while Avery remained situated on the couch with her laptop.

"Just some more chocolate and snack stuff, thanks." She replied flatly and bluntly without even tossing a single glance in my direction.

Whatever happened between us, I had a bad feeling about it.

After a trip to town and a bar, I finally returned home after a few hours, hoping maybe if I dragged time out long enough, I could avoid this situation with Avery altogether. It was my hope that Avery would be dead asleep by the time I got back past midnight. Maybe she would forget about it all and put it behind tomorrow morning, and we'd return to normal.

Sadly, it was wrong for me to hope for so much.

Like some brooding parent waiting in the dark for their child to come home, she sat on the couch with her arms and legs crossed, harsh gaze burning holes into me as I stood there stunned at the open doorway. "Are you cheating on me?" Her question came right off the bat when I walked through the front door.

"What?" Surely, I misheard.

"Are. You. Cheating. On. Me." She stated each word loud and clear with a tense jaw and hard expression.

Snapping out of my stupor, I shut the door, walked up to her, and sat on the coffee table across from her. "What? No! Why would you even ask or think that? What even gave you the idea or impression? Avery, what's going on? Talk to me, little raven, please." I sounded pathetic with how genuine I sounded; even I was surprised at my own voice when it bounced back into my ear.

Avery knocked my hands away with a scowl and hissing growl when I reached out for her. "You are home late more often than not, and you disappear at night. What do you think, Julian?" Scoffing out a dry chuckle, she ran a hand down her face. "But I believe you, and I know you are telling the truth, so you are capable of the truth." Now, I was utterly confused.

"Where do you go? What do you do?" By the determined look in her eyes, it seemed as if she knew the answer but wanted to hear it from me.

The smart move would be to give her what she wanted, but I turned into a stupid man. "I told you, work." I had to protect my image with Avery.

Scoffing, she let out a pathetic laugh that sounded mocking. "Work, huh?" Shifting in her seat, she reached into her back pocket, pulled out a bunched-up evidence bag, and slammed it right into my chest with an open hand. "Which one? The one where you run your company and build shit, or the one where you kidnap and murder people?"

Her hand dropped from me, and the bag landed in my open hands. Inside it was my necklace, the one she gifted me. Stunned and confused, all I could do was look at her dumbfounded as I bounced my wide eyes back and forth between her and the bag; a part of me hoped maybe the bag would disappear if I looked away enough.

"You wanna know where I found that?" Her words shook with anger as her breaths became heavier.

When I remained silent, she continued. "At a fucking crime scene. I thought surely it was a mistake, but no, not after I turned it around and saw our initials and date carved into it." Her body shot up from the couch in fury as she threw her hands up with a scoffing groan. "Just, what the fuck Julian?"

Pacing, she ran a hand down her face while keeping one hooked on her hip. "I can't believe it. This whole time, you have been lying and deceiving me." Stopping, she looked at me with disbelief and scoffed with a shake of her head before her pacing continued, "My fucking boyfriend is a fucking serial killer. Oh my God, I'm sleeping with a serial killer. Holy fuck, oh my God," freezing in her spot, she looked at me with shocked eyes, "I let you fucking chase me through the woods like a fucking psycho!"

Gripping her hair, she muttered to herself as she resumed her pacing. "Tell me, was any of this real to you? Us? This relationship? Or is it all some big sham or twisted sick game to you? Did you think it was funny to string me along? Oh, I bet it was just rich for you, of course, huh? Date the fucking CSI who works your scenes!" Letting out an empty laugh, she shook her head again. "Great, just fucking great! And of course I'm just a stupid fool who doesn't know any better and falls for your stupid charms. How could I not fucking see it? I see it in everyone else, yet I couldn't even see that my own boyfriend is a fucking serial killer."

Standing up, I closed the distance in a few strides and grabbed her arms. Bad move. "Don't fucking touch me!" She snapped and reeled back from me with a distasteful scowl and glare.

"Avery, listen—"

Growling at me, her hands burned my chest as she attempted to shove at me—and failed at it. "No! I won't be listening to anything you say!" Her voice lowered in volume after a few heavy breaths. "I can't believe it. It all must be some fucked up nightmare, but the evidence is there. I fucking touched it! I just... I can't believe this whole fucking time." The way her voice cracked broke my heart. "You lied to me, kept the bag over my head, strung me along, and played me like a stupid fiddle. And I fucking fell for it. For all of it. I let you in, let you close in more ways than just physically.

Why would you even do any of this? Why? You have any idea how hurt I am?"

"I love you!"

"I fucking love you!"

Stunned silence gripped us with our simultaneous confession.

"I love you." I broke the silence with my cracked voice, using her stunned silence to get my words in. "I did it all because I love you, Avery."

It wasn't for effect. My legs really did give out under me, sending me to my knees in front of her. "From the moment I saw you in the library, you stirred something within me, something no one has ever done before. I knew then and there that you were special. I searched for you until our date, and when I saw you sitting pretty, ready for my hands to steal you away, I couldn't help it. I'm too selfish of a bastard to let you go, so I took you. I took you because you made me feel things I never thought possible."

A weak chuckle broke out of me as I looked up at her with genuine eyes. "When I smile with you, it's a real smile, not the plastic one everyone sees. My words with you are never empty or filled with false promises to manipulate you. Never once have I wronged you in any way because I can't. The thought of hurting you or doing anything ill to you physically sickens me. I didn't understand these feelings at first, but over time with you, I realized that what I feel for you is what you neurotypical people call love."

Through shaky breaths, I continued to bleed my heart out to her. "I couldn't lose you. If I came clean to you, then I'd lose you, and I couldn't have that. The more I fell deeper in with you, the harder the thoughts of having a life without you became. So, I couldn't, I just couldn't. You have to believe me Avery. I swear, I am not lying to you now. I love you. I truly and genuinely do, and only you. The only things I ever lied about were my late nights out because that's when I'd be killing. Other than that, I have never lied to you about anything, especially now."

Desperate and broken, I continued to look up at her for any ray of hope that our relationship would be salvageable. Even though my gut sank to the depths of the ocean floor, my heart held out for that tiny spark.

But who was I kidding? This relationship of ours was doomed from the start. Who in their right mind would willingly choose to stay with a person like me? Especially someone like her.

This was it.

This would be the end of us, the end of me.

No way would she stick around me now, knowing the truth.

All I could do now was wait for the cops to show up, cuff me, and ship me off to death row.

I should be mad at the thought of it all, but I wasn't.

I got to taste a slice of paradise during my time with Avery.

Avery graced my putrid life with her warmth and love, and I will forever cherish it as I'd rot away in prison.

This was it.

I love you, my little raven.

CHAPTER 31
Avery

I STILL SEE HIM.

Even when he's not around me, his presence lingers. Well, that and I literally see him watching me from across the street from my apartment window.

Julian wasn't in jail, as crazy as that sounded.

"I can't do this." It was clear what should be done, but I couldn't bring myself to do it.

I should be running far away from Julian right now, straight to the police station to write up a report, to send my coworkers here to apprehend this monster.

No, that wasn't right, to call him a monster, to think of him as one, even if it was one.

"I need to go." My movements felt controlled, like a puppet on a string, as I grabbed my bag and made for the door.

"Wait!" Julian's body inserted itself between me and the way out.

"No! Back off, or I swear I'll punch you!" A pathetic threat, but I had to try.

"Please... Just... Just one last hug, and one last kiss, that's all I ask of you before you leave me for good." He begged with apparent desperation, which ached my heart.

His eyes were so broken and sad, but what, I don't know. Was he upset over our relationship ending? Or having his secret be out finally and being caught?

Well, even prisoners get their last meal before execution.

He could very well use this opportunity to kill me, bury his secrets with me, but I sensed no malice from him. All I saw and felt was a desperate man wanting some peace before being parted with.

Against my better judgment, I relented. Not because he requested it, though, but also for me.

The moment I walk out that door would be a chapter of my life going up in flames.

So, I threw my arms around him and leaned up, pressing my lips against his in a frenzy, shoving all my feelings of affection, devotion, love, and hurt into the deep and passionate kiss.

Our final kiss.

"I love you, little raven."

That was three nights ago, three nights since I had any contact with Julian. I returned to my apartment that night and have remained here since. The last thing I ever said to Julian was a text message the next morning.

> I need some time to think. I'm not gonna turn you into the police, but I'm also not fine with all of this… Just give me some time and space, please. This isn't the end, I just need to digest everything before I turn back to you… Hopefully.

I couldn't bring myself to do it, even if it were the legal and right thing to do. Well, right was debatable. Yes, him murdering people was most definitely wrong, and he really should be rotting in jail for those crimes. Yet, I couldn't. Why? Because I was still alive. Why hadn't he killed me? Besides the fact I was different than other people he's encountered in his life. But also, if I really think about it, he's only killed the 'bad' people really... Well, who's to say he killed those people? Bodies were never found, so there—wait, never mind, he blatantly confessed to me three days ago.

Fuck, how did I end up in this shit show? Things like this don't happen in real life, just the movies or books. I mean, in a book, this would be cute—actually, never mind again because it was basically my own fucking book that I'd published with his help. Oh God, he helped me with the scenes in my book, and I wondered why he was so perfect!

"Fuck!" I groaned out loud and ran my hands through my face before pulling my curtains shut with a quick scowl at Julian because I was pissed at him.

Why am I even entertaining any of this? There shouldn't even be an 'us' still. I can't be with a serial killer! Granted, he was handsome and dashing as hell and treated me perfectly. Besides the serial homicidal maniac part, he was a perfect life partner. But I digress: I can't be with a fucking serial killer!

Julian said he loves me, but can people like him even truly love someone?

Okay, stupid question because my search history was filled with those questions. So, yes and no. I mean, it flattered me to be his exception. Yet, at the same time, after knowing all of that, I couldn't help but wonder if it was only a matter of time before something would happen to his feelings. What if he grew bored of me? Then what? Dispose of me, then?

Also, I know he said he kept it all from me to protect me and keep our relationship alive, but did he plan on hiding it for the rest of our lives? Or did he plan to stop killing? I highly doubt the latter because people like him usually don't just quit it without significant repercussions. If he had intentions of ever coming clean to me, then when? How?

Honestly, I doubt he ever would because his secret coming out meant the end of our relationship and his livelihood. Or so I thought.

We were separated, but not officially or truly broken up because I was a fucking idiot who couldn't let go of the only good thing in my life, even if he turned out to be not so good...?

Yeah, he was a serial killer, but again, he was a very good man. And, I mean, how bad of a person could he really be if he only went after criminals who deserved what they had coming to them?

Lordy, what the hell was I even thinking? I shouldn't be siding with a criminal, even if he was my boyfriend. I worked for the law, for Pete's sake!

Ping!

Like clockwork, his message came through at 8 o'clock on the dot.

> Don't forget to eat a decent meal and drink lots of water, and no coffee or energy drinks until tomorrow morning. I'll be watching over you and keeping you safe like always, little raven.

I hated how my heart fluttered at his daily messages. I never bothered to reply to any of them, though, but I also didn't bother trying to block him or anything either. Needless to say, I've been a total mess ever since the blowout. I knew what *should* be done and, technically, what I *had* to do. But I couldn't.

The crazy thing, even after knowing everything, I still felt an immense love for Julian, and it didn't feel wrong, which was insane because I should *not* be remotely fine with being infatuated with a serial killer!

But he's a good serial killer.

Yeah, my heart refused to accept the horrid truth of this all. My logical brain screamed at me to go to the police, report his ass, and try to move on with my life because it was the right thing to do. Or at least right in the mind of the law and maybe morally. Unfortunately, life wasn't so black and white, no matter how much I argued with myself.

I must admit, he's been nothing but perfect still. Despite his obsession with me, he respected me enough to respect and abide by my rules and wishes. He's made it pretty damn clear and known to me what he wanted to do to me following my decision to put this distance between us. Hearing—reading—it all unnerved me a little, but at the same time, I couldn't help but feel some excitement over his possessiveness. Hell, I still read those messages late at night and pleasure myself to them.

Shaking my head, I cleared my mind of everything to unwind fully for the night. No point in stressing myself out when I knew damn well my mind won't be made up any time soon, or ever.

Honestly, it was childish of me to drag it all on at this point, but I wasn't ready to fully accept the baggage that would come with my decision.

An annoyed groan tore out of me at the sound of my phone going off. I, being an idiot, picked it up without checking the caller ID. "What? What happened to giving me space?"

I wished it was Julian, though, after hearing the shrill of the other side. "Excuse you, we taught you better than that. You see what happens when you don't live with us?"

Hanging up on my parents crossed my mind, and my nerves moved my thumb over the red button at the bottom of my phone screen. "I'm sorry mother. I thought you were someone else." The temptation pushed my finger closer to the screen.

As much as I wanted to be a brat and hang up, I was taught better and still had those teachings ingrained into my very being. "How are you and father? Is there a reason for your call?" I asked through gritted teeth as I fought with the demon on my shoulder.

"Well, if you keep in touch with us as you should, then you would know that your father is not doing well with his heart. We want to have dinner with you tomorrow to discuss some things and reconnect with you. Lao's Lounge, 7 o'clock. Do not be late. Oh, and put on something nice, not those pants or homeless outfits you wear." Not as much as a 'bye' before the line cut out.

I could just not show up. They didn't know where I lived, so they couldn't come by and literally drag me out. I didn't owe anything to them, not like they gave me anything besides a fuck ton of emotional and psychological trauma. On the other hand, a free fancy dinner was a free fancy dinner. Who knows, maybe they do want to try and mend things after all this time.

Yes, my parents were assholes, but I couldn't help but yearn for an actual relationship with them to gain some kind of genuine affection. It wasn't healthy to want for such, but I couldn't help it. One dinner won't kill me. If things went off the rails, then I could always get up and leave.

CHAPTER 32
Julian

I NEVER KNEW IT was possible to actually feel my heart break, because, well, a heart was just another organ—and organs don't 'break.'

I thought the worst of it was the lies I fed Avery, but the moment she left after our final kiss, she somehow ripped my heart out of my chest and took it with her. I felt so empty, so dead, even though physically I was alive. It truly felt as if there was a void in my chest where my vital organ should be. It was there still, doing its job pumping my blood throughout my entire body. Yet it felt dead.

And every time I thought about Avery, or even saw any mention of her around my place, the stupid fist-sized organ clenched and tore in half it felt like. I felt so pathetic, so low, so fucking human. I hated it. I hated how Avery turned me 'normal' when I built myself to be above everyone else. Yet, deep down below the anger and resentment, I felt immense gratitude towards my little raven. If not for her, then I would never have gotten to truly live and enjoy life. Only when I had fallen deeply for her did I realize the joys of life around me. Simple acts like home-cooked meals, cuddles on the couch, strolls around the backyard, and stupid shit like that became things I looked forward to every day besides my deadly hobby.

Avery became a facet of my life that I thrived for. Waking every morning with her in my arms was the most wonderful thing ever. I honestly never thought anything or anyone would ever come close to giving me the pleasure that killing gave me, yet everything I felt for Avery was so much more than the immense rapture I got from hunting and killing my victims. Dare I say it, I might even give up serial killing for Avery if I knew I could live without it. Unfortunately, if I tried to cut that part of myself away, then I'd be nothing but a husk. As much as I loved Avery, that was a part of me that could never be changed. To me, giving up serial killing would be the equivalent of ceasing to eat or drink—I'd survive, but not for long.

The mere fact of it all tore at me almost as much as Avery's decision to take a break from me. I can't ever change that aspect of my life, and I was afraid that because of my twisted side, I'd lose Avery for good.

Even now, I couldn't keep myself away from my sweet Avery. Like a desperate creep, I stood across the street from her apartment window and watched her through it until she noticed and shut the curtains. I know I agreed to give her space, and I have. I haven't physically approached her or tried to force a conversation onto her ever since that night. But I couldn't let her be. I needed to ensure her safety. So, I settled with watching her from afar.

I bugged her a bit with daily reminders to eat and to be healthy in an attempt to keep her from slipping back into her bad habits, and so far, she hasn't told me to shut up. Granted, she hasn't responded to me—not even once. Well, at least she still accepted the food I'd drop off for her at the station and at her doorstep. Now, I didn't know whether or not she actually ate the food, but she took it. So, I would count my wins in this matter.

It was probably stupid of me to torture myself like this, though, following Avery around like a lost puppy at the distance. But I only do so because I cared and worried for her and her well-being. Even if, by the end of all this, she chooses to completely sever our relationship, I'd still watch and care for her from afar. There would be no one else in my life that would ever take Avery's place. Avery would forever be my one and only, even if she didn't see things that way anymore.

If this scenario were to happen early in our relationship—well, it wouldn't have early on, actually. Old Julian would have never let her leave the house. She'd be chained up in the basement for all of eternity until she changed her mind or until she died of natural causes because no way in hell would the old me give her this grace. Unfortunately for my old self, Avery's changed me into a better person, more or less. Like I said before, I was grateful yet hated how she's made me more 'human' in a sense. She made me vulnerable, and I appreciated that in a way because it made Avery all that more special to me.

As much as I wanted to keep her locked away for myself forever. The thought of it now disgusted me because it would be such a wrong towards Avery. I'd truly lose her completely if I dared do such a thing. Though a forgiving person, there's no way she would ever forgive me for forcing her to remain in my life like some caged bird. Besides, I wanted Avery for Avery. If this was some physical obsession, then the kidnapping and imprisonment plan could work, but I wanted *all* of her. I wanted her smiles, giggles, the innocent and playful sparks in her eyes, her little witty tongue, her sarcastic remarks, the warmth and genuine affection from her touch and loving eyes. I would have none of that if I locked her away in my depressing basement. I might as well straight up kill her at that point because she'd be nothing but a resentful shell of a person towards me.

I also haven't killed a single person—or animal—ever since she separated from me. But that might very well change tonight. Although I'm not entirely sure how becoming of me it would be to murder my future in-laws, even if they were pieces of shit from what little Avery has told me about them. I don't know what her mother said to her on the phone call because I never got as far as hacking her phone or cloning it, so all I had to go off on was the video feed of the camera that remained hidden in her place still.

It concerned me with how Avery's demeanor changed when she picked up the phone and realized it was her mother on the other end. I wanted so badly to barge into her place and embrace her in my arms when

I saw her shoulders tense, and her lips pulled down into a frown. I wanted to cheer her up, make her feel better, and let her vent her anger.

I already knew she didn't have the best of relationships with her parents, so I doubt a call from them was any good, especially with how she reacted. I could easily make that problem of hers go away—I mean, no parents meant no more problems. Unfortunately, I highly doubt Avery would appreciate that kind gesture from me.

Well, whatever conversation happened between them got Avery going. I couldn't help but feel a spark of anger while I watched her throw on a cute knee-length dress that had a soft pink top whose halter top wrapped around her delicate little neck, making it look so much more delectable to me. Then the flowy cream skirt of it—fuck, I wanted to bunch it around my hands to gain access to her sweet cunt underneath her lace panties.

Why in the fuck did she need to dress up like that for? Surely it couldn't be her parents, right? Why would she dress up for her parents, whom she hasn't spoken to in nearly a year?

Whatever the reason, I would find out in a bit because I planned to follow her to her destination. Unfortunately, I only wished it was a welcomed sight. I only intended on observing from my table a few down from her family's, but I couldn't control my own motions and words when a pathetic man showed up—it all turned out to be some stupid hookup by her parents. Disbelief and rage filled my calm exterior when I heard her parents refer to the man as her fiancé—I honestly never wanted to vomit in my life until I heard those words from her parent. Then, everything turned up ten notches when Avery's precious body was struck by her own parent.

Would it really be *that* bad to kill my in-laws before they officially became my in-laws?

I mean, what was that saying? Better to ask for forgiveness than to apologize? Something like that? I mean, Avery couldn't get *that* mad at me for killing her parents, with whom she had a poor relationship with already, especially after they turned violent against her and tried to pawn her off into some marriage to better their business connection like she was some object or commodity to be traded.

CHAPTER 33
Avery

PERHAPS I HOPED FOR way too much.

Upon entering the fancy oriental restaurant, I was met with a set of cold eyes and fake smiles from my parents as I approached their little private table in the reserved section. "Hi mother, father." I returned their chilling gazes with a small but warm smile of my own as I reached my arm out to hug my mother, only to be met with a brush off from her.

Not gonna lie, that hurt. Yeah, I should have known better; they've never been big on displaying any kind of affection growing up. Again, I had my hopes way too high.

Taking the empty seat next to my mother, I kept my smile up as I looked at both of them. "I have to admit, this is a bit of a surprise. You haven't spoken to me in over a year about." Putting the timeframe out in the open gave me a dreadful feeling in the pit of my stomach.

Nothing.

An awkward silence later, my mother's unsavoriness broke it. "At least you do not look homeless, so you can listen still." My mother harped on me as she gave me a once over, taking in my soft pink and cream halter top dress that came down to my knees.

Sensing this dinner wouldn't go how I hoped, I got up from my seat with a crestfallen expression. "I think it's best I leave if this is what your attitude towards me the whole night is going to be. Goodbye, mo—"

A panting man appeared beside me before I could finish my farewell, turn around, and leave. "Mister and missus Le, I am so sorry for my tardiness. The business meeting ran behind."

"Grant, no, no, no don't apologize. We are glad you could still join us. After all, a C.E.O. like you has to have a lot on his plate." My mother's demeanor instantly changed with her bright smile, which irritated me to no end.

So, she could smile warmly, just not towards her own child. A knife stuck itself into my gut at the warm exchange before me with my parents and this young man. "I'm so sorry, I'm Grant, Grant Xu. You must be Averline." The man, Grant, turned his bright and smiling face towards me before holding out a hand for me to take in a shake.

Forcing my twitching lips into a smile, I reached out and took his hand in a quick shake before taking my limb back to my side. "Avery, my name's Avery." I corrected him before slinging the strap of my purse over my shoulder. "Have a good dinner. Obviously, you are more welcomed than me." I bit out in a cold and bitter voice towards my parents before turning around fully, only to be stopped by my mother grabbing me and forcing me to sit down at the table again.

"Oh, don't be silly, food is almost here, and Grant is here now." Judging by her overly friendly tone and talon-like nails digging into my shoulders, this whole thing was a setup.

"It's so lovely to finally meet you Avery—"

"Averline. Avery is such a childish-sounding name. I don't know why she insists on going by it." My mother interrupted Grant with an overly sweetened giggle and a silly wave of her hand.

"Because it's the name you gave me." I gritted out with a scowl, glaring at my mother with sharp, irritated eyes.

Taking a deep breath, I softened my face as I turned towards Grant. "Listen, I'm sorry for whatever lies they've told you about me to trick you into this little dinner date, but I am not interested. I'm sure you're a great guy, but I am taken, sorry." Well, it felt good not to lie about my relationship status for once, even if it was still in the air.

I didn't get up fully from my seat before a strong hand gripped and yanked me back down into my seat. "Averline, you will not be rude to your fiancé. Now, apologize and be good for once and sit." Shockingly, it wasn't my mother this time, but it wasn't like my father's harshness was any better.

"Excuse you? Fiancé?" Wrenching my arm from my father's hand, I narrowed my eyes at him. "Listen, I don't know what delusional game you and mom are playing at, but I'm done. Obviously, it was a mistake to come here tonight. A mistake to hope that this would be the reunion I dreamed of."

A sharp sting snapped my head to the side with my shocked gasp. "You insolent child, we are doing you a favor by setting you up with someone as great as Grant. You do nothing but crawl around in those stupid houses and run towards a dead-end with that stupid ambition of writing those stupid stories of yours. Grant here will take care of you. It's the least you could do for us to ease the burden you've been on our lives." No one in the place dared to move towards us, which was no surprise because this whole place was crawling with vermin businessmen.

Seems like Grant was no better either because his friendly demeanor dropped in an instant. "I hope she's not usually this disobedient and head-strong. I already told you what I wanted. If she doesn't deliver, then the deal's off, old man." His judgmental eyes glanced me over disgustingly with a scowl on his face.

"She is all you asked for. Just get her behind closed doors, and her tone will change." My father assured this deplorable man next to me with a dismissive wave of his hand.

By some grace of the heavens, my silent prayer was answered. "Hey darling, I know I said I couldn't make it to dinner with your parents, but I wrapped things up sooner than expected. I hope I am not too late or interrupting something too important?" I didn't give a damn if God sent me the devil, he was my devil, and that's all that mattered.

"I am sorry, this is a private dinner." Pissed would be an understatement to describe the murderous look and tone of my father's voice as he stood to size Julian up.

Not letting this miracle save slip, I shot up from my seat, wrapped my arms around Julian, and leaned up to press a grateful kiss against his lips. PDA wasn't our thing, but fuck it because I wanted to shove it into everyone's faces right now. "I'm so glad you could come, babe. You are just on time. I was about to tell them about my wonderful boyfriend and how we're about to celebrate our one-year anniversary." I lied without an ounce of hesitation as I smiled venomously at my parents, who looked like they just witnessed me grow out three heads.

"Mom, dad, and I guess Grant now too, this is Julian, my boyfriend." I dug the knife deeper into them by remaining glued to Julian and smiling at them with a shit-eating grin.

"Julian Smith? Owner of Black-Smith Inc.?" Granted seemed more stunned by Julian's appearance than the bomb I dropped. "Oh man, Grant Xu, it's amazing to meet you in person like this. Huge fan of you and your company, I mean, the things you guys work on, your projects, your net worth, and everything, amazing." Wow, this guy seemed more in head over heels for my boyfriend than me with how much he kissed Julian's ass.

"You know this man, Grant?" Now, my father's tone changed from hostile to interested as he fixed his suit jacket and straightened himself out. "Apologies, Averline hadn't told us about you, so—"

"Save it, old man." Julian snapped with a stone-cold glare, making my father flinch back a little. "*Avery* hasn't gotten a chance to say anything with how you and her mother have been bullying her around. Drop the sweet act. I saw and heard everything from the moment Avery walked into the place. Never have I been so disgusted by a human being until I saw your interaction with Avery, who is your own daughter."

Scoffing angrily, he scowled deeply at my family. "You know, I already knew you were bad from what Avery told me, but now I can see that she was being very generous. I can't believe you two disregarding your daughter's identity and well-being for your own sick gains, calling her up only to use her as a stupid pawn." His face softened lovingly when he glanced at me, but the anger came back when his eyes left me. "Avery is such a wonderful woman who deserves so much better than you two and this sham you're trying to set her up with. I bet you don't even know about how his company is tanking, which is why he's so eager to get into business with you as a fallback."

His last bit of information quickly turned my father on Grant, and of course, my overly dramatic mother nearly had a coronary at all of this. Then, like the snake she is, she recovered enough to give Julian a saccharine smile. "Listen, this isn't what you think or what it looks like. Why don't you sit down and join us for dinner? We can talk about all of this, and we can welcome you to the family properly." She reached a hand out toward Julian's shoulder, only to have him shrug away as if she were diseased.

"No, and soon Avery won't be related to you in any way, shape, or form once she changes her last name to mine." If I had a drink, then I would have spat it out with how much confidence Julian said all that, as if we weren't in an awkward separation with each other because of *his* secrets.

"You cannot marry my daughter. You do not have permission to." My father argued with a reddening face.

"Too bad we're in America and in the 21st century, so I don't need it. Nor is Avery your property. Now, if you'll excuse us, I am removing us from this unsavory scene and situation." Julian mocked my father with a proud smile, wrapping his arm around my waist and leading me away from my sputtering father.

After a few steps, Julian spun us around with a proud and smug smile at my parents. "Oh, and if you had even bothered to keep up with your daughter and support her like decent parents, then you'd know about her new-found fame as bestselling author with her newly published book. In fact, she's about ready to surpass this," Julian paused for a second to gesture lazily at Grant with a disgusted frown, "Thing in terms of fame and wealth with all the events she's booked out with along with the movie deals flooded her way." Julian didn't give my parents a chance to correct their stupid sputters as he turned us around and proudly walked out with me safely tucked in his arm.

"Thank you, but this changes nothing between us," I spoke in a soft voice to him as we exited to the street.

Turning to face me, Julian took my face in his hands and smiled at me almost sadly. "I didn't do it to get in your good graces. I did it because it was the right thing to do. I told you I will always watch over you and keep you safe. Even if you chose to end us, I will always be your shadow, your little guardian demon."

Taking a deep breath, he steeled himself. "I won't deny that I am not a good man, but to you, I will always be nothing shy of perfect because you deserve perfection and so much more. I'm not gonna be your hero who saves you. I am your demon who will slaughter anyone and everyone who dares to jade you. I am a killer, and that will never change either. But I am your killer, your tool, and I will forever taint my hands to keep your world safe and perfect." With such conviction and honesty, it was hard not to let my insides turn to mush at his sweet but twisted words.

"Stay the night with me."

CHAPTER 34
Julian

HOME. I ALWAYS SAID my home is my place to retreat, a shelter to keep me from the elements and to house my devious hobby. My house was my perfect home, so I thought. Truly, home was Avery, as stupid and cliché as it sounds, but she somehow became my home. My house never felt bare, empty, or sad until Avery left me for a month and a half. The life in my place went with her through that door the day she crossed it for—what could have been—the last time. Shameless for me to admit, but I haven't really been back to my house much throughout the last six weeks; I'd downgraded to living out of my truck, which was always situated across from Avery's apartment, and I'd wash up, and clean up at the employee locker room at work or in my private work bathroom.

When her message came through, I literally dropped everything and sped my way down the roads to Avery—to home. Her car, well technically mine, was parked out front by the time I arrived, and I only hoped I didn't keep her waiting too long.

Yet, all my excitement was killed with my engine. It didn't occur to me in my flurry of hope, but what if this was goodbye? What if she was here to cut it all off finally? Take her things back to her place and remove her very soul from this place and my heart. I should have thought more about the meaning behind her message instead of letting myself become blind to my feelings for her. This could very well go the other way.

A heavy silence fell upon me as I stewed inside my chilling truck, eyes warily locked on the front door. It was a stupid idea, but I could turn around and avoid her for the rest of my life. It's too bad my pride wouldn't let me become a coward. I had to see what she wanted, face the music and shit. Besides, maybe it was something good how I initially made it out to be; this could be the beginning of a new us.

The first step was to get out of the truck and actually get my ass into the house. Otherwise, I'd get nowhere—literally and figuratively. So, very reluctantly and with a bated breath, I climbed out of my truck and approached my own house as if it were some prison. Before I could change my mind, my hand swung the door open, and my feet carried my unwilling body into my foreign home.

Avery was nowhere in sight, but she was here judging by her purse sitting on the door side table with her keys. Her name hung on my tongue as I opened my mouth, refusing to come out because of these nerves and butterflies in my stomach—another thing I never thought possible for me to have or feel. Unable to call out for her, I slowly walked towards the hallway. It didn't feel like me, like my whole body, mind, and heart had a mind of its own.

I was a rational man; I shouldn't be losing control of myself like this, letting my mind and heart lead my body based on feelings. Soon, I found myself staring down the staircase that led down to the second basement door—the first that lined the hallway having been opened already.

Shit.

Sucking in a deep, shaky breath, I descended the stairs and mentally prepared myself for whatever Avery would throw at me once she'd discover my secondary holding area. I still haven't fully fixed up my primary one, so the basement has seen much use over the past few months.

My achingly tense face relaxed at the sight of her standing before the shut door. She didn't go beyond, and she didn't enter. Good.

"Is this..." Avery's shoulders rose and held for a second before her long exhale was heard as her head turned back towards me, burning me with her wary, scared, and curious eyes into me. "Is this where it happens? Your kill chamber? Is that the reason why you forbade me from going near the basement? So you could continue to hide your horrors from me?"

Not wanting to have this conversation in a dark stairway, I took her hand in silence and led her back up the stairs to the living room, where I sat her down on the couch next to me and faced her after twisting my body a little. "Yes, and no. The basement really is just that, a basement, for the most part, and I use it mainly for storage and all of that. I actually built a secondary place that's connected to the basement, where I have a secure holding area for my victims and where I keep my tools. I don't kill in my basement or my kill chamber."

Blinking a few times, Avery held a hand out for me to pause. "Wait, I'm not walking on bones and bodies out in the backyard and garden, am I? Please don't tell me you use them as fertilizer, which is why your garden flourishes so well." Her words were paced with worry, but she also sounded hopefully curious.

Unable to help it, I cracked a smile and chuckled with a shake of my head. "Sweetie, come on, I'm a professional. Bodies in my backyard garden? Come on, I'm kind of hurt you'd think I'd be that much of an amateur to be so risky." Keeping the amused smile on my face, I turned my tone serious, "I don't kill in the house or around the house."

"Where?" She deadpanned, looking at me as if she was done with me. "Where, Julian? Where did you kill people?" She continued to press when I didn't spit my answer out fast enough.

With a sheepish grin, I pointed a finger behind me. "There's a reason why I got thirty acres of land... There are lots of areas to safely dispose of someone... After a good chase..." Why did it feel so embarrassing to admit all of that to her? As if I was some child caught with their hand in the cookie jar.

"Show me." She demanded with a huff and cross of her arms.

"What?" Show her what? Where I killed people? Because that would be rather hard to do because I killed everywhere back there in the forest.

"Your routine. Show me what you do," she said in a determined voice as she leaned closer to me with a widening smirk and eyes buzzing with curious excitement. "You got me, I'm your victim, so show me."

Fuck, that shouldn't excite me so much, not when we were supposed to be having a serious conversation. But how could I deny her when she practically egged me on? "Little raven, you don't know what you're asking of me." I warned her with a grave voice as I ran a hand down my face and rested it on my lower jaw, which clenched tightly.

Unfurling her arms, she settled her hands on the tops of my thighs and leaned in real close to me until her face was a mere inch from mine. "I'm not asking. I'm telling." Leaning in closer, she brushed her lips against the shell of my ear. "So. Show. Me."

"Safe-word?" I knew what she asked of me, but even if I indulged her and let loose, she still had complete control.

Her breathy answer sent a bolt of pleasure straight down into my throbbing cock, making it twitch and strain against my tight work pants. "Guilty."

Unleashed, I grabbed her arms and pulled her off of me before standing up and dragging her over to the backdoor. The door nearly flew off its hinges with how hard I threw it open before shoving her across the threshold. "Ten minutes, fucking use it. If I catch or find you, then you're mine. Mine to do whatever I want." Excitement flicked my tongue across my lips as I held up my wrist and tapped my watch. "Tick tock, better spread those wings and fly little raven, while you can."

A flash of excitement spread on her giddy, grinning face, and she turned on her heels and sped off. Gripping the doorframe, I held myself back from going after her sweet little ass as it grew further and further away from me until she disappeared into the tree line with her black curtain of silky hair flowing out behind her. "Fuck, you don't know what you're in for, baby." I growled softly as I shed my coat and discarded it on the patio table.

Ten torturous minutes ticked by painstakingly slow, but ten minutes on the dot, and my feet took off before my brain registered anything. Did I have any idea where I went? No. I wasn't trying to pick up any trails or tells to lead me in the right direction; I couldn't; I was in too much of a hunting frenzy, which hazed my mind. Strangely, I knew where to go based on some unknown instinct. The bushes and tree branches whizzed past me, leaves scratched and slapped against my body as I plowed through the greenery like a raging bull at a red flag.

With every blink of my eye, I grew closer to my target; I just knew it. A rustle and snap off to the side had my body careening toward the source before I could pause to debate whether the sound could have come from Avery or some animal. It was faint, but I could smell her addictive scent lingering in the air, acting almost like a string leading me towards her. That or I hallucinated from my adrenaline, a notion I quickly shoved away when I caught sight of her flushed face darting around ahead of me.

Our bodies collided with winded grunts when my arms coiled around her, and I sent us both to the ground. With a vicious snarl, Avery grabbed a handful of dirt and threw it in my face before her hand connected with my cheek, sending a loud slap through the air around us before the sounds of her body struggling filled the space. Her legs kicked and flailed under me in an attempt to shove me off while her hands fisted and came down on my chest and shoulders. None of it hurt; whether because she held her punches or my body was numb with adrenaline was a debate for later.

Leaning my full body weight against her, I pin her body flat to the ground to take her wrists hostage and bind them with my belt after quickly removing it. With two of her limbs bound, I grab a fistful of her hair and drag her over to a tree, hauling her to her feet, and press her front side right up against it with her hands stretched above her. "You know, if I didn't know any better, I'd say you didn't take my good grace seriously. You wanted to get caught, didn't you?" My words rasped against her ear as my other hand pulled my knife out and held it against her side.

Taking in a full breath of her, I ran the tip of my nose along the length of her neck before pressing my tongue against her thrumming pulse and licking the length of that with my tongue while I carefully cut a slit into her top. "I warned you what would happen if I caught you. Well, let me rephrase that: *when* I caught you. Because, let's be truthful, you were never going to get away. You didn't have a hair of a chance. I let you out of your cage to fly, but I let you out into an aviary. From one cage to another, you really had no chance."

"Y-you're wrong, I didn't—ah!" A hard roll of my hips into her backside got her to shut up real quick.

"I thought we were going to be truthful." I chided with a soft 'tut-tut' of my tongue before gripping her cut shirt and tearing at it with a wicked grin at her gasp. "I caught you, so now you're mine. All. Mine." That possessiveness in me surfaced the more I ground my hips at Avery's after spreading her legs more to get better access.

"You do this to all your victims? Bind them up and fuck with them before killing them? Or do you keep them somewhere all on some fucked up little farm?" Avery snapped her head back at me with a soft scowl, trying to maintain her image even though I could see her pupils dilating and softening with each roll of my hips.

Chuckling deeply, I yank her head back by her hair until it looked uncomfortable for her. "No, but I do whatever I want with my victims. You intrigue me, and the thought of killing you brings me no satisfaction. I rather put you to use elsewhere to give me pleasure. But you like it, don't you? Being my special little case. You love the thought of me keeping you, don't you? Being my little pet, my plaything, my slut. You love the fact that I'm laying my claim to you, that you are mine."

Avery's shaking head quickly tried to deny everything, and failing horribly, the evidence was clear the moment I tore her pants away, trailed the blunt side of my knife up her thighs, and pressed it against her slickened folds. "You and I are going to have a lesson in being truthful, little raven." I sighed playfully with a chiding shake of my head as I held the glistening blade up to her face so she could see the obvious evidence of her arousal to my words and actions. "You wouldn't be this fucking wet if you didn't want any of that."

Her body shuddered under me as her eyes fluttered close with a shaky breath. Releasing her hair, I hastily undid my pants and pulled my hard member out, and pressed it between her hot pussy lips. Biting my bottom lip, I let out a soft groan when Avery's hips bucked back against me, rubbing herself along my length and slickening me up with her juices. "Good girl, such an eager little slut." I chuckled while weaving my fingers through her tresses again, pulling her head back.

Carefully, I tap her lips with my blade. "Lick it. Taste how excited you are for me to claim and own you. How excited you are to belong to a killer like me."

Trembling lips parted, and her tongue peeked out between the space to flick at the covered metal gingerly with a whimper. "Please, I need you," She begged, looking up at me with such a sweet face that pulled a lustful groan from me.

Too bad I didn't want this game to end yet. "Need me? How?" I teased with a smirk while rubbing against her more, dipping the tip of my dick right into her entrance but never entering before dragging all the way up to her asshole, then back down I went and repeated.

"In me, I need you in me, Julian. I need your cock in my needy pussy, fucking it and filling it. Please, Daddy." Avery's cute little face flushed red with her reply while her hips shamelessly moved against me to try and get me actually to slip into her.

"Oh?" Amused, I pulled her head back more until a hiss of pain passed her lips. "Now I'm your Daddy again?" My eyes traced her adorned neck, where she still proudly wore her little choker with the other half of the pendant. Avery never once removed the thing while we were separated, which gave me a lot of hope every time I saw her.

"You are always my Daddy, my Julian, no doubts or qualms about it." She whispered with softened eyes filled with sureness and adoration.

With a smile, I brought my lips down on hers with a passion like never before, kissing her as if this were our first and last time. Keeping her head peeled back, I forced my way into her mouth until she choked on my tongue from my frenzy dominance of her mouth. "And don't you dare forget that. You are mine." To further tease her, I positioned myself right at her entrance and gave her a little push but not breaking entirely into her. "Say it, say you're mine, and I'll make it so."

"I'm yours. I'm all yours, Julian, for now and ever." Her lips never moved so quickly to utter such sweet words that stoked the flames of lust and passion I had burning inside of me for her.

Not wasting another second, I buried myself balls deep into her with one hard thrust that jerked her body and ripped a small scream from her. Twisting and biting my tongue in my mouth, I held back my teasing words as I found myself bursting at the seams with immense pleasure. Fuck I wanted to spill right then and there, but I refused to have this moment be a short one. I guess I underestimated how much I missed and craved her because, fuck, she felt like pure bliss and paradise.

Pulling back, I snapped my hips back into her until she became flushed against me again and quickly worked myself into a hard rhythm, bouncing Avery's precious body with every thrust. Readjusting my grip on her hair, I held her firm and steady before ghosting the tip of my knife around her waist and up her midline, leaving a faint red trail behind until I slipped it under the center of her bra and cut it away. Then, I circled the sharp metal over the swell of her breast to her nipple.

The wicked idea of carving my name into her crossed my mind, and it was tempting to press the blade harder into her until my name became etched into her pretty body. Resisting the urge, I ran the blade across her upper chest and lightly trailed my name there; it wouldn't be permanent. It'd fade sooner than later, along with the others, because I barely broke her delicate skin. She may be fine with me scoring her body, but she made it damn clear the limit was surface level. Even if I was twice her size, I've no doubts she could lay my ass out in seconds flat if I dared to entertain the thought of crossing her.

"Oh fuck... I love you so much, Julian." She moaned deeply with a whimpering scream of pleasure as she came undone around my cock.

Her tiny body writhed under me to get some reprieve, but I trapped her firmly between myself and the tree, being mindful not to push her into the harsh bark too much to keep her body from being scratched up too much. As her orgasm shook at her body, I kept going, pushing her beyond the edge. Dropping the knife to free my hand, I slipped it between her legs to find her engorged pearl and stroked at it with the pad of my fingers. Shivers of pleasure threatened to spill my release before I was ready when her melodic sobs of pleasure graced my ears.

"Julian, too much! Can't—fuck! Stop coming!" She cried out between her tears of lustful anguish.

Fortunately for her, I couldn't hold out much longer because she squeezed at me tightly. *Unfortunately* for her, I was much too pent up for one single round. After spilling into her with a deep groan, I immediately pulled out and shoved myself into her unexpecting ass, making her scream and pound against the tree with her bound hands. "Daddy, too much!" She gasped through her strained breaths.

"You can take it. You can always take what I give because you're my good girl. My good little slut." I growled through a grin as I watched her bubbly cheeks bounce with every thrust of my hips. "Fuck, your ass feels so tight and good." It was hard not to pick up my pace and pound into her like there was no tomorrow.

As my dick wrecked her ass, my fingers found themselves inside her filled cunt, hooking into her sweet spot until she sang like a pretty little bird and spasmed around me uncontrollably from the rapture of her orgasms. Our combined juices dripped down her thighs as her walls quivered around my digits, and her juices squirted out of her when I pushed her to the peak of her pleasure. "That's it baby, just let go, let me give you all the pleasure in the world until you can think of nothing but the next orgasm."

Once again, it didn't take long for me to reach my release. As I emptied myself into her with a groan, I felt a little disappointed about not taking her mouth first. I could've filled all three of her holes if I'd used my brain for a millisecond. I was pent-up enough to go three rounds so that it would have been feasible. Oh well, next time.

Reaching up, I undid my belt and held her tightly against me for a moment to spoil her with loving kisses and praises. "I love you so much, Avery,

I really do. Words can't describe how my heart somehow flips around you and how my stomach churns in a good way. God, don't ever spend any time away from me like that ever again, don't ever leave me again. I'll do whatever you want, just don't leave me."

"What if I asked you to stop killing?" She didn't sound hopeful or curious, but she was more forlorn and disappointed as she gave me a concerned look.

Swallowing the lump in my throat, I let out a long sigh. "It'll be hard, but I will do my best to stop completely." I'd probably be miserable for the rest of my life in some aspects of it, but if it meant keeping Avery in my life, then I was willing to make that sacrifice. Well, I probably should mentally prepare myself to stop because surely that's what she'll ask of me to continue our relationship.

"Let's get you back to the house and cleaned up, and we can talk more." I needed a moment anyway.

Pulling out of her, I tucked myself back into my pants before picking her up in my arms and making my way back towards the house.

Being a killer was a huge part of me; it was like breathing to me. I needed it to live, to function. I'd have to find other means to occupy my dark side soon, though, for Avery. I love killing, but I love Avery more. The past month and a half proved to me I couldn't live properly without her, so if giving up killing is what she'd ask of me, then I'd do it.

An awkward calm washed over me when I entered the house with her in my arms. "Do you want me to start you a bath, or do you want to shower?"

"I think a nice b—"

THUD! THUD! THUD!

"Hello! Are you still there!? Help! Please! I'm stuck down here!"

Whatever calm, sweet moment we had broke into hell as Avery widened her eyes at me and punched my chest. "You have an actual person down there right now!? What the fuck Julian!? I could have opened that door earlier and seen someone!? How long have they been down there!? You fucking had someone down there, and you decide to sit me down and try to talk to me like a normal person!? Julian, what the fuck!? Then you chase me and fuck me in the forest like a damn psycho, all while you had someone chained up in the basement of our home!?" She wasn't truly upset and rageful with how she hissed at me almost playfully.

Flinching back from her soft hits, I set her down to grab her hands and hold them against me. "I uhh kind of forgot he was down there..." Something that had never happened before, but Avery's separation really threw my world into a hell I didn't know how to navigate.

"The fuck you mean you forgot you had a human being down in your basement? Oh my god, how are they still alive, then? You had to have fed them and shit." She continued to speak in a slightly raised voice.

"Well, I was about to dispose of him, but then we had our little argument and blowup, and I was more focused on you and everything, and I just kind of forgot... From the sounds of it, he probably broke free and has helped himself to my reserves. I've got months' worth of MREs and water stocked up in the basement, so he probably got into those." Otherwise, I couldn't see how he'd be alive still because, thinking back on it, I stopped tending to the prisoner a little over a week into the separation because Avery was a more important matter than keeping my target alive for slaughter.

"Oh my god, Julian, let me go and take care of that man. By the time I'm out of the bath, the basement better be body free. No more bodies in the basement from here on out, I don't care, well I do care, just I won't go crying to the cops or anything on you, but I do not want to see or hear—wait, oh my god, all the noises from before, they weren't animals were they?" Realization striking her face pulled an amused chuckle from me when I saw the gears turning in her head. "Oh my god, Julian! You were fucking me while you had people down there too!?"

Okay, now I was in full-blown laughter with Avery wailing at me with her fists. "Julian! That is not funny! You're such a jerk! Ugh! Just no more bodies in the basement. Go fix your holding area and keep them away from the house. I do not want to hear any more bumps and thumps in this damn house unless it's from us." She groaned, threading her fingers through her hair and throwing them in the air.

"Fine, fine, I'll make quick work of Harry," I responded with my dying laughter.

"Harry? As in?" Surprisingly, she didn't look horrified.

"Yes, the asshole who made a fool of you throughout high school and at the reunion. I don't ever go after people who aren't criminals, but he was an exception for how he hurt you." Well, that answer felt weirdly normal. Actually, this whole relationship kind of felt weird but in a normal way with everything out in the open.

"You know, just... Go take care of the problem, and we'll talk after dinner." Avery stopped me with a smile as she held out her hand at me.

"Enjoy your bath, baby." I chuckled, kissing her forehead before disappearing down the hallway.

CHAPTER 35
Avery

IT FELT SO WRONG for this to feel so normal.

Sitting here on the couch with my serial killer boyfriend. God, that sentence shouldn't even be in existence. I shouldn't be sitting anywhere near anyone who was a criminal, let alone a criminal boyfriend who could literally slit my throat at any given moment. We shouldn't be having such a normal conversation like a normal couple; I mean, discounting the fact he's a serial killer, he was by all means a perfectly normal and perfect man/boyfriend.

"So, let me get this straight: you only kill criminals, specifically those who were let off by the system or slipped by the system someway somehow." I reiterated after digesting everything he dumped out onto the table. "And the feathers, they are a symbolism of death, the last steps of life, and the scattered files is basically your reason to the police of why they are condemned?"

"Correct, yes," Julian confirmed with a firm nod of his head, tightening his hand around mine.

"And there's an aspect to it all in which we haven't figured out, which is the warning you leave beforehand, basically an omen." That part was a revelation, and it was unknown until now.

"Yes, I always leave a note with 'GUILTY' scribbled in red and pin it to their door with a feather, a sign that death was coming for them for their sins will be coming." Well, we never found any of the victims, nor did we discover the scenes until days after. Nothing ever got reported to us, so we knew nothing about the warning. I didn't blame the convicts for not coming to us, though. No offense, but a criminal coming to us to report a crime against them? In a perfect world, we'd take them seriously, but the cops around here were more than willing to put them on the back burner.

Also, if someone came into the station reporting an odd note with a feather, we'd probably file them as a nutcase and not take them too seriously. Even after a pattern of homicides inevitably emerged, we had nothing to go on besides the scene. We always assumed them to be dead, killed, because we could never find their bodies; Julian's victims seemingly disappeared without a trace, and after a while, we defaulted to 'yeah, they were killed' to shut the public up basically.

"And you gave me that idea for my story... Your real experience... Oh my god, everything you gave me was based on experience, holy shit." Yeah, I've been having a lot of those 'oh shit' moments tonight.

"Nothing better than experience." He replied with a sheepish chuckle. "But uhh, you're taking this a lot better than I expected... Though, to be fair, this whole thing is going very unexpectedly, in a very good way."

"And all your victims, all the bodies, they're all basically buried deep underground with a building on top of them?" Okay, I had to give him props because that was a genius method with a minute margin for error and discovery.

"Yes." Another methodic nod with a flat, grim smile.

Taking in a deep breath, I held it for a second to calm my nerves. "I'm gonna be honest with you, babe. This whole thing is still a huge pill for me to swallow. Logically, I should have reported you the moment you confessed, and you should be in jail right now, but I can't. I barely entertained the idea before throwing it out. I feel like an idiot for saying and admitting it but thinking about a life with you was painful. Logically, I should be running for the hills, flying a few continents over, and disappearing, but I can't, and I won't."

Sighing heavily, I ran a hand through my hair and laughed crazily to myself. "Yes, the fact my boyfriend is a damn serial killer is a bucket of iced water to the face, but, like, I'm fine with it...? Ish? I really shouldn't be rationalizing it, but at least you only go after the bad guys. In a way, you're just an unhinged Batman. And, I mean, you haven't tried to kill me, which brings up another thing: why me? Why even engage in a relationship with me and all of that?"

For the life of me, I couldn't figure out a reason for him keeping me around because a man like him could easily have anyone he wanted. If he wanted someone for sex, he could have gotten some bomb-ass Victoria's Secret model, not a plain Jane me. Okay, maybe I was his body type, but not like I was the only person with this build in this damn town. Yes, the fact he truly has feelings for me did hang in the back of my head, but he was a psychopath. So, believing all of that was iffy for me.

His tongue nervously darted out to wet his lips before he pulled me fully into his lap, making me straddle and face him. "You are different, like I said. The sight of you in the library stirred something awake within me, and when I touched you, I literally felt sparks. I have never had such an attraction towards someone before. What I felt towards you was akin to what I felt towards my targets, but not exactly the same."

Breathing deeply, he rubbed the back of his neck and looked seemingly in thought for a second. "While I wanted to cut the life out of my victims, I wanted to carve you up just to be feral. The mere thought of doing any harm to you, much less taking your life, physically pained me. I wanted you like I wanted to kill, and you became some strange obsession and compulsion for me that was only sated through intimacy, whether it be us in the bed or doing domestic things like cooking and other things like cuddling on the couch."

Another deep breath later, he cleared his throat and continued, "I don't know how to explain it fully, but you are different in an amazing way. You have changed me so much, and you have no idea. I've done things, felt things, and am willing to do things I never would have entertained the thought of before you graced my life. I just love everything about you so much, no matter how simple or silly it is. Like how you make the cutest faces when you work on your stories or the way you blow your ice cubes away before you drink."

Chuckling softly, he shook his head softly before kissing me quickly and looking at me with a warm smile. "I appreciate the normalcy you've brought to my life and how you've opened my eyes to everything. I'm finally living and enjoying life because of you. You are special to me, Avery, so much that I can't possibly explain with words because it would take an eternity. I love you, Avery. I truly and genuinely do. My little raven for now and ever."

"Oh, Julian." Somehow, I fell deeper in love with this man.

Okay, I may be severely deprived of attention and affection and clung onto Julian because he's the first person to ever show me this side of life, but deep down, I knew he was special to me too. It wasn't because he was the first to come along and pay attention to me. No, I truly felt a deep connection to him that ran deep into my very soul.

"I love you. I love you so much, you have no idea." I whispered against his lips with a smile before kissing him deeply, pouring everything I had into it with a soft moan as I pushed him back into the back of the couch.

"I swear, I will spend the rest of our lives and forever to prove to you that what I feel for you is true. You will never suffer or feel anything shy of happiness and content each and every day while I am by your side." Julian promised with a searing gaze.

"My Daddy, for now and ever." I giggled with a huge grin.

"And you will forever be my little raven."

Life was perfect.

Thump!

Never mind, scratch that. "Julian! I thought I told you I didn't want that shit in the house!" I gave out an annoyed groan with a roll of my eyes as I trudged over to the basement door and descended the stairs. "I swear to all that is holy, Julian, if I—oh, never mind."

Well, now I felt like an idiot.

Julian chuckled at my dumbfounded expression and gave me a smirk with a raised brow. "Okay, that one was a fluke, and I already apologized for it thoroughly with my tongue, or do you need a reminder of how you forgave me for it already?" He mused with a chuckle before stacking away a box onto a shelf. "Just restocking and reorganizing as I told you, and everything is secluded to the secondary chamber again as it has been, besides that one slip up when it was still being fixed up and renovated."

Stubbornly, I pouted at him with my arms crossed as he approached me with an amused expression. "I promised you already, you won't ever see or hear any of it, and it won't be in the house." He chuckled, taking me into his arms and kissing my forehead. "How's writing coming along?"

"Horrible, I can't get the words to word properly." I sighed heavily and dropped my arms before slumping into him, letting him support my full weight as I melted into his warmth.

"Go settle on the couch with your blanket, and I'll get some snacks for you to munch on while you relax and unwind. No more typing tonight unless your mind is sorted. You won't be doing yourself any good if you force yourself." He spoke into my hair, his hands rubbing my back as he spoke.

"Carry me?" I tilt my head back to shoot him my pleading eyes and pout, the one which usually gets him to cave.

Like I expected, he relented.

It didn't take long for me to doze off completely on the couch after stuffing myself full of chips and dip along with mini-corndogs. When I was startled awake, it was dark out. A quick glance at the clock showed 7 o'clock. "Shit." I groaned to myself as I sat up and rubbed the sleep from my eyes. I slept for five damn hours, which will make sleeping later tonight a bitch.

"Daddy?" I peep my body up from the couch, scanning the area with my half-open eyes.

"Good evening, sleeping beauty." Julian chuckled from the kitchen, briefly peering up from the stove to flash me a smile before returning to the task at hand.

"Why didn't you wake me?" I asked with a pout while rubbing my eyes again.

"I did, or I tried. You shooed me away and pulled the blanket over your head. I tried a few times, and you kept shooing me off and kicking me away. So, I just let you be. Besides, you needed the sleep anyway. I mean, I did keep you up pretty late last night." The cheeky smile on his face didn't go unnoticed by me, and neither did the little playful, teasing edge to his voice.

Huffing, I laid myself back down on the couch and buried myself in it. "Are you going out tonight?" Well, at least I rested a little easier knowing why he went out so late sometimes. Was I okay with it? Eh, not really, but there's not much I can do about it.

Sure, I could ask him to stop being a serial killer, but our relationship would surely suffer if I forced him to stop that side of him. At the end of the day, he wasn't abusing me; he just killed people—bad people! He kept it away from me and me away from it, so at least that was thoughtful of him. I might as well kill Julian myself if I asked him to stop. So, I've come to accept him for all he is and live with it. It wasn't easy, but adjusting and accepting got better with time.

"No, I've got no late-night plans for the next week." There was an uptick to his tone, which had me lifting my head to look over at him, catching his smiling face as he held a pan in hand with what looked like steaks on it. "I'm fucking you right into our anniversary, then taking you on a week-long trip to the coast. So, better be prepared to lose your ability to walk tonight."

"You scoundrel!" If the distance between us wasn't so great, then I would've chucked a throw pillow at him.

Damn. One year. Can't believe it.

365 days. 52 weeks. 12 months. It felt so surreal the more I thought about it. My first real relationship made it to a year. I made it a whole year with my serial killer boyfriend. Yeah, never gonna stop saying that: my serial killer boyfriend.

I couldn't help but laugh the more it hit me and sank into my disbelieving brain. "Lose some sanity over there, love?" Julian chuckled with a bit of concern while remaining in the kitchen.

"I went a whole year with a serial killer and didn't even notice. God, how do you put up with me? Man, I'm thinking about all the times you came home covered, dented your car with blood and guts on it, and just... How did you not look at me and go, 'Is this chick serious?' or 'Is she really this stupid?' when I'd believe your lies?" It seemed silly now as I thought hard about it, yet I was so stupidly, blissfully ignorant of it all.

"Well, if it makes you feel any better, I didn't enjoy lying to you, even if it was to cover my own ass, self-preservation, or whatever you want to call it." Guilt crossed his frowning face before his lips turned into an apologetic smile.

"You still have a lot of groveling to do." I teased with a giggle, sticking my tongue out at him before snuggling back into the couch with a content sigh.

And grovel he did until my brain was mush that night. We made love right into our anniversary, which, in my opinion, is a great way to start another stretch of our relationship.

Too bad life was a bitch.

Epilogue 1

"It's as if you were writing out your own life!"

Oh, you have no idea.

I kept the thought behind a kind and friendly smile, though, as I let my fan gush on about my books while I sat behind the signing table. "I'm so glad you enjoyed the stories I've written. You have no idea how nerve-wracking it was to think about my story not being enjoyed. I know everyone has their own preferences, but I just hoped not everyone would hate it because it is kind of strange." Seeing all these fans at my first book signing overwhelmed me a bit, but it was so lovely and refreshing all at the same time.

"Oh girl, no! Don't let that imposter syndrome get you! If someone doesn't like it, then it's their loss, but honestly, your story concept for these morally gray, blackish serial killers finding their matches in these kick-ass females is awesome. And the amount of detail and realism is just perfect." Another fan joined with a grin.

"Well, I hope I continue to have all the amazing support from you guys and others out there as they discover me and my stories. I love writing. It's my escape and everything, but knowing my books are making your days makes me all the happier and more motivated to keep going more." Providing people with their own escape through books made me happy at the end of the day, and it was now one of the top reasons why I continued to write and publish my stories eagerly. "The sheer amount of gratitude I feel for you guys is indescribable. Honestly, I really couldn't have done this without you guys."

Well, and Julian and Liz, but they were a given. I don't know how those two put up with my antics during my writing process, especially Julian because he was usually around when I would be complaining and drafting. He was the one to suffer all my random ass questions and ideas and had to entertain them. Although, speaking of Julian, where—

"Sorry, sweetie, the convention ran later than any of us expected." Speak of the devil, and he shall appear looking as dashing and handsome as ever and a little out of breath.

"Did you sprint the two blocks here?" I chuckled as I got up from my seat to hug him.

"Faster than waiting for an Uber." He joked back, though judging from the flat undertone of his voice, he was earnest.

"Well, I can see how your scenes are so accurate if this is the inspiration you have." My fan teased me with a giggle before we continued to chat for a little longer, and they left.

Sitting quietly beside me with a friendly smile, Julian anchored me with his comforting silence. "I don't think I've told you enough yet, but I am so proud of you." I would never grow tired of hearing his praises because they gave me a sense of security and affection from him.

"I still can't believe all of this." If someone had told me nearly two years ago that I'd be attending one of the biggest author events in the Pacific Northwest as a best-selling author, I would have laughed and shaken them off.

"Life does some amazing things sometimes," Julian remarked with a tender smile at me, taking my hand in his and bringing it to his lips to kiss the back of it. "I'll get us something to munch on and drink while you continue until your scheduled time."

Two incredible years with Julian, and he's never once slacked in caring for me. We've had our rough spots over the years, but our baseline felt like a constant honeymoon period. I hate to say it because no relationship is ever truly perfect, but for us, our relationship was perfect given everything.

Yes, Julian was still killing, and yes, I was more tolerant and accepting of it. True to his word, he kept his business away from the house; I knew he had his little chamber and did his killing on the property, but at least he didn't ever use the basement again or bring any of his activities into the vicinity of his house. Also, the soundproof headphones he gave me did wonders to block out the sounds of echoing screams.

Obviously, I still kept up with my thriving author career, but I still maintained my job as a CSI as well. I might have settled initially with my chosen career at the time, but I've got a newfound appreciation for it and the opportunities it has opened for me. Also, it provided a nice chunk of time for me to spend time away from Julian; don't get me wrong, I love my man, I really do, but spending too much time cooped up in the house or around him really strung me out a lot of the time. Too much of a good thing can be bad, as people like to say. Thankfully, between my day job, his, and his hobby, the amount of time we spent away from each other was perfect to maintain a healthy balance in our relationship.

Hours later, the convention was finally over. It was a relief but also bittersweet. It truly was amazing to meet all my fans and get the chance to talk with my favorite authors and many others. It amazed me at the amount of knowledge I've gained the past few days, and the new friends I've made really made me happy because I finally found my place it felt like.

The drive home was long, but thankfully, I wasn't the one who drove. Hours later, we arrived home, exhausted. So, we opted to crash after a quick dinner. I wanted to show Julian how thankful I was for him coming with me, but that could wait until tomorrow.

The funny thing about plans, though, was that they change.

Did I plan on waking up in the middle of the night? No.

Did I plan on waking up in the middle of the night to a gun pointed at me? Hell no.

Did I plan on waking up in the middle of the night to Carl Bornes jabbing a gun into me after dragging me out of Julian's arms? Hell fucking no.

"Remember me, you stupid bitch? Thought you could escape just because you got me booted off the force?" He seethed next to me, his acrid breath and spit hitting my ear and face with each spiteful word as he dug the gun into my head.

Julian quickly scrambled out of bed when I was jerked away from his embrace. Standing a few feet from us, he eyed Carl with disdain that softened with wary concern when they bounced to me. "Carl, let her go. Just let her go and leave. We won't press any charges or anything, but you have to let Avery go and leave." Julian kept his voice leveled and calm as he spoke with his hands held out toward the former detective.

"No, I'm not leaving until I put a bullet in her myself or take her down to the station for a live confession on TV. I am fed up with her getting away with all her crimes! And my whole life was ruined because of her." Then Carl rambled or mumbled something incoherent under his breath as he shifted the gun against my body.

"Carl, it's not her, she's not the killer, trust me, I know. I live with her. I have been with her for two years, and I would know if she was The Omen." If the situation wasn't so dire, then I would've laughed at the irony of Julian's words. "I understand, I get it. You want a definite answer, someone to put a face to this elusive killer who's gotten under everyone's nerves, but going after an innocent woman is not the answer."

"No! She's got you fooled! Of course, she has. Why wouldn't she? Listen, pal, I am doing you a big favor by taking out the trash for you. You may think she loves you, but people like her aren't capable of feelings like us. It's just all pretend. It won't be long until she sticks a knife through your heart, literally. So, I'm doing you a damn favor." His words hurt me more than the damn gun digging into my temple.

I love Julian, no doubt about it, but I had my moments of shakiness during my lonely nights. At the end of the day, Julian was a psychopath, and I knew the psychology of psychopathy. So, I knew better. Julian was more than capable of love, just maybe not in the typical sense as neurotypical people like me and Carl, but he was capable and did truly love me. Still, getting the jabbing reminder of people like Julian not being typical made my thoughts run the other way sometimes.

But those thoughts and feelings fell away when I would meet Julian's deep gaze. His hazel green eyes were always filled with such brightness, love, devotion, desire, adoration, passion, and so much more whenever he looked at me. Even when he stared off into space with his gaze on me, I could see the way his eyes sparkled. Julian may be able to fake a smile, fake a laugh, fake being friendly and charming, but he couldn't fake his eyes.

Click!

Tension in my body rose at the sound of the gun's safety clicking off. God, two years without a peep from Carl after he got let go from the department with half his benefits. Why now? I thought him getting axed with an assault and battery charge on his record would be enough for him to learn his lesson, but I guess not. Sure, I saw his face here and there in town, but he lived here, so that wasn't anything odd in our small city.

"What will it take for you to let her go?" Julian's defeated voice shook as he kept his... scared...? Eyes on me.

"A confession, so you better talk some sense into her—"

Julian's raised voice boomed across the room, stunning Carl and me with his following words. "Thane Gorlin, March 23rd, 2012. You won't find his remains because I fed him to pigs, but he was my first victim ever. He was charged with multiple counts of domestic abuse, child abuse, and neglect. The judge set him free with ten years probation and mandatory therapy and support groups."

Stunned silence strangled the air as he continued, "The snapping thread for me was when he sent his wife to the hospital with a knife wound to the stomach, and she nearly died. He was the turning point for me to act on my killer impulses when I acted on my ideology of justice needing to be exacted. The system is shit. Criminals who should be locked behind bars are free or get a slap on the wrist, and he was what made me snap when he went after my sister, who is nothing but a sweet woman who deserves someone good."

I never knew that. Granted, I never asked him about any of it. It became a silent agreement between us to not talk about his serial hobby, well, more of a me thing. I never asked or touched on the subject with Julian and vehemently avoided it to make it life easier. So, I never knew his beginning or if he had some reason or trigger, I kind of left the subject be.

"What?" Carl had never looked more confused and stunned in my life, and I've worked with this man for years.

"Thane Gorlin was my reason, my trigger. He tricked my younger sister into marrying him, and their marriage was a shit show, but my sister was too good of a person, too religious, to leave. I might not have the same feelings I do for my family as I do for Avery, but we have a mutual blood relationship. I couldn't stand the sight and fact Thane put my sister at Death's door like that, and it could have all been prevented had this justice system of ours not failed her." Taking a deep breath, he let his shoulders fall in defeat.

"So, I took matters into my own hands. After that first taste of blood, animals didn't do it for me anymore, so I kept going after I honed my skills and methods to the utmost perfection. I thought surely I'd get caught for Thane because he was a spur-of-the-moment kill, but after seeing him slip through the cracks because of his record and everything, I continued after a whole year of studying and honing. Ten years and counting, that's how long I've been at this game. If you want a confession, then I'll give it to you along with every victim and the spot I disposed of them, but you have to let Avery go. She really is innocent in all of this. She didn't know any better, and I kept her in the dark as well." His eyes begged me to play along, and it hurt me to see the gloom descend over his face and body.

"Julian, no..." My voice cracked at the reality of the moment.

This was it; this was the end of us because Julian would finally be caught.

"I'm sorry. I thought I could continue to hide this from you for the rest of our lives because I love you so much. I truly do care for you and have an instinctual attraction towards you, but I guess that cat's out of the bag now. I'm just sorry for all the blame that's befallen you because of my actions." Even though his lies were sweet, they were true, and they sounded like a confession of a dying man.

The pressure around my body slackened, and I used the chance to slip from Carl and run straight into Julian's open arms. "Shh, I got you. Everything will be okay. I'll take care of all of this, don't worry. I am not leaving you." He whispered into my hair between his peppering kisses.

Carl's maniacal laugh chilled the room and my body; he truly lost it. "Are you fucking serious!?" His laughter didn't stop, which really unnerved me.

"Carl, please, let—"

My body flinched when Carl cut me off with his raised voice and aimed his gun at me. "Shut up! Not another peep out of you. I want Julian over here, now! I want him to write down a full confession, names with dates and locations of his victims, and anything and everything he can give. And it's all going to happen right here, right now, because I am not letting you out of my sight until I have everything from Julian."

Great, from one hostage situation to another. Was it too much to ask for a break?

Julian darted his body in front of me, shielding me from Carl and the gaze of his gun. "Carl, I will give you everything you want, but you have to promise me that Avery remains unharmed and unscathed. She has no part in it, and I don't want her getting hurt or harmed because of me."

"Julian, please, don't." My hands clung to the back of his shirt as tears stung my eyes. "I don't want to lose you."

Looking back at me with a grim but reassuring smile, he leaned down and kissed the top of my head. "You won't." His hands knocked mine away, and he approached Carl with his hands raised in the air.

Just when I thought the end was near, Julian bolts into action. In the blink of an eye, Julian's hand shoots out and slaps Carl's gun out of his hand, sending it to the floor with a *clatter* and sending the room into chaos. Carl reacted immediately and grabbed at Julian's shoulders, shoving him back against the nightstand and sending both of them to the ground with grunts. Fists flew back and forth, some nailing and some missing as the two men rolled around on the floor in a struggle until Carl somehow ended up on top of Julian and wailed on him nonstop with a flurry of punches at Julian's upper body and face.

"Carl, stop!" I was quickly thrown off when I threw myself around Carl's pulled-back arm, landing a little ways away with a pained grunt when I landed on my ass.

"Avery, don't, you're going to get hurt." Julian half shouted at me through his own grunts as he kept his arms up to protect himself from Carl's blows.

Frantically, my eyes and head darted around the room in search of something to use. I lunged for the fallen lamp but found myself snatching up the discarded gun at the last second.

I'd never shot a gun or any kind of weapon directly at a live human being in my life, nor did I ever have the desire to. Yet, I pulled the trigger without an ounce of hesitation after pointing it at Carl. The aftershock of everything trembled at my body and hands as I stared at the scene in disbelief. "I..." I didn't mean to? I'm sorry?

Why didn't I hesitate? Why was it so easy for me to take Carl's life? I wasn't a killer.

With a grunt, Julian shoved Carl's literal dead weight off to the side, where he continued to bleed all over the floor. "Little raven, put the gun down, it's over, he's dead, it's over, so put the gun down."

My thoughts escaped me mindlessly. "I... I had to. He was going to take you away. He was going to make you leave me... He wouldn't stop hitting you. He doesn't get it, and he was going to ruin something good. I had to do it to protect you, protect us. Oh my god, I killed someone." Terrified of myself, I instantly dropped the gun.

Shocked, I couldn't tear my eyes away from Carl's bleeding body. My whole body felt numb as the entire situation fully sank into my very bones; I barely felt Julian's arms take hold of me, and his words sounded so muffled to me. I knew love made you do the craziest things, but I never knew the full extent of that saying until tonight.

For Julian, I would do anything. I went against my own morals for this man, and I had no regrets about it. Because of my love for Julian, I chose to turn a blind eye to the fact he was a homicidal maniac, basically, let him go on killing. I've become more diligent as a CSI whenever it came to his crime scenes to ensure nothing left behind could be led back to him, helping the criminal and breaking the rules and protocols for him. And just now, I killed a man out of fear of losing Julian. I killed Carl because he became a threat to us.

I really would do anything for this man because I love him, just as he has done for me.

Julian turned his life upside down because of me and went down a crazy avenue of experiences he never felt or been through before because of his love for me.

He became human, for me, because he loves me.

And I became undone for him.

I love Julian, and I will let nothing stand in the way of that.

Epilogue 2

EXCITEMENT BURNED AT EVERY fiber and nerve ending in my being as I rocked on the balls of my feet.

Attempting to ease my anxiety over the situation, I took another walk through the scene I just created to ensure nothing was out of place. Everything had to be perfect. It won't be long now; Avery should be here any second now.

"You jerk, you're lucky it's my day off when you decided to do this." My little ball of sunshine bounced up to me with an unamused frown and glared as I exited the house with a sheepish grin. "Honestly, babe, I thought I told you to be careful. I don't care if you've been at this shit for fifteen or so years now. That doesn't mean you should get complacent because then shit like this happens, and I have to clean up after your ass."

Huffing, she grumbled something under her breath before turning her attention back to me. "Seriously, how the hell did this even happen? Please don't tell me this is as bad as the last one." She grumbled to herself again before pushing past me with her little suitcase of equipment trailing behind her. "Oh my... Julian! Did you even clean up at all? It's going to take us all damn day to comb through this damn place. Julian, what the fuck? I'm your girlfriend, not your damn maid or cleanup lady."

If this were a serious situation, then I wouldn't be snickering like a little asshole as I was now. "It was just an off day for me. I don't know what happened. Things just kind of happened." I lied with a small shrug of my shoulders. This time, I didn't feel guilty about hiding the truth from her because it was a good kind of deception.

Groaning softly with a roll of her eyes, Avery opened her suitcase and pulled on a pair of gloves after tying her hair up. Then, she started to get to work while I stood back and watched with a smug smirk as I leaned against the doorframe with my arms crossed. "You so owe me for this." She huffed with a pout at me. "The fuck did you two do? Summon a tornado to tear through this place?"

"Like I said, things just went haywire," I replied with a subtle shrug of my shoulders, keeping up my nonchalant front.

Honestly, I have no idea how this place got so torn up; none of it was my doing. The only thing I did was clear the area some and set the needed items around. The place was already abandoned and sacked by squatters and transients, and it was set to be demolished along with some other dilapidated places around the area. This whole block was scheduled to be flattened for some kind of strip mall and new business buildings, a new and big project my company just signed onto.

"He threw something over on the shelf, then something in the pile of cushions, and then something under the couch. The spaces are kinda too tight for me to reach into, so I figured it be best to leave it to you." Avery was not amused by that answer one bit, a fact made evident by her intensifying grumbling.

Her tense body slackened with a small chuckle after she picked a book off the shelf and saw the title of it. "Something good?" I inquired with a quirked brow.

"Just something silly." She dismissed herself with a deflated voice and a wave of her hand.

"No, tell me, nothing is silly when it comes to you, you know that little raven." I encouraged her to speak her thoughts.

Slowly, the corner of her lips curled into a dopey smile as she admired the book in her hands for a few more seconds before looking up at me and showing me the book. "I don't know if you remember, but this was the book I was looking for the day I ran into you at the library, Serial Methods and Madness. It's a silly thing and a small detail from years ago, but it's one of my first memories of you, kind of the start of us... So, it's just kind of sentimental to me." Her fingers danced along the spine and edges of the book before opening it when she saw something sticking out.

Five years with this amazing woman, and she never ceases to amaze me. I don't know how it was possible, but I found myself falling deeper and deeper in love with her every passing day. Somehow, our relationship grew deeper the night Avery committed her one and only murder of Carl Bornes. Something changed with her that night; pulling the trigger pulled something else within her. She looked at me in a new light, almost like she had some newfound appreciation for me. The depths of the passion in her eyes became even more indescribable—newfound freedom and love.

Our relationship before Carl's murder was good, but there had always been this silent, lingering tension between us, mainly regarding my deathly hobby. It was something Avery kind of accepted and lived with it. After the incident, though, something immediately flipped within her. My serial killing activities may not be some common dinner conversation, but she has inquired more about it than before. Everything completely fell into place after that fateful night—we became bonded at the soul in a way.

"Of course, I remember. I remember everything when it comes to you, to us." No lie, I really did remember every little thing of our life.

"Oh? Then what did I get on our seventeenth date?" I'm pretty sure she picked a random number, but the smug little pouty smile on her face was too amusing not to entertain.

"Well, for breakfast, I made us eggs benedict, which you had two of, along with a glass of orange juice. Then I dropped off an Italian sub from Geraldo's along with some mango nectar for lunch. Finally, for dinner and dessert, I took you out to Old Bay for seafood, where you got the seafood platter and some alfredo on the side. You ate nearly two baskets of the biscuits, had some red sangria, and then we got ice cream at Frozen Stiles, where you got some mango sherbet and a scoop of taro." Okay, saying it out loud kind of made me sound a little creepy with how much I recalled, but I couldn't help it when it came to Avery. I wanted every second of her branded into my mind.

"Holy shit, you really are a little serial stalker killer psychopath." She joked with a chuckle before tucking the book under her arm.

Coming up to me, she quickly kissed and grinned goofily at me before going over to a corner of blown-out walls. A moment of peaceful silence fell upon us as she searched the area. "Bub, where's your necklace?" She gave an annoyed, groaning sigh as she lulled her gaze back at me.

Placing a hand on my chest, I pretended to feel for the necklace that I knew wasn't there. "Oh, guess I forgot it at home." I feigned innocence, shrugging my shoulders.

Rolling her eyes, she propped her balled-up fists on her hips and glared at me softly with calculating eyes before huffing and crossing her arms with a suspicious twinkle in her eyes. "Julian, what's going on here?" The little game lasted longer than expected, so I couldn't complain about the lack of entertainment.

"Go check the couch. I really couldn't get under there." I chuckled, gesturing at the only full piece of furniture in the area that was still usable.

As she was on her hands and knees with an arm stretched out under the couch, I slowly positioned myself behind her and watched as she stood up with a tiny little box in hand. The smirk on my face turned into a full-blown smile at the sight of her eyes widening when she opened the box and saw its contents. "Jul—oh my God!" Avery dropped the box—which I caught—when she turned around and saw me kneeling on one knee before her.

"From our very first encounter to the start of our true relationship when everything came out of the dark. I know this isn't the most romantic place, but you always did love your little crime scenes and following me around sometimes. Honestly, it went a lot better in my head, but plans don't always work out." Nervously, I licked my lips and chuckled. "Well, doesn't matter now, and I'll do this over if you want, but I have to ask the question now." Why was I stalling? Four simple words refused to leave my mouth as I held the ring out to her.

"I honestly never saw myself doing this, and I mean, I knew I wanted us to last forever, but you and I have talked about this a bit. Marriage isn't some deal breaker for us. We're fine with domestic living and our relationship where it is now is perfect and all." Is this how Avery felt when she rambled? "But recently, the thought of being able to call you my wife, officially, just grew on me. And now, I can't think of anything else but to change your last name to mine and officially make you mine in the face of the law and whatnot."

This anxiety was maddening. "You really are the best thing to ever happen to me, and I already planned on spending the rest of my life with you, but it would be an honor, and you would make me the happiest man ever if you say yes." Taking a deep breath, I recollected myself. "Allow me to care for you for the rest of our lives. Let me love and cherish you, show you why and how you're the exception to my madness, why you are the most special and only person in my life. Please, will you marry me?"

The round alexandrite shined and glittered in my trembling fingers, along with the black diamond-encrusted feathers of the band. Everything sat on/in rose gold, which would match very well with her fair skin. It took a while to get the custom ring made, but I knew a few people who I did some work for and called around until I found someone reputable and good.

Giggling and sobbing, she nodded her head while squeaking out her answer. "Yes, but please, do this in some place that doesn't smell like stale piss. But yes! Always and forever, my answer will always be yes."

"Good, because I have an appointment set for us down at the courthouse in an hour." I chuckled with a cheeky grin, laughing a little when Avery playfully slapped my shoulder.

"Julian! You didn't even ask yet you made the damn appointment?" She laughed while pulling me up by my arms.

"Well, I was pretty confident of the answer," I admitted with a sheepish chuckle.

"God, you are lucky I love you so damn much," Avery said with a roll of her eyes.

Wrapping my arms around her, I pulled her close and cupped her face with one hand to tilt her head up into a deep kiss.

"I love you so much, my little raven. Can't wait to see your name as Avery Smith in an hour."

"Cheeky asshole. I love you too, Daddy. Can't wait to be Avery Smith."

Afterword

If you enjoyed the story then please leave a review to support me!

Thank you so much for reading Killer in the Sheets, the first installment in my Serial Lovers series, an interconnected but standalone series of books about the twisted tales of serial unalivers finding their happy endings. If this dark little rom-com was your cup of tea then I hope you will enjoy the next installment about a cop's daughter and a court judge; Guilty of Love will be coming late fall 2024 or beginning of 2025.

In the meanwhile, if you enjoy mafia romances then I would love and appreciate it if you gave my other books, The Bratva's Bride and The Bratva's Beast, a read.

Support me further by following me on my social media platforms to keep up with my author musings along with sneak peeks at upcoming books, my works in progress, and just my author antics!

tiktok.com/@rose.chase.author

instagram.com/rose.chase.author/

facebook.com/rose.chase.author

amazon.com/author/rose.chase

About the Author

Rose Chase, a dedicated nurse and loving mother to two boys, discovered her passion for storytelling in middle school on online forums and Wattpad. Despite her busy life, she delves into the captivating realm of contemporary romance, with a particular fascination for dark romance and morally gray characters. Through her skillful storytelling, Rose navigates the intricate dance between love, desire, and the shadows of human nature. When not saving lives or caring for her family, she immerses herself in the world of fiction, inviting readers to explore the depths of love and passion while confronting the complexities of the human heart.